Before anyone woke, he scrubbed down his room twice with the strongest cleansers he could find. Removed anything, seen or unseen, that said, "Jessica White Was Here." Then he tried to sleep, but his heart was beating too fast. Every time he closed his eyes he saw Jessica rise like a zombie from the grave.

He went to the kitchen and made himself a hearty breakfast. He was famished. When he was done, he felt so much better.

It's over.

When he returned to his clean room, he saw a note on his bed. Something was wrong.

It was a plain white card in a blank white unsealed envelope. He slowly removed the card.

We know what you did last night.

Something else was in the envelope. He poured it into his hand.

Dirt. And a single earring.

Praise for Allison Brennan

"Brennan's powerful, gut-wrenching thrillers show a talent for plotting that's evident from page one. Gritty and intense, these suspense stories are not for the faint of heart." —*Romantic Times*

"Brennan does murder better than almost everyone writing in the suspense genre." —*Armchair Interviews*

Also by Allison Brennan

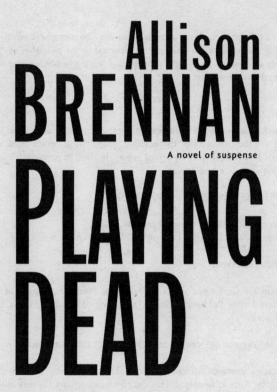

Allison BRENNAN

A novel of suspense

PLAYING DEAD

BALLANTINE BOOKS • NEW YORK

Playing Dead is a work of fiction. Names, characters, places, and incidents are the products of the author's imagination or are used fictitiously. Any resemblance to actual events, locales, or persons, living or dead, is entirely coincidental.

A Ballantine Books Mass Market Original

Copyright © 2008 by Allison Brennan
Excerpt of *Sudden Death* copyright © 2008 by Allison Brennan

Published in the United States by Ballantine Books, an imprint of The Random House Publishing Group, a division of Random House, Inc., New York.

BALLANTINE and colophon are trademarks of Random House, Inc.

This book contains an excerpt from the forthcoming book *Sudden Death* by Allison Brennan. This excerpt has been set for this edition only and may not reflect the final content of the forthcoming edition.

ISBN 978-0-345-50273-5

Cover illustration: Hankins & Tegenborg, Ltd.

Printed in the United States of America

www.ballantinebooks.com

OPM   9 8 7 6 5 4

For the FBI Special Agents
in the Sacramento regional office
who live up to their motto:

Fidelity, Bravery, and Integrity

ACKNOWLEDGMENTS

As always, many people helped with the details of this book.

First and foremost, my husband Dan for helping me figure out how to make a conspiracy work.

A special thanks to morgue supervisor Phelan Evans from the Sacramento County Coroner's Office for not only the tour, but answering all my questions without batting an eye. C. J. Lyons once again saved my butt with her sound medical advice. My friend Trisha McKay who reminded me that the Fox & Goose serves Guinness on tap. And Virna DePaul who answered many of my legal questions.

Of course, I can't neglect to mention Dan, my husband, for making many sacrifices, including eating cold or late dinners—and sometimes having to make his own dinner—during the writing of this book.

I especially want to thank the Sacramento Regional FBI Office, in particular SAC Drew Parenti, SA and Citizen's Academy leader Steven Dupre, and the fabulous agents who shared their knowledge and experience. This book is much better because of their generosity in giving of their time and expertise. I especially want to thank SSA Mike Rayfield of Squad 8, who makes fugitive apprehension sound like fun. Any errors are mine and mine alone.

Under the "I couldn't do it without you" heading: my fabulous editor Charlotte Herscher (thank you for helping me be the best writer I can be); Dana Isaacson (thank you for both your criticism and praise—your fine-tuning is invaluable); Kate Collins, and the rest of the Ballantine team who work so hard behind the scenes—thank you for everything. Of course special thanks to my agent Kim Whalen, who surprisingly has a calming effect on me, and the entire Trident team.

And I would be remiss if I didn't finally recognize the loyalty and support of my husband of fifteen years, Dan, who still makes me laugh.

PROLOGUE

He buried Jessica White's body in the vast open space on the west end of Stanford University.

He hadn't meant to kill her. She'd been intoxicated, but coherent. He pretended to be tipsy, but in truth he'd replaced his beer with a nonalcoholic variety he kept in his room. He needed to be in control.

They fucked like animals and he couldn't climax. He'd had this problem before, knew what had to be done to bring relief. She laughingly agreed to "play the game," as she called it. But tying her to the floor spread-eagled was no game to him.

She was beautiful. Long, lean body, round tits, perky nipples, dark hair spilling around her.

So he had closed his eyes, wanting to remember the woman who had loved him, who had taught him everything about sex.

Bridget had seduced him when he was twelve. Told him what to do, what she liked, made him do things he didn't want to. But he'd loved her. Loved her breasts. If she'd just let him suck her breasts, he would have been happy.

She knew he liked it, and only let him touch them

when he finished his other duties. She said only young men made her feel good. Only young men like him.

The week before he graduated from eighth grade he went to her house like he did every Wednesday after school. He waited for her in the backyard. Leaving together would have been unseemly, she always said. After all, she was the principal.

He waited and waited and then heard laughter from inside. He walked around to her bedroom window and saw her with another boy. He was smaller and younger and had no pubic hair.

Bridget had told him last time he was getting too old.

She let the boy—a kid who'd transferred midyear and was a grade younger—touch her breasts. Like she'd done when she first brought him to her house. It was only later, after she hooked him, that she denied him until he satisfied her. Until he hurt her.

Outside her bedroom window, he hated her.

He went back late that night. Snuck into her bedroom. He wanted to kill her, but he loved her so much. She needed him.

She was expecting him.

"I saw you watching. I'm sorry we can't see each other anymore. You're leaving for high school in the fall. But I'll give you something to remember me by."

Then she hurt him and he thought he would die.

After that, he couldn't have sex like a normal person. He watched porn movies, he spied on his father and stepmother while they did it—quick and fast. Later, he spied on his hypocritical father when he learned about the young mistress.

He tried to re-create that urgent copulation with Jessica, but it hadn't worked. It never would.

He didn't even realize he'd strangled Jessica until he climaxed and collapsed on top of her. She wasn't breathing. He stared in shock at her neck, saw the bruises, the thumb impressions so deep they had to have crushed her larynx.

He looked at his hands as if he didn't recognize them as his own. They had been around her neck, his thumbs pushing, but he didn't remember.

He wasn't a murderer. It was an accident, just a terrible accident. Who would believe it? Jessica's wrists and ankles were red and chafed, probably from straining while she suffocated. No one would believe that she'd allowed him to tie her up. That he'd just gotten carried away. That's what happened, things got out of hand because she wanted him so bad. She'd asked him to tie her up. She'd begged him to do it rough, saying she liked it that way. It was all her fault. *Sick bitch*.

So he waited a few hours until everyone in the fraternity was drunk or passed out, then brought his car around to his ground-floor window, taking Jessica out that way instead of through the door.

No one had seen them together. Jessica had made a big production about leaving the party earlier—she didn't want her ex-boyfriend to know she was going to screw someone in his own fraternity. Then she climbed in through his window and . . . she died.

He drove to the west end of the campus into the rolling hills toward the Dish, a radiotelescope built a couple years back. When he could drive no further, he walked along a jogging path with a shovel he'd taken from the fraternity basement. He veered off the path about twenty-five yards, shielded by trees and shrubs, until he found soil soft enough to dig.

He was stronger than he looked, which surprised anyone who decided to pick on him. Digging the grave gave him time to clear his mind, to focus on the task at hand, and to formulate answers to any questions he might be asked regarding Jessica's disappearance. She hadn't told anyone she was coming back to his room because her ex was insanely jealous. She lived nearby, in an off-campus sorority. She had walked to the fraternity.

If she had told anyone about meeting him, he'd lie. He'd lied most of his life. He was good at it. He'd brought all her personal effects and tossed them into the grave, along with the ropes he'd used to bind her. He'd go back and make sure there was nothing of her in his room, not even a hair. He was a neat, orderly person. No one would be surprised if he deep-cleaned his room Sunday morning.

He had to move her body from his car to the grave. Not yet dawn, the quality of night was changing almost imperceptibly. He didn't have much time.

He'd wrapped her body in a wool blanket. As he removed her from the trunk, her body was stiff and difficult to bend. Rigor mortis. It hadn't even been six hours! He pulled her out, falling backward and dropping her body in the dirt. Jessica rolled out of the blanket, stiff legs bent at an awkward angle from the time spent in his trunk.

Frustrated and angry at himself for his clumsiness, he pushed her back onto the blanket and carried her like a baby to the grave. He dropped her in and quickly shoveled dirt over her. Seeing her dead again had unnerved him. He wanted to get back home as quickly as possible. He needed to shower.

Relieved upon finally finishing the unsavory task, he

returned to the fraternity his father had insisted he join. He was to continue the proud family legacy. "You'll major in biology, enroll in the premed program, then you can choose your discipline. Surgery would be the smart decision." As if he wasn't smart enough to figure out his father wanted him to follow in his big, fat footsteps.

He had no desire to go into medicine. He'd tell his father to go to hell. Someday. He should have done it a long time ago.

No one was awake when he returned just as the sun crept over the horizon. He went to the bathroom, locked the door, and flipped on the light.

Something was caught in the buttons of his shirt. He pulled at it, inspecting it carefully. Slightly greasy, what on earth . . .

He bit back a scream. It was her skin! Jessica's skin had come off in a chunk on his buttons. What other parts of the dead bitch were on him that he couldn't see?

He stripped and jumped under scalding hot water in the shower, scrubbing his body over and over until he was red and raw. Images of Jessica rising from the grave, her skin sloughing off in greasy chunks of flesh, haunted him.

Before anyone woke, he scrubbed down his room twice with the strongest cleansers he could find. Removed anything, seen or unseen, that said, "Jessica White Was Here." Then he tried to sleep, but his heart was beating too fast. Every time he closed his eyes he saw Jessica rise like a zombie from the grave.

He went to the kitchen and made himself a hearty breakfast. He was famished. When he was done, he felt so much better.

It's over.

Though he'd killed Jessica only hours ago, the event seemed surreal, as if he'd been an observer of the brutal act, not a participant.

When he returned to his clean room, he saw a note on his bed. Something was wrong.

It was a plain white card in a blank white unsealed envelope. He slowly removed the card.

We know what you did last night.

Something else was in the envelope. He poured it into his hand.

Dirt. And a single earring.

ONE

Claire was an expert bullshit detector. That's what made her so good at her job investigating insurance fraud.

This morning she'd been called to a warehouse fire in West Sacramento, at the Port of Sacramento near the docks where the Deep Water Ship Channel connected the Sacramento River to the San Francisco Bay. The port predominantly handled agricultural products, but container goods from China and beyond were not uncommon. They didn't have customs or any serious inspections, which were taken care of at the port of entry. As far as docks went, they were relatively clean and quiet, even at seven in the morning. Most of the activity was at the far end where a ship was being loaded with produce Claire couldn't identify from this distance.

She breathed deeply, the lingering scent of burned wood, scorched metal, and ash making her grimace. Best to get this out of the way now, before the temperature rose. It was only the second week of May, yet summer had arrived. While the rest of the country enjoyed spring, yesterday Sacramento had peaked at ninety-five. Today would be even hotter.

Claire was supposed to meet the arson investigator

here at eight, but she liked hitting the scene early to do her own walk-through. She'd already done everything she could from the office; the two final pieces for the report were the walk-through and interviewing the claimant.

Five-shot Starbucks latte in hand—as much to combat the mild hangover from her late night as to wake her up—Claire grabbed her backpack from the backseat of her Jeep, absently brushing dog hair off her jeans. She had to remember to cover the seats with towels when she took Chewy and Yoda on car rides.

Crime scene tape cut across the front of the warehouse—but since it was a mere shell and incapable of being locked up, she slid under the tape. Arson. She smelled it.

Warehouses sometimes burned down by accident. A careless employee left a cigarette butt burning, lightning struck, homeless people tried to get warm in the frigid Sacramento winters.

But accidents were rare.

The building owner hadn't even been smart about it, Claire thought as she walked around taking pictures and notes. There was no evidence of burned goods. They could have been stolen before the arson, but Claire suspected the merchandise had never arrived or had been sold before the arson. She'd already pulled the financials of Ben Holman and Holman Medical Supply Company, Inc. Operating on the wrong side of a razor-thin profit margin, Ben Holman was three months late on his personal home mortgage and his creditors all had 90- to 120-day lates on him.

Convenient timing for an insurance claim that would give him half a mil for supplies and damage.

Holman would likely claim faulty wiring . . . possible, of course. These dockside warehouses were old and rarely did the owners upgrade the interiors. They were used for the temporary storage of goods that came down the Sacramento River shipping lane. Product came, product left—cogs in the wheels of the economy. But in this instance? No way. It was arson, and Claire just needed to wait for the fire investigator to show up and confirm it.

Holman Medical Supply Company, Inc., would soon be one less cog to muck it up for legitimate business people.

Claire deeply breathed in the fresh air as soon as she cleared the building, then leaned against a cement wall to write up questions for warehouse-owner Holman.

He didn't know Claire had security tape from the warehouse three doors down that showed him driving up the day before the fire started. He didn't know she had a copy of the manifest filed with customs in San Francisco. And he would certainly deny knowing where the missing goods were, though she had a contact who said an unusually large supply of syringes had shown up on the streets yesterday.

Ben Holman was just one more pathetic human being who proved that no one could be trusted.

Claire drained the rest of her lukewarm latte, stuffed her notebook and camera back into her pack, and stretched, hoping the investigator wouldn't be late. She wanted to write up the report and meet her veterinarian at her house at noon. Dr. Jim made house calls, at least for her. She had started toward her Jeep when she heard a deep male voice.

"Claire."

At the familiar voice, she dropped her cup and pack, reaching for the gun she carried in a belt holster in the small of her back, and began to turn when someone from behind grabbed her arm, bending it up and back. She aimed a perfect kick to her attacker's balls, but he anticipated the move and sidestepped it, spinning her around and pushing her against the cement wall she'd been leaning on, knocking the wind out of her.

"Claire, stop. I need five minutes. Please."

Daddy.

Raw anger and deep sadness always accompanied any thoughts of her father. But here—now, in person— the anger and sadness were magnified. She heard nothing, felt nothing, saw nothing, except the familiar stranger in front of her. Heard him breathing, felt his heart beating as her arms were trapped between her chest and his, saw the plea in his vivid blue eyes, eyes like her own.

Once, she had loved him. Trusted him. Worshipped him. She remembered the past with such clarity that it took her breath away.

He looked so much older now. Of course he did. She'd never visited him in prison. She hadn't seen him in fifteen years, since the trial, since she'd testified for the prosecution against her own father.

It had been nearly four months since Tom O'Brien had escaped from prison during the San Quentin Earthquake. Four months and no word except that her father had become some sort of a dark hero, helping authorities capture the other escapees, while slipping away undetected. She'd talked repeatedly with local and federal cops, endured weeks of stakeouts outside her home, sacrificing her privacy. For a while, she even thought he was dead. And when she finally believed he had disappeared for good, he showed up here. Now. Like a ghost.

Love and hatred for this man overwhelmed Claire.

Tears welled up in her eyes. To force them back she pictured the dead, bloody body of her mother. Fifteen years might have seemed like a lifetime, but the sight and smell of blood was as fresh in her senses as if Claire had walked in on the murder this morning.

Daddy.

She pushed against him, but he had her pinned tightly to the wall. Her gun dug into her back, and the pepper spray on her keychain was in her pocket, out of reach.

"Claire, I don't have a lot of time. The Feds are watching you."

"Were," she said.

"Are," he contradicted. "I know you don't believe me, that you never believed me, but I didn't kill your mother. And I have proof."

"I didn't believe you then, and I don't believe you now."

His face hardened, but his eyes watered. Looking at her father was like looking at an older, masculine version of herself.

They'd done so much together before that awful, life-ending day. Biking. Skiing. Camping. She desperately wanted to believe him because they'd been "two peas in a pod," as her mother used to say.

The mother *he* had killed.

Claire knew the truth. It was as much her fault as his, but he was the one who'd pulled the trigger and coldly killed two people.

"I'm sorry, Dad," she said, surprising herself as her throat swallowed the tremble in her voice. "I should never have told you about Mom's affair. It was childish of me. I just didn't know then that everyone lies, cheats, and steals for personal gain."

He looked as if she'd hit him. "None of that was your fault, Claire. Your mother had had affairs before."

"That's what you said at the trial, but—"

"It's true."

"It was convenient for you. And would it really matter? Even if she'd screwed around with a dozen men it wouldn't change the fact that Mom and her current lover were screwing in your bed when you walked in and shot them."

She was on a roll. She stared at him, remembered that he had been convicted in a court of law by twelve jurors. He'd been convicted of murder, and few innocent people went to prison.

"You would have said anything to get out of prison. The D.A. offered you a plea. You didn't have to get the death penalty! You could have pled guilty. Maybe if you'd just admitted the truth I could have lived with it, I could have forgiven you, but you just lied and lied and—"

"I wasn't lying," he insisted, his jaw tight. "Everything I told you then was the truth."

"The evidence showed—"

"The evidence was circumstantial. Someone framed me. I have proof."

"What proof? If you had proof, why didn't you bring it up during one of your half-dozen appeals? Have your attorney petition the court? There is no proof that you're innocent."

"And there was no proof that I was guilty!" he

shouted in her ear, his voice shaking. "It was all circumstantial, Claire. A setup. A frame—"

"Yeah, so why don't you go find the *real killer*?"

"Dammit!" He took a deep breath. "I need to find
Oliver Maddox. I know he spoke to you in January before"—he paused—"the earthquake."

"Before you escaped from prison? Let's call a spade a
spade, Daddy, okay? No bullshit. You're an escaped
killer and they'll shoot first, and frankly, no one gives a
shit about your answers."

Claire's insides were twisted and burning. She'd never
talked to her father like that, had never raised her voice
or sworn at him.

*Don't think of him as your father. He's an escaped
prisoner. A convict. A murderer.*

His face hardened, but pain lit his eyes. "Oliver Maddox has information I need to prove my innocence. He
works with the Western Innocence Project. I tried calling
him, but his phone isn't working. I can't very well go
looking for him. I think someone scared him into hiding.
I need your help to find him. I don't have anyone else to
turn to, Claire."

She blinked back tears. More lies from her father.
"After I talked to Maddox, I did a little research. I'm
good at that. He's just a law student, not even an attorney.
Doesn't even work for the Western Innocence Project—he
was an intern last summer. They were never going to
take up your case."

Her father shook his head. "That's not true. Oliver
planned on meeting me the week before the earthquake.
He said he had information about Lydia's lover, Chase
Taverton. Evidence that *he* was the primary target.
Taverton was a prosecutor. If he was the target, that

opens an entire pool of suspects, and the detectives barely looked at that possibility."

"You're grasping at straws—"

"Oliver has even more information," he continued quickly, "but he never showed for our meeting, and I couldn't reach him. The next day, I was transferred into the general prison population."

"They don't put cops in with the general population."

"Something happened. Someone got to him—"

"I haven't spoken to Oliver Maddox since I kicked him out of my house months ago when I found out he'd lied to me. He lied to me, and he lied to you. He was just a kid jerking your chain, he didn't have the Project behind him, and he probably didn't know anything that would help you unless he made it up. You were a cop once. You should know how many killers claim they're innocent."

"*I am!*"

"So who did it? In the twenty minutes between when I left the house and called you and you walked in, who broke into our house and killed them? And why? You know, Dad, usually the most obvious answer is the correct one."

"I'm so sorry, Claire, but you have to believe me. The only reason I care about proving my innocence is to prove it to you. I don't want you looking at me the way you are right now. I want my little girl back."

"I'm not a little girl." She found it hard to catch her breath. She couldn't think, she just wanted him to disappear.

"I know." His voice quivered. "Please, Claire, I'm risking everything coming to you. I need your help. I can't do this on my own. I went to the campus, his house, couldn't find him. I couldn't ask more questions without drawing attention. I need to find out where he went and exactly what he knew, get him to tell the truth no matter who threatened him. Working for Rogan-Caruso Protective Services, you have access to far more information and resources than I do."

"Why would I help you? I could lose everything I've built since you went to prison," she said. "My career, my PI license, my home. I don't want to go to jail."

"Claire. Please."

The quiet plea twisted her heart. "Go away. Leave me alone."

"I don't have anyone else," he whispered.

She spoke equally quietly. "Well, then, you don't have anyone, Dad."

A truck turned onto the road heading for the warehouse.

"Think about this, Claire. Think about *me*. I'm not a killer. You know that in your heart."

To prevent her from pursuing him, he pushed her down. "I'm sorry," he called as he ran in the opposite direction of the approaching truck.

Claire slowly pulled herself up. She might have been able to chase after and catch her father, but what would she do? Shoot him in the back?

Instead she put her hands on her knees and fought to regain some semblance of control over her emotions. To try and forget the pain in her father's eyes. To try and forget the pain twisting in her heart.

The truck belonged to the arson investigator, Pete Jackson. He got out, looked at Claire with a frown. "You okay, Ms. O'Brien?"

She faked a half smile as she stretched. "Fine. The sooty air just got to me."

"I told you not to go in until I got here."

"Sorry. Why don't you walk me through it?"

"You must already have your own conclusion."

"I need you to prove it."

"Lucky for you I already have the proof your company needs. Found the hot spot and identified the accelerant. The burn pattern indicates not only arson, but an amateur."

"Too cheap to fork over for a professional," Claire muttered.

As she followed Pete Jackson into the warehouse, she glanced over her shoulder, looking for her father. Tom O'Brien was nowhere to be seen.

That didn't mean he wasn't around.

The Feds had made it perfectly clear to Claire that she needed to report any contact from her father, or be considered an accomplice. They'd threatened her—jail time, loss of her private investigator's license, her concealed-carry weapons permit. Her dad said that the Feds were still watching her. Agent Donovan had come around a couple times, but it was routine. She'd answered his questions and told him to get lost each visit. She didn't think they had someone on her 24/7 after the first two weeks since the quake, but maybe she was wrong. Maybe she'd been so preoccupied with trying to forget about her father, she'd missed the obvious.

Remembering the look on her father's face gave her pause. And his words had sounded . . . truthful. But he'd had fifteen years to perfect his act. How could she believe him now when she hadn't believed him then?

But what if he *was* telling the truth?

For fifteen years she believed, she *knew*, that he was guilty. After the trial she learned to block everything out to prevent the nightmares from creeping in. If it hadn't been for Detective Bill Kamanski and his son Dave, a young street cop who had been her dad's friend, she would have probably turned to drugs or worse. They taught her to be strong, to accept what had happened and move on. She'd almost changed her name to forget who her father was. But in the end, she'd realized that if she changed everything about herself, she'd be living a lie. So she remained Claire Elizabeth O'Brien, accepting the truth, at the same time forcing that horrific day and the trial from her memory. Most of the time it worked.

Seeing her dad again after so long, especially with the panic in his face and voice, made her question everything she believed. *Stop that.* She knew her father was guilty. There could be no other explanation. Her mother was having an affair and her father snapped. It happened all the time throughout the world.

But would it hurt to find Oliver Maddox? Talk to him? Learn what he knew? Maybe the kid had proof of her father's guilt, and that's why he hadn't shown up. If that was the case, Claire would call the Feds and set up a meeting to put her father back in prison.

At least then she could tell her father he had nothing to hold on to. Maybe she could get him to turn himself in. She didn't want him to die, gunned down by an overzealous cop.

Who was she kidding? His execution date was six weeks away. If not for the earthquake, his days would have been numbered anyway. Why had he foolishly re-turned to Sacramento when he'd managed to stay under the radar successfully for the last four months? He should have kept on hiding. He was obviously good at it.

Still. Oliver Maddox had told her father he knew something about her mother's lover Chase Taverton. Taverton had been a Sacramento County prosecutor who, from what Claire remembered from the trial, was successful, charismatic, and well liked. Still, prosecutors acquired enemies—criminals they put in prison, victims who didn't get the justice they deserved. Or maybe it was personal.

Her heart twisted at the thought of turning in her father, and she doubled her focus on Pete Jackson's comments as they walked through the burned-out warehouse.

Why couldn't you have just stayed away, Dad?

TWO

Tom O'Brien was grateful when Nelia didn't say anything on the drive back to the motel. He needed the time to think.

He'd unintentionally manhandled Claire. Though she hid her fear well behind those suspicious blue eyes, he'd scared her.

He squeezed his eyes shut, the hot burn of unshed tears reminding him of everything he'd lost on that horrific day fifteen years ago.

"I'm so sorry, sweetheart," Tom whispered. If Nelia heard him, she didn't comment, her eyes focused on driving in morning commuter traffic, knuckles white as she gripped the steering wheel. He'd tell her everything—they had no secrets—but now, he had to regain control over his past, over his emotions.

Fifteen years was a long time, but when you lived day in and day out remembering every minute of the hour that destroyed your life, you didn't forget a detail.

He remembered exactly what he had felt when Claire called him that day about Lydia and Taverton. Pain. Anger. And a deep, soul-shattering sadness that his marriage was, in fact, over.

But he'd never imagined Lydia dead.

*   *   *

It wasn't the first time Lydia had cheated on him. Tom had learned of another affair five years before. That time she'd been screwing another cop. From his own division. He'd told Lydia he could forgive her if she promised never to stray again.

"If you don't love me, tell me," he'd said. Divorce was foreign to him—his parents had been happily married for forty years before his dad died—but he wouldn't live in a loveless house. He wouldn't keep her trapped just because they had a life together, a child together.

That first time, Lydia had cried and begged for Tom's forgiveness. She'd met the cop at the hospital where she worked as an emergency-room nurse. It was the adrenaline of the moment, she claimed, she didn't know why she had let it continue. Tom forgave her. Lydia had seemed so sincere.

But that horrible day, knowing she was in his bed with another man, the insidious self-loathing returned. That voice that said, "You're a sucker. She cheated on you once, Tommy Boy, you knew she'd do it again."

Was she fucking another cop? How many had there been? Had everyone been laughing at him behind his back? Poor Tom O'Brien, his wife was a whore.

He went to the house that day not only to confront her, but to see the truth for himself. That his wife had spat on their wedding vows again, that they meant nothing to her, that his forgiveness had meant nothing, that their eighteen years of marriage meant nothing.

Maybe if Tom was the only one who knew of Lydia's infidelity, he could have lived the lie until Claire went off to college. Quietly gotten a divorce. But their fourteen-year-old daughter knew. Had known for weeks. It had all spilled out when Claire called him in tears.

"I've seen the car before, two months ago. I asked Mom who was at the house and she said just a friend, and then I saw her kissing a man at the park last month. Mom didn't see me. I wanted to tell her to stop, but . . ." Claire's voice trailed off. "I saw the same blue car then."

Tom was ill with the thought that Claire had been living with this knowledge, that it hurt her.

"Mom brought him home today," Claire sobbed into the phone to her dad.

"Why aren't you in school?" he'd asked.

"Missy and I came home for lunch."

He'd learned later that was a half-truth. Claire and Missy had come home during lunch, but had planned on cutting classes the rest of the day.

"Daddy, I hate her!"

Claire didn't hate her mother. It had been a statement born of anger and frustration. Nor did Tom hate Lydia, but any love he'd had was a diminishing memory. Tom told Claire to stay at Missy's house and he'd talk to her after he spoke to Lydia. "Don't worry," he'd said. "Everything is going to be fine."

He didn't believe it. Claire didn't, either.

He parked his police-issue motorcycle down the street from their bungalow in South Land Park, not wanting the copulating occupants to hear the sound of his bike. He walked up to the front door rather than using the garage-door opener. An unfamiliar blue car— an older-model BMW—was parked in the narrow drive.

Tom inserted his key, but locked instead of unlocked the door. Claire hadn't said whether she'd gone into the house, only that she recognized the man's car. Why *would the door be unlocked? Had Claire seen more than she wanted to admit?*

Tom turned the key again and went inside, knowing instantly that something was very wrong.

He reached for his gun, its weight comforting as fear-laced adrenaline rushed through his veins. It was the acrid smell—not of sex, but of death. Blood mixed with the lingering scent of gunpowder.

His rubber-soled boots made no sound on the worn wood floor of the narrow hall. The mirror over the living room mantel reflected his profile—hard, chiseled, tough. A cop. If he dared look at his eyes, they would have been a wild, fearful blue.

Every door was closed. The bathroom. Claire's room. The linen closet. The small guest room that Lydia used as an office. And the door at the end of the hall. Their bedroom.

Not closed, he noticed while approaching, but ajar. Pushing it open with his shoulder, Tom stepped over the threshold.

The queen-size bed, lit by the midafternoon sun oddly filtering through the half-closed blinds, was in disarray from a rowdy session of sex. Both victims were naked, the male lying facedown on top of the female. Both bloody, the attack so quick and efficient that the male victim didn't have time even to think about a defense.

Lydia was on the bottom—had she seen the killer? No—she always made love with her eyes closed. At least she had with her husband.

Her dead lover was sprawled on top of her. Four bullets in his back, one in the back of his head. He certainly hadn't seen the killer. Tom hadn't seen so much blood since he'd been the first responder at a brutal Korean gang shootout in Del Paso Heights. Lydia was drenched in it. His and hers. The killer had placed a single bullet in Lydia's head. Why? Wouldn't he have known the bullets penetrated the man's body?

Of course, Tom realized with sick knowledge. He had wanted to make sure Lydia was dead. Just in case.

Tom had to leave. Call for help. Do something, dammit, anything but stand here and look at his wife dead and naked in the bloody arms of another man. He was a cop, he knew to leave the scene undisturbed. But he had a burning question. He had to know who. What man had Lydia turned to because Tom wasn't good enough? What man had slept with his wife? Did he know him? Was he a friend? Another cop?

Tom's eyes were dry, but his throat constricted as the brutal slaying of his wife hit him. She didn't deserve this, didn't deserve to die an adulteress.

Tom didn't touch anything. The man's face was turned away from the door. Barely breathing, Tom walked around the bed to look at his face. Pent-up rage ate at his gut. He would have yelled at Lydia had she been alive. He'd been prepared to confront her and her lover. Throw her out of the house. Now? Guilt and anger battled with a surreal sense that this could not be happening.

Tom stared at the dead man, one eye full of blood from the bullet behind it. But Tom recognized him—a man he'd never met personally but had seen in action in the courtroom. A prosecutor, Chase Taverton.

He turned to leave, to call in the murder, to give himself five minutes of fresh air before he told Claire her mother was dead.

Then he saw it. His personal firearm, a Smith & Wes-

son .357. On the nightstand, not in the drawer. He always stored it in the nightstand on his side of the bed.

It was on top of the nightstand, on Lydia's side of the bed.

His gun.

His wife.

Her lover.

This wasn't right. His gun was in the wrong place. Had someone used his gun to kill them? His feet were like lead as he stared, trying to make sense of what had happened in his bedroom.

He heard the front door slam. "Daddy?"

Claire.

He couldn't let her see her mother like this.

He quickly left the bedroom, pulling the door closed behind him. "Claire, don't—"

"What's wrong?"

"We need to leave." Get her out of the house, protect the crime scene. Protect Claire.

"Is Mom gone? What happened? What—" Tom's little girl stared at the gun in his hand.

Fear crossed her young, pretty face. Was she afraid of him? No, not his Claire Beth. He'd walked into a nightmare.

"Claire, I came home and found her. She's dead, honey."

"Dead? Who? What happened?" She said the words, but confused and scared, hadn't comprehended what he meant.

His own gun had killed his wife. The shock hit him and he realized he was in serious trouble. He didn't want Claire to know but the truth was certain to come out.

"Claire Beth, we have to leave now. Your mother—God, I wish I didn't have to tell you like this—she's dead, honey. Someone killed her and Taverton. They're both dead."

Claire shook her head, her eyes wild, her jaw clenched in denial. "No. No! I don't believe you!"

Tom hadn't been holding her tightly enough and she broke free, stumbled around him, bumped against the wall, ran to the end of the hall.

Sirens sounded in the distance. A neighbor must have heard the shots and called the police. How long ago?

Tom followed his daughter, reached for her as she flung open his bedroom door. She stared.

"Claire—"

She screamed.

Tom grabbed her by the shoulders and turned her to him. "We have to leave."

"Daddy—what happened? What did you do?"

"I didn't do anything."

Tears streamed down Claire's cheeks. There was doubt in her blue eyes. She didn't believe him. She didn't believe her own father.

"I would never do anything to hurt you."

"But—" She looked at the gun in his hand, her entire body trembling.

"I didn't kill your mother."

The sirens were closer. On their street. "We have to talk to the police. Tell them everything. The truth."

Claire's bottom lip quivered. She pushed away from him and ran from the house. Through the open front door Tom saw two patrol cars pull up. One cop—a rookie named Adam Parks—jumped out and ran to

Claire, pulling her to safety behind the car, peppering the distraught girl with questions.

Tom holstered his service weapon and stepped from the house, hands in front of him, palms up. He was in uniform of course. He was on duty. Parks looked at him quizzically. "O'Brien?"

"This is my house," Tom said. "There're two dead bodies in the bedroom. I didn't touch anything." Not that it would matter, Tom thought. It was his house, his gun, his wife in bed with another man.

He knew what the crime scene looked like. He knew what these cops would think as soon as they saw the naked bodies.

Worse, he knew what Claire thought. How could he convince her he'd never hurt her mother?

Parks and another cop—Reynolds—went in and searched the house, came out, and said, "Detectives are on their way, and the chief of police."

Tom nodded.

"What happened?" Reynolds asked quietly. "You came home for lunch and found your wife in bed with another man? Just lost it?"

"I didn't kill anyone."

"It's just you and me, Tom."

Tom turned. He wasn't going to answer any questions. He knew better than to talk without an attorney.

Seventy-two hours later he was arrested on two counts of murder.

THREE

When Mitch Bianchi trained in underwater forensics, he thought he'd find something he was not only good at, but enjoyed.

He was very wrong, at least on the latter point. He was good at it—combining his love and skill of diving with his innate law enforcement savvy. But recovering floaters was the worst job in the Bureau, even worse than his work identifying remains in the mass graves in Kosovo early in his FBI career.

But skill trumped desire every time in the Bureau, and this time Mitch had a stake in the investigation. If Oliver Maddox was dead, it gave Mitch one more direction to turn in his private investigation into the murders of Lydia O'Brien and Chase Taverton.

"You're quiet this morning," Steve Donovan said as he turned onto River Road heading toward Isleton, where Maddox's white Explorer had been found in the river. According to the sheriff's diver, the victim in the driver's seat had been there for a while. Four months? Possible. And it would confirm Mitch's suspicion that Oliver Maddox had found out something that made someone nervous enough to kill. Again.

"Just thinking."

"Funny how you never mentioned you were house-sitting for Nolan while he's at Quantico."

Mitch didn't show a physical reaction. "How'd you hear?"

"Nolan called in last week for some of his files and mentioned it in passing. I remembered he lives only two blocks from Claire O'Brien. So I drove by a couple times, just to check it out, and surprise, I saw you sitting and talking with her at Starbucks Sunday morning. I didn't have a chance to call you on it in private until now."

Trying to come up with a lame excuse or lie would only damage Mitch's friendship with Steve. "You knew I was looking into O'Brien's case."

"I didn't think you were playing with O'Brien's daughter."

"It's not like that, Donovan."

"Don't jerk me around, Bianchi. You're playing a dangerous game here. Meg will draw and quarter you if she finds out you're working the O'Brien case after you were removed. The only reason you're on this assignment is because you're the only diver we have in-house."

"It's complicated." Mitch had to tell Steve the truth. In some ways, he was grateful that Steve had confronted him. Mitch could use a fresh mind to go over the details.

"We have a twenty-minute drive," said Steve.

"We'll talk later. I need to lay it out for you. I still don't know enough to draw any solid conclusions."

Steve's mouth tightened. "Don't screw with me anymore."

"I won't."

"Seven o'clock, tonight, Fox & Goose, and you're paying."

"Fair enough." Mitch didn't want to meet at the Fox

& Goose—he and Claire were supposed to go there tonight to listen to friends of hers who had a band—but Mitch wasn't picking Claire up until eight. An hour with Steve, then he could drive the five minutes to Claire's place. Steve would be long gone.

He planned to tell Steve all about his deception. Everything from his research into the O'Brien-Taverton murders to O'Brien saving Mitch's life to Mitch befriending Claire under false pretenses. The truth about everything, except for how close he and Claire had become over the last couple months. Mitch couldn't acknowledge to Steve—to anyone—that his feelings for Claire had moved far beyond professional interest.

They drove in awkward silence. Mitch looked through his notes on Oliver Maddox. He first learned of O'Brien's connection with the law student through the prison visitor logs. Mitch had looked for Maddox after the prison break, ostensibly because O'Brien might have tried to contact him. But he'd been pulled from the O'Brien case almost immediately. Politics or jurisdictional grandstanding, he didn't know which. He should have stopped then, but when Mitch found out that Maddox had been missing since a week *before* the earthquake, his instincts told him something was rotten. He put a BOLO on Maddox with his license plate and description.

Now they had Oliver Maddox's car and a grossly decayed body at the wheel. After four months the victim would be impossible to positively identify at first glance. Hell, a floater after twenty-four hours was green and sloshy and hard to ID.

Mitch's instincts told him it was Maddox. Disappeared without a trace, and now his car was found underwater.

Accident? Or murder?

The narrow, two-lane road to Isleton that followed the meandering Sacramento River was one of the most dangerous in the county. Accidents were common, especially during rain or the deadly fog that often descended upon the San Joaquin Valley. There was no guardrail to protect a motorist from going into the river. Once in the water, most accident victims didn't survive.

The California Delta covered over 738,000 acres. Hundreds of miles of waterways cut through the Delta, the water coming from the Sierra Nevadas through not only the Sacramento River, but numerous smaller rivers and creeks. They all eventually converged before merging with the San Francisco Bay. Isleton was a small river town of fewer than a thousand residents in the southwest corner of Sacramento County. It was known for its annual summer Crawdad Festival and not much else. Mitch didn't want to think about what those crawdads had done to the body in the Explorer.

Maddox's vehicle had been found in the river two miles north of the city limits. The Sacramento River flowed steadily, but today's current didn't look too bad.

A crowd had gathered alongside the river: local cops and their FBI team. Steve pulled up next to the emergency vehicles and said, "Ready?"

"Always," Mitch replied.

They got out and a deputy sheriff—Clarkston on the badge—approached with the sheriff's diver. The local diver was older than Mitch and a foot shorter, graying, with a craggy face and unusually large hands. "Harry Young. Thanks for coming out."

They shook hands, exchanged credentials, and Young said, "I didn't disturb the car. It's a white 1998 Ford Explorer, registered to Oliver Maddox. A missing person report was filed by Tammy Amunson on January 23 of this year. One victim in the driver's seat, been under for a time—eyes gone, fingers missing. A lot of critter damage, but the trunk and limbs are intact. No visible wounds, seat belt intact and engaged, windows down or broken on impact."

"Was there any evidence along the riverbank of a car going into the water?"

"If there was, it's long gone. Four months, rain, weather, growth."

"Who found it?"

"Fisherman. Early this morning, at dawn. His line got caught and when he freed it, he got a chunk of clothing with it."

"Where's the evidence now?"

"Bagged," the deputy said. "It'll go to our lab."

The deputy was more antagonistic than the older, easygoing diver. Mitch smiled at him. *Play nice with the locals,* he could hear Meg's stern lecture. The FBI had better relations with local law enforcement in recent years, but some cops were old school.

"How deep?" he asked.

The diver responded. "Thirty feet. We got someone from the EPA on the way since this is an environmentally protected area."

"It's now a crime scene."

Young grinned, patted Mitch on the back. "I'm gonna like you. I got the crew waiting to haul the car up, but your office said don't touch the vehicle. Don't much see what you can do down there."

"We want as much evidence as possible intact before we haul up the vehicle. We may bag the body underwater and bring it up separately to minimize damage." But if it was too difficult to remove the body from the vehicle, they'd bag what they could and haul up the body with the SUV. "What kind of fish activity do we have here?"

"Sturgeon, stripers, crawfish. Hell, this is a terrific fishing spot."

"It was an accident," the deputy interrupted.

Mitch raised his eyebrows. "You have a witness who saw it?"

"No, but—"

"Don't assume anything."

The deputy bristled at Mitch's tone. Mitch kept his expression calm: Diplomacy wasn't his strength. Action was.

Steve smoothed the tension, saying to Young, "Why don't you dive with us? You can see what we do, maybe it'll help in future investigations."

"Doesn't look like you need us," Clarkston said.

Young interjected, "I'd like to go back under. Good practice."

Mitch took Steve's lead. "Great. I need an experienced partner."

Steve pulled Young and Clarkston away from Mitch and showed them the sophisticated underwater camera the ERT unit had purchased last year with their limited discretionary budget.

Mitch walked over to Special Agents Duncan and Morales. Though both were young—about thirty, coming into the Bureau under the age of twenty-five, a rarity these days—he didn't have to tell them what to look for.

"Split up and take a Sheriff's deputy with you." He pointed north and south of their location. "We're look-

ing for where the Explorer went in, but based on the remains it was months ago. Anything you find, mark it
and inform Donovan. I'll be underwater."

When Mitch first joined the FBI more than a decade
ago, the Violent Crimes Squad had been one of the best-
staffed and funded units in the Bureau. They'd have had
a full squad of eight out here to recover the body and evidence. After 9/11, resources for their unit were minimal
and staffing was barely twenty percent of what it had
been. Priorities had shifted to counterterrorism and
counterintelligence. Mitch had mixed feelings about the
changes, but he'd adjusted accordingly. They all had.

Mitch finished putting on his diving gear. Even
though he was about to enter murky river water and
face a dead man, a rush overcame him.

He met up with Young and they checked and double-
checked the equipment, then went out on the boat over
the spot where the Explorer rested beneath the surface.
Steve and a deputy manned the boat while Young and
Mitch fell back into the cold water.

Maddox had been missing since the end of January.
Chances were he'd been in the river the entire time. But
proving it was homicide instead of an accident would be
difficult at best, unless they were lucky enough to find a
bullet entry wound or obvious stab marks. The fish and
crustaceans would feed on any exposed areas first,
which often made it more difficult to determine *how* a
body had been assaulted. But a gaping wound no matter
how gnawed by river life would point toward foul play.

The water was icy, having traveled from the Sierra
Nevadas where the snow had been melting all spring,
filling the creeks and tributaries, merging to make this
river. The ninety-degree weather did little to warm the

thirty-foot depths where the Explorer rested, its wheels buried deep in the sediment. The wet suit protected Mitch from the worst of the cold, and he took a moment to acclimate himself to the water pressure, diminished light, and temperature.

He approached cautiously, taking the time to inspect and photograph the front of the vehicle—there were no obvious collision marks. They'd need a more detailed inspection, but it appeared that nothing had hit this SUV, front or back. There was some minimal damage on the passenger side, but nothing to indicate a collision so violent it could push a car into the river. One problem with water was that it carried evidence away from the scene. If there had been branches or leaves embedded in the undercarriage of the car, suggesting perhaps where the vic went in, the evidence could easily have been washed away under the constant pressure of the flowing river.

The Explorer was fully submerged and held fast, the front end sinking deeper into the muck because of the weight of the engine. The water wasn't too murky at first, the sun above cutting through, though as they walked along the bottom of the river and disturbed the sludge, their field of vision deteriorated. The underwater lights he and Young used cast an odd illumination around them, making the shadows darker.

Only the windshield was intact, which suggested the driver hadn't hit the water with any great speed. Mitch ran his finger along the window edge, felt the top of the retracted driver's-side window. The smooth edge told him that it had been down when the vehicle went in. Mitch inspected the other windows. They'd all been down on impact; none had broken under the pressure.

Who drove with all their windows down in the frigid cold of a Sacramento January? He indicated the evidence to Young, who did his own inspection and nodded.

The victim was strapped into the driver's seat. Most victims would unbuckle themselves and attempt to escape, unless the accident rendered them unconscious.

It was virtually impossible to tell anything about the victim, though with the constant movement of the fresh, cold mountain water through the car, decomposition wasn't as advanced as Mitch would have guessed. A recent body would have been dark green, but this body was extremely pale, almost translucent, as the gases in the body had leached out over time. The body was intact for the most part, though Mitch knew if they tried to move it, skin, hair, and potential evidence would be lost. The vic's eyes were gone, as well as his ears, nose, lips, and a good chunk of his face. The vic's fingers were also missing. The body could have fed the fish for some time. Clothing offered some protection because it could take years to disintegrate.

The vic wore jeans, sneakers, and a lined jacket. Under the jacket appeared to be a turtleneck. No one in the Valley had been wearing turtlenecks since early March.

The vic was the same general size and build as Oliver Maddox. Mitch's preliminary conversations with the Davis Police Department shortly after the earthquake had given him little—the detective assigned to the missing person case said there had been no physical evidence of foul play. Mitch would have followed up with friends, teachers, neighbors—except that he'd been pulled from the case.

Oliver Maddox had gone missing in late January—about the same time that Tom O'Brien had been moved from a safe area of San Quentin into the general prison population.

Mitch didn't buy into the coincidence. Maddox had probably been working on something related to O'Brien's conviction, but the only person who knew what was the fugitive himself. Still, how both events connected eluded him.

When Mitch looked inside the car, he was certain he had a homicide on his hands. The car was in neutral.

He photographed the interior, the control panel, and the buckled seat belt. He mentally walked through different scenarios, including suicide, but kept coming back to murder.

Mitch decided to leave the body in the vehicle, suspecting that the corpse would fall apart if they tried to extract it. They had special waterproof body bags for the floaters that could be sealed to prevent evidence loss. He pulled plastic evidence bags from his equipment belt and strapped them to what remained of the vic's hands and head to prevent not only trace evidence but body parts from washing away when the vehicle was raised.

Mitch and Young bagged as much loose evidence in the Explorer as they could for fear it would disappear or disintegrate. Then Mitch caught Young's eye and pointed upstream to indicate where he was heading to search for potential evidence. He used his underwater light to illuminate the depths.

The bridge pillars were only forty or so feet from where the vehicle had come to rest. Mitch pictured the damage on the passenger side and inspected the left side of the pillars extensively. There was no evidence that the vehicle had collided with the pillars either above or below the surface, but with the rise and fall of the water level, paint chips would have been rubbed away. Still Mitch took a lot of pictures—perhaps a collision expert could match up the unique marks on the door with these pillars.

Cars submerged quickly in water, but not instantaneously. Inside air needed to be displaced, and the current of the river would move the vehicle as it filled with water. Maybe a minute or two. Still, forty feet from the bridge, windows down, Mitch figured the car had gone in relatively close to the bridge. Most likely not more than a hundred feet upstream, probably less. If they could pinpoint the entry point, they could use the known water currents from January to estimate what day the vehicle had gone in.

He surfaced and floated. Though there would be seasonal variations, and in a storm the current would be completely different, today was clear, windless, and gave him a good sense of the natural flow of the river.

It was a hunch, but Mitch suspected that the Explorer had gone in approximately eighty feet from the resting spot. He swam upstream, draining his energy. Agent Duncan saw him, but didn't approach. Mitch wasn't surprised.

He hadn't made a lot of friends in the two years he'd been with the Sacramento regional FBI office. Everyone knew that he and Supervisory Special Agent Megan Elliott used to be married. It wasn't like he had announced it, but Meg insisted that everything be on the up-and-up when Mitch came on board.

It was no one's damn business, as far as Mitch was concerned. They'd made a mistake, it was over, no one needed to know anything more. But Meg insisted that someone would find out anyway, and then it could make both of their jobs more difficult, especially since they were both on the violent crime squad.

He still had respect for Meg. Hell, Mitch liked her a lot. They'd met at Quantico, become good friends because of common interests, and ended up in Kosovo together four years later, digging through mass graves as part of a national evidence response team. When they returned to America six weeks later, they both felt out of touch with everyday concerns. The weight of Kosovo tormented them, and they turned to each other for solace. They were two busy people with the same career and they thought that marriage was the answer to loneliness.

They were wrong. The marriage officially ended three years later.

Mitch pulled himself out of the water and sat on a rock at the edge of the river, looking for the most likely point of entry. The killer would want an easy place to push the car into the river. Mitch looked up. This was a curve, but the river meandered in at this point, not out. If the Explorer went in at this spot, it was coming from Isleton. Had Maddox come down here to meet with someone?

According to the locals, there was good fishing in this part of the river. A small restaurant and tackle shop was nestled on the road next to the bridge. Potential witnesses might have seen the car go under. But Mitch sensed that this killer wasn't stupid. No, the car went in at night. Cloudy or moonless or stormy. Minimal traffic. No witnesses.

There was no perfect murder. If they couldn't find

physical evidence here or in the vehicle, they would officially identify the victim and go from there. Retrace his final days. But Mitch didn't intend to wait for identification. He'd start his investigation presupposing it was Maddox.

He motioned to Special Agent Duncan who was not so discreetly staring at him from across the inlet. What did he expect? He'd probably had more face-to-face time with the Office of Professional Responsibility than any active agent. And since the last visit was only three months ago when he returned from Montana after tracking down two fugitives, he was lucky to still have a job.

But what was he supposed to do, sit on his hands? Even though he'd been given a direct order not to cross state lines to follow the fugitives, he'd done it anyway. Under the same circumstances, he'd do it again. He was *good* at his job, he had to act. Sitting around playing bureaucratic games and shuffling paper from one desk to another wasn't in his job description.

Mitch understood his primary flaw: He had a hard time following orders he disagreed with. He'd had the same problem in the military. His issues with authority stemmed from his conflicts with his dad, a bigwig prosecutor who had seemed all-powerful and righteous while Mitch was growing up. Only when it was too late for Mitch to change his path did he learn the cold truth about his father.

When Duncan was within hearing distance, Mitch said, "Go over this area again. The turnout, the dock. The guy's been under for a while, look for any sign of new growth—it might indicate the spot he entered the water. Talk to the owners of the tackle shop and restaurant. Find out how often this dock is used, and specifically about any regulars—people who come out and fish at least once a week. I'm sure there're a few. There may be a witness who doesn't even realize it."

Mitch didn't think so. Probably nobody but his killer had seen what happened the night Oliver Maddox went into the river. But Mitch had to cover all the bases.

He went back under, letting water wrap around him, as he slowly swam back to the Explorer's resting place.

What were you doing that got you killed, Oliver?

FOUR

"Tom?" Her voice sounded far away. "We're here, Tom."

He hadn't been sleeping, but he'd been trapped so far in the past Tom hadn't realized they had already arrived back at the motel.

"Sorry."

"Let's go in." Nelia's voice was quiet and lyrical. It calmed him, grounded him, like nothing else could.

My angel.

She'd saved him, physically and emotionally. He didn't deserve her, but he wasn't about to give her up. He drank in her trust, her support, her *faith* in him as if she were wine to the dying man.

It was quiet and they walked to the room together. Nelia had checked in two days ago, paying up front for a week. He'd hidden in the truck, sneaking into the room when it was clear. Acting like the fugitive he was; hating every minute of it. Without Nelia, her truck, her money, her faith, he wouldn't have survived this long. Coming back to Sacramento to prove his innocence would have been suicide. But Nelia was his eyes and ears. While it still wasn't easy, with her it was definitely safer than if he'd traveled alone. She bought the food, she reserved the motel, she drove.

His angel.

They walked in and Tom went immediately to the bathroom. He wasn't being fair to Nelia, but he needed to run his head under cold water and think.

The earthquake seemed so long ago. He'd run because—no use lying to himself—he ran because he was a dead man. At the end of January, he'd had five months before his date with the executioner. His appeals had been denied, over and over. Oliver Maddox had given him cautious optimism, then disappeared. Tom's thin thread of hope had been severed.

When the quake struck, others ran as well. Cold-blooded killers. Tom had to do something to stop them.

So he had pursued them. He was one of them, after all. They trusted him as much as they trusted anyone. And he ended up capturing seven of the bastards before catching up with Doherty and Chapman in Idaho. He'd been cocky. Cocky because he'd done a damn good job and saved lives. He felt like a cop again. He felt like he was doing something positive after fifteen years behind bars.

It had been three and a half months since that bastard Aaron Doherty had shot him in the stomach and left him for dead in the middle of a snowbank in Idaho. Tom had played that situation wrong—he'd thought he needed to watch Chapman more closely, that he was the more dangerous of the two. Misjudging that psycho had almost killed Tom.

He would have died if Nelia hadn't found him in the snowbank along the frontage road.

It had been touch and go for a while. For over three

months, Nelia nursed him back to health. He rubbed the gnarled scar on his stomach. It was still touch and go; the bullet remained in his body. For the past two weeks, he'd been having periodic sharp pains. But it wasn't like he could go to the doctor.

Nelia hadn't asked questions, at least not at first. She wasn't scared of his blood or his story; she was simply a sad and beautiful woman. And last week when he said he was leaving to find his daughter and prove his innocence, she had simply said, "I'm coming with you."

Tom O'Brien couldn't die knowing Claire believed he'd killed her mother. He would find a way to convince her of the truth she'd been too young and emotional to accept when she was fourteen.

Having Nelia, a stranger, believe him gave him the strength to make a stand. He knew he might die in pursuit of the truth. He'd accepted that fate when his last appeal had been denied. He was already a dead man. He had nothing else to lose.

He left the bathroom and his eyes rested on Nelia. Seated at the small Formica table in the corner, she was drinking coffee. When she saw Tom, she poured him a cup from the thermos she had earlier filled at a nearby coffee shop. She pulled muffins from the bag. "You didn't want to eat before, but you need your strength," she told him.

Sitting across from her, he took her hand. She stared at him, brown eyes sad and worried. "I don't know what I did to deserve you," he said, voice cracking. He cleared his throat and sipped warm coffee to swallow the emotion.

She shrugged and glanced down. She hadn't told him everything about her past, but he knew she'd lost her son twelve years ago. He'd been murdered. She hadn't shared any other details, but even sharing those few had been like ripping open her heart.

Her loss had sent her into a self-imposed exile. It was why she lived alone in the woods, but didn't explain why she'd helped him, or why she believed him. She'd tell him in her own time.

"Claire is—" What could he say? "—not what I expected."

"She is who she is. You can't expect that the horrible things that happened in the past wouldn't affect her."

"No, but I—I wanted her to be . . . open. She was cold. She's believed all this time I'm guilty. She was angry and scared. Scared of her own father! I love her more than anyone, and she—"

"Tom."

He caught her eye. Nelia never raised her voice, but her tone commanded his attention.

"You can't expect to change her mind during one surprise confrontation. Give her a little time."

"Unless she turns me in to the cops."

"Do you think she will?"

Did he? "I really don't know." He bit back his fearful frustration. "I need her help."

"I can look for Oliver Maddox," Nelia offered, not for the first time.

"Claire has the resources and training to do this. You've already risked too much for me."

"You saved me as much as I saved you, Tom. My cabin in Idaho was as much a prison to me as San Quentin was for you. You freed me. I'm not leaving you now. Not until we find out what happened to your wife."

"Nelia, tell me the truth. How did you find me?"

"I told you. I saw something out of the corner of my eye. I went to investigate, found you."

"But you were hours away from home. And you never leave, or so you told me. Why that day? Where were you going?"

"Back home."

"From where?"

He knew all about how she'd found him—she'd stopped for gas, the snow was coming down harder, she feared she wouldn't make it back to her cabin before her road became impassable, even with four-wheel drive. She saw what she thought was an angel, did a double take, and saw him lying in a ditch. He'd crawled out, trying to make it to the road, but passed out.

But she'd never told him why she was three hours from home, or why she was driving in the storm, or where she was coming from.

"On the anniversary of my son's murder I visit his grave. In San Diego," she whispered. "For the last twelve years. I've never told anyone."

"No one? Not your family?" She spoke to her mother every Sunday afternoon. It was a formal, one-sided conversation, with Nelia cutting it off after ten minutes.

"My ex-husband knows. He found me at Justin's grave the third year I went." She looked down at their clasped hands. "I swore him to secrecy. He owed me. Like Lydia, he was having an affair. But unlike you, I knew about it and didn't care. I didn't love him. Never had. We married because of Justin . . . and we divorced when we no longer had him." Her voice cracked. "I want you to reclaim your daughter, Tom."

"Nelia." He kissed her hand, squeezed it. "I couldn't

have made it this far without you. I'm going to make Claire listen. I didn't have time to tell her everything Oliver told me. I need to go to her house and—"

"Her house? That's not a good idea. You said yourself you saw one of the FBI agents in her neighborhood yesterday."

Mitch Bianchi. He'd been at the Starbucks kitty-corner to Claire's house yesterday morning. Tom had considered approaching him. After all, Tom had saved the FBI agent's life during the raid on Blackie Goethe's gang.

But he'd decided against it. He needed more information before talking to anyone in law enforcement, even Bianchi.

"Tom? Let me go to Claire."

"I don't want anyone, even Claire, knowing you're helping me. You may not care, but I won't let you risk anything more than you already have. Please. I don't want to worry about you, too."

"I need to do something!"

"You can. Talk this out with me as I write a letter to Claire. Help me find a way to convince her in writing what I failed to get across today in words."

FIVE

Claire was certain that Oliver Maddox was some pie-in-the-sky liberal public defender wannabe who'd encouraged her father's hopes of getting away with murder.

What she should do is contact the FBI and inform them her father had made contact. Or maybe phone Bill and Dave Kamanski. They'd know what to do. Both cops, they had told her more than once that all she had to do was call if she needed anything.

She didn't want to drag them into it. The Kamanskis had been her only family since her father's arrest. Dave was the big brother she never had, and Bill . . . she had often wished he was her father. Because she hated the real one who was sitting on death row.

Actually, she didn't hate him, and that's why she felt so miserable much of the time. She *wanted* to hate him. She wanted to hit him, yell at him, throw things at him for killing her mom, for ruining their lives. Making her sit through a public trial for weeks, through his sentencing. It had been the worst time of her life. From the minute she saw her mother's dead body, and knew her dad had shot her, to when he was sentenced to die, it had been hell.

Guilt twisted in Claire's heart. She'd spent more time over the last fifteen years trying to hate her father for his crimes than mourning her mother's death. She'd been so angry with her mom about the affair, furious that she could be so selfish as to hurt the family. And then she was gone. Claire never had the chance to talk with, argue with, love, or hate her mother. It was so much easier to focus on the trial and hating her dad than it was to focus on the pain and guilt over her mother's murder and remembering every fight, every disagreement she and her mother had shared. She wanted to go back and tell her mother she loved her.

A part of Claire wanted Maddox to be right. She had believed for so long that her father was a killer, but she never stopped loving him, even when she wanted so much to hate. It had made his crimes that much harder to accept, and transformed her love into confusion and misery.

The only really good thing in her life right now was Mitch Bianchi. She'd been moving from guy to guy for so long without any commitment that having someone sort of steady was nice. More than nice. He was the sexiest, safest guy she'd ever dated. A writer, perfect. She didn't want to think about her long history with other underachieving men. She shrugged it off whenever Dave Kamanski teased her about the "dumb blonds" she dated: good-looking men who didn't tax themselves mentally, often not holding down regular or "normal" jobs.

Mitch was different. He was surprisingly smart. He didn't seem like she'd imagine a writer to be, but he did have a way with words. And he was so hot, so sexy, his body hard as a rock. He worked out, and they had spent many hours together playing racquetball on the weekends. He didn't let her win and he played hard.

And damn, he looked doubly hot when he sweated in his cutoffs and faded T-shirt.

Chewy and Yoda liked him. Funnily enough, that made Claire a little less comfortable. She was growing attached to Mitch, and she didn't want to get close to anyone. Her life was a mess. *She* was a mess. But she didn't want to get rid of him, either.

There was no way she was dragging Mitch into this situation. She didn't want him being charged as an accessory or harassed by the FBI. She was going to have to figure out what to do about her father's contact on her own. She didn't believe her dad, but she wondered if he had actually convinced himself he was innocent. Or maybe . . . he was.

Her stomach churned, the latte turning sour. What would it hurt to talk to Oliver Maddox again? Find out exactly what he'd been feeding her father? Maybe then she could convince her dad to turn himself in. She didn't want him gunned down or arrested in a big standoff. She was tough, she'd withstand the media scrutiny, the way her life would be turned upside down like it had been after the prison break. She'd avoided more reporters than cops that awful week in January . . .

She didn't want him to die. Not like that.

What do you want? Him to die by lethal injection? Does that make it better?

She had time before she had to meet her vet. As always, Claire's curiosity bested her. She tried the private phone number Oliver Maddox had left her four months before. Voice mail picked up.

"Mailbox is full. Please try your call again later."

The Port of Sacramento was halfway between the Rogan-Caruso offices downtown and UC Davis. She might as well head to the university and try to track down the law student. Maybe find out that he was no longer a law student, that he'd moved cross-country and taken up medicine.

For fifteen years she'd believed her father had killed her mother. And the guilt remained after all these years. That it was her phone call to her father about her mother's affair that had started the time bomb that ended with two dead lovers and a man on death row.

She might as well have pulled the trigger herself.

Claire stifled a sob as she pulled in to a parking space in the UC Davis visitor parking lot ten minutes later. She slammed the Jeep into park and banged her head on the steering wheel as if that could force the memories from her mind and the stench of blood from her senses. If she hadn't called her father to rat out her mother's infidelity, her mother would be alive and her father would never have gone to prison. They might have divorced, they might have hated each other, but they would both still be in her life.

When Oliver Maddox came to her to ask her to help with an appeal of her dad's case, she rejected him immediately. She'd been at the trial. She'd walked into the house only minutes after her father killed two people. Maddox said, "There's a chance your dad was framed. And I think I can prove it."

Was she willing to go through it all again on "a *chance*"?

She'd be lying to herself if she said Maddox's visit hadn't given her more than a few sleepless nights. What did he know? Why was he doing this? But when she found out he wasn't working with the Western Innocence Project, was just a law student, she'd discounted everything he'd said. One more lying fraud in the world, why was she surprised?

She banged her head one more time and wished she could just forget she'd seen her dad.

He'd looked old. Sad. Defeated.

She couldn't be wrong about that day. She *wasn't* wrong. She'd heard her mother and Chase Taverton alive having sex, called her father, and less than twenty minutes later walked in and they were dead. Who else could have gone into the house and killed them during that short time? Without her or her father seeing anyone? Without leaving any evidence?

She'd been a coward. If she had walked in on them, her mother's lover would have been long gone before her father came home. If Claire had had the courage to confront them herself, she'd never have had to call her dad.

She jumped out of her Jeep and started across the UC Davis campus. She was a proud college dropout after three semesters. College hadn't been one of Claire's wisest choices. Not because she couldn't make the grade—she'd dropped out with a 3.7 GPA—but because she'd hated college almost as much as she'd hated high school. The interpersonal drama irritated her and she tended to get into trouble because she shined the light on truths that people preferred to keep hidden. "Playing nice with others" had never been high on her to-do list. Why play nice when everyone lied?

Five minutes later, after a brisk, head-clearing walk, she stepped into the main administrative office building and said to the secretary, "My name is Claire O'Brien and Oliver Maddox contacted me about an appeal he's working on."

Everyone lied. Even she did. She was quite good at it when she was searching for the truth.

The secretary's eyes widened. "Recently?"

"A few months ago."

Her face fell. "Oliver is no longer here."

"He transferred?"

"No. He's missing. No one knows where he went."

"When?"

"End of January. I don't know the exact date. His girlfriend filed a missing person report with both campus security and Davis police."

Oliver had been missing since January? Claire asked, "Do you know where I can find her?"

The receptionist frowned. "We can't give out private information."

"What about her name? I'm an alumna, I can get her contact information from the student directory." She showed her Davis ID, glad she'd always kept it in her wallet.

"Well, since you're an alum." She walked over to a file cabinet and flipped through some folders. Pulled one, wrote information on a sticky note, and handed the note to Claire.

Tammy Amunson, Clark Hall #25A.

Beneath was a phone number.

"She lives on campus?"

"Yes."

Claire glanced at her watch. She might have time to talk to her, if she could find her now. Clark Hall wasn't far. "Did Oliver have an advisor?"

"I'm sure he did, but I don't have those records here.

I can have someone call you with the information later today."

"That's okay, thanks."

Claire didn't push it. Oliver's girlfriend might know, and if she didn't Claire could go to the law school herself. The fewer people who knew she was looking for Oliver, the better.

She left the administration building and walked briskly while dialing Tammy's number. A sleepy voice picked up. " 'ello."

"Tammy?"

"No, it's Jennifer. Who's this?"

"Claire. I'm looking for Tammy."

"Wednesday . . . she has biology at some god-awful hour. She's out at 10:30."

"At Messenger?" It helped having a familiarity with the campus.

"Yeah."

"Who does she have?"

"Oh, God, I—Thompson."

"Thanks."

It was nearly 10:30 now. Claire had no idea what Tammy looked like, but she hightailed it to Messenger Hall where the science labs were. She put her blazer back on to look more professional, even though it was far too hot for a jacket. She brushed her hair as she walked, glad that she'd left her backpack in the car. Backpack said student, not private investigator.

Claire mentally thanked her boss at Rogan-Caruso for urging her to get her PI license. With it came official-looking documentation, when all being a PI really meant was using common sense.

The first student she asked about Professor Thompson's class gave her the room number, and Claire walked into the classroom three minutes before class was over. She marched up to the front and the professor—an older, gray-haired woman with a stern face—frowned at her. Claire didn't falter. She showed Professor Thompson her PI license and whispered in her ear, "Name's O'Brien. I'm looking into the disappearance of a student here, Oliver Maddox. I was told his girlfriend Tammy Amunson was in this class."

The stern face softened, and the professor glanced at a blonde in the front row. "Tammy, you may leave with Ms. O'Brien."

Tammy looked skeptical and a bit skittish, but she gathered her things and followed Claire from the classroom.

"Hi, Tammy, I'm Claire, a private investigator looking into Oliver's disappearance. You filed the missing person report, correct?" She showed her the license, but pocketed it quickly. If Tammy knew what Oliver was working on she might connect Claire's name with her father and become suspicious.

"You haven't found him yet?"

"No. Let's go outside and talk."

They sat on a bench a ways from the main doors and Tammy said, "I'm so worried about Oliver. Something was wrong, but he didn't want to talk about it."

"Let's start at the beginning. Why did you file a missing person report in the first place? How long had he been missing?"

"The last time I saw him was January 20. It was Saturday night and we had a date. He'd been so busy I—" Tears sprang to her eyes. Normally, when a woman started crying, Claire became suspicious. Girls used tears to get any number of things they wanted, or to avoid getting into trouble. But watching Tammy—her demeanor, her posture, the way her hands clenched and unclenched her biology book—Claire decided the emotion was authentic.

"It's okay," Claire said, not sure how to console her. Claire never cried. *Especially* in public.

"I told him I was going to break up with him if he didn't spend more time with me. That was awful of me, I know, but I missed him, and I missed us."

"What was he working on that kept him so busy?"

"He's a third-year law student. He had a full schedule, plus he was working on his thesis." She paused. "You know, I told all this to the police when I filed the report. Did you talk to them?"

"Yes, but they're not actively looking for Oliver. It's been nearly four months, it's a cold case. And he's an adult." Though Claire hadn't actually talked to the police yet, it was sad but true that the missing persons department in many cities was understaffed. Children were, rightfully, given priority. And while the police always looked into a disappearance, the more time that passed, the colder the case got.

Several tears escaped and Tammy wiped them away. "That doesn't seem right."

"It's not," Claire agreed. "What was Oliver's thesis on? I have down that he was working on something for the Western Innocence Project. Could he have left to do research? Maybe not told you?"

Tammy looked down. "Oliver lied about that."

"Excuse me?"

"He wasn't working *for* the Western Innocence Project. That's his dream job. Oliver is so compassionate.

That's why I love him. He cares so much about people and doing the right thing. Sometimes too much."

"Why would he lie?"

"He interned for the Project last summer and found a file when he was boxing up cases for storage. He read the whole thing and went to the director and asked to look into it. The director said the case had been reviewed and they'd decided not to get involved. Oliver tried to change his mind, but couldn't. So he thought he'd look into it himself. He was obsessed, decided he would write his thesis on the case. He called it 'The Perfect Frame.' "

Claire's heart thudded. "Why?"

"I'm studying to become a veterinarian. Legal stuff doesn't interest me so I really didn't pay much attention to the details. All I know is that he was really excited about it, and thought he had it figured out. He said he was going to talk to his advisor Monday morning, try to convince him, but even if he didn't, he planned to go to the director of the Project with another appeal to look into the case."

"Was it urgent?"

"Oh, yeah, the guy's on death row. He has no appeals left."

"And you didn't talk to him after Saturday?"

She blushed. "Well, Sunday morning. I stayed at his place. He has a town house on F Street."

"Rented?"

"Owned. His parents died when he was just a kid. He lived with his grandmother most of his life, but he had an inheritance—wrongful-death lawsuit. His parents were killed by a drunk driver."

"How awful."

"The police went there and said it looked like he'd packed up, but I know Oliver wouldn't have left without talking to me. I *know* it."

Claire believed her. She was starting to get a very bad feeling about Oliver Maddox's fate.

"Who's his advisor? It wasn't in the report."

"It wasn't? I thought I gave that information to the police. Professor Don Collier. He's a law professor and does pro bono work for the Project. Oliver absolutely worshipped him."

The assassin was not happy.

He drove fast, away from the opulent, gated mansion where he'd just met with two of the three men who'd blackmailed him into murder. They called him "our assassin" and it pissed him off. Not that they thought of him as an "assassin," but because they considered him their *property*.

Fifteen years ago he'd made a choice—and huge sacrifices—to stay near the woman he loved. He'd thought one murder (okay, *two murders*) would have bought his freedom, so when he made the decision to stay in Sacramento after killing the prosecutor and his whore lover he expected to be left alone.

But they wouldn't let him go. Holding that one ancient *accident* over his head, they made him their hatchet man. And they had the evidence to send him to prison. Or to death.

He shivered involuntarily as a glimpse of his body, dead and rotting, flashed in his mind.

He feared death. In death there was nothing but cold, damp dirt and carnivorous bugs. In death, he would watch his body be devoured with time and the elements.

His skin would slough off. He knew what happened to the dead. He'd seen it.

When he was a rookie, the first time he went to the morgue to view an autopsy he saw firsthand what they did. The pathologist cut the body open. Removed everything—stomach, brain, heart—and weighed it. They looked at everything, a fucking full-body rectal exam. Then they put everything they took out back in, dropping the mess into the torso, and sewed the body up. Put it on a metal gurney and twenty-four hours later the body was taken to be buried or burned.

He also knew what happened to the dead after they were buried. After the flood in 1997 when he had major drainage problems around his house, he had to move one of the bodies. She'd been underground fourteen months.

He didn't know why, but he had expected her to look pretty much as she had when he'd dumped her in the hole. He thought she'd be dirty, maybe a little foul-smelling, but he hadn't expected her to be half-skeletal. And then the worms . . .

Rubbing hands over his body as if brushing off an ant attack, he almost crashed the speeding car. He still had nightmares about that day . . . sometimes, his body was being eaten, and his skull stared back at him with empty eye sockets.

His own future death gave him frequent nightmares.

It wasn't because he killed people—he didn't really mind that. And they paid him—pretty well actually, after he'd called their bluff. The assassin learned who one of the principals was, and the slimy developer certainly didn't want his dirty secrets spread around town. Yeah, they paid him now, but that wasn't the *point*. The *point* was that they controlled his life. They knew his true identity. It didn't matter that he cleared twenty grand with every killing; he was stuck in involuntary servitude, which sucked.

Now he knew who all the players were and he considered taking them all out. *Pop pop pop!* They'd be sorry they fucked with him. He was a better killer today than fifteen years ago. They'd made him one.

But they had leverage on him. Solid evidence that he had killed Jessica so long ago. And that was what made the bastards so good at the conspiracy game: blackmail.

But everything would come crashing down if Thomas O'Brien wasn't stopped. And now that Oliver Maddox's body had been found, there could be other people looking into things better left dead and buried.

What had angered him was his blackmailers' reaction to the discovery in the river. That they felt Claire had to be watched, that she would be a threat if she got wind of what that idiot Maddox had been working on.

He would not let them touch Claire. Claire was his. He'd protected her, taken care of her, practically raised her since her father went to prison. He made sure unworthy men stayed away. He felt no guilt for killing her mother and framing her father—her mother was a slut, and obviously her father couldn't keep that whore in line. If it had been his dad? He'd have punished her. But his mother would never have strayed in the first place. His mother knew her place.

And then she died.

He would never let them touch Claire. If she had to die . . . he would personally take care of it. It would be another sign for him, that the time was right for sacrifice and change.

Claire was living on borrowed time, anyway. He hadn't killed her fifteen years ago when he had the opportunity. So that meant that the assassin owned her.

And he could take her whenever he wanted.

SIX

Claire thanked Dr. Jim for coming during his lunch break to examine the stray dogs she'd taken in while she found their owners or new homes. In addition to Yoda and Chewy, Claire had two strays right now: a Lab mutt and what Dr. Jim was certain was a purebred Jack Russell terrier. She couldn't pronounce the veterinarian's last name, but it didn't matter since he had DR. JIM emblazoned in blue on the breast pocket of his white lab coat.

"I might have a home for the Lab mix," Dr. Jim said.

"Really?" Claire glanced into her small backyard where the year-old stray was chasing his tail. Yoda, a rather serious beagle, watched the visiting mutt with what she could only think of as a look of disdain. Yoda simply didn't know how to have fun.

"Family with three boys. I had to put their shepherd down after a hit-and-run last week. They were devastated, of course, but I think they really want another dog as soon as possible, and they're good people."

"They can come by anytime. Just let me know when and I'll be here."

"Still nothing about the terrier?"

She shook her head. "I put notices up in all the usual

places, with the pound, all over the park. I went to every house in a four-block radius. No owner, and no one recognized him."

"He's a smart dog."

She smiled. "You want him?"

"I have four dogs, three of which I took from you. April will shoot me if I bring home another. Besides, I think he's more your style. Even Yoda seems to like him."

True, Claire thought. "We'll see what happens. It's only been two weeks. Maybe his owners went on vacation and the house sitter lost him." She could hope. But the truth was a lot of people simply abandoned their dogs and cats when they moved, or when the pet became too much work. She wanted to strangle those people. Instead, she found good homes for the animals, no matter how long it took.

"Do you want to come over for dinner tonight?" Jim asked. "April is making lasagna."

Claire liked Jim and his wife, but she always felt like a third wheel. They'd been married for years, but still acted like newlyweds. It reminded Claire that no matter how many guys she dated or friends she went club-hopping with, in her heart she felt isolated and alone. Until Mitch.

"I have a date, but thanks for the invite. Tell April I said hi."

Claire watched Jim drive off, then closed the door and walked down the hall to her office.

Facing the rose garden in McKinley Park, her Tudor-style house wasn't large, but it was charming. She kept her dogs outside, though they had access to the enclosed sunroom. Neelix, her orange and white cat, had the run of the place. It was because of Neelix that she'd met Dr. Jim in the first place. She'd just bought the house in McKinley Park four years ago when she'd witnessed a teenage boy throwing rocks at a stray cat in the park. The cat was shrieking. Claire had wanted to chase down the punk, and she'd certainly had enough adrenaline to get in a few good licks, but the poor, undernourished injured cat was lying there, trying to get up, dazed. The cat's back leg was broken. Claire picked saving his life over revenge.

She didn't always choose so wisely.

No one claimed Neelix, so she'd kept him. Nursed him back to health. He went from a six-pound skeletal feline to a thirteen-pound fat, lazy cat.

Neelix opened his eyes, not moving from his spot at the end of her bed when she walked in. She scratched him behind the ears, then turned into her office, a converted walk-in closet. Her bedroom originally had two closets—a large walk-in, and a smaller closet. She had taken the doors off the walk-in, removed the shelves and poles, and turned it into her office. It fit a desk, a small file cabinet, and a short bookshelf. Comfortable and functional.

She flipped on her computer screen and Googled the Western Innocence Project. Nearly every state had an "Innocence Project," which was generally affiliated with a law school where lawyers and students took on criminal appeals pro bono if they felt that the convict had been unjustly convicted. Many of the cases came from DNA evidence, often older cases where new forensic technology enabled them to extract DNA from a rape or murder and match it—or not—to the individual convicted of the crime.

She didn't know what she was looking for. She'd talked to the director, Randolph Sizemore, Esq., once before when he had told her that Oliver Maddox wasn't an employee of the Project nor was the Project working on the O'Brien case. However, it might be worth talking to him again. Maybe he knew where Maddox went. Maybe she hadn't asked the right questions.

Spontaneously, she dialed Sizemore's direct line. She'd uncovered it after speaking to him in January, but hadn't had cause to use it.

"Randy Sizemore."

"This is Claire O'Brien. I'm calling about Oliver Maddox."

Silence at first, then, "Hello, Ms. O'Brien. How can I help you?"

"Do you remember me?"

"Of course. I made a note of our conversation in my journal. You claimed that Oliver said he was working with my institute on behalf of your father."

"That's what he told me, but I know that he was an intern last summer."

"True. I have no new information."

"Do you know that Oliver Maddox is missing? He's been missing since January 20."

There was silence on the other end. "I didn't know. I'm sorry."

"I spoke with his girlfriend. She said that he came to you last summer and asked if you would look into my father's conviction. You didn't tell me that the first time I spoke with you."

"That's not exactly what happened. Hold on. I remember talking to him about it, but . . ." Claire heard pages flipping in the background. "Oh, right. Yes, O'Brien. It was over five years ago that we put together that file. The file was reviewed by a practicing attorney and it was determined that we had no cause to believe Mr. O'Brien didn't get a fair trial or was wrongfully convicted. The file went to archives."

"And you told Oliver this?"

"Of course. I have so many cases on my desk. I have three full-time attorneys working for me, plus many others who work pro bono. We give a thorough look at the case file, court transcripts, evidence. If there's anything at all that we can sink our teeth into, we file a motion. Put it on the record, even if we don't have the time or resources to pursue it."

"Did Oliver tell you why he thought the case should be looked at again?"

"To be honest, I wasn't paying much attention. That was a busy time, and I had a half-dozen serious cases I was working on, all with legitimate problems. I didn't have time to revisit a case that had been vetted by an attorney I thoroughly trust."

"Who was the attorney who originally looked at the file? Maybe Oliver spoke to him."

"Can I ask you something?"

"Yes." His sympathetic tone had Claire on edge. She hated when people pitied her.

"Do *you* believe your father is innocent? In your heart, what do you think?"

She hadn't expected the question. But in the months since Oliver claimed he could prove her father was framed, she'd been thinking about it, and after seeing him this morning . . . She said honestly, "I don't know. Up until I saw my mother's body I would have said he'd never kill anyone. But Oliver was so convinced he was innocent." She didn't mention "The Perfect Frame" to Sizemore. "I want to see what he saw and draw my own conclusions."

"Don Collier."

"Excuse me?"

"Professor Collier does pro bono work for me, and he reviewed the case. He had been a criminal defense attorney before he started teaching at Davis."

"Thank you." Her head was spinning at the information, but she asked, "Can I get a copy of the file?"

"It's in archives. I let Oliver make a copy, but I made sure the original was appropriately refiled. It might take me a day or two."

"That's okay. I really appreciate it."

"I'll have my secretary call you when it's ready."

She thanked Sizemore and put down her phone, wondering what was going on. Having gotten Collier's name from Maddox's girlfriend, Claire had already left a message for him, but he hadn't returned her call.

She tried digging deeper into Oliver Maddox, but there was very little about him. He had a paper posted in the archives of the UC Davis newspaper website. As an alum—even though she'd never graduated—she could access it using her former student ID. It was a paper on the criminal justice system, more than twenty pages. She skimmed it to see if it mentioned her father's case. It appeared to be an indictment against the current appeals process. She didn't see anything related to her dad, but she printed it out to read over more carefully later.

Claire's father had been convicted because of opportunity and motive. His gun was used, but there were no prints on it. It had been wiped clean, which the prosecution claimed was O'Brien's attempt to cover up the murders. There was GSR on his hands, but he'd been at the gun range earlier that morning. The prosecution claimed he'd premeditated the murders, and therefore made sure that he had a good reason to have gunshot residue on his hands.

Other than the timeline, there was no other hard evidence. The jury, like the prosecution, didn't believe that anyone else had the means or motive to kill two people at that exact time. No one had seen anyone else— stranger or friend—in or near the house.

Claire had trusted the prosecutor, Sandra Walters. Ms. Walters wanted justice for her mother and Chase Taverton. She'd been kind and supportive from the beginning, treating Claire with kid gloves both on and off the witness stand. Dave and Bill Kamanski, whom she stayed with during the trial, made sure that Claire was treated well. Everyone seemed overly nice to her then, but those months were a blur.

Bill hadn't wanted her to come to the trial at all, but Claire had to. She had to hear everything, to try to understand how her father could have killed two people. How he could have killed her mother.

Claire didn't remember the specifics of the trial. It was as if she'd listened to every word, and imprinted the transcript in her mind, but when she tried to recall details of testimony they were fleeting, just snippets of conversation here and there.

Two weeks before she started her sophomore year in high school, her father had been convicted. The trial had only lasted eight days, but it had taken nine months to build the case.

Three days after the conviction, the judge sentenced Thomas O'Brien to death.

In the courtroom, her father had turned and stared at her, his eyes haunted.

She'd run to the bathroom and dry-heaved.

"I've told the truth." Her father's flat plea bounced in her head. *I've told the truth. I've told the truth.*

She could not accept it. Who else? Who else could have killed them? And why?

Her father had never admitted that he killed Lydia O'Brien and Chase Taverton. Even fifteen years of prison time and a half-dozen appeals hadn't changed that.

And today, he'd said the same thing.

Oliver Maddox had found *something*. At one time, the Western Innocence Project had been interested in the case, otherwise why would they have had the files in their office?

Still, maybe Maddox was just trying to grandstand and come up with some brilliant thesis, or get himself some press, but he had to have a reason to tell his girl-friend that he had proof of "The Perfect Frame." He had to have a solid reason to come to Claire and tell her he believed her father was innocent. He had to have something to convince her father that proof of his innocence was attainable.

She owed her dad—Claire owed *herself*—the truth. If not now, when? When her father was dead? When it was too late?

Tammy said Oliver was supposed to meet with his advisor, Professor Don Collier, that Monday. The missing person report would have been filed with the Davis Police Department. She needed to talk to the detective in charge and see if she could get copies of his reports—who he talked to and what they said. She didn't know if it would help, but it might give her another path to travel.

Right now, all she had was the advisor. She'd left a message for him after talking with Tammy. She tried his number again, but when voice mail picked up, she immediately hung up.

She glanced at the time in the lower right-hand corner of her computer screen. Damn, she had to put this aside and go to her interview with Ben Holman, the owner of the warehouse that had burned down. She turned off her monitor, washed her face, and reapplied the light makeup she wore during the day.

She left in her Jeep and just as she merged onto the Business 80 toward Roseville, her cell phone rang. She glanced at the caller ID and saw that it was Dave Kamanski's cell phone number. Normally she loved talking to her "brother"—the son of the man who'd taken on guardianship duty when her father had been sent to prison. Dave was ten years older than her and had been a rookie cop when she'd moved into Detective Bill Kamanski's house. Dave had trained under her father and they'd been friends. Tom's actions had hurt him nearly as much as they had Claire.

But now . . . Claire didn't dare tell Dave her dad had contacted her. He was still a cop, a solid cop, and he'd insist she report it.

"Hi," she answered.

"Kings game, seven o'clock, my house. Phil, Manny and Jill, Eric. Phil's cooking."

"I sure hope so," she teased.

"Think Jayne is free tonight?"

Jayne Morgan was the computer expert at Rogan-Caruso and the closest thing Claire had to a best friend. She suspected that Dave had a crush on Jayne, but sadly it wasn't mutual.

"I can ask, but don't count on it," Claire sidestepped.

"But you're game?"

"I don't think I can." Mitch was picking her up at eight. She hadn't introduced him to her "family." That would necessitate her explaining to Mitch about her father being a killer—and a fugitive. Not to mention that Dave and Phil Palmer, his longtime partner, always gave her boyfriends a hard time. Mitch could probably hold his own, but they'd jab at him about being a freelance writer with no visible means of support, and no real job.

"Okay, 'fess up. What are you doing?"

"I have a date."

"Bring him by. Someone we know?"

"No."

"New guy?"

"Sort of." She'd been seeing Mitch for a few months.

"Well? Doesn't he like basketball?"

"He likes to play, not watch."

"You're dating an athlete now?"

"No, though I'd bet he can beat you at racquetball."

"Bullshit. Your boyfriends are all wimps."

"That's not true."

"You should date someone who's your equal, Claire, not someone you can mentally and physically run circles around."

"Yeah, yeah, tell me something new."

"So you're not going to bring him?"

"Not yet. I haven't told him—well, I just like things the way they are, okay?"

Dave softened. "Claire, if you want to talk about your dad—"

"No," she said quickly. Too quickly? She cleared her throat. Oliver Maddox had also talked to Bill, but Claire hadn't wanted to listen to what they'd discussed. But now she needed information . . . Would they realize something was up if she started asking questions? She'd have to tread carefully. Dave, Phil, and Manny were all smart cops. She needed to get Dave's dad Bill alone. Bill had a soft spot for her. She didn't feel good about exploiting him, but right now she needed all the information she could get.

"How about if I come by for the first half?"

He snorted. "Your date won't mind?"

"No need to be snide, David."

"Ouch. You must be pissed to call me *David*."

"Later. I have an arsonist to interview."

"The West Sac warehouse fire?"

"Yep."

"Be careful."

"Always."

She hung up and pulled off the freeway, then turned into an upscale development in Roseville, a sprawling suburban city with over one hundred thousand residents, halfway between Sacramento and the quaint Gold Country town of Auburn.

Before walking up to pound the final nail in Ben Holman's proverbial coffin, she dialed Mitch's cell phone number. Though she didn't have time to talk, she hoped he'd answer. She loved his voice. No matter what mood she was in, talking to Mitch always made her feel good.

Voice mail picked up.

"This is Mitch Bianchi. Leave a message and I'll get back to you."

He sounded far more formal on tape than in person. She said, "Hi, Mitch. It's Claire. Slight change of plans. I need to make a stop tonight and it'll take me awhile. I'll meet you at the Fox & Goose about nine. Sorry. Call me if there's a problem or . . ." *if you just want to talk*. That would sound stupid. "Or whatever," she finished lamely. " 'Bye."

She pulled together her file and clipboard, checked her weapon, and walked up to interview Holman.

SEVEN

The assassin was anxious and excited. He'd be seeing Claire tonight. In the flesh.

When he came off duty he rushed home to shower and change. He didn't want to be too early, so he tried to calm himself. He poured a glass of wine and sat on the edge of his bed, a towel around his waist. He turned on the television via remote.

The TV in his bedroom wasn't connected to cable or an antenna; instead, it was hooked up only to his DVD player where he had one special disk. A compilation of the secret tapes he'd made of Claire. A "Best of Claire" movie.

He savored every moment. Every movement Claire made was burned into his mind; her every sigh, every word vibrated between his ears. It didn't matter what she was doing as she lay in her bed. As long as he could see her, he was happy.

He'd had to be careful, play it cool, make sure that if the camera was found, it couldn't be traced back to him.

When she'd been living in the apartment downtown, it had been much easier to tape her. It had been an old apartment with high, ornate ceilings. He'd planted the camera in the attic, a small hole drilled through an edge in the molding. It was perfect: virtually undetectable. The camera equipment had been expensive, but well worth it—and he had the money, considering he killed annually for the blackmailers.

But he'd been taping her since long before she moved out on her own.

The disk's first scene was of Claire undressing. She'd been sixteen at the time. Perfect in every way.

She came out of her private bathroom wrapped in a white towel, black hair wet, slicked back. Her hair had been long then, very long and lustrous.

She sat on the edge of her bed, brush in hand, combing through her thick hair. She was looking off into a corner, and he'd always wondered what she was thinking about just at that moment. She'd looked so wistful.

When her hair was tangle free, she braided it down her back, as she often did before she went to bed.

"I really should cut my hair," she said to her reflection in the mirror.

"No," he said out loud, thirteen years after the tape had been made. She ended up cutting her hair short when she was twenty, never letting it grow past her shoulders.

She dropped the towel and stood naked in the middle of her room.

Perfect.

Her skin was white, with very faint tan lines from the bikini she had worn the summer past. Her brown nipples tilted up slightly, her breasts round and heavy. He loved those breasts, how he longed to touch them. She was slim and curved, a faint hourglass figure on her petite frame. She was a hair over five foot three, though she'd put five foot four on her new driver's license.

Then she turned and he saw her magnificent backside, her beautiful shoulders, shapely hips. She bent over to pull underwear from a basket in the corner. One foot in, the other, sliding lacy panties over her hips. She grabbed a shirt out of the same pile, pulling it over her head, her body twitching, unknowingly seductive as she slid it down. A little shirt, it ended at the top of her panties. She sat at her desk and opened a book. Homework.

The disk cut to a scene in the same room, except that Claire was nineteen and not alone.

She was with a boyfriend. Because the assassin had watched her closely for years, he knew that this was the first time she'd had sex.

He hated it and loved it. He pictured himself in the role of Ian Clark, the asshole who'd taken Claire's virginity.

Kissing her lips.

Licking her breasts.

Spreading her legs.

It was him, only him.

As he watched the disk, he pulled the towel off and took his hard cock in hand. He'd had the camera perfectly aligned with her bed, so he saw everything. The look on her face when the dipshit put his mouth on her breasts. She looked both nervous and excited.

Because she was Claire, she ended up taking over. She let the fool start, then she positioned him beneath her and controlled her own deflowering.

The assassin couldn't see her face, so he closed his eyes. Listened. Claire's moans. Gasps. Her "awww" as she controlled entry. Her "ummms" as she enjoyed new sensations.

He pictured himself taking Claire's virginity. Felt himself entering her—but he would be on top. He would be in charge. He pummeled her, over and over, making her his, making her want him.

Closing his eyes, he watched Claire beneath him. Her black hair, long and silky, just like Bridget's. Her eyes looked into his, so blue, so bottomless, so expressive.

It's always been you.

With Claire, he never had problems with release. In his mind, he climaxed into her, then opened his eyes as the image that sent him over flashed in his head.

His hands around her neck. Her bloody eyes bulged, her hands clasped around his wrists in a death grip, her mouth open, lips blue.

No!

He didn't want to kill her. Unlike the others, Claire was meant to be with him forever. But he wasn't ready for her yet because he *would* kill her, and he didn't want to, which is why he had to practice on others.

He wanted to protect Claire. The runaways died so she could live.

He opened his eyes, turned the DVD off, whipped the wet and sticky towel from his waist and tossed it in the hamper. He needed another shower.

He turned the water on cold. Dammit, he didn't want it to be like this. He didn't want to have to kill Claire. He wouldn't. That's why he hadn't touched her in fifteen years. He'd had opportunities, but he never touched her inappropriately.

Fifteen years ago fate had stepped in and saved him. He'd never admit that to the blackmailers, but sending him to assassinate Chase Taverton had changed his life for the better.

* * *

He'd followed Chase Taverton three days to get a feel for his routine. Taverton didn't have one, other than working long hours at the district attorney's office. He'd considered taking him out that first day, but the black-mailers were concerned about the circumstances of Taverton's death.

It was Judge Hamilton Drake who had proposed he should frame someone. Drake knew Taverton was having an affair with a married woman. He didn't know who, but it was a not-so-secret secret in the building.

It didn't take the assassin long to learn the identity of Taverton's lover. Taverton went to her house Monday during lunch, stayed just under an hour, then left. He did the same thing on Tuesday. While he was inside fucking the whore, the assassin carefully broke into Taverton's snazzy BMW and read his schedule for the week. Taverton had "Lunch w/ L" written every day that week. Scanning back, he'd been having the affair for a long, long time. They even had a weekend trip planned in two weeks. The assassin called his blackmail-ers and suggested they wait until the trip to kill him.

Negative. Taverton had to die as soon as possible. He was working a case that would get the judge and other important people in deep shit.

So the assassin promised he'd be dead Wednesday by one in the afternoon.

Lydia O'Brien was a nurse and she worked the night shift, twelve hours, from six p.m. until six a.m. four days a week. Her husband was a cop and left at seven thirty. The assassin didn't know about a daughter until he broke into the house while the adulteress slept. That was the curse of rushing the job. He'd have known *about the daughter if he'd had more time. He swallowed his nerves. It was as if he'd never killed before. But he'd never killed for reasons that weren't . . . more personal.*

He had his own gun, but he also knew cops. They always kept a gun in their bedroom. He wished he had more time—one day to steal the gun, the next to kill the prosecutor and his whore. But the blackmailers wanted no delays, which meant no more planning time.

If he had to use his own gun, he'd have to leave it, otherwise the frame wouldn't work. They'd try to trace the gun, but it was old, long ago stolen, and had no murders attached to it. He hoped to get his hands on the cop's gun.

There was nothing that connected the assassin to the two people he planned to kill. The blackmailers wouldn't talk, because they had as much—or more—to lose. And he knew enough about why they wanted Taverton dead to keep them uncomfortable. He'd recorded his conversation with Harper and Drake just to be on the safe side. He didn't want them to think he was expendable.

He was too smart for that.

He didn't even live in Sacramento, he had no reason to be here, and he was staying under an assumed name in a hotel down in a seedy Stockton neighborhood forty minutes south of the capital city. He could disappear and the police would look for people who wanted Taverton dead. That's why killing him with the whore made so much sense. The police would look at the obvious: her idiot husband. When the assassin told Harper about his plan to take out both Taverton and his lover, within twelve hours Harper learned that O'Brien worked solo. He was normally a training officer, but had no rookie currently assigned to him.

A lot of things could go wrong. O'Brien could be on a call. Taverton could cancel his rendevous. But the assassin took comfort in the fact that he wasn't connected to anyone and could slip away. If it all went south and the blackmailers exposed him, he'd have to disappear and assume another identity. Self-preservation was key.

He refused to think about his own death.

He waited until the working neighborhood was quiet. The old woman next door might be a problem, but the assassin came in through the garage door on the opposite side of the house, which was also the easiest lock to pick.

Slowly, he walked through the house. Silence. The whore was sleeping. But if today was the same as the last two days, she'd be in the shower by noon. It gave him only a few minutes to find the gun and hide before Taverton arrived at 12:30.

The house was homey and quaint. Nothing like the huge mansion where he'd grown up. Pictures on the walls of the family that lived there. Pictures . . .

His heart pounded as he stared at a photograph of the most beautiful girl he'd ever seen. Her long black hair, her big, round blue eyes, her smile . . . it was as if a huge spotlight was illuminating her framed picture. It was the sign he'd been searching for.

He'd made three major moves in his life. The first was when he dropped out of college after killing—accidentally killing—Jessica. Each time he made a move, he had heeded a sign. But nothing had been nearly as powerful as this. There was nothing like this girl.

She was his fate.

Now he felt good about killing Taverton and the whore. What was that slut doing sleeping around? She had a daughter, someone who looked to her for moral guidance, someone who needed her. And what about her husband? He was either a stupid fool or he didn't care. Either way, he deserved to go to prison for his ignorance.

That would leave the daughter. She would need his guidance. A strong shoulder to cry on.

He would stay in Sacramento for the black-haired beauty.

He waited in the girl's room while her mother slept. Carefully, with gloves, he went through her things. Discovered her name was Claire from the colorful animal letters on her door. Her room was cluttered but not messy. She'd made her bed before leaving for school. She was a good girl. There was no real theme or color scheme—her down comforter was red with several throw pillows in all colors. One of her walls was painted bright pink, the others sky blue. She had movie and teen heartthrob posters on the walls. In the corner was a basket with stuffed animals.

In his search, he learned she was a freshman at St. Francis, an all-girl Catholic high school. There were dozens of snapshots of her with her friends on a large corkboard on one wall.

A worn floppy bear on the bed with one eye missing.

A white bathrobe hanging on the back of the door.

A shelf lined with well-read books, thin romances as well as thick fantasies, like Tolkien's trilogy.

On her nightstand was a photo of Claire dressed up for Halloween as Princess Leia, with her father as Darth Vader. It was a few years old, judging by the newer pictures with her friends. Princess Claire didn't have breasts yet.

He knew he shouldn't, but he took one of the pictures from her wall of friends. There were at least a hundred pinned up. After her mother was shot dead, would Claire notice that one was missing?

He also took a pair of her panties. Bright pink, like her wall. Lacy. The underwear a teenage girl would wear to feel like a grown woman, but still in her favorite little-girl color.

A loud, metal grinding sound vibrated the house, and he tensed. Then came the sound of running water through pipes in the wall that separated Claire's bedroom from her parents'.

Realizing the noise was simply an old plumbing system, he left Claire's room and stood outside the master bedroom, looking through the open door. The adulteress was in the shower, evidenced by the sound of water hitting flesh. He quickly strode across the room, looked under pillows, under the bed, then in the nightstand drawers.

He grinned. He was right: There was a gun.

He returned to Claire's room before her mother finished with her shower. He sat on her bed and waited. Waited for the perfect time to kill.

He imagined a life with Claire.

The assassin turned off the icy water. Fifteen years had passed and now he was an important part of Claire's life. But if Tom O'Brien knew what Oliver Maddox knew, he, too, could put together the truth of that long-ago day. And if that happened, the assassin's well-planned life would crumble around him.

Then he'd be forced to kill Claire. He refused to leave town without her, and he knew she wouldn't go with him voluntarily.

EIGHT

Nelia was napping, her back to him, while Tom sat at the table near the covered window reading over the letter he'd written to his daughter. Nelia had wanted to deliver it for him, but Tom wouldn't allow it. The more she risked exposure, the greater her chance of being tried as an accessory.

Wasn't that what he was using Claire for? To have Claire become an accessory to help him find Oliver Maddox? To help him prove his innocence? Was it a double standard? He'd told Nelia that Claire's training and resources made her the perfect person to dig for the truth. And on the one hand, that was true. But Tom also desperately wanted Claire to learn for herself that her father was innocent. She was a doubting Thomas, had to see it to believe. She'd always been like that, and he wanted her to figure out the truth so she'd believe him. He didn't want to hurt Claire or get her in trouble. He hoped that if worse came to worst, the fact that he was her father and she was a distraught daughter would weigh in her favor if things got hairy.

Hopefully, it wouldn't come to that. If she could just find Oliver Maddox, then she could step aside.

Tom rubbed his head. If Maddox had learned the

truth about what happened, why hadn't the kid turned it over to the police? Why had he missed his meeting with Tom the week before the quake? Someone must have scared him into hiding, or scared him into quitting the investigation. Maybe Tom was making a huge mistake bringing Claire into this mess.

His lower back burned and he absently rubbed it. He didn't have a lot of time. His days were numbered either way. The only thing that mattered now was that he didn't die a guilty man. Claire had to believe he was innocent. Then, maybe, he could die in peace.

Seeing Claire again had hurt. He hadn't expected the physical pain in his heart, twisting his insides like a constrictor until it squeezed the breath from his lungs. The pain in her face, the distrust in her eyes. Claire was no longer the bright-eyed, too-smart-for-her-own-good, inquisitive daughter he'd been raising. As a child, she'd wanted to know how everything worked and why. She would marvel at something as basic as a toaster or as complex as the stars in the sky.

At least once a week on a clear night, Tom and Claire went out in the backyard and looked at the stars. Tom made a point of learning about astronomy because it pleased Claire that he knew about the universe, and it pleased him to make his girl happy. When they went on their summer camping trip—without Lydia, who didn't like sleeping in a tent—they often stayed up well past midnight watching the sky and talking. About everything and nothing. Sometimes they were just quiet together.

Being a father had grounded Tom like nothing else in his life. His family was the most important thing to him. Lydia—he'd loved her, even after her infidelity. If that made him weak, he didn't care. He'd have divorced her had he known about Taverton, not killed her. No matter how much anguish he endured because of Lydia's choices, not for a second had he considered shooting her.

It was a few days before Christmas when Oliver Maddox had visited Tom at San Quentin for the first time. Tom had lost hope that he'd ever be able to clear his name. His last appeal had been rejected. He was scheduled for execution on July 1. Six and a half months and he would be dead. Being convicted of a crime he didn't commit had enraged him for years, but his anger had dissipated. He would be executed an innocent man, but surprisingly he'd come to terms with dying.

What he couldn't accept was that he would die a guilty man in the eyes of the only person he cared about.

The guard led Tom through the North Seg section of San Quentin. Tom glanced at the cage that held Scott Peterson. Peterson looked up, gave him a brightly dazed smile, then went back to the book he was reading. There was a guilty bastard, Tom thought. People equated Tom with scum like Peterson. A wife killer. But he didn't care about public opinion. Tom only cared about the opinion of one person.

And, if he was honest with himself, he wanted to know who'd framed him. Who'd destroyed his life and why. Why, dammit?

He hadn't been sentenced to Quentin. He'd spent the bulk of his fifteen years in a secure area of Folsom, where the warden segregated cops like him from the general prison population. It was lonely, and he still wasn't completely safe. There were multiple attacks on him, and he didn't know if they were because someone had found out he was a cop, or if he'd racked up more enemies.

When Tom's last appeal was denied, the warden at Folsom asked if he would like to do a final good deed. He was asked to transfer to San Quentin to befriend a killer who police suspected of murdering more than the eight young girls he'd admitted to. Tom agreed.

Terrence Drager didn't tell Tom squat about the unsolved cases in the months Tom was in the North Seg talking to him. But after he was executed, one of the guards handed Tom a letter. "From Terry. Wanted me to give it to you after he went to hell. You'll be joining him there in a few months."

The letter was a list of locations. Twenty-seven locations, each identified only by a month, year, and the color of the victim's panties. Tom retched at the information.

Tom sent the information to the Folsom warden. He hadn't heard whether any of it panned out, or about when he'd be transferred back to Folsom. His work here was done, and even though the North Seg was safer for him than other areas of San Quentin, he didn't feel secure.

Tom learned later that Oliver Maddox had identified himself as an attorney working for Tom's counsel, which was the reason why they were left alone in the interview room. Tom's hands and feet were shackled, and a chain secured him to the floor. He'd never get over the feeling of being a caged animal. And still, bulletproof glass separated Tom from Maddox. They spoke through closed-circuit phones.

On the other side of the glass was a boy—well, he

was probably in his mid-twenties, but he didn't look more than eighteen. He had close-cropped hair except for a long tail in the back, and silver wire-rim glasses. "Oliver Maddox," he said. "Thank you for agreeing to see me."

"Your letter was interesting."

Though the guard stood outside the door once Tom had been secured, Tom didn't believe for a minute that the guards didn't listen to the allegedly "privileged" conversations.

Oliver had sent Tom a letter asking for a meeting. Tom didn't know the kid, but he identified himself as a new lawyer working for the Western Innocence Project. "I have reviewed all your case files and identified several oddities," he had written. "I believe that you were wrongly convicted and would like to discuss a possible appeal."

When Tom received the letter last month, he read it over and over in disbelief. After all these years, he had lost hope that anyone would learn what really happened that day.

It didn't make him feel any better that God knew the truth. Tom had a few choice words to say to the Almighty, and expected when he said his piece he'd be spending additional time in purgatory, which certainly couldn't be worse than prison.

But now, an outsider believed him. Believed he was innocent. He met with Oliver Maddox.

"I'm still working on getting to the governor," Oliver said, averting his eyes. Tom wondered if Maddox was telling the entire truth. "I'm hoping he'll not only stay your execution but release you."

"Why?"

"I think once the governor sees the evidence, he'll realize that you were framed."

"I mean, why are you helping me?"

"I think you're innocent."

Tom stared at the kid. This stranger believed Tom hadn't killed his wife and Chase Taverton. He was helping him for only one reason: It was the right thing to do. He was a young idealist. Tom hadn't met one of those in a long, long time.

"Do you know, in your gut, that I am innocent?"

Oliver's expression bespoke sincerity. "There was an article in a law-review magazine about your trial, your appeals, everything. There were several irregularities in the investigation, and when I reviewed the case files I thought for certain that the Western Innocence Project would get behind it. But my advisor felt there wasn't enough to get a stay from the governor or a new trial." Oliver shook his head. "The Project wants wins. DNA evidence, a new witness, lack of due process, something solid."

"Not the word of a man convicted by a jury of his peers." And his daughter, Tom thought.

"If Lydia O'Brien was the target, then your guilt would make more sense. She was your wife and she was having an affair. On the surface, it seems logical. Do you know how many men kill their wives in any given year? There were—"

"I know." He didn't need to hear it again. "The husband, the boyfriend, the ex-boyfriend always top the suspect list."

"Right. Well, have you ever considered that maybe Chase Taverton was the target?"

Tom shrugged. "For years I tried to make it about

Taverton, but it didn't make sense to me. No one knew I was coming home that day. I was on lunch break when Claire called me. How could someone plan it so that I would be in the vicinity at the time they were killed? It was an unknown, as far as the killer was concerned."

"What happened when you took a lunch break?"

"I don't understand what you mean."

"I mean, did you call it in? Tell anyone you were off the clock?"

"Of course. I called dispatch."

"And did you do this the same time every day?"

"Roughly. Depended what calls I'd been on, what I was doing."

"Who knew when you were on lunch?"

"I guess everyone on the clock. I reported my unit number and where I was. I had to keep the radio on in case I was called to a scene, but it was just background noise."

"What about your partner? Where was he?"

"I was on day shift, I didn't ride with a partner. I often had rookies with me—I was a training officer— but I was studying to make detective, and I hadn't had a rookie in weeks."

"So you were alone, and everyone on duty or with a police-band frequency would know that you were signed out for lunch."

"You think that someone in my department—no. I can't believe that anyone I knew then had anything to do with Lydia's murder."

But the seed was planted. Who hated him so much that they'd frame him for murder?

"Maybe, or maybe it was just someone who knew a lot about Chase Taverton and enough about police procedures and codes to monitor police frequencies. You

*were on break and everyone knew it. The killer could
have been waiting to kill Taverton and your wife while
you were unavailable."*

"But if Claire hadn't called me, I would have been at
lunch and—" He stopped.

"Right. You were eating alone and everyone knew, or
could have known. No big secret."

"You're making a lot of leaps, Maddox. You're making the leap that someone knew about Lydia's affair, and
my studying over lunch, and they knew that Lydia
would be home with her lover during the same time as
my lunch break? A jury didn't buy my defense, which
was along the same lines—that I just happened to come
home within minutes of my unfaithful wife being murdered by someone else. I'm surprised you do."

"You testified that you saw your personal firearm on
the wrong nightstand in the bedroom when you walked
in and saw the bodies."

"Yes."

"My dad was a cop. He put his gun in the same place
every night. He checked it religiously. He kept his in a
holster attached to the side of the bed. He would never
have put it in the wrong place. Ever."

"I could have been in a rush," Tom said, using the
prosecution's argument. "I was in a rage. Not thinking.
Heard Claire come in. Or, as in the closing statement,
was trying to cast doubt that I was the killer."

"Cops and their guns . . . no, you wouldn't have been
so stupid as to leave it there. You would have either dis-
posed of it or put it back where it belonged. But even
more likely, you wouldn't have used your own gun."

"They call them crimes of passion for a reason," Tom
said. "The killer usually isn't thinking."

"Even a crime of passion—I just couldn't picture you being so stupid. Your daughter calls you, you go home and kill two people? It doesn't make sense to me, but yeah, on the surface, it was an easy prosecution. One of their own was killed and they jumped all over the most likely suspect."

Oliver stared him in the eye, leaned forward and whispered, *"I think it's all about Chase Taverton. I think he was the target, and I'm going to prove it. I have a lead. I just wanted to meet you, see if you were who I thought you were."*

"And?"

"You pass."

Oliver hadn't visited him again, but they set up a weekly phone call so Oliver could ask questions and tell Tom what he'd uncovered. On that last call, two weeks before the earthquake, Oliver was excited.

"I think I have it, Tom," he said. "I don't want to say much over the phone. But I have Taverton's personal journal. Everything is in here—everything he was working on. Details. Some of it is in Taverton's own cryptic notes, but I'm working on it. There's a guy, a criminal informant, Taverton was working a plea deal with the week he was killed. Frank Lowe. Know him?"

"No," Tom had said.

"He's the key. I feel it. I think this is a conspiracy, Tom. Based on his notes, I think that Taverton was using Lowe as a witness against someone very, very big."

"Who?"

"I have ideas, but I don't want to say right now. Not until I find Lowe and do some more research into this. If

I'm wrong, it'll be even worse for you. But if I'm right . . . let's meet again. I'd rather tell you in person."

They arranged to meet on Monday, January 21. But Oliver never showed, and the day after, Tom was moved to Section B.

Tom couldn't retrace Oliver's steps, and even knowing now that Oliver had lied to him about his position with the Western Innocence Project, Tom had hope that there was truth in what Oliver had uncovered. That Taverton had been the target and Tom had been deliberately framed.

If Claire believed him, she could bring in the power and resources of Rogan-Caruso. The security company was the best in the business. With them behind him, Tom might finally learn the truth. More important, Claire would.

He folded the letter and put it in his pocket. He glanced at Nelia, still sleeping. He'd told her the truth—he didn't deserve her or her trust. But without it, he would be lost, or dead.

He loved her.

He prayed she'd forgive him.

Tom pulled a piece of notepaper from a small stack and wrote:

Nelia,
   You've already gone above and beyond for me. I'm not going to jeopardize you further. I'm taking the letter to Claire, and I'll be back as soon as I can.
   I love you.

                                                    Tom

NINE

When Claire arrived at Dave's house on the far side of his father's rural property off Bader Road in Elk Grove, she was still fuming over her interview with the warehouse owner. Holman had lied through his teeth, but she took down his statement verbatim.

Now her real work began. Holman insisted he had nothing to do with the arson. She already had the report about the medical supplies on the streets, but Holman was right about one thing—she couldn't prove someone else hadn't stolen and distributed them.

Liars and thieves like Ben Holman pissed her off.

She frowned, thinking about her conversation with Oliver Maddox's girlfriend earlier in the day. Was Claire no better than Holman? She'd misled Tammy Amunson about why she wanted to find Oliver. True, she hadn't really *lied*, it was more a sin of omission. She really *did* want to find Oliver and she *was* concerned about his disappearance. She *did* have a private investigator's license. But she'd never used it deceptively before.

Did a good reason justify her dishonesty?

Dave bent over to hug her when she walked through the unlocked door. He was nearly as tall as Mitch and broader. Claire didn't know why her friend Jayne didn't like him; Dave was both a good guy and good-looking.

"You're late." He messed up her hair.

She wrinkled her nose at him and grabbed his beer, finishing the rest.

"I hate it when you do that," he said.

"I know. Where's your dad?" She'd hoped to pull him aside and ask about Oliver Maddox. She knew Bill had talked to the college student back in January, but at the time she had been too raw to discuss the conversation in depth. Then the earthquake hit and they both had other things to think about.

"He's *at* the game. An old buddy of his got some prime tickets."

"Good for him," she said, though she was disappointed she'd have to wait until tomorrow to talk to him. Dave might know something . . . if she could get him alone. "Who's all here?"

"The usual—Manny and Jill, Eric, Phil."

Claire tried to rid her body of the day's tension. She rolled her shoulders, said hi to everyone, grabbed a beer from an ice bucket. These were her friends, she reminded herself. Why did she feel so uncomfortable, like an outsider? She always tried, but never felt like she quite fit in anywhere.

She pushed aside her father's haunted expression.

Her lies to Oliver Maddox's worried girlfriend.

Her growing confusion over her father's guilt.

A timer went off, and Phil jumped up. "Hey, Claire, have a second to help?"

"Sure."

She followed Phil into the kitchen. He popped open the oven and took out a delicious-smelling Mexican dip, then popped in garlic bread and adjusted the temperature.

Phil tossed her a bag of tortilla chips. "Go find a bowl."

Also a cop, Phil was a few years older than Dave and his friends, but he was a fixture in the group. Especially after he saved Dave's life during a domestic disturbance call the week before Claire graduated from high school. If Phil hadn't intervened at the right moment, Dave could have been dead. The bullet ended up grazing his arm, but it was only inches from his heart. Bill called Phil his adopted son.

Claire rummaged around the cabinets. Dave was not organized.

"Dave says it's getting serious with your new boyfriend."

"Dave has a big mouth." She found a big bowl and dumped the chips into it.

"He's just concerned because you haven't introduced him. You usually aren't so secretive."

Eric came in as Phil spoke. Eric was Dave's age and they'd been close ever since Eric joined the force more than ten years ago. "Yeah, and I think this is a record. Dave said you've been seeing him for a couple months. Long time for you."

She rolled her eyes, but she was getting irritated at the interrogation from the cops. Dave, okay, he was practically her brother. But Phil and Eric?

"Okay, a week from Friday, the Kings are playing the Lakers in L.A., we'll all meet at my place and I'll invite Mitch, okay?"

Dave walked in. "Is this *the* Mitch Bianchi you have yet to introduce to Dad and me?"

"Oh, stop," she said. "I didn't think you cared."

Dave squeezed the back of her neck. "I'll always care about who you're dating."

Claire felt claustrophobic with Dave's overprotective, brotherly attitude, and Phil and Eric's intrusiveness. "Get over it," she said, trying to sound light, but her tone was flat.

Dave dropped his hand and grabbed the plate of chicken off the counter. "Game's started, we're down six already."

"Dave, I'm sorry, I—" Claire frowned as he walked out. "I didn't mean it the way it sounded," she ended lamely.

"He knows," Eric said, rubbing her shoulder. "I'll take this tray—anything else?" he asked Phil.

"The bread has a few minutes. I'll wait for it." Eric left, and Phil took up rubbing her shoulder where Eric had left off. "Dave just worries about you. He wants you to be happy. So is it serious? You and this Mitch Bianchi?"

She shrugged. "The usual." That was such a lie, she realized as she said it.

"So it is," Phil stated.

"What? Please. I don't have time for serious relationships. Worry about Dave. He's a lot older than me, he should be thinking of settling down."

Her cell phone rang. She glanced at the number. *Mitch.*

"Go ahead," Phil said. "I'll take care of this. Grab the bread when the timer buzzes." He took the bowl of potato salad from her hand and left the kitchen.

"Hi," she answered, feeling giddy when she heard his voice.

"Change of plans?"

"Yeah. I need to make an appearance at this thing. I hope it's okay that I meet you at the Fox & Goose."

"I'll be miserable the entire hour you're late, but I'll manage as long as you don't cancel on me altogether."

"No chance. I missed you this morning."

"Ditto. Coffee doesn't taste the same without you."

She laughed. "I highly doubt that. So nine is okay?"

"I'll be waiting."

She hung up, a rush of anticipation running through her veins. She considered leaving now and catching up with Mitch before he left his house, but decided against it. She'd been practically ignoring Dave and his friends since she'd been seeing Mitch, and Dave would be ticked if she bailed earlier than she planned. Plus she had to make it up to him for jumping down his throat earlier.

The timer went off and she took out the garlic bread. She decided one beer was plenty, and started a pot of coffee. That's what it was: She was worn down from today and the stress of the confrontation with her father. A cup of coffee or three and she'd be back to her old self and ready for a night of dancing.

Dave walked into the room. "I'm sorry," Claire said to him, glad they were alone for a minute.

"It's okay."

"Are you sure?"

Dave walked up to her, kissed her on the cheek, and said, "Yes. But I could tell something was bothering you from the minute you drove up. Want to talk about it?"

She glanced at the doorway. Everyone was in the great room, the television loud enough to drown out their conversation.

"Do you remember a few months ago, before the

earthquake"—she preferred to say "earthquake" rather than "when my father escaped from Quentin"—"when we had dinner with your dad, and I told him about my conversation with the law student Oliver Maddox?"

Dave tensed and straightened. He went from friend to cop in a split second. "Yes. Dad had a visit from Maddox as well."

"Right. And I was too angry and upset to listen to him."

"I remember that, too."

"But I need to know what they talked about."

"Why now?"

"I—" She couldn't tell him about her father. Not yet. "I found his card in my desk this morning and it's been on my mind. He told me he was close to finding proof that my father is innocent. I didn't believe anything he said then, especially when I found out he lied about who he worked for. But now—"

"Now what?"

She said, "I just need to know what he meant; if there's anything he found out that might, I don't know, confirm my father's guilt or give me something new to look at, maybe—"

"Are you buying into Maddox's theory?"

"I don't even know what his theory is, not completely, which is why I wanted to talk to Bill."

Dave stared at her flatly. "A bulletin came into the station today from the sheriff's department. Oliver Maddox is dead. His body was found this morning in the Sacramento River near Isleton."

Claire couldn't have heard that right. "Dead?" she whispered.

"His identity hasn't been confirmed, but it was his car

and a body in the driver's seat, badly decomposed, but it's likely Oliver Maddox." Dave watched her closely, too closely, like a cop viewing a suspect. "So I ask you again, Claire, why are you interested in Oliver Maddox now?"

"I haven't been able to sleep," she said, not completely lying. She'd had problems sleeping ever since her mother was killed. "It's been worse since the earthquake." Again, the truth. "And I've been thinking about what Maddox said, and wondering if I should have listened to him. If maybe he knew something that . . . that proved my father is innocent. What if it's the truth? What if I ignored Maddox because of my own guilt?"

"Guilt? For what?"

She laughed without humor. "What? You know damn well that I called my dad that day and told him about the man in bed with my mother. I set in motion the entire chain of events. For fifteen years I've believed that I ignited my father's fuse. He may have pulled the trigger, but I baited him. What if I'm innocent?"

"Claire, you *are* innocent. What your father did had nothing to do with you—"

She interrupted. "It had everything to do with me. And my dad. And my mother. But if my dad has been telling the truth all along, no matter how crazy it sounds, it means that someone else *did* kill my mom and that prosecutor. And Oliver Maddox was onto it. He must have known something, otherwise why would he come to me—and your dad—" She paused. "How did he die?"

"I don't know," Dave said. "The autopsy is tomorrow and the investigation is ongoing. I heard the FBI is involved, but this isn't a Sac PD case. I don't have any details."

She looked him in the eye, asking without words.

He nodded. "I'll see what I can find out." He took both of her hands in his and squeezed, his face stern. "Don't get your hopes up, Claire. This probably doesn't mean anything. Your father was convicted. The evidence was solid."

"It was largely circumstantial."

"He had a half-dozen appeals, every one of them a failure. No one thinks he's innocent. And"—Dave implored her with his expression—"I don't want you throwing away your life helping him."

Tom sat in the park across the street and watched Claire's house.

She wasn't home, but he had no idea what her schedule was. In the few days he'd been back in Sacramento, he'd only learned that she had no regular habits except hitting Starbucks every morning.

She could be home any minute, or not for hours.

He should have listened to Nelia and not come here. He'd seen Special Agent Bianchi twice; he was obviously watching Claire at least periodically. But Bianchi didn't appear to be anywhere nearby now, and Tom wore a fairly decent disguise. He'd been using a rinse to hide the silver, making his hair browner than its natural black. He also took Nelia's suggestion and didn't crop it short as he'd worn it both before and after going to prison. She'd trimmed it into what she called a conservative businessman's cut. The day's growth of beard—though coming in threaded with silver—helped hide the shape of his face. And Nelia had bought him a pair of gold-rimmed glasses to wear. He had a newspaper under his arm, and wore sneakers, jeans, and a black polo shirt. At first glance, no one would suspect that he was Tom O'Brien, the last fugitive from San Quentin. But if Claire or a cop saw him, the disguise wouldn't buy him much time.

He sat on the bench and watched. Nelia would have woken up by now and be worried about him. Or be angry. Probably both. He didn't want to upset her, but he'd already decided that if she were caught helping him, he would tell the authorities that he'd threatened her. Forced her to help. Confuse them enough that maybe they wouldn't push it. It also might help that Nelia was on decent terms with her ex, a district attorney in San Diego.

The park closed at sunset, and Tom didn't want to chance hanging out there long after. Patrols increased in the evenings, primarily as a deterrent to juvenile crimes like vandalism and graffiti and petty theft.

Being back in Sacramento had shoved the past right under his nose. He'd brought Claire to this very park when she was not even three, an inquisitive toddler who enjoyed feeding the ducks. He remembered when one of the mallards had nipped her finger. Instead of crying or chasing the bird, she'd lectured him, pointing that hurt finger at the duck.

"That was not nice. I fed you already, let the other ducks have a turn."

While in prison, Tom tried to remember the good times, but inevitably he'd see Claire's young, stricken face when she cast her eyes on Lydia's dead body.

Traffic in the area diminished as the commute ended. Claire still hadn't returned home.

Tom didn't need a lot of time. Go in, leave the letter, get out. Hell, he could leave the letter in her mailbox. It would be safer that way.

But the truth was he wanted to see how she was doing, and a person's house said a lot about how they lived. Five minutes. Go in, put the letter on her refrigerator, glance around, leave. The dogs might bark, but he wouldn't be there long enough for the neighbors to call the police.

Just as he was about to get up from the bench, Claire's Jeep pulled into the driveway. She jumped out, ran into the house. That had been close. He wasn't ready for another confrontation.

He'd put the letter in her mailbox after she went to bed. Hope she checked it early. He could call her, tell her it was there.

Less than ten minutes later, Claire emerged from the house once again. She'd changed from her slacks and blazer to black jeans and a lacy tank top. As she walked to her car in spike heels, she pulled a purple T-shirt over her head. She drove away, speeding through a yellow light and turning onto the on-ramp of the freeway a block over.

Now. What are you waiting for?

He crossed the street, trying not to walk too fast or too slow. His heart pounded. She was his daughter, but she also believed he was a killer. He had to accept the fact that she might turn him in or set him up.

He expected that she'd have an alarm, and was surprised when he didn't encounter one. Maybe she didn't have one because of her animals. Perhaps he could stay a little longer.

The dogs in the back barked. There were three or

four. A golden retriever gazed through the glass pane on the back door, tongue hanging out, looking as if he'd much rather lick an intruder than attack him. Claire always had a soft spot for animals. Lydia had been severely allergic to dogs and they'd never had one.

An orange and white cat wound around Tom's legs and he bent to scratch the animal behind the ears, tears burning behind dry eyes.

Bill Kamanski, a detective and the father of a good rookie cop Tom had trained, had become Claire's guardian. Tom didn't want to go to prison and leave his daughter with anyone. He'd wanted to be her father, dammit! He'd raised her, he loved her. He hadn't killed anyone . . .

After sentencing, but before Tom was transported to Folsom Prison, Bill met with him in lockup. Reality had finally hit Tom. He was going to be in prison for the rest of his life—until he was executed. He had appeals, but for the first time since he was arrested, he realized he might never be free again.

"Tom." Bill sat across from him, his face hard but his eyes compassionate.

"What do you want?" he'd asked. This man already had his daughter. Tom was no longer a father to Claire; the court had given—with Tom's reluctant approval—custody of his only child to a virtual stranger.

Not completely true. Claire had known Dave Kamanski for three years. Tom liked Dave, but he was too young to accept the responsibility. His father Bill was a widower, owned a home, and was a respected member of law enforcement.

There really had been no other choice. Lydia had

never gotten along with her sister Joyce, who lived three thousand miles away in Boston. How could Tom send Claire cross-country to an aunt she'd seen maybe three times in her life?

"I wanted you to know that I'll take good care of Claire," Bill said. "I'll do everything I can to protect her from the media, to give her as normal a life as possible."

Tom said nothing. He wanted to hit someone, rage against the injustice of being sent to death row an innocent man. But he couldn't. No one had believed him during the trial, no one would believe him now.

He had wanted desperately to testify on his behalf, but he knew that would have been foolish. The D.A. wanted him on the stand, and anything he said they'd twist and turn to set his temper off. That's what they wanted to do, his attorney insisted. And Tom became convinced his attorney was right. Now, he couldn't help but wonder if it would have made a difference. He'd never know.

"This is hard for you," said Bill. "No matter what happened, I know you love your daughter."

Tom's voice cracked. "Don't—don't talk about me to her. She already believes I'm guilty. Don't rub it in."

"I won't say anything negative about you to Claire, Tom. I promise."

He nodded, unable to speak.

"Claire doesn't want to see you."

Tom had feared that. The court had allowed a thirty-minute visitation with his daughter before his transfer. But his daughter didn't want to come.

"That may change, and I'll bring her when she wants to—"

"No. I don't want her to step foot in a prison."

"Be that as it may, if she wants to see you, I'll bring her. But if she doesn't—I'll write to you and let you know how she's doing."

Tom nodded.

Bill stood and started for the door. *"Watch your back, Tom."*

"I didn't kill them," he whispered.

Bill left.

True to his word, Bill sent him letters twice a year, sometimes with photos of Claire. It was a kind of bittersweet hell receiving them. He craved the information, then he'd fall into a dismal depression. It should have been him, not Bill, who was there for Claire's graduation, when her best friend was killed by a drunk driver in college, when she got her PI license, or when she bought her house.

Swallowing the bitterness, Tom looked around Claire's cozy home. He could see his daughter here, while at the same time realizing how much he didn't know about her, Bill's letters notwithstanding. The house was clean but cluttered, much like her old bedroom. Hardwood floors and simple furniture, with brightly colored pictures of Ireland decorating the walls. Claire had told him she wanted to go to Ireland, where his mother had been born. Before she died when Claire was twelve, Deirdre O'Brien had doted on her only granddaughter, and told her stories of Eire, real and made up.

Tom wondered if Claire had gone. He hoped so, but Bill had never said anything.

In her bedroom, classic movie posters dominated the

walls, from *Casablanca* to *The Wizard of Oz* to *Star Wars*. Claire had always loved the movies.

Her room was more colorful than the rest of the house, with a dozen brightly colored pillows scattered on a white down comforter. She'd done a half-ass job making the bed, the blankets hanging askew. The cat jumped onto the bed as if he owned it, sat down and stared at Tom.

Being here, seeing how she lived, disturbed Tom on so many levels. He needed to get out of here. Maybe he should never have come back. Claire was better off without him in her life.

You're innocent. Claire needs to know it, believe it, prove it.

Claire had a small office off her bedroom. It might have been a large closet with the doors removed. He placed the folded letter under her keyboard, leaving half of it protruding. He grabbed a sticky note from a stack and wrote CLAIRE in block letters, stuck it on the edge.

Turning, he glanced over at a picture on the wall separating her makeshift office from her bedroom. It was framed in pewter and placed in such a way that it could only be viewed if you intentionally pivoted to look at it.

He crossed over, took it off the wall, tears clouding his vision.

It was a picture of him and Claire when she was eleven. They'd gone camping in Yosemite for a week that summer. Lydia had even joined them because they'd rented a cabin and she had a real bed to sleep on. It was the last family vacation they'd shared, and they had an incredible time. He and Lydia had reconnected—or so he'd thought then—and Claire was still a little girl, though she'd begun to show signs of the beautiful woman she'd become. The picture reflected a perfect moment in time.

He and Claire sat on the porch swing of the cabin. The colors at sunset were vivid and surreal. But the sheer joy on their faces was something Tom hadn't remembered until now.

If Claire had hung this picture in her office, even in an out-of-the-way corner, somewhere in the back of her mind she must still love him. Still believe in him.

He clung to that hope. It was all he had, but it was more than he'd had this morning.

He put the picture back on the wall, walked away, then turned and pulled the picture down again, taking it with him. He left the house the same way he'd come in, locking the door behind him with the pick he had opened it with.

TEN

Parked in the lot next to the Fox & Goose, Mitch rested his head on his car's steering wheel. He'd called Claire for the sole purpose of finding out where she was, where she was going to be, and to confirm when she planned to arrive tonight. All so he could get rid of Steve long before she showed up.

He was in way over his head with Claire.

Mitch walked into the bar early, claiming a small table. Antique wood doors—some with ornate knobs or etched glass—split the bar in two to allow more private seating, but Mitch wanted to see the entire room and the main entrance, so he preferred a spot in the far corner.

A waitress stopped by and he ordered a pint. He was off duty, and he needed a beer about now. First the dive this morning and the subsequent investigation—he and Steve hadn't left Isleton until after four that afternoon. Steve had to follow up on another case, so Mitch had taken care of the ubiquitous paperwork at headquarters.

Tomorrow morning he'd observe Maddox's autopsy. Though not required to attend, it would get him a cause of death and an ID faster than if he waited for the report. The sheriff's department had jurisdiction and was handling the evidence, but Deputy Clarkston had extended the invitation, and Mitch jumped at it.

Why had Maddox gone down to Isleton in the first place? The canvass by the cops hadn't yielded anything useful, and if the body had really been underwater for nearly four months, a casual witness would probably not remember anything helpful. Still, Mitch had suggested to Steve that they go back with Maddox's picture and canvass Isleton again. Flash the photo around, see if anyone recognized him. Before leaving headquarters, Mitch had also put in a request for Maddox's phone records.

They had an appointment with the Davis detective in charge of the missing person case, then they'd track down the girlfriend who reported Maddox missing and find out what, if anything, she knew. Confirm her statement to the Davis PD and see if she remembered anything else.

He was relieved that Meg had cleared him to work with Steve on this case, knowing that it could wind back around to Thomas O'Brien. Maybe his "punishment" was over and Meg wanted his eyes on the case. Or maybe Steve had put in a word for him. Whatever the reason, Mitch was glad to be back on the case. Something was going to break. Maddox had been murdered—of that Mitch was certain—and he hoped that the discovery of Maddox's body would flush out his killer.

If they found out who killed Maddox, Mitch was certain it would lead back to Thomas O'Brien's case fifteen years ago. It was no coincidence that Maddox had gone missing two days before O'Brien was moved to San Quentin's dangerous Section B.

The waitress placed his pint of Guinness on the

coaster in front of him. He sipped, remembering his first date with Claire.

After weeks of flirting and conversation and spontaneous dinners when they "ran into" each other in the evening at Starbucks, he and Claire had come to the Fox & Goose on an official date. Her favorite local band was playing, she said, and asked him if he wanted to join her.

"Do you want to meet there?" he asked.

"Well, I thought maybe we could make a date of it."

He should have said no. Instead, he'd said, "I'll pick you up at eight. We can have dinner first." Why had he agreed? What was he thinking? He knew damn well what he was thinking. He was deeply attracted to Claire O'Brien. He could tell himself he was doing it for the job, but the truth was he wanted to be with her.

Everything that came before that night nearly two months ago Mitch could have justified, even if he had to stretch his arguments. After that night, he had no more excuses.

He'd put everything on the line: his career, his heart, Claire's trust.

He picked Claire up just before eight that evening. She came to the door in jeans, a red spaghetti-strap tank top, and spiky sandals. Her black hair loose around her face, dancing above her shoulders, and she'd done something to her eyes to make them seem a darker, sultrier blue. A green Celtic knot tattoo decorated her upper right shoulder blade. He wondered if she had any other tattoos, and where they were.

All Mitch could think about was taking her to bed. His face heated. She'd hate him when she learned who he was and why he'd befriended her. Okay, just this one date. He wouldn't sleep with her. He wouldn't kiss her.

He should make an excuse that he had to work late. That wouldn't work, he'd told her he was a writer. Maybe he had a deadline? He didn't know. Hell, he should walk away, tell her he was ill, and never return to her Starbucks. Disappear from the face of the earth. He had to stop this right now.

Instead, he kissed her. Just a light kiss on the lips. A hello kiss. But that hello kiss whetted his appetite and he wanted more than just one. He stopped himself. She smiled. "Hello."

She tossed a blazer over her arm and a bag over her shoulder. He told himself it was for the job. But it was no longer about the job. He had originally planned to befriend and keep tabs on Claire on the chance—the good chance—that her father would eventually show up. O'Brien was likely waiting for enough time to pass where he thought it'd be safe to approach his daughter, his only living relative.

But now Mitch saw the flaw in his plan. When O'Brien showed up—and he would, statistics put the odds firmly on that eventuality—Mitch would have to arrest him. It didn't matter that Mitch had reviewed the evidence and thought there was merit to O'Brien's claim of innocence. The fact was O'Brien was still a fugitive and Mitch would be risking not only censure, but imprisonment if he didn't apprehend O'Brien when he had the chance.

And Claire would discover the truth. He'd misrepresented himself. He'd lied. She would hate him. And he wouldn't blame her.

Deep down, Mitch hoped O'Brien never showed. He

wanted Claire to himself, and he never wanted her to find out the truth.

Stupid. She would find out sooner or later. That first night out, while they ate, Claire said, "You know, when I first met you I thought you were a cop."

Mitch's blood ran cold, but he kept his face casual. "You did? Why?"

"I've been around cops all of my life. And a lot of Rogan-Caruso employees are former cops or military. Two things stood out. First, every time someone walks into your peripheral vision, you glance at them. Quickly, but it's a habit. And when we sit at Starbucks, you always have your back against the wall. Just like you do now."

"I was in the military for three years."

She nodded. "That explains it."

He didn't know if it explained it. He'd almost forgotten who he was dealing with. Claire O'Brien was not stupid.

"Marines."

"Semper Fi."

He grinned.

"Why'd you leave?"

He didn't want to talk about himself, but he wanted to share something real with Claire. And it didn't get more real than this—his past, the past that made him the man he'd become. The good, the bad, and sometimes the ugly.

"The real question should be, why'd I join."

"Okay. Why'd you join?"

"My dad."

"He was in the Marines?"

"No. The Air Force."

She didn't say anything, but he saw her mind working behind those incredible blue eyes.

"When I was growing up in Santa Barbara, I didn't have plans for my future. My dad was the district attorney, and I was a beach bum."

"Somehow, that doesn't fit. I don't see you lying around on the beach working on your tan."

He laughed. "No, lying around wasn't my style. Surfing was. Surfing and diving. Travis—Travis Cole, my closest friend since we were six—and I spent every afternoon on the waves or under them. And we cut enough classes that I had to study my ass off to pass my finals."

"Your dad didn't like that."

"Hell no. He didn't like Travis, who was from a wealthy family. They had the kind of money that seemed to grow on trees. I didn't have the same advantages. We weren't poor by any stretch, but putting me through college and law school like my father planned would wipe out their savings account." Mitch heated with regret remembering when he told his dad he'd be a lawyer over his dead body. Rod Bianchi was dead less than a year later.

"I joined the military right out of high school to get away from Dad. It was the military or college, and I really didn't want to go to college. I wanted to travel the world with Travis on his yacht, diving in the tropics and surfing waves that hit empty beaches. But I couldn't do it. I told myself it was because my mom would be devastated, but in truth I was still under Dad's thumb. No matter how many shenanigans I pulled with Travis, I kept going home and asking for forgiveness."

"You probably would have gotten bored with that after, oh, ten or twenty years."

He nodded, gave her a half smile, though his memories were of an unhappier time.

Something passed across Claire's expression that told Mitch now was the time to get her to talk about her dad, but then it was gone and she said, "So you joined the Marines because he had been in the Air Force."

"Yeah."

"And why'd you leave?"

"My dad died. Heart attack."

"I'm sorry."

"He was a workaholic. On the job 24/7. He didn't know the meaning of the word *relax,* and his doctor had been warning him for years that if he didn't slow down or take care of himself, he would die early. Rod Bianchi didn't believe him. He was in shape, worked out at the gym every morning, ate healthy. He died at his desk."

"And you came home to be a beach bum?"

"I considered it. But I ended up going to college. Travis got tired of traipsing across the planet, so he joined me. We got a place on the beach and spent a lot of time on the waves, and a little time in class."

"How'd you end up becoming a writer?"

Now they were getting into the lies. It had felt so good to tell Claire the truth about himself that he dreaded the next sentence that came out of his mouth.

"I worked on the campus newspaper. I liked it, and when I graduated I took a job on a paper in the south. Then moved my way up the Eastern Seaboard. Came back to California when my mom died. When my grandmother passed a year later and I had a bit of money, I decided that if I was ever going to do something big, I needed to try now. So I'm trying to write the Great American Novel."

The lies came off his tongue effortlessly, but he wished his heart wasn't so twisted. He wanted to tell Claire everything—how he joined the FBI because he thought that would have pleased his father, the man he had fought with only days before he died. How his mom had blamed him for his dad's early death.

Instead, he created a fictional past for Claire and hated himself for it. He couldn't tell her he thought her father was innocent, or that he had intentionally befriended her in order to capture Tom O'Brien.

Claire took his hand and kissed it. "You'll have to teach me to surf someday."

"There're no beaches in Sacramento."

She raised an eyebrow. "Really? Guess we'll have to head to the coast for a weekend sometime."

His heart did a flip and his hand tightened within her grasp.

"Guess we'll have to," he said thickly.

Instruments were being tuned in the bar, and Claire smiled. "That's Finnegan's Wake."

"What?"

"The band. Named after the classic Irish folk song. A homage of sorts. This is their first time here."

"I thought this was a British pub." He pointed to the British flag hanging on the interior glass windows of the converted warehouse. "And isn't that Queen Elizabeth?" he said, gesturing toward a mural.

She laughed. "Come on, let's dance."

Mitch had seen Claire dance before, but not when they'd been together. When he'd been watching her, following her.

Her body moved erotically back and forth to the fluid tempo of music as he danced with her. Seeing her so free was a treat. Every morning when they talked she was on guard and cautious. Now . . . was this the real Claire? Was this the woman she'd have been had her life not been turned upside down when she was fourteen? Or was this the woman she'd become because of the murders? She danced for herself, no one else. Tonight, she seemed relaxed. Almost . . . happy. Happy with him.

She couldn't possibly know how her movement affected him. Her eyes closed and she wore that half smile Mitch loved so much. At this moment, her entire demeanor said "peace," when usually Claire seemed to struggle so.

She opened her eyes, looking right at him, all her beauty and charm and those seductive bright blue eyes focused on him. She wrapped her hands around his neck and closed her eyes again. The music had changed to something more folksy. Whatever it was, she liked it and moved accordingly.

"I love . . ."

"What?" he said, unable to hear her over the noise.

She stood on her tiptoes and leaned against him until her lips practically touched his ear. Her warm breath had him holding his. "I love this song."

She rested her head on his shoulder and his arms wrapped around her waist, pulling her tight against him. The dance floor wasn't large, about ten feet square, and more people joined them, pushing them closer. She kissed the side of his neck and Mitch held her tighter, one hand on the small of her back, the other on her neck.

Throughout the evening they danced, they drank a bit, and Mitch wanted to be nowhere else in the world but with Claire.

She wrapped an arm around his waist at the end of the evening and said, "That was fun."

"I agree."

They walked out to the parking lot, arm in arm. Mitch unlocked the passenger door for Claire. He'd taken out everything that might identify him as an FBI agent. His gun was in his trunk. He felt naked without it, but Claire would have been able to see—or feel—the piece on him.

"Wow, chivalry," she said and turned to face him.

She kissed him. Everything about Claire was larger than life, and her kiss was nothing less. Her mouth parted and her tongue found his. She tasted of hops and peppermint. Her hands wrapped around his neck, pulling him down to her, her fingers rubbing his muscles, his hair, his shoulders. Her lithe body molded to his and all Mitch wanted to do was take her to his bed, right now.

His mouth opened to suggest it, but he stopped himself. He was staying at Nolan's house. Nolan had a damn congressional medal of honor on his wall with the salutation "Special Agent Nolan Cassidy" plus a bunch of news articles in his den, extra guns in his bedroom. Damn.

"Come home with me," Claire murmured.

Was she drunk or just tipsy? What was he thinking? It didn't matter! She was Tom O'Brien's daughter. He couldn't sleep with her, no matter how much he wanted to.

He was about to protest, but instead pinned her to his car and kissed her as hard as she'd kissed him. Their bodies were as close as possible while still being fully clothed. He held her chin, kissing her repeatedly, not wanting to give up this moment.

Reluctantly, he pulled himself away. Her blue eyes

looked black in the yellow light of the parking lot. Her skin was flushed, breathing heavy, lips red and lush.

"I want to." He swallowed. "But—"

She put her finger to his lips. He kissed it and she smiled. "No buts. No promises. I want to, you want to." She gave him a feather of a kiss that was as erotic as the deep kiss a moment before.

"Claire."

He wanted her.

He couldn't have her.

"I'll take you home," he said.

If she was hurt by his rejection, she didn't show it. The last thing he wanted to do was hurt her. He wanted to make love to her.

But not like this. Not with lies between them.

He drove the short distance to her house.

"Thanks," she said, making a move to open the door.

"Claire—" He took her arm, pulled her across the middle seat, and kissed her. Long and hard, showing her his feelings when he couldn't speak the whole truth.

"I'll see you tomorrow morning, okay?" he whispered as his lips pulled back, lightly touching hers, teasing both of them.

"Okay." *Her voice was hoarse.*

"Good night."

" 'Night."

He watched her walk into her house alone, and he prayed he had the willpower to resist her next time they went out.

And he knew the only way he'd be able to resist her would be if he never saw her again.

But that wouldn't happen.

ELEVEN

Steve walked through the door of the Fox & Goose at seven thirty. Mitch had to get him out of there before Claire showed. He doubted Claire would be early, but he wanted Steve gone by eight thirty.

"You started without me." Steve slid into the chair next to him and motioned to the waitress to get him what Mitch was drinking.

"You're late."

"Got a lead on the Pinter case, but it didn't pan out. Arrested one of his minions, though, practically a kid—but with two hundred counterfeited credit cards in his possession."

"No shit."

"Credit-card fraud is out of control, and until we get the big players like Pinter we'll never even make a dent." He shook his head. "Here we are, at one of Claire O'Brien's favorite hangouts. But of course you already knew that."

Mitch said nothing. What could he say?

"If Meg finds out about your off-duty investigation of Tom O'Brien, that's one thing. You get a slap on the wrist. But if you're *involved* with Claire, that's a whole different ball game."

"It's not like that."

"So what the fuck is it like?"

"It's complicated."

Steve sipped his beer. "Dammit, Bianchi, I went to bat for you today with Meg. I told her I needed you as a partner, that you are invaluable to the squad. So no more bullshit."

"I wouldn't put you at risk, Steve."

"Why are you obsessed with Tom O'Brien? Just because he saved your life three months ago? Or is there something else you're not telling me?"

Mitch didn't want to talk about his own father railroading another innocent guy into prison. It still burned him and he hated that he came from the same gene pool as Rod Bianchi. But Steve was smart, maybe he'd see the same problems with the O'Brien conviction that Mitch saw. That while Mitch couldn't right the wrongs committed by his father long ago, he *could* help another wrongfully convicted man find justice and exoneration.

"Let me lay out what I know," Mitch said. "The fact that Oliver Maddox is dead makes it even more suspicious." Mitch filled Steve in on Maddox looking into an appeal of O'Brien's death sentence. "What if Maddox had real information?"

"And the *real* killer didn't want it to get out?" Steve shook his head. "This is a wild-goose chase. Maddox's death was probably an accident. Dozens of people drown in the Delta every year. Most are accidents."

"Convenient accident," Mitch said.

"Could have been suicide."

"By drowning? Rare. Let's wait until the autopsy tomorrow. And we have the meeting with the detective in Davis. But look at the facts. Maddox disappeared two days before O'Brien was moved into the general prison population. He was actively looking into the O'Brien case, had met with O'Brien at Quentin, and phoned him *six times* after that meeting. There was a meeting scheduled on the books for the Monday *after* Maddox disappeared."

"How'd you find that? I didn't see it in the file from Quentin."

"It wasn't, but when I interviewed the warden and the head guard of North Seg, I got a copy of the schedule. It wasn't in the file because Maddox never showed up. He was already dead."

"You're certain it's murder."

Mitch nodded. "Steve, I'm sure as hell not perfect, but you know I'm a good cop. I smelled murder the minute I saw the body."

"I'm not going to doubt your instincts, Mitch. They've been right on the money in the past. But this time you're too close to it."

"Maybe, but there's more than Maddox being dead."

"What? Just because O'Brien helped capture the Goethe gang, that psycho up in Montana, and a bunch of other prisoners, he's redeemed from a double-murder charge?"

"That wasn't what I was going to say, but now that you mention it, I think those actions say a lot about his character."

"What it says is O'Brien isn't a repeat offender. He killed in a crime of passion. Most spouses who off their unfaithful wives aren't out to kill a half-dozen other people."

"He risked himself—his freedom and his life—staying close to San Francisco to set up Goethe's gang."

"But he's a dead man, Mitch. His date with the executioner is only weeks away. Maybe he wanted to do something noble to go out in a blaze of glory or whatever." Steve shook his head in disbelief and drank some beer.

"Put that aside for now and look at the facts of his case. O'Brien was convicted solely on circumstantial evidence."

"He had motive and opportunity," Steve countered. "That isn't circumstantial."

"Bullshit. A lot of people have the motive and opportunity to kill and they don't do it. Why use his personal weapon?"

"Crimes of passion aren't well thought out."

"Did you look at the crime scene photos?"

"No. Why would I have? I'm not obsessed with this case." Steve motioned for the waitress to bring two more pints. Mitch stole a glance at his watch. 8:10. He needed to wrap this up within thirty minutes and get Steve out of here before Claire walked in and saw them talking like they were best friends. Mitch didn't want to confirm Steve's suspicions that his feelings for Claire went beyond his need to prove O'Brien innocent.

"The bodies were in bed. Taverton on top of Mrs. O'Brien. The killer walked in and shot them without hesitation. Without Taverton even having a chance to move or defend himself. That, to me, says cold-blooded premeditation."

"And a betrayed husband could have planned it just like that. What if he knew about the affair for a while? Fumed over it? Then his daughter calls and she's upset because she walked in and heard her mom in bed with a stranger. It set him off. He might have been thinking about it, maybe planning it, and now he just goes and does it."

"No rage? No yelling and fighting?"

Steve shrugged, sipped the new pint the waitress brought. Mitch tossed a twenty and a five on the tray and thanked her.

"What I'm saying," Mitch continued, "is that the police never investigated Chase Taverton's life, not in any depth. He was a prosecutor. He must have racked up a long list of enemies, and to not even walk down that road—if only to check it off the damn list—seems not only irresponsible, but flat-out wrong. It's like they saw what they wanted to see—crime of passion—arrested the husband, and tossed away the key."

"Usually the most obvious suspect is the killer," Steve said.

"And sometimes the obvious suspect is innocent."

"He was convicted by a jury."

"You know as well as I do that jury instructions and what is admissible and inadmissible in court holds a lot of sway over what the jury hears and thinks about a case."

"I didn't realize you were such a bleeding heart."

"It has nothing to do with that, it has to do with due process. So yes, I think O'Brien is innocent." It was the first time Mitch had admitted it aloud.

"Well."

Mitch said nothing for a long moment. "We know that Oliver Maddox was digging around in the events of fifteen years ago. And he disappeared at the same time O'Brien was moved from the safer North Seg to Section B. That tells me that someone wanted O'Brien dead, and it was only a matter of time before word that he had been a cop leaked out. A couple other facts: There were three separate attacks on O'Brien at Folsom Prison the first year he was there, even when he was in a secure section of the prison. I've asked for the records on those attacks, but so far I've been stonewalled by bureaucrats who say they don't know where they are."

"Could be the truth."

"O'Brien has never wavered from his version of the events. And one more thing: The court records are a mess. There're missing documents, missing witness statements, missing evidence."

"O'Brien had several appeals. The documents could have been misfiled or lost."

"True. But there's one thing that's very interesting."

"Shoot. You've piqued my interest."

"The call to the police about shots fired wasn't made to 911."

"I don't follow."

"Someone called the Sacramento PD phone number, not 911. There's no trace or tape on the main number. It goes to the receptionist. All 911 calls are automatically taped and located."

Steve thought on that. "Unusual."

"The police canvassed the neighborhood and found no one who had made the call."

"Was any of that brought up at trial?"

"No. But the defense had to have known it. I'd think a cop like O'Brien would question it. His counsel sucked."

"By that, do you mean corrupt or incompetent?"

"I have no idea, but there were other minor problems. The call to the station is the biggie, though, in my mind. Steve, it's not just *one* thing. It's a series of problems with this case. I couldn't live with myself knowing I didn't do everything I could to make sure an innocent man doesn't die."

Anyone can convict a guilty man; it takes a brilliant prosecutor to convict an innocent man.

The voice of Mitch's father came back and Mitch swallowed the anger and disgust that arose every time he thought back to the files he'd found in his father's office after he died.

Steve stared at Mitch, his dark eyes unreadable. "Okay. You've convinced me, not of his innocence, but that maybe there's something here worth looking into. But I want your assurance that you're going to be a cop first. You see Tom O'Brien, you don't let him go."

"Of course. In fact, I want to find him first. I'm worried when he's in police custody he'll end up dead. If we have him, we can protect him until we find out what Maddox had uncovered."

"And if it doesn't have anything to do with O'Brien?"

"I'll live with it."

"Good." Steve leaned back, crossed his legs. "You know, before you came to Sac two years ago you had a reputation for being a hard-ass, but you're a softie at heart, Mitch. Hell, you and I both know that guys like O'Brien can crack and take the whole family with them."

"But it wasn't a murder-suicide. It was a double homicide with the daughter just down the street."

"O'Brien had a history," Steve reminded Mitch. "Written up several times, probation twice."

"For roughing up suspects."

"And that justifies it?"

"No, but the first suspect was a child molester, and the second suspect had beaten his wife to a pulp. Kicked her with steel-toed boots. She had a miscarriage and nearly died."

"So he's known to snap. What's the difference when he sees his wife in bed with another man? He snaps, has his service pistol on, shoots them."

"Without a fight or confrontation? And he didn't use his service weapon. It was his personal firearm. And it was left on the nightstand. And according to his report, the gun was found on his *wife's* side of the bed next to an open window."

"There were no footprints or fingerprints on or near the window," Steve said. "He could have opened the window and made it look like an intruder. Put the gun down because he heard his daughter come in."

Mitch was off and running now. "C'mon, Steve, don't you think that it's odd there were *no* fingerprints on the windowsill? Like it was wiped?"

"O'Brien could have easily wiped it to set up his story, or maybe his wife was one hell of a housekeeper."

"How could O'Brien get to his gun in his night-stand—where both he and his daughter testified he kept it—without the lovers seeing him?"

"He moved it beforehand."

"That was the prosecution's argument."

"It makes sense."

"What if the killer was in the house when the wife brought in her lover? Retrieved the firearm and waited for them to get naked, then killed them?"

"O'Brien could have done the same thing. Maybe he knew about the affair, was following her, was in the house—didn't expect his daughter to come home."

"But he talked to Claire on the phone. While he was in the house killing her mother? He planned it all out, but didn't give himself an alibi? Now that *is* stupid. You have to look at the photos. It looks like an execution."

"The work of a cold-blooded killer," Steve countered. "A man who can kill his wife and her lover while his daughter waits for him down the street.

"The job is still the same," Steve continued. "We apprehend O'Brien and put him back in prison. We're not the judge, or the jury, or the appeals court."

"He's out of appeals."

"And the Western Innocence Project dumped his case, too. They must have realized there was nothing to it."

"And Oliver Maddox, the law student working on it, is dead and has been since before the earthquake, if the autopsy goes like I think it's going to go tomorrow," Mitch said. He sat ramrod straight, looking at his nearly empty pint of Guinness. He'd been in front of the Office of Professional Responsibility so many times it was almost a joke. Disobeying orders or not following established protocols. He had friends in high places, though they'd only protect him for so long. But every rule he broke was because he was searching for the real truth in the cases he worked. Professional? Maybe not. Responsible? Mitch didn't see any other option.

The truth may not have mattered to "Hang 'Em High" Rod Bianchi, but it mattered to his son.

Steve looked at his friend. "I agree, the way you laid it out I'd be interested in digging deeper. Okay, this is what I'll do. I'll look the other way while you play undercover neighbor with the daughter. I can't get close to her anyway, she knows I'm a Fed. I've done the routine stop-bys and talked to her a couple times. I got the impression that she wouldn't be very receptive if her father does make contact."

"I appreciate it—"

"But—" Steve interrupted. "You can't play the maverick. We're in this together or not at all. I went to the mat for you with Meg. Though I'll be damned if I can figure out your relationship with that woman. She goes ballistic when she thinks you screwed up, but then tells everyone that you're an ace investigator, one of the best."

He and Meg had always respected each other's abilities. "We've always been friends. That was sort of the problem with our marriage—we liked each other, but you know, that's not really the foundation a marriage needs." He shifted uncomfortably. He'd never talked about his past relationship with Meg to anyone, especially someone from the office.

Steve nodded. "If Meg finds out that you're that close to Claire, you'll be on a plane to Quantico before you can pack a bag."

"Fair enough." Mitch nodded. "And if we do take Tom O'Brien into custody, we keep him in our custody. No locals. Federal holding." He glanced again at his watch. 8:40.

"I think I can work that. I'll do what I can."

"That's all we both can do. Thanks."

"Now tell me the truth—why do you keep looking at your watch?"

Mitch could have lied, but after bringing Steve over to his way of thinking he needed to lay everything out on the table.

"Claire is meeting me here at nine."

Steve nodded, as if he knew the complete truth.

"Then I'd better get the hell out of here."

Nelia was sitting at the table in the dark when Tom walked in with fast food he'd grabbed at a nearby drive-through. He put the food down and said, "Hi."

She just stared at him with her large eyes, darker in the dim artificial light filtering through the creases in the blinds.

He turned on a light and saw that her eyes were bloodshot. His stomach flipped. The last person he wanted to hurt was the woman who had saved his life, who believed in him.

"You're angry because I went to Claire's without you."

She tilted her head but remained silent.

"You're angry because I left in the first place."

Nelia dipped her head in acknowledgment.

"I'm sorry."

"No you're not."

He sat across from her. "I had to go. I had to see how Claire lived. I had to be near her."

"I understand that, but we had an agreement. You lied to me."

"I didn't lie—"

"You planned all along to go on your own. Don't make it worse by repeating the excuses you thought up on your way back here."

"You're right. But you've risked so much to help me. I can't have you risk anything more."

"That isn't your choice, is it?"

"I couldn't live with myself if you got in trouble—or

hurt—because you helped me. Nelia, you have to understand that! I'm an escaped convict. They're not going to
play nice if they spot me. To me or anyone with me."

"Don't think I haven't thought about it. But this is
bigger than you and me, this is about the truth. I never
knew the truth about what happened to Justin. Never!
His killer was never caught. The police never even had a
suspect. There were no similar crimes in the area, nothing in the state, nothing in the damn country that they
could find. It was as if some phantom killer walked in,
killed my baby, and disappeared. I never knew why.
Why Justin? Why me?"

"Nelia—"

"Now I have the chance to find the truth for someone
else." She slammed her fist on the table. "For you. You
were a cop. You know the first person they look at when
a child disappears? His parents. Andrew and I were
under investigation. They had to clear us before they seriously started looking at other potential suspects. For
days the police looked at me as if *I* had killed my son. As
if *I* had something to do with it. And Andrew. Either
separately or together. They tried to get me to tell them
that I knew my husband had killed Justin, implying that
I was protecting Andrew. Then in that stupid good-
cop/bad-cop game, a vile detective flat-out said we'd
conspired to kill Justin. Why? Why would I kill him?
But they didn't care *why*, they figured if I'd confess
they'd uncover the motive later. Maybe I was just crazy.

"Andrew and I didn't love each other, but I never believed he could hurt Justin. But for a while, after all the
questions, after Andrew's affair became public, after the
police showed me the ph-photos—" Her voice cracked
and Tom wanted to wrap his arms around her, but Nelia

had never talked of this. Tom doubted she'd spoken to anyone about what happened during the weeks after her son was murdered.

"I thought maybe . . . and then I thought about my sister. She was babysitting for me that night. What if she had a boyfriend over? Was protecting him? What if she was part of it?" Nelia's voice trembled. "I blamed everyone. I know Andrew didn't kill Justin any more than I did, or Carina, or a phantom boyfriend. But when I saw—" She rubbed her face roughly, squeezed her eyes closed, and sank into the chair. Tom took her hand. She was shaking.

"The crime scene photos." Her voice was barely a whisper, the anguish in every breath. "And." She cleared her throat. "For a minute, I looked at Andrew. As a killer." She opened her eyes, stared at Tom. "I knew he wasn't. He was far from perfect, but he loved Justin with his whole heart."

"I hate that you went through that." Even though Tom understood it all too well.

"I was a suspect because I didn't have an alibi," she said. "I was working alone at my office."

"No one believed—"

"Yes, they did. Strangers believed. People who didn't know me. And for a while, I thought my family—"

"They didn't think you'd killed your own child."

She sighed, some of the pain and anger escaping. "No, but for a while they questioned just like I did. Because there were no suspects, there was no one else, and it came down to why? Why would someone randomly break into a house and steal a child and kill him? It wasn't a pedophile, he wasn't abused that way." Her head fell to the side, downcast, tears streaming down her face.

Tom stood and pulled her up and into his arms, holding her tight. She clasped her arms around him, her body shaking with silent sobs.

Several minutes later, as Tom stroked her hair and murmured soothing nothings in her ear, Nelia said, "I know the pain in your heart, having someone you love think you are guilty. I believe you, Tom. I want Claire to believe you, too."

Tom found her lips with his, kissed her, tasted the tears caught in the crevice of her lips. His hands fisted in her hair and he gently pushed her down to the bed. The love, the trust, the faith this woman had in him undid him. He didn't deserve it, but he would protect it with everything he had, including his life.

"I love you, Nelia."

She whispered in his ear, "You're the only person who has ever been able to dull the pain in my heart, pain I've lived with for twelve years. You saved my soul, Tom. I love you."

TWELVE

Claire drove to the Fox & Goose after changing at her house. The conversation with Dave had depressed her, making it clear that there was no one on her side in this situation. She wished she could confide in Dave, but he was a cop first. Yes, he cared about her, and he had once been close to her father, but she still didn't expect him to forget that her father was a fugitive. She couldn't.

But . . .

Oliver Maddox's death couldn't be a coincidence. She wished she had been thinking clearer when her father cornered her that morning, asked him more questions, like what exactly did Oliver Maddox know?

She swallowed thickly. She had been in no frame of mind then to ask anything coherent. If only she had a way of contacting him, finding out—

Wouldn't Oliver have kept records? Files? Notes on his thesis? Something where she could pull out threads to follow on her own? But where to start?

She was no longer a scared high school freshman who'd had her entire life blown up. She'd be thirty this year, she had a career, she was smart. She should be able to look at the evidence on her own, dispassionately, to see if maybe there was something—anything—missed the first time around.

What did Oliver see that no one else saw? Where did the Western Innocence Project fit in? Or Professor Collier?

Tomorrow, she'd catch up with Collier in his office bright and early. She didn't think she'd learn anything by hitting Oliver's house—the police would have gone through it after the missing person report was filed. But she'd go by, see if something stuck out to her. Talk to Tammy again, ask more questions about Oliver's thesis and whom he had spoken to. Though she said she hadn't known any details, Tammy probably knew more than she thought. It was all about asking the right questions. Then Claire would head into the Rogan-Caruso offices and use their vast computer resources to search for more information. Investigation was legwork and questions. And more legwork and more questions until the truth emerged. That she could do. She felt better having a game plan.

In the bar's parking lot, she turned off the ignition. She wished she had canceled her date with Mitch. Not because she didn't want to see him—on the contrary, she'd been looking forward to it all day—but because she was so twisted inside that she knew Mitch would ask her what was wrong. He was unusually perceptive, and while she appreciated his attentiveness in conversation, she didn't like being the brunt of anyone's scrutiny.

Still, she needed to unwind. She couldn't do anything more about Oliver Maddox tonight. A pint of stout, a little dancing, and Mitch. It sounded like just what she needed.

It was a quarter to nine when she opened the door of

the pub. She saw Charlie and the Finnegan's Wake band setting up and was about to say hi when she saw Mitch.

He sat at a table near the back, looking tense, while another man loomed over him, hands on the table.

Claire recognized the bastard harassing Mitch. FBI Special Agent Steve Donovan. He'd come by several times since the earthquake to threaten her about her father. As if she would harbor a fugitive, especially after what her father had done.

What are you doing now, Claire? You're keeping your mouth shut about seeing him, aren't you?

Donovan had also harassed Charlie and the band and even talked to her boss at Rogan-Caruso, further embarrassing and enraging her.

Had he been following her? Did he know about her relationship with Mitch?

She stomped over to them, insinuated herself between the cop and the writer. She pushed Donovan in the chest. "Didn't I tell you after you harassed my friends"—she jerked a thumb toward the band—"to leave me and mine alone? I told you I'd call if I heard from my father."

Donovan glanced at Mitch, then said, "I'm just following up, Ms. O'Brien. I told you I'd be checking in periodically."

"Just go away." She blinked back what she feared were tears. She didn't want to tell Mitch about her father, but now she had no choice. What must he think of her keeping such a big secret? Not that she'd done it on purpose, it wasn't typical conversation to open with, *"Hey, my father is an escaped killer, wanna go dancing?"*

"I'm leaving," Donovan said. He nodded to Mitch, then left.

Claire turned and looked Mitch in the eye. "I'm sorry about that."

"It's okay."

She slapped her hand on the table. "It's not okay. I don't like talking about it, okay? I hate it. I just hate it." She swallowed. "I'll tell you everything." She walked over to the bar, hoping Mitch would follow at the same time she wished he would just tell her, *"Sorry, I don't like complications."* It was so much easier not letting anyone inside. Sharing her pain made it more real.

Mitch followed, sat next to her. She motioned for a pint of Guinness for her and Mitch and waited for the bartender to serve them before saying, "That damn Fed probably told you everything." She took a long swallow.

"Not really. Just enough—"

"To make you think I'm a liar."

"You've never lied to me."

"By omission."

Mitch took her hand, squeezed it. That quietly intimate, sweet gesture had Claire's heart. "You don't have to tell me anything you don't want to. I still like you. A lot."

As if to prove it, he kissed her softly. Sweetly. She stared into his eyes. He possessed a deep-seated aura of compassion, in contrast to his square-jawed, rugged appearance.

"Fifteen years ago my father was convicted of murdering my mother and her lover," Claire said quietly. "He escaped from San Quentin during the earthquake. That guy who talked to you is with the FBI. He's been coming by now and again to make sure I'm not keeping my father locked in the basement."

"Somehow I don't see you doing that."

She shook her head. "I was there," she whispered.

"Where?"

"At the house. Right after—I saw my father leaving the bedroom where they were dead and—shit!"

"It's okay, Claire."

"You shouldn't have had to hear about this from that man. What did he say to you anyway?"

"Not much. Just wanted to know when was the last time I saw you and if I had seen a man. He showed me a photo. A mug shot." He stared into his beer. Claire feared this situation bothered Mitch more than he was saying.

"My father?"

"Told me it was Thomas O'Brien, a fugitive. He didn't tell me about the earthquake, but I'd heard about that on the news. I put it together."

"I'm sorry, Mitch. I really thought it would be over by now, but . . ."

"But what?"

"It's never going to end until they find my dad. And I'm scared."

"That he's going to hurt you?"

"Me?" She shook her head rapidly back and forth. "Hell no, he'd never hurt me. I'm scared that they'll kill him. He's a fugitive. He escaped from prison. But did you know he captured nine of the other escapees? Or led the police to their capture? I didn't know anything about it until a reporter cornered me outside the Rogan-Caruso office and asked if I'd heard anything about my father tipping off the police about one of the escapees. Then I talked to Bill—he was my guardian—and he looked into it. Found out my dad was a hero, then the media broke the story. He's still my father—and I never visited him in prison. Not once. I never wrote to him, or answered his letters to me."

Why was she talking like this? She'd never told anyone about the letters, she tried to never think about them. She'd read them, of course she had to, she was too damn curious by nature. All were the same. *How are you? I love you. I'm innocent.*

She'd hardened her heart against her father because she couldn't handle the emotions that battled within, the guilt, the fear, the anguish, the betrayal. And the love. She had loved her father so much . . .

And now she had hope. That's where all this was bubbling up from, a new idea that she might have been wrong for half her life.

Mitch wrapped his arms around her in a hug. At first Claire stiffened. She hadn't been hugged—not like this— in longer than she could remember. Protected. What a silly thought. Mitch was a writer—sure, he was physically fit—but she had far more self-defense training than he had. She had no reason to feel protected or anything else with him.

He tilted her chin up and said, "Claire, nothing you could tell me is going to change the way I feel about you." He kissed her. "We all have said and done things we regret. I've done my fair share. But I'm telling you right now, Claire O'Brien, that what's inside you is a passionate, smart, beautiful woman I'm lucky to be here with."

This kiss was warmth and passion. This kiss was a prelude to bed. A promise.

The bond she'd felt with Mitch, almost from the first time they met, was strong. It scared her, and that, she realized, was why she didn't want him to meet Dave,

Bill, and the others. She didn't want anyone or anything to hurt this new and powerful relationship. Didn't she deserve to be happy? To find someone she wanted to spend her time with? She was so tired of being alone. In her heart, she'd been alone since the day her mother was murdered.

With Mitch, she felt whole.

Mitch had that aura of a loner that she knew all too well. And for the first time, she wanted to get closer to someone. To *really* let someone into her heart, not just her bed.

But she also wanted him in her bed. She needed an hour of nothing but a physical connection. She had to clear her mind, to feel something other than pain and confusion.

"Let's get out of here," she said, her voice unusually deep.

"Claire—" His voice was thick, eyes searching hers, desire for her as strong as her own.

"Follow me home," she said, taking his hand.

He sat in his car in the far corner of the parking lot and watched the entrance of the Fox & Goose, waiting. The door opened and he leaned forward in anticipation. It wasn't Claire.

She'd said she was meeting her boyfriend—Mitch Bianchi—but she'd refused to share any more information. He'd known she was seeing someone—he made it a point to check up on her whenever possible—but she'd sounded *enamored* with the asshole. And why had she not brought him by the house for the game? Why was she being so secretive about this relationship? He was a writer—a nothing, like all the other losers she picked.

He'd never been threatened by any of them. He understood Claire better than she knew herself. He'd made it a point to study her, learn about her, understand her. She dated men who were her intellectual inferiors. She used them for sex and nothing more. And as long as none of them were a threat to *him,* he could quench his thirst with other women.

His hands clenched the steering wheel. He hated that she slept with men other than him. He'd wanted to be her first and only. But that would have tipped his hand too soon. It was better this way, watching her from afar. Being there for her when she needed him. And then . . . he'd know when the time was right. He'd know when to show her that fate had brought them together. They were meant to be.

He had his girls to keep him from moving on her too soon.

Too soon? It's been fifteen years!

He didn't want to kill her. He wanted her, but if he took her he would have to kill her. Instead, he protected her by standing back and not sharing his love. His love would kill Claire, and then he would have nothing left to live for.

She was everything to him.

Until she got serious with another. When she took another man not only to bed, but into her heart, when she opened up her soul . . . that was for him, and him alone.

The door opened again and he saw her. She wore the dark jeans, and had added strappy high-heeled shoes and a lacy black tank top that hugged her breasts like a leather glove. Her fair skin was so white, especially against her shiny black hair. To touch her hair, her skin, her breasts . . .

His eyes whipped to the man with her, his heartbeat quickening. Mitch Bianchi was not like the rest. He had the same good looks, but was taller, more physical, older than other men Claire had dated. He had an air about him . . . a familiar appearance. Did he know this asshole? No, he didn't think so. It was more the way he moved, the way he scanned the parking lot. Maybe he was in security, worked for Rogan-Caruso, though Claire said he was a freelance writer. Odd.

They were talking, then suddenly Claire wrapped her arms around her boyfriend and kissed him. A full-body kiss, up against the side of the building.

No, no, no! This was not good. The jerk had his hands on her ass, then her back, then her hair. What was he going to do? Fuck her right there in public?

He desperately wanted to confront them, arrest them for public indecency, kill them. He should be the one with his hands on Claire, but not up against the wall of some filthy bar. He'd pour rose petals on her bed, treat her like a princess. His princess.

They stopped groping each other and walked—together—toward Claire's Jeep. She'd been drinking. That's why she was acting like a slut. She'd been drinking and he was going to take her home. Except that she slid into the driver's seat. He walked three cars away and got into a rather nondescript American car.

With clenched fists he wrote down the license plate, then followed. Discreetly.

Bianchi followed Claire home. Parked in her driveway behind her Jeep. He was going to screw her. *Bastard.*

"She's mine!" he shouted in the safety of his car.

He drove off, angrier than he'd been in a long, long

time. He almost stormed into her house. Almost . . . to confront her. He wanted too much to kill her.

I sacrificed for you! I protected you! You're mine!

But he continued up H Street, turned down a side street, and then made another right and headed back downtown.

He'd had these urges before. There was only one solution.

He went on the prowl.

THIRTEEN

As Claire led him across the threshold of her house, Mitch told himself he needed to extricate himself from this situation. When Claire learned the truth she would be hurt and furious, and he didn't want to pile on any more pain.

She kissed him. Those soulful blue eyes fluttered closed and he lost himself in her lips.

She pulled his polo shirt out of his jeans and ran her soft hands up his chest, her thumbs skimming his nipples, her fingernails digging lightly into his skin.

He pushed her up against the wall, pressed his body against hers, her hands trapped between them. He kissed her, over and over, hard then soft then hard again. His hands were flat against the wall on either side of her head, keeping her aligned where he wanted her.

Mitch tried to tell himself this was just about sex, but that was a lie. He needed Claire like a man needs sustenance. He couldn't explain it, didn't want to think about it. Deep down, under his protective shield, he realized that Claire was as important to him as breathing. He couldn't *not* make love to her. Kissing her, holding her, listening to her pleasure as they made love would revitalize him. He'd been functioning on autopilot for so long. Until Tom O'Brien saved his life, Mitch had been on the fast track to burnout.

O'Brien had saved his life, and Claire was saving his soul.

"Claire," he breathed into her lips. "I don't know—"

"I want you, Mitch."

Last time he'd had a battle within himself to stay out of Claire's bed. He'd resisted, but tonight the battle was over before it had begun. His hand grabbed her hair and he devoured her lips, his teeth skimming along her jaw, his tongue tasting her flesh.

She gasped as his tongue dipped into the hollow of her neck. She wiggled her arms up and pulled off his shirt.

In the dim light of her entryway, she frowned. He tensed. He hadn't thought about his scars. More lies on top of the ones he'd already told. He was drowning in his own deception.

She ran her finger over an old scar from a bank robbery gone bad ten years ago.

"This looks like it's from a bullet."

"It is," he said. "Friendly fire during basic training."

She kissed it warmly, then continued the kisses across his chest, her tongue moving in moist circles as she licked him from left to right. Her hands reached under his waistband and squeezed his ass, sending heat up his spine. He wanted her.

Claire was surprised when Mitch pivoted and picked her up as if she weighed next to nothing. His hard muscles pressed against her thin shirt. He had no fat on him, and while he didn't seem unusually buff with his shirt on, when off? he was hot. She loved how physical he was, how he didn't treat her like a delicate rosebud, but a desirable woman. She had never shied away from her sexuality, but she rarely found a partner who equaled her passion.

Maybe because she'd never cared about anyone as much as she'd come to care for Mitch.

He glanced around and she realized he had never been to her bedroom. She pointed him down the hallway, then to the right.

They turned the corner into her bedroom and she hit the wall with her hand a couple times until she found the light switch. The two bedside lamps came on, not bright, just enough light to cast shadows across the room, so she could see him and he her. Visual stimulation was almost as powerful as physical stimulation.

Mitch tossed her on the bed with a grin as he followed, holding his body over her as if he were about to do push-ups. He dipped his head toward hers and nipped her bottom lip. Shivers went up and down her nerves. One small bite on her well-kissed lips and she was at his mercy.

She reached down and unbuttoned his fly, pushing his jeans around his hips.

"This doesn't seem fair," he said. "I'm nearly naked and you're fully clothed."

"Life isn't fair." She pushed at him until she was on top. She pulled his jeans off, then ran her hands up hard, muscular legs. Mitch looked like some sort of Greek god. His skin was on the olive side, but not so dark that she thought Mediterranean. Whatever the combination of genes, they'd created a perfect specimen.

She ran her fingers up his thighs, skimming over his hard penis. Her heart was beating so fast—she wanted to jump all over him. But she also wanted to go slow, to savor this connection, a melding with Mitch that she couldn't explain and didn't want to overthink for fear of it disappearing in a puff of smoke.

She swallowed uneasily as her heart flipped. Her life was in total disarray and she was stepping over the line into an area of relationships that, for her, was still unexplored. Sex, yes, but this . . . this sense of *more* scared her. Scared her but she wanted it nonetheless.

"Claire, sweetness, is something wrong?" Mitch touched her chin, pushed it up to look at him, his dark eyes concerned.

She shook her head. "You're gorgeous." Keep it light, keep it flirtatious.

Don't fall too hard, Claire.

Too late.

"You're rather gorgeous yourself." He pulled her up until their lips met. He kissed her softly but consistently, not pushing but not shying away. Her brief melancholy passed and she nipped his lip, then skimmed her tongue along his strong, square jawline to his ear, then back again and up the other side.

Mitch sensed something had disturbed Claire, but then she flipped an internal switch and turned more passionate, heating up his easy kisses. Her hands didn't stop moving, squeezing his biceps, his triceps, grasping his hands as her mouth moved from his mouth down his neck, down his chest, her tongue skimming his navel as Claire traveled further south.

"God, Claire."

"Don't you mean goddess?" she teased, then ran her tongue over his hard cock.

"You don't play fair," he said.

"You're right. I don't."

"In that case . . ." Mitch reached down and grabbed Claire under her arms and pulled her right up to him. He kissed her as if it were for the last time. He rolled her over, to give himself better leverage and more control. He pulled off her lacy black tank top and bright pink bra, then filled his hands with her breasts. They were perfect. He tasted one, then the other, then back again, until Claire squirmed beneath him.

Mitch loved that Claire wasn't timid in her nakedness, nor did she play games with sex. She took what she wanted and gave back twice as much. He slid off her jeans, only marginally surprised to find a mischievous fairy tattoo—Tinkerbell?—high on her outer right thigh, right below a very sexy bikini line. He kissed it. First an Irish icon on her shoulder, then a fairy on her thigh. Mitch eagerly anticipated what else he would discover as he explored.

Claire's defenses fell completely away as Mitch moved his mouth from her outer thigh to her inner thigh, his warm breath caressing her most sensitive spot. She gasped as he nibbled, his mouth moving closer and closer until he pushed his tongue into her and sucked.

Her hands grasped the down comforter as she moaned, "God, Mitch."

He raised his head and in a husky voice said, "You called?"

"You tease." She reached into her nightstand and felt around until she found a condom. She threw it at Mitch.

Claire wanted to keep it light, but she was spiraling further out of control. She wanted to keep sex with Mitch easy and fun, but it was dark and sexy and needy. She *needed* him as much as she wanted him.

Their hands and limbs moved constantly, touching,

squeezing, caresses hard and soft, teasing and urgent, both fun and all business.

"Claire."

As soon as she looked into Mitch's eyes, he plunged into her. Her eyes closed and she wrapped her arms around his neck, pulling him down to her. He didn't move at first, just held himself deep inside her, while he kissed her. Warmly, with a deep affection Claire craved.

"Look at me," Mitch said.

She did. Mitch's chocolate brown eyes stared at her with such intensity, his face revealing a layer of emotion she hadn't seen before.

He started moving inside her. Slowly. Exquisitely. Their hands clasped as they focused on watching the pleasure their bodies generated in each other's eyes.

Claire gasped from the intensity of their coupling. Here and now wasn't only about sex and mutual pleasure. It was as if they'd become one person, their hearts beating in rhythm, their bodies completely in tune with each other. She'd never had this sense of completeness with anyone. Lust was turning into something else, the *more* she both wanted and feared.

The slow tempo of their lovemaking increased. Bit by bit, together, by unspoken consent, their bodies moved faster. Sweat glistened on their skin as they held back in order to make the finale more powerful. Claire wrapped her legs around Mitch's thighs, to urge him to go deeper, to be even closer to him. With every thrust, she shook. With every grunt deep in his chest, she gasped.

Mitch licked his lips as he watched the waves of pleasure on Claire's flushed face. He loved how Claire gave herself so completely to him without holding back. She was as physical in bed as he, loved the foreplay, wasn't afraid to touch him anywhere and everywhere. As if reading his mind, her hands pulled from his and wrapped around his neck, over his head, down to his shoulders where her nails cut erotically into his back when he adjusted his position to rub against her in just the way she liked.

Foreplay was the time for teasing and games; now was the time for focus. For love. To show Claire that this wasn't an isolated moment in time. That they had something together that they didn't have apart.

Her hands moved down to his ass and squeezed as her body tensed beneath him, her breathing quick, sounds escaping her throat that hit him deep in his cock. They were slick with sweat, their bodies raw and exposed, as Mitch positioned his hands under Claire's beautiful ass and pushed her as far as she would go. Her orgasm came with several high-pitched moans, and he followed with a loud groan.

He lay on top of her for a minute, panting. Then he pulled her into an embrace, side by side. He kissed her all over her face and shoulders and neck, not wanting to pull out, but knowing he had to break the spell. He wanted this time, this raw exposure, between him and Claire. He brushed her hair off her face. She was looking at him, her blue eyes bright and satisfied and warm. Mitch drank in that content, blissful expression on Claire's face. He wanted to make her happy, protect her from the pain she lived with day in and day out. They had found each other, and together they had something too powerful to ignore.

Even though half of it was built on a lie.

Mitch knew he'd fallen in love, and fallen hard.

FOURTEEN

Claire couldn't sleep. Mitch's even breathing was soothing, and she was lulled into a comfortable drowsiness, but she still couldn't cross over to the other side.

She watched Mitch while he slept, sprawled comfortably across her bed on his stomach. Too good to be true, but here he was, in the flesh. Her body still remembered just how good he was, and he *was* in her bed, generating about a thousand watts of heat. Maybe that's why she couldn't sleep, she was too hot. He wore his boxers and had only the sheet draped over his legs. Neelix was curled between his feet. Mitch was a good sport about her cat.

The bullet wound he'd gotten while in the military hadn't made it to his back. In the faint light she saw another scar, lower on his back, above his left kidney. And another scar on his arm. That one was new—it still bore a reddish appearance. She'd seen it many times before; it was on his forearm. He'd never told her what it was from, and she'd never asked.

Now, she wanted to know everything about him. They had time. She wanted to savor each moment and every revelation about Mitch.

Carefully, so she didn't disturb him, Claire slid out of

bed. Her hair was still damp from their midnight shower. After the intense first time, playful sex in the shower was a welcome diversion from her thoughts—her feelings—about Mitch. But now sleep wouldn't come and those thoughts and fears came back.

Bill Kamanski used to brew her hot tea when she hadn't been able to sleep after the trial. Sometimes it had worked.

She made the tea as quietly as possible using only the stove light for illumination.

She'd have preferred to stay in bed with Mitch and block out the real world, but Claire didn't have the luxury of avoiding her responsibilities. She had to follow up on her contacts for the Holman arson investigation and check her office e-mail to see if she had a new assignment waiting.

But in all honesty, her job was the last thing on her mind. She had a trail to follow. Professor Don Collier hadn't returned her call, but she didn't know if he'd even received it. Maybe he hadn't even been on campus yesterday.

Hot mug of tea in hand, Claire made a small detour into her makeshift office and turned on her screen, glancing through the doorway to her bed, where Mitch hadn't moved. The screen didn't shine on the bed, so she hoped she wouldn't wake him. Gently, she tapped the keys and brought up the UCD website. A few clicks later she learned that Collier's first Thursday class was criminal law at eight a.m., and lasted ninety minutes. If she rushed out by seven in the morning, she'd make it to Davis in time, even with traffic. She glanced at the clock. 2:30. Now that she had a set plan, she might be able to get a couple hours' sleep.

She looked for her notepad to jot down the time and location of Collier's class. She picked it up and saw a folded piece of paper protruding from underneath her keyboard with a bright green sticky note with CLAIRE written in large block letters.

Someone had been in her house.

Blood rushed to her head as she unfolded the note with shaking hands. An overwhelming sense of violation hit her.

In the odd light of the computer monitor, she read the letter.

Dad. He hadn't signed it, but she immediately knew her father had been here. Not only from the small block letters he used, but from the way he addressed her.

Claire Beth, it began.

Short for Claire Elizabeth. Her dad was the only one who sometimes called her Claire Beth.

She glanced at the narrow wall where she'd hung a picture of her and her dad. She blinked, at first seeing it, then realizing it was missing.

She stared at the letter, her ears ringing. Her father had been here.

Claire Beth,

I wish I had approached you at another time and place, but my opportunity was limited. I understand why you don't believe me. If I had been in your shoes then, at fourteen, walking in on what you did, I would probably feel the same way. And please believe me, I would have done anything to have spared you sitting through the trial.

The pain you've endured all these years tears my heart. It shows in your eyes. You once enjoyed every moment of the day. Now, all I see are barriers and skepticism. How I wish I could change the past, change everything that happened.

I did not kill Lydia or Chase Taverton. I am not a killer, Claire, and I will prove it to you. Somewhere a killer walks free and he is the proof of my innocence. I believe the way to find him is through Chase Taverton.

I didn't want to get you involved. I only wanted to find Oliver because he has the information about Taverton that could exonerate me.

Oliver believes that Taverton was the target, not your mother. I don't know exactly what he found, but it was big. He called me the week before I was transferred to Section B and said as soon as he tracked down a man named Frank Lowe, he'd have the evidence he needed. All Oliver told me about Lowe was that Taverton had cut a plea with him and he disappeared right after Taverton was murdered. I have no idea who Lowe is, but Oliver believes he can clear my name.

Find Oliver or find Frank Lowe.

I can face death if I know, in my heart, that you believe in my innocence. Until then, I'm in hiding. The police aren't going to reopen this case without clear evidence I'm innocent. Even then, I don't know what's going to happen. But I have to fight. This is my last chance. This is my stand.

Consider this, Claire Beth, because I have thought of it every day and every night for the last fifteen years. When you came home that day and heard your mother with a man, they were alive and in the bedroom. Twenty minutes later, I came in and they were dead, killed with the revolver I kept in my nightstand drawer. You know I never carried my .357 with me. I always kept that gun in my drawer. I taught you to use that gun. I taught your mother how to use that gun. It never left the house.

If you believe that, believe that I didn't premeditate murder, then you know that I am innocent.

What continues to haunt me every day of my life is that I know you almost died that day. I know I didn't kill anyone, but my gun was used. That tells me that the killer spent time in the house. He took my revolver, and hid. Waiting for the right time to kill Taverton and your mother. Taverton was the target. I'm certain of that.

You're a grown woman. A beautiful, smart woman. You work for one of the best security companies in the country. Help me. You're my only hope. Be careful! Someone framed me and if they know you're looking into the case, your life is on the line. I would never put you in danger if I could avoid it, but you're my only chance.

I love you.

Claire read the note three times. She'd ignored him, pretended he didn't exist. It was much easier to think that he was guilty and she was doing the best she could.

Her father's written plea was far more compelling than his restraint at trial. She felt emotion in this letter. Fifteen years earlier, he had seemed to exist on autopilot.

Oliver was dead. Where was Frank Lowe? How could she prove her father was innocent?

"Working late?"

She jumped and pivoted in her chair. Mitch sat up in her bed watching her.

"I didn't mean to wake you," she said.

"It's nearly three. You need sleep, sweetheart." He patted the spot next to him.

She refolded the letter and put it under her keyboard, turned off the monitor, and went back to her bedroom. She slid between the sheets and Mitch took her into his arms.

"You're tense."

"I'm an insomniac."

He kissed her neck and pulled her to him so their bodies were spooned together. She snuggled against him, not wanting him to know anything was wrong. Showing Mitch the letter would risk his freedom and safety. Claire wouldn't do that.

She couldn't do that to the man she was falling in love with.

FIFTEEN

Guilt washed over Mitch as he rifled carefully through Claire's desk.

She'd left before seven—took a quick shower and asked him to lock the door when he left. She said she had an appointment in Davis.

Davis. While her appointment could be innocent, related to her job with Rogan-Caruso, it was an odd coincidence that Oliver Maddox had lived and gone to school in Davis.

Mitch's gut said there was something else going on. She'd been deeply upset and preoccupied when she'd come back to bed at three in the morning. What had happened?

He found nothing about her father. No day book, no messages, nothing. On her computer monitor was a bright green sticky note with CLAIRE written across it. He didn't know what had gone with that note. It was not her handwriting.

He booted up her computer and first checked her e-mail. Nothing in the last forty-eight hours struck him as suspicious—most was work-related. He checked her browser history. It automatically erased every twenty-four hours, and Mitch didn't have the technical skills to retrieve her old e-mails and web history from the hard drive. But what he saw gave him pause. Last night she spent time on the UC Davis website, including a page with Professor Don Collier's class schedule. Collier was Maddox's advisor. He'd been interviewed as part of the missing person investigation months ago.

Claire was surfing Collier's pages. Had she learned that Maddox was dead? Had he come to see her? While looking into Tom O'Brien's conviction, Maddox would likely have spoken with everyone who knew O'Brien, including his daughter.

Claire had also looked up the address of the Davis Police Department. Yesterday afternoon she had been at the Western Innocence Project website.

She'd done searches on not only Don Collier and Oliver Maddox, but Chase Taverton. Mitch wrote everything down, then realized he was late to meet Steve. He left, taking care to leave everything exactly as Claire had left it.

Claire had somehow been in contact with her father, Mitch was certain. He prayed he could keep her out of hot water, but feared she was already simmering.

Claire rushed to Davis, driving recklessly to make it before Collier's eight a.m. class. She risked a ticket by parking illegally and ran to the campus building where Collier's criminal law class was scheduled to begin in five minutes. If he was already inside, she was screwed. She knew what he looked like from his photo on the website, and suddenly realized that he was walking right in front of her. He certainly played the part of law professor: pressed slacks, button-down shirt, no tie, and a tweed—who wore tweed anymore?—jacket with leather patches on the sleeves.

"Professor!" she called.

He glanced over his shoulder at her, slowed his pace. "Are you in my class? We're almost late."

"Actually, I'm Claire O'Brien. I called you yesterday."

He stopped walking. "You didn't need to visit in person. The phone would have sufficed."

She flashed her identification. "I'm a private investigator looking into Oliver Maddox's disappearance. I understand that you were his advisor."

He raised an eyebrow. "So you're here because you're a PI, not because you're a felon's daughter?"

If he was trying to throw her off her game, it was a good effort, but she'd withstood far worse over the last fifteen years. "I work for Rogan-Caruso Protective Services, Professor. My job always comes first."

He nodded. Rogan-Caruso had a certain reputation, Claire knew, and she used it without remorse. "So," she continued, "I understand that you were the last person to see Oliver before he disappeared."

"You understand wrong." He gave a dramatic sigh, and Claire's instincts went on high alert. Collier avoided looking her square in the eyes and she watched him closely.

"I never saw Oliver that day," he said. "We had a meeting scheduled on Monday morning but he never showed. I assumed he'd forgotten. His girlfriend came to me on Wednesday to see if I'd heard from him because he wasn't answering his phone and he'd missed classes. I told her I hadn't talked to him since the Thursday before. She then said she was going to talk to the police. They spoke with me, and I told them what I just told you. You could have saved a trip if you had read the missing person report."

"That wasn't my only question," Claire said. She didn't like Collier. He was too slick, too highbrow, too unconcerned about one of his students missing. And his answers were too perfect.

She said, "How did you feel when Oliver told you he thought you were wrong in rejecting my father's case for the Western Innocence Project?"

"I—I don't understand what you mean."

"I spoke with Randolph Sizemore yesterday and you're the attorney who reviewed the case evidence in the Thomas O'Brien trial and determined that there was no sufficient cause to have the Project look into filing an appeal. I thought it was ironic that Oliver picked that case to investigate. Did he share his findings with you?"

"No. I never discussed it with him after our initial conversation where I explained my reasoning."

Claire saw in his averted eyes that he was flat-out lying. He moved ever so slightly left to right, looking for escape. A thin line of sweat formed on his scalp.

"Yet he was writing his thesis on this case." She continued to push. "He believed Chase Taverton was the intended victim, and my mother was in the wrong place at the wrong time. Which pretty much throws the prosecution's claim that it was a crime of passion out the window. Change the motive, and a whole world of suspects emerge."

"I think you're a desperate young woman trying to cling to the false hope that your father is innocent of two brutal murders."

"Why are you lying?" Claire said, hackles raised. Collier went on the offensive when cornered; so did she. She tried to slow her heart rate, but she was angry.

"If you don't leave, I will call for security."

"I'm not stopping you from getting to class." She glanced at her watch, mostly to prevent herself from decking him. "You're already late."

He glared at her, turned, and walked briskly to the lecture hall.

Claire went back to her Jeep and took several deep breaths to calm down. She rested her hot head on the steering wheel. Maybe she'd played him wrong. Maybe she should have gone in all honey and sweetness and asked if he had a copy of Oliver's thesis, or his notes.

Collier would never have given them to her. If he was involved in Oliver's disappearance, he had either hidden or destroyed everything Oliver had shared about the case. But why would a college professor be involved in hiding information about her father's case? Why would he even care? Or maybe he was just a touchy, crabby guy. Had she misread his reactions to her questions?

Might Collier lie because he'd made a mistake in reviewing her dad's case and his weak ego couldn't handle it? There had to be something else, something more.

The key was finding out more than just who wanted Chase Taverton dead. Who had the means and the *motive* to kill Chase Taverton? Claire had to learn everything she could about her mother's dead lover if she was going to figure this out.

Time was her problem. Fifteen years had passed since the murders. Memories faded. People moved or died. Criminals whom Taverton prosecuted might not even remember the man who put them away. Unless, of course, they had been involved in his murder.

Was Taverton involved in any gang- or mob-related prosecutions? Sacramento didn't have a "mob" problem in the traditional way New York and Chicago and, to a lesser degree, nearby San Francisco did. But there was a powerful criminal Russian community in Sacramento and Stockton. But would they or any other petty criminal have set up such an elaborate frame?

She pulled out her father's letter. Frank Lowe. She knew nothing about him except what her father said: that he was someone Chase Taverton had cut a deal with. How would Lowe be able to clear her father?

Was he dead, like Oliver?

She needed to see the evidence against her father. She was an investigator and while she didn't investigate murder, she knew what was staged and what was real. Like Ben Holman's arson. Obviously arson, staged to look like a theft.

Claire broke out in a sweat. Her father's guilt made sense on the surface, but there were so many layers when Chase Taverton was added to the equation as more than her mother's lover. There was a damn good chance that everyone had drawn the wrong conclusions. And Claire saw a new reality, one where she'd been deadly wrong.

Claire now saw flaws in the prosecution's argument. Flaws that a good defense attorney should have exploited. Or was she seeing the flaws only because she *wanted* her father to be innocent? She rubbed her temples, feeling the pressure of a growing tension headache.

A criminal lawyer named Prescott had represented her father. She made a note to track him down and find out what, if anything, he knew or remembered from the

trial, perhaps something that Claire had been too cata-
tonic to notice at the time.

She had told the truth on the stand. The whole truth
as she'd seen it. That alone may not have been enough to
convict her father, but it had destroyed his life.

She would discover the truth about that terrible day
no matter what it took. Once and for all, Claire had to
know for certain that her father was guilty . . . or innocent.

SIXTEEN

Mitch had only worked in the Sacramento regional FBI office for two years, but until now he hadn't had reason to observe an autopsy at the county coroner's office. Generally, the FBI simply reviewed the reports if they were involved. But Mitch wanted to be hands-on. Steve came along.

Deputy Clarkston greeted Mitch and Steve when they arrived. "Thanks for letting us come," Steve said diplomatically.

Clarkston shrugged. "You did the heavy lifting yesterday. If you want to watch the autopsy, fine by me. My boss said whatever you need, to help. But we're working the case, just so you know."

"Good," Steve said when Mitch wanted to argue. "We'll give you whatever help you need, but it's all yours."

Clarkston relaxed and opened the door to the observation room.

The small room was cramped for three broad-shouldered cops. They stood, pushing the two chairs to the corners. A television high in one corner was blank. Mitch flicked a switch and static ensued.

Clarkston tapped on the window and caught the attention of a young forensic pathologist. He turned on the mic. "Can we get a visual here? And we will need two copies of the tape."

She nodded and switched on the camera above the body.

The pathologists all wore face masks, gowns, gloves, and booties, but that was the extent of their protective clothing. The three of them in the room were all women.

Mitch wanted to tell Steve what he'd learned from Claire's computer, but the information had been obtained illegally. Meg would have a meltdown: She was a stickler for constitutional law. You don't bend the rules—any of them.

Mitch glanced at the dead body. They would have confirmation within the hour—the dental records from his hometown dentist had been overnighted and the chief pathologist was off right now comparing the corpse's dental X-rays to those of Maddox.

Just last night he'd promised Steve that he would keep nothing from him, nothing that could jeopardize the capture of Thomas O'Brien. But what did he know now, really? Claire had done a few Google searches on the principals of the case. What did that tell them? It wasn't illegal for Claire to look into her father's case.

But Mitch knew there was more to it than that.

The external exam now over, the internal exam was beginning. The senior pathologist made the first incision.

Maddox's body was pale, the skin having dissolved. The body was a lumpy mass of human Jell-O. Because it had been in fresh, cold water, putrefaction had slowed, but bacteria had still done severe damage. If Maddox had drowned, there was no way to prove it. Only through external investigation—accident site, damage to the car, mental state of the victim prior to disappearance—could they determine it had been an accident rather than murder. A bullet would be nice, Mitch thought, but there had been no obvious wounds on the body when they'd bagged him underwater yesterday.

And looking at the body now, Mitch couldn't see anything obvious. There were no visible wounds that would indicate cause of death. No bullet or knife wounds. But with the skin slippage and advanced putrefaction, obvious wounds might be unnoticeable.

Mitch watched in silence as the pathologists removed and weighed organs that no longer had the color and shape they should have. How they knew what section was the heart and what was the lungs, he didn't know.

When the senior pathologist removed the brain, she said, "Now this is interesting."

"What?" Mitch asked.

She pulled the camera in closer and Mitch focused on the television screen over his head. "See it?"

"No." All Mitch saw was a lump of dark mass that had the basic form of a brain.

"Here." She took a scalpel and touched a section of the brain that was a slightly different color than the remainder.

"Okay, you got me. What?"

"This is discolored because it was bruised prior to death."

"Are you saying he was hit on the back of the head before he died?"

"I'm saying that his brain was bruised prior to death, but there were no open wounds."

"How can you tell?" Clarkston asked, nose wrinkled in disgust.

"The fish would have attacked his brain if it was bleeding externally at the time of death," the pathologist said. "Though you might want a professional marine biologist to consult."

"You're right," Mitch said. "Fish and other organisms in the water would have focused their feeding activities on any exposed areas. You can see that they primarily ate the face and fingers. What about his skull?"

"I'm getting to that," she said, slightly irritated. Mitch swallowed a snide comment.

"There wasn't anything as obvious as a bashed-in skull," she continued, "when we made the external examination." With the help of one of the assistants, she turned Maddox's body on one side. She examined the skull closely. "Hmm."

"What?" Mitch couldn't help but ask.

"There is a fine crack in the skull. Here, right at the base." She pulled the camera closer. Mitch could see the damage only when she pointed it out using the sharp end of her scalpel.

"That's interesting," Clarkston said.

The chief pathologist stepped into the room and said, "I'm done with the comparison. Your victim is Oliver Maddox. I'll write up a report and send it to your office." Then he was gone.

Nothing that Mitch didn't already know, but it was nice getting the confirmation.

"What's that?" the assistant pathologist said from the room.

Mitch turned his attention back to the table. The

stomach had been removed—or what was left of it. Inside was something bright pink.

The senior pathologist placed the stomach on the scale and cut it open. She removed the object and frowned.

"It's plastic."

"It's a flash drive," Mitch said, incredulous, staring at the thin device half the length of his thumb. "That was in his stomach?"

"Yes," the pathologist said.

"You're sure, right? Stomach and not the intestines?"

"Yes, I'm sure."

"Why is that important?" Steve asked.

"Because it would have passed through within twelve to twenty-four hours. If it was in his stomach, he likely swallowed it within six hours of death."

"Swallowed a flash drive?" Clarkston asked. "What on earth for?"

"That's what we need to find out," Mitch said. He looked the deputy in the eye. "Will you let us work the drive? I'll send you a report as soon as we know what's on it."

Clarkston frowned. "Well—"

Steve said, "Our Silicon Valley lab is state of the art. Twenty-four hours or less."

Clarkston was reluctant, but said, "Okay."

"Pink," Mitch said. "I'll bet it was his girlfriend's. Maybe she knows what's on it."

"Twenty bucks we get nothing from that," Steve said to Mitch.

Mitch didn't want to take the bet, but said nonetheless, "You're on."

SEVENTEEN

After getting a copy of Oliver Maddox's missing person report from the Davis Police Department, Claire drove back to Sacramento and headed to the county archives. She'd been so tense after her conversation with Collier she decided to postpone talking to Oliver's girlfriend Tammy. She needed to go over her father's trial transcripts and see if Frank Lowe had played a role she didn't remember. But more important, to truly follow in Oliver's footsteps, she needed to know these case files inside and out. Something in the files Oliver found at the Western Innocence Project had piqued his interest. Maybe she'd see the same thing.

The archives housed most county records and Claire had been there many times in the course of her investigative work. Generally, she'd have to wait to access files—they needed to be researched and pulled. Depending on workload, it could take a few minutes or several days. But Claire played the grieving daughter card and it worked. The bureaucrat behind the desk took pity on her and pulled the O'Brien case file out of order.

Twenty minutes later, Claire sat in the far corner of the public area staring at the outside of a brown file box. One box. The entire case against her father had been reduced to a box. Murder trials often had dozens of archived boxes. Everything went inside—police reports, crime scene photos, depositions—anything used in the trial.

She breathed deeply and opened the box.

It was obvious that a bunch of stuff was missing. She took everything out, trying to figure out what *wasn't* in the box. There were motions, transcripts from jury selection, and the sentencing hearing.

The entire court transcript of the trial was gone. There was no witness list, no crime scene report, not even the coroner's report.

There had to be another box. She looked on the outside of the box. It was labeled "The People of Sacramento County vs. Thomas M. O'Brien." In the bottom right-hand corner was the notation "2 of 2."

She walked back to the lady who had helped her before and told her there was another box.

The woman sighed. "If there's another box, it's filed wrong and there's no way I can find it now. Fill out this form and I'll have someone research it."

"Thank you," she said, repressing her frustration.

Claire took the form back to her table and went through the documentation that was in the box. Most of it was motions, but she noted her father's attorney— George Prescott, Esq. She wrote down his contact information. Maybe he'd have a copy of the transcript.

While there was no crime scene report, the original police report and photos were inside. Claire took a deep breath and opened the folder.

Officer Adam Parks had filed the following report:

Responded to an anonymous call of shots fired at 1010 35th Avenue. Upon arrival, a Sacramento Police

Officer, Sergeant Thomas O'Brien, was exiting the resi-
dence with a minor female, later identified as his daugh-
ter, Claire O'Brien. It was quickly determined that the
residence belonged to Sgt. O'Brien. Sgt. O'Brien in-
formed this responding officer of two bodies, presumed
dead, inside the residence in the rear bedroom. He vol-
untarily handed over his service revolver, which was
logged in to evidence. Inside, this officer ascertained that
there were two victims and they were both deceased. We
searched the house and garage to ensure there was no in-
truder on the premises, then secured the scene and called
in the possible officer-related shooting.

That was the only police report in the file. There
should have been reams of paper—interviews, follow-
ups, a canvass. Who had made the anonymous call? A
neighbor? That should have come out in the canvass.
What about the detective assigned?

Claire thought back to the trial. It physically pained
her—she'd spent years working hard to forget every detail of the nine months between the murders and her
father's conviction. She recalled that the sheriff's department had been assigned the investigation because of a
conflict of interest since the primary suspect was a
Sacramento Police Officer.

Again, she realized that she should talk to Bill. He'd
been with the sheriff's department for thirty-two years.
He'd know far more about her father's case and the subsequent investigation.

Also in the box were four unmarked photos, which
made Claire think they hadn't actually been used in
trial. They were snapshots, and that in and of itself was
odd. Where were the crime scene photographs? There

should have been hundreds of them. If the murders occurred now, there might simply be a disk of photos, but fifteen years ago they were still using film and archiving the hard-copy photos.

The photos were in color, and though faded, were still disturbing.

Her mother and Taverton were in a deadly embrace. Blood was everywhere, just like Claire remembered. The blood had seeped from the gun wounds, but there was no battle, no fight, no movement of the dying. Death was as instantaneous as you could get. If she had either the coroner's report or the crime scene report, she'd know how far away the killer had been when he fired and from what angle. But those reports were also missing.

She looked at the next photo and gasped. She stared into the dead eyes of her mother. Her face had been obscured in the first photo, but this was taken from another angle.

Mom.

She'd always been closer to her father than her mother. Growing up, she had not understood why. She and her mother argued about everything. Claire blamed herself. She'd been an obstinate kid. A brat. And when her mother was dead, she could no longer tell her that, even with everything they fought over, Claire loved her. They may never have been friends, but Claire loved her nonetheless.

And because she knew, even at fourteen, that she'd been so wrong about her mother. The good and the bad.

Waves of agony washed over Claire. "I'm sorry, Mom. I really did love you."

I'm sorry, Dad. I should have believed you from the beginning. But it looked like you'd killed them.

Maybe if Claire had been more open to listening to Oliver Maddox, he would have shared with her his theory. If she had just given him half a chance, she could have been working this for the last four months. Oliver might not have died.

Maybe she would have.

The facts jumped around in her brain. The killer must have known what Oliver had found, and feared exposure. But maybe Oliver didn't realize the importance of what he had, otherwise why wouldn't he have gone to the police? Oliver had been murdered—she was certain of it, no matter that Dave told her last night that his car crash into the Sacramento River could have been an accident.

She needed the coroner's reports. Both for her mother and Chase Taverton, and for Oliver Maddox. Fortunately, she knew the supervising forensic pathologist at the morgue.

Mitch and Steve walked into the Davis Police Department at 10:30 Thursday morning after finishing up with the autopsy and working out jurisdictional evidence issues with the sheriff's department. The flash drive was already on its way to the FBI's computer forensics laboratory in Menlo Park, less than three hours away. They figured the best way to preserve any information that had been saved on the chip within the submerged stomach of Oliver Maddox was to have the best computer minds in the Bureau work it.

Detective Theo Barker introduced himself to the

Feds. "I made you a copy when you called earlier," he said.

"Thanks," Mitch said and glanced through the report. Standard missing persons—the girlfriend called it in three days after she last saw Maddox, which was approximately noon on Sunday, January 20 when she left him, alone, at his town house on F Street. A neighbor reported seeing the white Explorer pull out of the driveway at dusk—which put his departure roughly at 5:30 p.m. That was the last reported sighting of Oliver Maddox.

There were interviews with the girlfriend, his advisor, classmates, neighbors, and his grandmother who lived in the Midwest. Nothing unusual, but Mitch would need to read it in more depth.

"Sorry to hear he's dead," Barker said, "but that's what I suspected. Young college student like that without financial or female problems doesn't just walk off. But what is the interest of the FBI? Your people don't investigate routine traffic fatalities."

"The cause of death is possible homicide," Steve said.

"The FBI doesn't usually investigate routine homicides, either."

"We're working with the Sacramento County Sheriff's Department," Steve said. "Maddox was a person of interest related to one of the fugitives from San Quentin."

"Think a convict killed him? I hadn't heard of any in this area."

"No, he was dead before the earthquake," Mitch interjected.

"By the way, there's a private investigator interested in the file. A real looker."

Mitch knew it was Claire, but asked anyway. "Do you have her name?"

Barker slid over a business card. "I didn't know Rogan-Caruso would take such a small case, but live and learn."

Mitch picked up the card. CLAIRE O'BRIEN, LICENSED INVESTIGATOR. Steve glanced at him without expression. "Thanks," Mitch said. "Appreciate the help."

They left the police station and drove over to the university. Steve asked, "How did she find out Maddox was missing?"

"Maybe she knows he's dead," Mitch said. "She has a lot of friends on the force."

"She's walking into the gray area," Steve warned.

"I know."

Steve's cell rang and while he talked, Mitch ran through last night. Claire was definitely more on edge than she'd been in the recent past, but he couldn't pinpoint any one thing that made him suspect she had been in communication with her father. Yet it looked as if she'd taken on her father's cause.

Steve hung up. "That was Meg. Five days ago O'Brien was possibly spotted in Redding."

"Five days? Why'd it take so long for us to get the call?"

"The Shasta County Sheriff's Department took that long to pull the tapes and look at them. They didn't give a lot of credence to the sighting. It was a truck driver at a diner off the interstate. But they reviewed the tapes and think it might be O'Brien. A deputy is driving down with the tapes, should be here early afternoon."

"If it was O'Brien, that means he's in town by now."

"You're thinking something," Steve said.

"There was a sticky note on Claire's computer with her name printed on it. It wasn't her handwriting. I couldn't find anything that looked like it that came from O'Brien, but she did searches on Maddox and Collier." He glanced at his watch. "She left at seven this morning. Collier's first class was at eight. What if she went to talk to him?"

"About Maddox? Why?"

"To see if he knew what Maddox knew about her father. Maddox thought O'Brien was innocent. I know for a fact that Claire gave Maddox no credence—believe me, she believes her father is guilty." *Believed.* "At least until recently. And I don't know about now, but it looks like she's trying to learn exactly what Maddox knew."

"To clear her father?"

"To decide whether he's telling the truth."

"Fuck," Steve muttered. "I put the fear of God in that woman, why is she screwing around with her future like this? She knows she could be charged as an accessory."

"She blames herself for the murders, but if her father is innocent, she'd blame herself for not standing by him," Mitch said.

"She told you that?"

"Not in so many words, but she did talk about the murders last night."

Steve glanced at him. "And she left at seven in the morning? You slept with her, didn't you?"

"I don't see—"

"Dammit, Mitch, what are you thinking?"

"Steve—"

"Don't bother making excuses."

"I wasn't going to." He should have, but he didn't regret his relationship with Claire. He only regretted deceiving her.

"I knew you'd fallen for her, but you're going to get yourself in deep shit if you persist in this. What if she is working with her father? What if she knows where he is and is helping him evade the authorities? Can you honestly tell me that your judgment isn't clouded? That you can—oh, this is really fucked. Anything you learn we can't even use to prosecute. You've contaminated the entire case!"

"Whoa, hold off a minute, Donovan," Mitch said. "O'Brien is a fugitive, and we can pursue him using any means possible. There is no contamination, other than the fact that Claire will hate my guts when she finds out I lied to her."

"We sure as hell can't use anything you've learned to—"

"To what? Prosecute Claire for talking to her father? Is that what you really want to do? We don't even know that she *has* seen him. What we've *guessed* is that somehow he got a message to her, told her something that prompted her to track down Maddox."

"She's supposed to report any communication, not just physical contact."

"I get that. But we agreed that the most important thing was putting O'Brien in federal custody to protect him. Wrongly convicted or not, he is in danger on the streets. If Claire is in contact with him, being close to her will help us find him. If we push her, I won't be on the inside."

His deception suddenly took a darker focus. He was not only watching Claire, but actively using her. It made him ill, but it was the single best way they had right now of finding Tom O'Brien.

"Think she's on to you?"

"No." Claire wasn't the type to keep her opinion to herself.

"You're going to have to push."

"She'll know."

"What do you think this is, Bianchi? A game?"

"I'm not playing any fucking games. I think O'Brien made contact with Claire, but I can't for the life of me figure out what he could have said that would have her working with him. I searched her computer and desk this morning when I sensed a change in her demeanor, found nothing from him, but lots of research on Oliver Maddox and the Western Innocence Project. And this guy"—Mitch tapped the file he was reading as Steve drove—"Professor Don Collier, which I already told you."

They'd arrived at Maddox's town house. "Okay, we work this but I'm going to be sitting on Claire," Steve said. "I have to. If the tapes suggest that O'Brien was heading to Sacramento, I need to put this case on the front burner, which means authorizing surveillance on Claire."

That would mean Mitch's position would be made known to his colleagues.

"Shit."

"You'll have to tell Meg what you've been doing. I have your back on this, Mitch."

So his career might be saved, but his personal life was going to go to hell, and fast.

They entered Maddox's town house. It was messy, but it didn't appear to have been tossed. There was no rotting food in the refrigerator—only condiments were on the shelves. Had someone come in here since the disappearance to clean it out?

"Maybe his girlfriend cleaned it out," Mitch said.

"We'll ask," Steve said. "No computer."

"There was no computer found in his Explorer."

"There was a computer here," Steve said and pointed to a printer and cables next to the desk. "Someone grabbed it. Could be Maddox took it. The windows were down in the Explorer. Maybe it floated out in the crash."

"I searched the floor of the river extensively. I would have found it. Silt builds up, but in four months it would have been visible, and it would have been too heavy to float downstream."

They searched the desk, Maddox's bedroom, kitchen, every possible hiding place for sensitive information. Nothing. Except for the empty refrigerator and the missing computer, the house seemed in order.

"So we can assume that Maddox hadn't planned to leave town," Mitch said. "He didn't stop his mail, shut off his electricity, water, anything. He may or may not have had the computer with him. He didn't say anything to his girlfriend, based on the report. The last known meeting he was supposed to have had was with his advisor, Don Collier, who said he didn't see Oliver Monday morning when they were to meet. If we assume that he is telling the truth, we can't account for Maddox's whereabouts from 5:30 p.m. Sunday—when his neighbor saw the Explorer leaving. If he didn't show up for the meeting with his advisor, he was probably already in the river."

"Why Isleton?" Steve asked. "There're maybe a thousand people living there. A bar, a restaurant, not much else."

"The way his Explorer was facing, he was heading *from* Isleton when he went under. On his way from meeting someone possibly? If so, we just need to figure out who."

"That's the million-dollar question." Steve shook his head as he gave the place one more glance. "There's nothing here."

"Do we have his phone records yet?"

"Yeah, I have them in the car."

"Let's find out the last person he spoke with," Mitch said. "Looks like the only evidence we have is Oliver's stomach contents."

"If we can get anything off the flash drive."

"Think of this, Steve," Mitch said. "Why would he swallow something like a flash drive unless he was desperate and thought that was the only way to save valuable information?"

"Maybe he was hungry," Steve said lightly.

"Hungry for the truth."

Jeffrey had known Hamilton since they met rushing the same fraternity. And for all those years, Hamilton had held over his head all the times he'd saved his ass. Whiny Richie jumped on that same bandwagon, pointing to all the money he made them and laundered to fund Jeffrey's political campaigns.

Now, Jeffrey was in the position of saving the day, and he would make sure his longtime friends knew it.

"It's all coming undone," Hamilton said over the phone. "I had a flag on the O'Brien file at archives. And guess who just pulled them? Claire O'Brien!"

"I told you we should have taken care of her a long time ago."

"If O'Brien was dead, this wouldn't even be an issue," Hamilton snapped.

"That was *your* job. You're the one who's tight with all the lawyers and judges and prison wardens."

While listening to Hamilton rant, Jeffrey watched the pretty young campaign intern finger-fuck herself like he had commanded. They were in his hotel room between appointments with big money donors. Jeffrey was furious that Hamilton had called during the short time he had to play, even though he reluctantly admitted that the situation in Sacramento was getting out of control. The fact that someone had found Oliver Maddox's body was unfortunate. But there was still nothing to tie Maddox back to them. They just needed to keep their cool.

"—and then there's Harper," Hamilton was saying. "Jeffrey, are you listening?"

"Of course."

"Are you alone?"

"Yes," he lied smoothly. He watched Julie turn herself on. He was fully clothed, of course. He didn't have time to go through the motions of foreplay and seduction. He didn't care if Julie or whoever he decided to favor that day got off or not. Jeffrey would be the first to admit that it was all about him and his pleasure, and if the woman didn't like it, he had plenty to choose from.

Hamilton warned him repeatedly about a potential sexual harassment scandal, but Jeffrey was careful. He paid his staff well and he paid *extra* well for favors like the one Julie was doing for him now. She looked at him and he motioned for her to keep going. He was getting hard, but Hamilton was worse than a cold shower.

"Jeffrey, what if the O'Brien girl makes the same connection between Taverton and Lowe?"

"She won't," Jeffrey said. "And don't use names. You should know better. We have it under control. Don't panic. As long as we keep our cool, we're fine. Got it? I have to go, I have another major donor meeting and I don't want to be late."

He hung up before Hamilton could protest.

"Spread your legs more," he told Julie.

"Like this?" She bent her knees so they were flush against the couch, spreading her wet pink lips. He loved young, limber girls. Julie was twenty. Hardly jailbait. He was *extra* careful about that.

Jeffrey was also single, so adultery was not even in the picture. He had several high-profile "girlfriends" for the paparazzi, and it was well-known he was a bit of a playboy. But he used his easy charm and powerful charisma to parlay that into somewhat of a following. Women came to *him* for sex. He never had to go looking for it.

"Good." His cock twitched. "When was the first time you fucked yourself?"

"I don't remember." She was growing a little flushed, but he sensed she was still nervous about being caught. That was part of the thrill.

"Take your fingers and push them in."

"I'd rather have you do it."

"I'm sure you would." He took his cock out of his pants. He was semi-hard. "Like it?"

"You know I do."

"Maybe I'll let you suck it later. Go deeper."

She inserted two fingers and pushed them deep inside her. What he really wanted was to watch Julie and another woman go at it, then take them each in turn. He liked having power over many women, having lots of choices.

But he had to be careful about that. The last time he'd gone too far into his fantasy he almost lost everything. Hamilton had to fix it. Jeffrey didn't like having to call Hamilton in to fix anything because he held it over him forever.

He watched Julie and thought about a different blonde.

Another problem Hamilton had to fix.

Jeffrey had picked up the hitchhiker on Highway 80 on the California-Nevada border. He was on his way back from Reno where he'd lost fifty thousand and change. He was angry, at the casinos and the cheating blackjack dealers.

Fifty thousand. From the campaign. Fuck. He'd have to talk to Richie about how to replace it without anyone knowing. Richie was good at that kind of stuff.

He pulled over because she flashed a little leg. He needed a diversion. He rolled down the passenger window and she ran over. He didn't unlock the door yet. "Hey," she said.

"What's your name?"

"Niki."

"Where're you going?"

"San Francisco."

"I'll take you as far as Sacramento."

"Great."

"What'll you give me?"

She rolled her eyes, then smiled. "How about a blow job?"

"Deal."

He drove forty minutes. They were still east of Auburn. "Let's pull over here."

"I'll do it while you drive."

"I don't want to crash the car."

"Oh, you really get into it."

Yes, he did. And he knew what he really wanted from this cheap whore who offered him a blow job for a ride. Girls like Niki would do anything.

He turned off the highway, then made a couple turns and parked off the road among the redwood trees. Perfect. He unzipped his pants and his semi-hard dick popped out.

He looked at her. "It's all yours."

"I don't think so."

She had a gun in her hand. It was pointed at his lap. "You guys are all the same. You'll do anything to have your cock sucked. Get out. You can hitch your way home. Maybe offer to eat out some lonely housewife." She laughed.

No one, no girl, talked to him like that. No woman pulled a gun on him.

He opened the door slowly. Got out of the car, hand on the door. Niki slid over to the driver's seat, grinning, like she'd bested him.

"Sorry, Jeff, you'll learn not to pick up hitchhi—"

He grabbed her by the hair and yanked her out of the car. She screamed, and turned the gun toward him. He grabbed her wrist with his other hand and slammed it against the car. He disarmed her easily.

And if he had just hit her and left her, he wouldn't have needed Hamilton to clean up his mess.

But Niki had promised him a blow job, and she was going to give him one.

He picked up the gun and pointed it at her head.

"I'll take that blow job now. And you so much as nip me, I'll blow your fucking head off."

She was crying. Crying! The bitch had pulled a gun on him and she was crying because he'd taken it away? But she got down on her knees and took him in her mouth and he was happy. When he was hard, he pushed her away. "Take off your pants."

"Please, don't. Just go—"

"Now."

She did. She looked pathetic with her shirt and jacket and a naked ass.

"All fours like the bitch you are."

She complied. He almost wished she would fight him.

He knelt behind her and raped her. Rape? No, he didn't think so. She'd offered her mouth, this was just another female hole.

He closed his eyes. He put the gun behind him, but said, "If you try to get away, I'll break your neck."

She didn't try. She'd accepted the fact that she'd fucked with the wrong person.

He pushed down on her shoulders to get better leverage. She wasn't very big, he realized. "How old are you?"

"Sixteen, you fucking pervert."

"You started it."

Sixteen. Perfect. He shouldn't do this, this was forbidden. The forbidden excited him. He came much too quickly.

He withdrew, getting hard again. He'd take her twice. She owed him.

She jumped up. He reached for the gun and held it on

her. She was sniffing, her eyes red, leaves in her hair. She pulled on her pants.

"Don't," he commanded.

"Leave me alone. Go away."

"I'm not done."

"Yes you are. Done for good, Mr. Jeffrey Riordan, license number 3ABB688."

"Don't threaten me."

She realized she'd made a mistake. She turned to run. He shot her in the back.

He almost didn't believe he'd shot her. He walked over to her body. Her mouth was moving, but only blood came out. She tried to get up, then collapsed. He couldn't stop staring at the dying girl.

He called Hamilton from his cell phone. "I have a bit of a problem."

Jeffrey shook his head to clear his mind when he heard a voice. Julie was talking to him. "Jeffrey?"

He was ready.

"Get down," he growled.

She knelt in front of him. As soon as her mouth wrapped around his cock he came.

He held her head to him for a long moment. He had a solution to their problem. Why did he always have to make the tough decisions?

If Tom O'Brien were dead, none of this would have happened. But since Hamilton had fucked that up, the next person in the food chain had to go. The only person, really, who could be a threat to them.

Claire O'Brien.

EIGHTEEN

Claire drove around to the back of the Sacramento County Morgue. Most people—unless they were cops or morticians—didn't know about the rear entrance. But Claire had met the head supervising pathologist when she was working a life insurance case for Rogan-Caruso a couple years ago. She'd witnessed her first autopsy then, and she and Phineas Ward hit it off. They'd never been romantically involved, but a few times they'd hit the club scene together platonically.

She handed her card to the receptionist, who said without looking up, "Paperwork and name of the deceased."

"I'm here for Phin Ward, not a body."

The woman glanced up, then called over her shoulder, "Phineas, you have a visitor."

Claire glanced around. The office was cluttered but organized. In the far corner was a fish tank with goldfish and a submerged plastic skeleton. Similar pathologist humor added levity to what could have been a depressing place to work, including a fake brain that looked real on a shelf, next to the snack food, and a life-size artificial skeleton hanging in the corner wearing a pirate's hat and eye patch and holding a plastic sword.

Phin emerged from the rear office and smiled at Claire as surprise lit his eyes. "It's been awhile." He walked out and greeted her with a hug, then escorted her into the staging area. This was where they first tagged, weighed, and logged in the bodies.

"I know, I know. I've missed hanging out with you. How've you been?"

"Sad and lonely without you, but I'll live. Better than being him." He jerked his thumb toward a cadaver in the hall outside the freezer. "Came in fifteen minutes ago. John Doe, hit and run."

A mortician walked by pushing a cadaver on a trolley. He handed his paperwork to Phin. Without looking at it, Phin walked back into the office, handed it to the woman, and returned.

"Is there a place we can go talk in private?" she asked.

He reached into a box and tossed her two booties for her shoes. She slipped them on, then followed him through the large autopsy room—currently unused—to a small office on the far side. The smell was mostly clean and antiseptic, with a very faint, underlying hint of something akin to rotten eggs. Like the first time she'd been here, Claire didn't think it was that bad.

The office was crammed with equipment used to preserve tissue samples and containers with a colored fluid that held, primarily, brains. "You don't mind, do you?"

"No," she said, partly lying. Phin had a morbid sense of humor and probably wanted to get a rise out of her. "What's this room used for?"

"We have a neurologist who comes in every Tuesday to examine abnormalities in autopsied brains. Primarily for genetic research."

She picked up a jar, brows furrowed. "Don't tell me this is from a child."

He took the jar from her, read the label, gave her a half grin. "Naw. It was removed from a grown man three days ago."

"It's so small."

"Yeah, that's why the neurologist needs to look at it. Abnormal." He put the jar back. "Okay, what brings you to my neck of the woods? Work or pleasure?"

"Neither. I'm not here about Rogan-Caruso business."

"And you're still seeing that Mitch guy?"

"Yeah, but—"

"So I guess you're not asking me out on a date." He sat on the edge of the metal-topped desk and crossed his arms, revealing intricate tattoos on his biceps.

"Date?"

"I'm just teasing you. You should have seen your face, though." Phin grinned. He picked up a jar and absently turned it slowly around in his hands, the preserved organ turning inside. Looked like a kidney, but Claire wasn't positive. "So why are you here?"

"I need a favor."

"Ah. The truth comes out."

"Two favors."

"What are you going to give me in return?"

She didn't know what to say. "Kings tickets?"

He laughed. "I'm joking. Damn, you're serious today. You usually come back with a great retort."

"I'm preoccupied."

"Okay, what? Seriously, I'm at your disposal."

"I need the coroner's report from two autopsies fifteen years ago."

"Fifteen years? Those are in archives."

"But you can get to them a lot faster than I can. When I called, they said it would take weeks. I don't have weeks. I need them like, um, today."

"You don't ask for anything difficult, do you?"

"Is it possible?"

"I'll get them. Who?"

"Chase Taverton and Lydia O'Brien. They were killed on November 17, 1993."

"O'Brien. Your mother?"

"Yes."

"Why?"

"I need to read the reports. They weren't in the court records."

He stared at her, wanting more information, but she didn't say anything else.

"I'll get them, but I might not have them until tonight."

"I really appreciate it. Call me on my cell phone and I'll pick them up wherever."

"What's the second favor?"

"There was a guy hauled out of the Sacramento River yesterday. You probably did the autopsy today."

"I know the body."

"Did you work on him?"

"No. What do you know about it?"

"I know who he was."

"He wasn't identified until this morning when the chief compared dental records. How do you know?"

"Well, I know the owner of the car that the body was recovered in, and Dave—my quasi-brother the cop, you met him at the Monkey Bar last year—told me last night they were nearly certain it was Oliver Maddox."

"A friend of yours?"

"Not really." She almost lied, made up a story for Phin, but she didn't want to lie to a friend, and didn't see what it would gain her now. "He was a law student researching my father's trial and conviction. He believed that my dad was innocent."

"I didn't think there was a question." His voice held a hint of compassion. One reason Claire had always liked Phin was because he was straightforward and relatively unemotional. He rolled with the punches and liked to have fun in the process. But just his mild concern had her throat constricting.

"There is. At least now there is."

"What do you want to know about the body?"

"Was Oliver Maddox murdered?" She could get the information from Dave, but Claire didn't want to ask. Dave was already suspicious.

"Inconclusive. Molly was the senior pathologist on the case and said there was possible brain damage at the back of the head, consistent with a blow, but the body was badly putrefied. We're ruling it a possible homicide. Because there are no external injuries that we could find, Molly put the preliminary cause of death as suffocation by drowning. But there's no way to tell if he was alive when he went into the water."

"Dave said he'd been there for a few months. He was reported missing the end of January."

"That sounds right, but it's nearly impossible to establish time of death after a couple days. He was under for months."

Possible homicide. Great. That didn't get her any further than she already was.

"Thanks for your help. And if you'll call me about the reports, I'd appreciate it."

"One thing was weird, other than the attention the victim was given."

"Attention?"

"Yeah—the FBI was here. I can't think of any other autopsy since I've worked here that the Feds came in to witness."

"That is strange." Why would the FBI be interested in Oliver Maddox? Were they tracking him because of his connection with her father?

"The other weird thing?"

"When Molly pulled out the organs, which were pretty much Jell-O from decomp, she found a flash drive."

"A flash drive?" Claire repeated, incredulous.

"Bright pink. The Feds took it with them."

"Was one of the FBI agents named Steve Donovan?"

"I don't know, I can check."

"Did you see them? Blond, six one, midthirties, about a hundred eighty pounds, has a mole on his right cheek." She pointed to the center of her own cheek.

"Yeah, he was here."

"Shit."

"Know him?"

"Yes. I just don't know what it means."

Driving from Maddox's town house to the campus, Mitch reviewed the phone records he'd ordered last night. The student didn't have a residential phone—more and more people were dropping their landlines for the convenience of a single mobile phone number.

"Last call was made at 9:45 p.m. Sunday, January 20," Mitch said. "He also made calls at 2:10 p.m.,

3:08 p.m., and 4:49 p.m., all to the same number. Then received a phone call from that number at 5:15. It lasted six minutes."

"Which puts that about the time he was seen leaving his residence," Steve said.

"He called the same number—an Isleton prefix—at 5:22 and again at 9:45, his last call. The first lasted three minutes. The second call less than a minute. If he was meeting someone in Isleton, it wouldn't take four and a half hours to get there."

"I'm not following you."

"We know he was driving from Isleton when he went into the river. Could be the last person who saw him alive. But we don't know if this last call was made before or after he left Isleton."

"So who's the other number?"

"It matches Professor Collier's home phone."

"Maddox called him three times, no answer, and then the prof calls him back."

"Collier said in the missing person report that Maddox was calling to cancel their Monday meeting."

"Why?"

"Oliver allegedly didn't say why."

"Why a six-minute conversation? What'd they talk about? The weather?"

"Collier said it was class-related. The Davis cops didn't know what Maddox was working on. Collier said it was his thesis."

"A thesis seems innocuous. Who would kill over a college thesis?"

"Maybe it's not even related. Could be he hadn't been working on his thesis because of all the time he spent trying to clear O'Brien."

"Now *that* makes sense."

"So he has to cancel the meeting because he doesn't have anything to show."

"I follow you," Steve said. "But one thing I can't figure out. In all this, why didn't Maddox go to the police? Or talk to someone? If he honestly believed that O'Brien was innocent—if he had found evidence to that effect—why wouldn't Maddox have turned it over to the authorities?"

"I—" Mitch didn't have an answer. "Maybe he didn't have proof. Or he could have had unsubstantiated theories. Knowing something to be true in your heart and proving it to be fact are completely different."

"Then perhaps his girlfriend or advisor will be able to shed some light on this."

Steve pulled into a security-vehicle-only parking place at Davis and put his official FBI business placard in the window. Mitch dialed the last number Maddox called the night he died.

"The Rabbit Hole."

"Where are you located?"

"Corner of 2nd and B Streets right off River Road. Can't miss it. Gotta white rabbit on the sign."

"Thanks." Mitch hung up.

"Well?"

"Bar, from the sound of it. Want to make a stop?"

"Worth checking into, but it's been nearly four months. If Maddox met someone there, the bartender may not remember."

"It's the only lead we got right now."

They exited the car, walked into the administration building, and showed their badges. "We need to speak with Professor Don Collier regarding one of his students."

"One moment." The receptionist left the room and Mitch said to Steve, "Do you have Tammy Amunson's contact information?"

"Yes, and her class schedule." Steve glanced at his watch. "It's 1:30. Her last class was over at noon today. I have a mobile number."

"I'm sure as hell not looking forward to giving her the bad news."

The receptionist returned. "I'm sorry, Professor Collier canceled all of his classes today."

"Canceled?"

"Yes, sir. I can direct you to his teaching assistant, Shelley Burns. She has a desk in Professor Collier's office at King Hall." She handed a card over on which she'd already written the name and number.

"Where the hell is King Hall?" Steve muttered as they walked out.

Mitch handed Steve a map of the campus he'd pulled from the receptionist desk. "Now I know why they pay you the big bucks," Steve said.

Shelley Burns's office was more like an oversize closet, not much bigger than Claire's home office, Mitch thought. She had a desk and a narrow wall of tall filing cabinets. Shelves on three walls were full of thick legal tomes. One shelf tilted precariously to one side. If anyone tried to remove a book on the left, Mitch was certain everything would slide off the right.

There was the desk chair and one more chair that the door hit when it opened. She gave a shrug when they walked in and stood shoulder to shoulder. "Sorry, I'd offer you the professor's office, but he locked up and I don't have a key."

"We're trying to reach Professor Collier about a student of his who has been missing."

"Oliver." Shelley frowned as she bobbed her head. "He was such a geek, but I liked him. I was shocked that the pressure got to him. I mean, he lived for this stuff."

"What do you mean about the pressure getting to him?"

"Don—Professor Collier—said that Oliver's thesis wasn't going well and he was panicked. Don thought he just left, couldn't take it. The thesis has to be vetted by not only his advisor, but a committee. He might have had to stay another year. There's a lot of pressure on third-year law students."

"I'm sorry to tell you that Oliver's dead," Steve said.

"Oh, oh no!" Shelley looked stricken.

Mitch sat in the one guest chair and put his elbows on his knees. "We're sorry. We'd wanted to tell the professor the news in person."

"Maybe he heard and that's why he canceled his classes," she said. "Though I can't imagine that he would do that without telling anyone about Oliver."

"You don't know why he canceled?"

"I thought it was a fight with one of his girlfriends. I was late to his eight a.m. class and was running across the lawn. He was standing in the middle of the walkway arguing with some woman. He walked off, angry by the looks of it, and she shouted something at him, but I couldn't hear it. I got into class like ten seconds before he did. He went to the front of the room and said that he had a personal emergency and was canceling the lecture today. Didn't even give an assignment. I mean, we only have two weeks until finals. He just walked out."

"He's never done something like this before?"

"Don? No way. He's never sick."

"What was his relationship like with Oliver?"

"Like, would he be distraught about his death? I guess he'd be upset. I used to be jealous of them—Oliver was his pet, everyone knew it. But then I suspected they had some big disagreement."

"Over what?"

She shrugged. "No idea. But it had to have been major. I mean, they used to talk for hours in Don's office, Don got him a choice internship two summers in a row, and Oliver had a key to his office so he could use Don's personal law books. Then it just stopped. They barely spoke to each other anymore."

"Just like that? Do you know when this argument started?"

"Hmm, not really. After classes began for the new term. That would have been end of August . . . maybe October? Early November? Definitely before Thanksgiving."

"Why do you say that?"

"Oliver didn't have any family nearby. Don always has his best students over for Thanksgiving, unless they go home. I was there with about eight or nine others. Oliver wasn't. And Don said he hadn't been invited. Really flip, very unlike Don."

"That's very helpful," Mitch said. "Did you—"

She cut him off. "If you're from the FBI, is that because Oliver was, like, murdered? And why aren't the Davis police here?"

"I can't really share that information with you as it's a pending investigation," Mitch said. "Do you have any of Oliver's things here? Research? Perhaps notes or an outline? His thesis?"

"Oh, no. Oliver was very hush-hush about it. He wasn't sharing anything. He wasn't even talking to Don about it. "

"Thank you for your time," Steve said.

"One more thing," Mitch said. He knew the answer, but he had to ask the question. "Can you describe the woman Professor Collier was arguing with before he canceled his classes?"

Shelley said, "Pretty, dark hair. Caucasian. Twenty-five or thirty. Older than a college student. She was wearing jeans, I think. A long beige blazer. I don't remember anything else. Oh, she was kinda on the short side. Don's on the short side, so I noticed she was at least four or five inches shorter. Five two maybe?"

"Thank you for your time."

They left King Hall.

"Dammit," Mitch said. "Claire was looking at his class schedule and left early. I knew it. What does she know that we don't?"

"I wish I knew," Steve said.

What was Claire up to? What did she tell Don Collier that had him canceling his classes and acting strangely?

"We have to track down Collier," Mitch said.

"Got his home address right here. He's not too far from campus. And now I have a good reason to talk to Claire O'Brien again. Two people have identified her. It sounds like she's a step ahead of us, too. I don't want her to get in over her head."

Neither do I, Mitch thought.

Steve called Oliver's girlfriend as they walked, and Tammy Amunson agreed to meet them on the ground-floor of her dorm. Tammy was a petite blonde, pretty, though she dressed on the plain and dowdy side. She wore small, smart glasses. Someone that an equally brilliant geek lawyer would fall for, Mitch thought.

"Tammy?" Mitch introduced himself and Steve. "Let's sit down where it's private." He led her to a sitting area in the corner. There weren't many people inside on this beautiful May afternoon.

Her face fell as she shrank into the chair. "It's about Oliver."

"I'm sorry to tell you this, Tammy, but he's dead. His body was found yesterday morning."

Her bottom lip quivered, and she bit it to make it stop. She blinked back tears, then said in a shaky voice, "Wh-what happened?"

"His body and his Explorer were in the Sacramento River near Isleton."

"Isleton? Where's that?"

"A small town in southern Sacramento County, in the Delta."

"I've never heard of it. I'm not from around here. I can't believe he had an accident like that. Oliver was such a good driver. I mean, sometimes he got distracted, especially when he was talking, and he'd get excited about something, but he didn't drink and drive, never, and he was never reckless and I don't understand how this can happen. When? Where has he been since January? Are—" She gasped. "Oh my God, he's been dead. Since then. Since January? I knew it. I knew something bad had happened to him!" She couldn't stop the tears from flowing, and batted them away with her hand.

"We have a few questions, if you have a moment."

"Anything. I—" She stopped talking and stared at them, blinking rapidly. "Was it an accident?"

"That's unclear right now, but we're treating it as a possible homicide."

She started shaking. Mitch put an arm over her shoulders, felt her body racked with sobs he couldn't hear. Somehow that made her grief worse.

When the worst of the shakes subsided, Mitch said, "You said in the missing person report that the last time you saw Oliver was about noon on Sunday, January 20."

She nodded.

"Professor Collier had a meeting with him on Monday, but Oliver canceled it."

"Canceled it? No. That's not right." Tammy squeezed her eyes shut. "No," she said more emphatically. "Professor Collier told me that Oliver never showed up for his meeting. I'm positive. That's what had me going to the police. Because no one had seen Oliver for days, and when Professor Collier said Oliver missed his meeting— Oliver was excited about the meeting. Really excited. He and Professor Collier had a dispute ages ago, and Oliver thought this would put things right. I told the— oh. I should have known something was wrong yesterday. I got my hopes up that she would find Oliver."

Mitch wasn't sure he was hearing correctly. "What happened yesterday?"

"A private investigator came to me after class. She was looking into Oliver's disappearance. I told her everything I told you, plus how excited Oliver was about his thesis, 'The Perfect Frame' he called it. He said he finally had the information to prove his hypothesis. I just got my hopes up that Oliver was okay. She seemed so determined to find him. I think in my heart I knew he was already gone, but—" She took a deep breath and the tears started running down her face again.

"Do you remember the PI's name? A company?"

"Claire. Um, Claire something. From Rogan-Caruso. I have her card in my desk upstairs."

"That's okay," Steve said. "We're familiar with the company."

Mitch's stomach felt like lead. What was Claire doing?

"Thank you for your time," Steve told Tammy. "Would you like me to call someone for you?"

She shook her head, wiping her nose with her sleeve. "My roommate is upstairs. I just want to go home." She sniffed. "Do you have any idea who would want to hurt Oliver?"

"No, Tammy, but we're working on it."

NINETEEN

Claire walked through the glass doors of the Renaissance Towers at 8th and K Streets—known to locals as the Darth Vader Building because the top dozen floors had a shape reminiscent of the Sith lord. She showed her Rogan-Caruso badge to the guard, who waved her through. She was still mulling over the information she'd learned from Phineas at the morgue.

On the elevator, Claire punched the 18 button. It was 1:30, past the lunchtime rush, and she had the ride to herself straight through to the eighteenth floor.

Guilt washed over Claire. She was about to violate someone's trust, and it didn't make her feel good. She worked through a cover story—something close to the truth, but without mentioning her father had contacted her or left her a letter. She'd simply heard that Oliver Maddox was dead and she wanted to figure out what he'd learned about her father's case. She had a right, didn't she? Her mother had been the victim.

Half-truths were still half-lies.

Rogan-Caruso Protective Services took up the entire floor, but you wouldn't know it when you exited the elevator into the simple yet comfortable waiting area surrounded by designer bulletproof glass, the Rogan-

Caruso logo of a sword and shield etched in the center. Though the office was thoroughly modern, the logo harkened back to the days of white knights to the rescue.

Claire always felt inadequate coming into the offices. She had a small workspace that she used primarily to access protected computer files, and she briefed her boss, Henry Opacic, twice a month on her assignments or before testifying at trial if one of her investigations went that far.

But today she was coming in to use the Rogan-Caruso state-of-the-art computer system to find out everything she could about this mysterious Frank Lowe.

She hated being deceptive, but she didn't want to bring her boss or anyone else in the company under the scrutiny of the FBI. And while Rogan-Caruso played hardball with the government, they also took jobs from the same. Claire wasn't exactly sure of everything the company did, and that was fine with her. She was happy with her low-level, below-scrutiny position, and she hoped that because of that no one would notice the computer time.

She stuck her badge into the slot that opened the first door. Aggie, the receptionist, glanced up. "Good afternoon, Claire. How are you?"

"Good, thanks."

"Henry is out of town."

"I'm just doing some research."

"Go right in."

Aggie knew everything about Rogan-Caruso. *Receptionist* was a misnomer. She buzzed Claire through, and Claire knew before the end of the day Henry would know exactly how long she'd been in the office and what internal files she'd accessed.

She wasn't planning on looking at internal files beyond the Ben Holman investigation.

Claire walked down the quiet, plush hall, around the corner, and hesitated outside the office of the only person she truly considered a friend, Jayne Morgan, the computer genius Dave had a crush on. But Claire didn't want to abuse her friendship, and she hated asking anyone for favors. This was her problem; she would handle it the way she preferred to handle all her personal problems: alone. Still, she peeked in and was both relieved and disappointed that Jayne wasn't in.

She sat at her desk and quickly wrote up the report on the Holman arson investigation, scanned in Pete Jackson's report, her interview with Holman, and what she'd learned from her informants about the medical supplies on the black market. She sent the whole report to Henry.

Claire then logged in to the Rogan-Caruso system and the world appeared at her fingertips. Jayne had created the intensive computer system which pulled public records and archived information from the Internet into a powerful database, which could be combined with secured data maintained internally or through their memberships and associations.

She typed in "Frank Lowe Sacramento," figuring that if Lowe was involved somehow with Chase Taverton fifteen years ago it would have been local. She could expand the search if nothing came up.

Immediately, more than a dozen Frank Lowes popped up. She wished she had more to go on because she didn't know *which* Lowe was the man Maddox had referred to. There had to be a better way to weed out the information.

She surmised that if this Lowe knew anything about Chase Taverton and the murders, he'd have been in Sacramento County in the early 1990s. That eliminated two potentials. Next she looked at ages. One Lowe had been a child in the early '90s. She took him out.

Using similar methodology, she eliminated half the Frank Lowes she'd uncovered. Then she started going through the remaining individuals more carefully, making notes. She was particularly interested in any jail time or arrests. If Taverton had made a plea agreement with Frank Lowe, he had to have been arrested at some point.

"He's dead," she said out loud when she came to a petty thief who had done time for burglary. She almost deleted his records from the search except for one thing: He'd died in a fire in the early morning hours of November 18, 1993. Less than a day after Chase Taverton was murdered.

She switched to LexisNexis, where she pulled up all newspaper articles related to the fire. Lowe had been a bartender who lived above a bar called Tip's Blarney in downtown Sacramento. The fire was ruled arson, but the owner, Tip Barney, had been cleared of any wrongdoing and no one had been arrested. The building was a complete loss. One body was recovered, burned beyond identification. There were no dental records for Frank Lowe, but Barney said Lowe was the only person who lived in the building, and he'd left him there at one a.m. when Lowe closed for the night.

Maybe she had the wrong Frank Lowe. Oliver had told her father that Frank Lowe had information. How could a dead man have information?

She made notes on the remaining Frank Lowes, but she kept coming back to the dead bartender. He'd died the night after her mother and Taverton were killed. In an arson fire. She ran a search on Tip Barney, not knowing what, if anything, would pop up.

She almost jumped out of her chair. Barney now owned a bar in Isleton. Oliver's Explorer was found in the river outside of Isleton.

That was a coincidence Claire planned to follow up on. Tonight.

She glanced at her watch. It was nearly four!

She was supposed to meet Mitch at her house at six, but first she needed to see Bill. She'd told him she'd stop by this afternoon. She had questions about Oliver Maddox as well as about her father's trial. Questions that Bill might have the answers to—she'd just never wanted them before.

Four o'clock was shift change, from day to swing. Dave walked into the locker room and caught up with Phil and Eric arguing about the Kings game from the night before.

"It's over," Dave said. "There's another game tomorrow."

"Want to get a beer?" Eric asked.

"I told my dad I'd stop by," Dave said. "He's having problems with his air conditioner again."

"He needs to hire a real repairman," Phil said.

"How's Claire?" Eric asked. "She left early last night."

Dave didn't want to talk about what he thought was going on with Claire. He had talked about it with his dad this morning, and Bill was concerned as well, but said Claire had called earlier and asked to come over that afternoon. Maybe it was a good sign. Claire had always been able to talk to Bill about what was troubling her. Bill was a great father, and Dave was glad he could share him with someone who needed a great father figure.

Tom O'Brien's crimes had hurt everyone who knew him. Dave had respected the older, wiser cop. Tom had trained him, and Dave thought he'd known him. But he hadn't. Dave had never thought Tom was capable of murder.

And worse, Dave hated that Claire paid the price, and was still in turmoil.

"Claire's fine," Dave said. "She had a date."

"She should have brought him over for us to meet," Eric said, then winked at Phil. "We'd have made sure he was good enough."

"Why didn't she bring him?" Phil asked Dave. "That's unlike her. Especially someone she's been seeing for a while."

Dave tried to dismiss it with a wave. "She's tired of the third degree on her boyfriends."

"She's never cared before," Eric said.

"Maybe this guy's different," Dave said, feeling uncomfortable with this conversation. "Look, Claire is practically my sister. I can give her a hard time, but I think we should leave this alone until she's ready to share."

"Aren't you curious?" Eric asked.

"Yeah," Dave admitted.

"We can check up on him," Phil suggested. "Just a quick look. Make sure he doesn't have a record or anything."

"Last time we did that we learned what's-his-name had two DUIs."

"She was pissed," Eric said.

"She thanked us later," Phil reminded them. "She was madder at the jerk than she was with us."

Claire's best friend in high school had been killed by a drunk driver. She had zero tolerance for it, and Dave had known that when he told her about the boyfriend. His dad had jumped down his throat when he found out, telling Dave to stay out of Claire's personal life or she wouldn't forgive him.

People need to screw up on their own. That's how they learn.

But Dave was overprotective of Claire, he couldn't help it. He remembered when she first came to live with them—she never slept through the night, waking to terrifying nightmares that had him and Bill running to make sure she was okay. She'd been a scared teenager who needed them. Just because she was a grown woman who carried a gun and Taser didn't mean she didn't still need them.

"Just a quick look," Dave said. "Make sure he's clean, and we don't say anything, okay?"

"Unless he's a wanted mass murderer," Eric teased.

Dave hit him on the arm as they walked to Dave's desk in the bull pen.

"Mitch Bianchi isn't a common name," Dave said as he sat down at the computer. "We should have something—or nothing—pretty quick."

He brought up the DMV database and typed in the name. Nothing. He typed in "Mitchell" for the first name. Nothing.

"Odd," Dave said. "Maybe Mitch is a middle name or something."

"Or he never got a driver's license," Eric said.

"In California? Rare," Phil said.

"Maybe he's not from California," Dave said. "Claire said he was house-sitting in her neighborhood. He's a writer."

He put a search into the criminal database. Nothing popped up. "He's clean," Dave said.

"Except he doesn't have a California driver's license," Eric said.

"Okay, what about a broader search," Phil suggested. "Noncriminal."

Dave was curious as well. He went into the full files. Nothing.

"Shit," Dave said. "Who is this guy? There's nothing on him."

He played around a bit more with the database. He could find nothing. He broadened the search nationally. Nothing. Then he decided to Google Mitch Bianchi and opened an Internet browser.

Fewer than two dozen webpages had the name. Most were genealogy related.

One article popped up.

It was a newspaper article from the *Dillon Tribune*, a small weekly paper out of Montana.

Sheriff Tyler McBride credited agents with the FBI in helping track the two San Quentin fugitives during the worst blizzard of the season.

"Hans Vigo and Mitch Bianchi went above and be-yond helping protect residents of the Centennial Valley. I commend both of them, and consider them friends."

*   *   *

"He's an FBI agent?" Phil asked, shocked.

"Claire's going to flip," Eric said. "Why did he tell her he's a writer? Is he undercover?"

"He's using Claire to get to Tom." Dave wanted to strangle him. How *dare* a Fed insinuate himself into Claire's life, date her, lie to her?

"Shit," Eric muttered.

"Bastard," Phil said. "Do you think Claire knows where Tom is?"

"No," Dave said, though after his conversation with her last night he wasn't so sure. "I have to tell her." His heart sank. The last person he wanted to hurt was Claire.

"Of course you do," Phil said.

"Damn straight," Eric concurred. "Do you want us to go with you?"

"No," Dave said. "I have to do it myself."

TWENTY

Claire rushed to Bill's house, opening the front door as the big grandfather clock in the entry struck once to mark half past the hour. The warm aroma of fresh-baked sugar cookies filled the house. Bill had taken to baking after his wife died, when Dave was barely a teenager.

Bill walked down the hall from the kitchen and greeted her with a warm bear hug. "I thought I heard that Jeep of yours in the drive."

"Sorry I'm late."

"We didn't have a set time. Come into the kitchen. I have cookies in the oven."

She loved Bill, more like a grandfather than a father. He was in his early sixties, had retired eight years ago. Gained a bit of weight around the middle, but otherwise looked the same as he had when she came to live with him after her father's arrest.

"Missed you last night," she said as she followed Bill.

"Waste of a night. Lost in overtime by three points." He shook his head. "They'd better have their game on tomorrow."

"You going to be at the game?"

"Yep, I have tickets for Friday and Saturday nights.

Then they go back on the road. Why don't you join me Saturday?"

"I'd like to, but—" She didn't know what she would be doing Saturday. Claire didn't want to make any plans for a while.

"Thirsty?"

"Water."

"Milk. You're too skinny."

"Am not."

Claire loved Bill's sunny kitchen with the cheerful blue-and-white checks. Grover, a retired police German shepherd, raised his head and smiled at Claire—at least that's what she liked to think.

She scratched Grover between the ears and sat at the table. Bill put a fresh-baked muffin and a tall glass of milk in front of her. She hadn't had lunch, and devoured the muffin while Bill watched her from a seat across the table.

"Okay, that was good. I miss your baking. But I thought I smelled cookies."

"You did. They're in the oven. I made the muffins first, knowing they were your favorite."

"It was delicious."

"I'll send some home with you." He poured her a second glass of milk. "Dave called me this morning."

"About Oliver Maddox."

Bill nodded.

"You know he's dead."

"Dave told me. A tragedy. I liked him."

She straightened. "How well did you know him?"

"Not well. But there's something endearing about a young idealist searching for answers. I was an idealist when I became a cop. Thought I could protect and serve and be proud of every decision I made." His voice trailed off and he glanced out the window, then back at Claire.

"Oliver lied to me," said Claire. "He told me he was an attorney with the Western Innocence Project and they were looking into my father's conviction. But when I called over there, I found out he had been an *intern* and was no longer even with the Project. So I didn't listen to him, Bill, and I now regret it. You talked to him. What did he know?"

Bill said nothing for a long minute. Then, "If you're looking for a clear indicator of guilt or innocence, I don't have it. But I did listen to what Oliver had to say, and it was compelling."

"Did he have proof that my father is innocent?"

"You need proof?"

She didn't understand the question. "Of course I need proof. He was convicted of a double homicide. He killed my mother. But if he didn't—yes, I need proof."

"There wasn't a lot of proof during the original trial. Tom was convicted on circumstantial evidence. Solid, to be sure, and back then I believed he was guilty. Weapon, motive, and opportunity."

"What about now?"

"Oliver said the police investigation into Taverton was on the surface, at best. They never looked beyond the obvious—threats made against him, criminals he had prosecuted who were at the time out of prison. Yes, they covered their bases, but it wasn't a thorough investigation because the district attorney believed they had the killer in custody. The investigation was more to prove Tom was guilty than to pursue any other possibilities.

"Truth is, that's the way it is most of the time. While we do our best to look at all potential suspects, usually we know who the killer is and work our butts off to prove it. That was the way it was with Tom."

Claire's heart fell. "So Oliver had no proof."

"What do you think, Claire? Knowing that the police didn't follow up on Chase Taverton or his potential enemies, what do you think about the case?"

"It doesn't matter."

"Yes, it does. It matters a lot. Because there *is* reasonable doubt. I used to be a lot more hard-nosed about the criminal justice system. I hated how some of those bastards got off because of a ridiculous technicality, only to rape or rob or kill again. It made me so angry and fueled my younger self to be a diligent, hard-ass cop. I didn't want any of the criminals I arrested to get off on a stupid loophole, or because I didn't do my job correctly. And the truth is, the detectives in charge of the O'Brien-Taverton double murder closed every loophole so Tom couldn't even wiggle. Remember, only a few weeks before Tom's trial started O. J. Simpson was arrested for murder, ridiculously claiming there was another killer. It made Tom look like a guilty man grasping at straws when his attorney stood up and claimed someone else killed those two people—because there was no other reasonable motive, no other reasonable suspect.

"Claire, do you need black-and-white proof that your father is innocent or do you believe that he is innocent absent proof of another's guilt?"

Claire let out a pent-up breath. She had never thought of it that way. She couldn't quite wrap her mind around it. She needed to blame someone for destroying her family. "Someone is guilty."

Bill nodded. "And I think Oliver figured it out. But he didn't share his conclusions with me. We spoke twice. The first time was right before Christmas. He explained his findings and theory to me and asked some questions about police procedures."

"What did he know?"

"He *knew* very little. He had reviewed the police reports and discovered that no one had seriously looked into the Chase Taverton angle back then. He thought that was odd, and I concurred. I didn't know it at the time, but I was out of the loop because I had a conflict of interest. And, frankly, most of the cops I knew suspected Tom was guilty. He had always been a bit of a hothead. I didn't know him personally, but it all came out during the trial. You know that."

"He never hurt me or my mom."

"I don't doubt that, Claire. He loves you."

She frowned. "Anything else? I'm trying to figure out what Oliver Maddox knew that got him killed."

"You think it's murder? Not an accident?"

"He disappeared after telling his girlfriend he was almost done with his thesis on 'The Perfect Frame.' But she didn't know where his thesis went. I'm certain that Oliver was referring to my dad's case, that he believed my dad was framed. And I—" What did she *really* believe?

"I think he might have been right," she said.

Bill leaned forward. "Might have been? Are you still qualifying your answers? If Oliver was murdered, he uncovered something big enough and dangerous enough that he was a threat to someone with the ability and lack of conscience to kill. And that person most likely killed your mother and Taverton."

"Do you think my dad is innocent?"

"Yes."

"Did you always think so?"

"No."

"What made you change your mind?"

"Time."

"I don't understand."

"Time away from the trial. Time away from the impact the trial made on the community, on you, on the people I worked with. When a cop goes bad, it's hard. You want it to go away. But listening to Oliver brought it all back, and I saw the holes in the case."

"Why didn't anyone else see them? All the appeals?"

"Appeals are a very limited redress. You have to appeal specifics, like an un-Mirandized confession or false testimony or incompetent counsel. Tom didn't have the money to pay for a separate investigation. He relied on an overworked criminal defender—and that still cost him tens of thousands of dollars. Probably more. He put fifty thousand in a trust fund for you and used the rest for his defense. But when the money was gone, he went to public defenders. The appeals were routine, delaying the inevitable. Nothing substantive came from them. When Tom thought the Project was taking his case, he had hope."

"You talked to him?"

"Yes. He called after Oliver Maddox came to see him."

"But Oliver wasn't with the Project."

"No. He lied, I realize now, but his heart was in the right place. He recovered Chase Taverton's day planner and told me he was retracing Taverton's steps based on what was written in there."

"Why didn't the police do that?"

"The day planner was his personal calendar. His public calendar only had active cases on it, and that's what the police were using. His personal calendar was apparently in the possession of his sister."

"What's her name?"

"Janice Krause. She lives in El Dorado Hills."

"Maybe she remembers something. Maybe she still has it."

"Claire, be careful. Oliver believed that your father was framed by someone who wanted to kill Chase Taverton. The killer must have learned about Taverton's affair, and the best person to frame is the husband. But if Taverton hadn't been having an affair, he would have faked an accident or had Taverton killed in a manner that would divert attention from the true motive.

"And that is what Oliver never found out, at least not to my knowledge. The motive of the killer. Believing that Taverton was the target and knowing *why* are completely different."

Claire absorbed the information. "Did he mention Frank Lowe to you?"

Bill started. "Yes. He called me and asked if I could look into a petty thief named Frank Lowe for him. He never told me why."

"And did you?"

"Yes. I asked Dave to pull his records. Didn't tell him why—I don't want Dave to get in trouble because I have this curious streak. It seemed like a dead end—Lowe was killed in a fire at the bar he lived above."

"Did you tell Oliver that?"

"I called him when I had the information, and said I

didn't know what good it would do because Lowe was dead."

"Did you know he died the night after Taverton and my mom were killed?"

"That's what Oliver had said. And he said one other interesting thing. He thought Lowe was alive."

"Did you give him the files?"

"No. Never had the chance. He was going to come by, never did. I left a couple messages, but never heard back from him."

"Why didn't you go to the police?"

Bill frowned, shook his head. "And say what? I have no evidence of anything. And I didn't know he was missing until this morning when Dave told me he was dead." He seemed to age in front of her.

"I'm sorry, I didn't mean—"

"Believe me, Claire, I wish I had pushed Oliver harder. I wish I had told him to be more careful. But the truth is, I was hopeful that he was going to find something to help Tom, and I let him go at it. He was a law student. I honestly didn't think he would get hurt digging through archives and court cases."

"When was he supposed to meet you to pick up the files?"

Bill sighed and stood. He walked over to a small desk near the back door and flipped his calendar back to January.

"Monday, January 21. He wanted to come by first thing in the morning, and I said anytime after six. I get up as if I'm still working the day shift."

"He went missing that Sunday night."

Bill blanched. "Claire—"

"I need to go."

"Claire, be careful. Talk to Dave."

"I can't."

Suddenly Bill straightened. "You're talking to Tom."

"Don't."

"Claire, you need to—"

"Don't tell me to go to the police. I can't do that. Maybe two days ago I could have—two days ago I would have—but everything my father told me you just confirmed. Something is going on here, and I need to figure it out. But I can't tell Dave. I love him, but he's a cop. He'll risk everything to help me, and lose everything as well."

"Because he loves you, Claire. You're the little sister Maggie and I could never give him."

"I need to do this."

He nodded. "I understand. But Claire, watch your back. And don't be afraid to call for help."

"Do you have the files on Frank Lowe?"

"I'll get them." He left, then returned moments later and handed her a thick manila envelope.

"Thanks."

"You know you can always call Dave or me. We'll be there in a heartbeat."

"I know." She hugged him. "But you see why I can't call the authorities now."

"No—" He stopped. "They want Tom in custody."

"And they don't care about the theory of a dead law student. At least not now. And the execution date is six weeks away. Dad has no more appeals." Tears coated her eyes and she blinked them back. "He's innocent, Bill." Her voice cracked. For the first time, deep down, Claire knew that her dad was innocent. "I don't need proof to know it. But I need proof to get him out from under the needle."

She walked to the door. Bill followed her and said, "Remember, you're following in Oliver's footsteps. Which means someone he talked to is involved. Oliver may not have known he was interviewing a killer. You might not, either."

"I'll remember."

TWENTY-ONE

It was nearly five when Mitch and Steve walked into the Sacramento regional FBI office to meet with their supervisor, Megan Elliott.

Meg was at her desk. Mitch suspected she worked longer hours than anyone else here, but even if he was concerned about her workaholic lifestyle he didn't feel right commenting on it. "Come in," she told them when Steve knocked on her open door. She finished up the report she was typing and turned to them. "I hear you two have been busy."

They sat in the chairs across from Meg. Her blond hair was pulled back into a long, sleek ponytail. Her casual look. When she was in the field, she wore her hair up tight. Having it down made her look softer and more like the woman Mitch had cared for all those years ago.

A lifetime ago. It was all water under the bridge.

Steve began, "Like I told you earlier, we have a positive ID on Oliver Maddox. I sent off the flash drive found in his stomach to our office in Menlo Park. Don't know that we'll get anything off it, but it was in a titanium case. Instead of screwing with it here, I thought it best to get an expert."

"Good." She made a note. "I'll follow up first thing in the morning."

"We have a missing person of interest. Professor Don Collier, Maddox's advisor, made a conflicting statement to the police. Maddox told his girlfriend he had a meeting scheduled with his advisor, but Collier told the police Maddox canceled the meeting. The girlfriend said Maddox was too excited about his project, and that Collier told *her* that Maddox didn't show up—he said nothing about Maddox canceling. We went to clarify with the professor and found out that he canceled his classes for the day. We went to his residence, but he wasn't there."

"Do you have enough for a warrant?"

"Doubtful," Steve said. "We're digging a bit more into his background."

"I'll get in contact with the U.S. Attorney's office and give them a heads-up."

As always, crossing her t's and dotting her i's, Mitch thought. Meg wouldn't allow anything to slip by under her watch.

Steve filled Meg in on everything except their suspicion that Claire O'Brien was working on something related to Oliver Maddox. However, he said, "According to his girlfriend, Maddox was still working on the Thomas O'Brien case."

"The file says that the Project didn't take the case."

"True, they didn't. But Maddox was writing his thesis on it nonetheless, and he told his girlfriend that it was called 'The Perfect Frame.' "

"O'Brien's guilt was established in a court of law," Meg said. "We are here to uphold those laws. Whether he was wrongfully convicted is not something that our office considers."

Mitch leaned forward. "Hypothetically," he said, catching her eye, "if O'Brien was framed and Oliver Maddox found evidence for such, that is a strong motive for his murder."

"As far as I'm concerned, you have two separate cases here. You have a fugitive, and you have a homicide. Whether Maddox had information that may have exonerated Mr. O'Brien is irrelevant to the fact that O'Brien is a fugitive. I expect you both to be equally diligent on both assignments. And don't forget that the Sacramento County Sheriff's Department has jurisdiction on the Maddox case. The only reason you two are still on it is because they asked for our assistance with the evidence, and they haven't told you to back off."

"If we find O'Brien, can we keep him in federal custody?" Mitch asked spontaneously.

"We have no cause. We'd keep him at the county jail until transport back to San Quentin or wherever the State of California wants to send him is arranged. We don't have jurisdiction over him. He was convicted in a California court, he is the state's problem. The only reason he's on our radar is because they asked us to help in tracking down the escapees. His crime wasn't federal."

"What if I could prove O'Brien is in danger if he's remanded to state custody?"

"What proof? More of the same you gave me when justifying disobeying my orders in February?"

Mitch let that dig slide. "Megan, there's something here. I can't prove it yet, but—"

She put up her hand to silence him. He hated when she did that. "Hard evidence, Mitch. I'm not going to go to bat for you without something solid. Not again."

He nodded. "Full disclosure," he said, glancing at Steve. "I befriended Claire O'Brien."

Meg stared at him, her jaw tightly shut. "Against my direct orders?"

"Yes, ma'am. I agreed to house-sit for Nolan while he's teaching at Quantico, and I ran into her by accident." Small lie. "I took the opportunity when I saw it."

Steve interjected. "Mitch informed me of the encounter and felt that he could learn more from Ms. O'Brien by working undercover than I was getting out of her during my periodic visits. I told him as long as he kept me in the loop, I thought it was a good idea. It's my case," Steve added.

Meg stared at the ceiling. Mitch recognized the posture. Frustration, but with a fatalistic *what can I do about it* demeanor. She turned her ice-green glare at Steve. "You knew I wanted Mitch off this case."

"Yes, ma'am."

"Agent Donovan, what do you think about the Maddox homicide? Does it relate to Thomas O'Brien in any way?"

"Based on our interviews to date," Steve said carefully, "it appears that in the course of researching Thomas O'Brien's trial, Maddox uncovered information that was damning to someone. It was during his private investigation that he disappeared. Whether directly or indirectly, whatever Maddox uncovered is related to O'Brien. And the fact that none of his research—his notes, his computer, his books—is anywhere to be found is another tip-off that there's something important in those documents. He swallowed a flash drive. That suggests that he knew he was being followed and feared he'd be assaulted for what was on the computer chip, and he had no other place to hide it.

"We have his phone records and he called a bar in Isleton the night he disappeared. Based on where his car was found in the river, we believe he did in fact reach his destination. We're heading there tonight to see if anyone remembers him, and if he met with anyone."

Meg had her hands on her desk. Authority suited her, Mitch realized. Even though she was a stickler for rules, she understood investigations. She was one of the best in the field because her instincts were so sharp. But she never admitted she had good instincts; she said it was a combination of intelligence and experience. But to Mitch, intelligence plus experience equaled old-fashioned street smarts.

"Follow the trail as long as it'll keep you moving. But we're not here to exonerate a convicted felon. We are here to apprehend him. And as far as the Maddox homicide is concerned, we are assisting the sheriff's department. Keep them in the loop. These are two separate cases until you find evidence that they are connected, and you'll treat them as such, understand?"

"Absolutely," Steve said.

She turned to Mitch. "Does Claire know where her father is hiding?"

"No. But I think she's heard from him recently," Mitch answered truthfully. "I suspect it was written communication, but I have no proof."

"Push her."

"She doesn't know I'm an agent—"

"I meant Donovan. You already screwed us on getting her for an accessory. She could pull out that you befriended her under false pretenses and didn't identify yourself as a federal agent. But I'm not interested in the daughter. I have some sympathy in this case. I just want O'Brien back in prison. And"—she added before Mitch could interject—"I'll keep him in our custody as long as I legally can." She made another note on her legal pad.

"I appreciate that."

"One more thing," Meg said and swiveled her chair. She picked up a remote and turned on the television behind her.

On the screen was a grainy black-and-white security feed.

"The tape from Redding came in," Steve said.

"Exactly. There's not a lot here, but I've watched it twice and there's no mistake. It's O'Brien."

They watched as a white, full-size American pickup truck pulled into the parking lot. Looked like a Dodge Ram, but Mitch wouldn't swear by it. A man exited from the passenger side. He was unidentifiable, wore a baseball cap low. He went around the side to where the restrooms presumably were.

Meg fast-forwarded, then stopped right before the man came into view.

There was no doubt about it. They only had one good glimpse, but when Meg paused it, Mitch recognized O'Brien. He'd darkened his hair a bit, sported a couple days' growth of graying beard. But it was him.

He jumped into the passenger seat and the truck pulled out.

"He's with someone," Mitch said, shocked.

"Bingo. Someone's helping him," Meg said.

"Who?" Steve asked.

"The driver isn't on tape. The license plates weren't visible. Believe me, I tried every which way, they aren't on tape. But there's no doubt a second person is in the car with O'Brien."

Mitch didn't know what to say. He had never considered that Tom had help on the outside.

"This makes it harder to track him," Steve said. "If he has help, that person may be able to hide him indefinitely."

"True, but it's clear that he's on the move. And from what you're telling me about his daughter, I'd say he's in town and made contact."

Mitch nodded. "We're on it."

"Good."

They left. "Thanks, Steve," Mitch said as they got back into Steve's car.

"We need to talk to Claire first. Or, rather, I do."

"I have an idea," Mitch said.

"Shoot."

"I'm meeting her at her place at six. Let me go there first. Then you come by about six thirty. Push her, and she's not going to give. But maybe—"

"I get you. Maybe when I leave, she'll vent to you."

"Exactly."

Steve started the car and shook his head. "Damn, Mitch, she's going to hate you."

"I know."

"What are we going to do about Isleton?"

Mitch wanted nothing more than to go to Isleton and see if anyone remembered Maddox. But right now, the more pressing case was Tom O'Brien's whereabouts. "Like Meg said, two separate cases. If we can't get down to Isleton tonight, we go down tomorrow."

*   *   *

Claire spent the entire drive home from Bill's house talking on her cell phone.

First Dave called. "Hey, I saw you driving away from Dad's. Why the rush?"

"I have plans." The truth. Sort of. She didn't want to cancel on Mitch, but she desperately wanted to go to Isleton and talk to Tip Barney, Frank Lowe's former employer and the owner of the ill-fated Tip's Blarney.

"I really need to talk to you."

"About what? Oh, I got the autopsy information from Phin, so if that's it—"

"No. What if I stop by tonight?"

"Can't you tell me over the phone?"

"Not really."

"Tonight is bad. I have to follow up on a Rogan-Caruso–related investigation." The lies were flowing easier now, and Claire shifted uncomfortably as she merged into heavy traffic on Highway 99. "Tomorrow?"

"I'm on duty."

"Call me when you're getting off and we'll meet up someplace, okay?"

"All right. Is everything okay?"

"Yes. I should ask you the same thing. You sound so serious."

"After our conversation last night—did you get the answers you needed from Dad?"

"Some of them. Dave, call me tomorrow, okay?"

She hung up and dialed information for the number of Janice Krause, Taverton's sister. Unlisted. She then called Jayne Morgan on her mobile for the phone number. Again, fibbing to Jayne about why she wanted it. Jayne didn't seem to care, and rattled off both a cell phone and home phone after a few moments.

"So I saw you were on the database this afternoon," Jayne said.

"I didn't see you, why didn't you say hi?"

"*Saw* is a relative term. I was monitoring the network from home. Who's Frank Lowe?"

"Some guy who died in a fire. I was just doing research."

"Hmm. Whatever. Need anything else?"

"Nope, thanks." She hung up. Odd. She dismissed her worry. She hadn't done anything illegal, and if the company got mad that she'd used their resources for personal business, she'd apologize and hope they didn't think it was egregious enough to fire her over.

Employment security was the last thing on her mind, however.

She was about to dial Mrs. Janice Krause when her cell rang. Caller ID read Phineas Ward and his cell number.

"Hi, Phin," she answered. "You work fast."

"Not fast enough."

"What?"

"There is no coroner's report on those homicides."

"What?" She sounded like a parrot.

"It's gone."

"How?"

"Good question. There's no way it can just disappear. If someone requests the report, we make a copy. It's kept in a digital file. It's easy to print a certified copy. The original backup reports are also digital, and a paper copy is kept off-site. The digital file is the easiest to access, and it's not there. I checked our internal records to make sure the case numbers matched. There's a gap in the numerical file. They were erased, or they were never archived electronically."

"How is that possible?"

"Hell if I know. I'm not a computer nerd. But I've never once heard of a missing report. Then I called the warehouse and asked them to pull up the original paper copies. Lied through my teeth, saying they were needed ASAP for an appeal case."

"And?"

"They're not there."

"Could they have been misfiled?"

"I'm having the archive supervisor research it personally, but I swear, Claire, I've never encountered a problem like this. *Both* the digital and the paper files missing? It's like they never existed. What did you want to know about the bodies anyway?"

Claire was still absorbing the information. Missing coroner's reports on both her mother and Taverton. "Bullet trajectory. I wanted to see at what angle and distance the bullets were fired."

"Why?"

"Information. I don't know exactly why, but because they were missing from the case files, I became curious. Now I'm more curious."

"You and me both. I'll let you know what I find out, but don't hold your breath."

"Thanks, Phin."

She hung up and dialed Janice Krause. It was no coincidence that both her mother's *and* Chase Taverton's autopsy reports were gone. What was in them that *didn't* come out at the trial? How could they disappear with no one being the wiser?

"Hello?"

Claire had almost forgotten she'd called Taverton's sister. "Mrs. Krause?"

"Yes? Who's this?"

"Claire O'Brien, with Rogan-Caruso Protective Services. I'm an investigator looking into the death of a law student from UC Davis." She spoke fast, hoping Mrs. Krause wasn't taking good notes.

"I don't understand."

"According to my interviews, Oliver Maddox, the deceased, had met with you earlier this year—in December or early January—regarding the personal calendar of your late brother, Chase Taverton."

There was a long pause. "What does—I'm confused. Are you saying Mr. Maddox died?"

"Yes, ma'am."

"I'm sorry. He was a nice young man. But what does this have to do with my brother? Chase was killed fifteen years ago."

"According to Mr. Maddox's notes, he retrieved Mr. Taverton's calendar from you. Correct?"

"I gave him a copy, yes. I didn't even know I had it, but when he called and asked if I had any of Chase's personal effects, I recalled several boxes my mother had in her possession before she died in 2001. He came to my house and went through them."

"You made him a copy of the journal? Do you still have the original?"

"No."

"No?" Claire repeated, stunned.

"A couple months ago, someone from the district attorney's office called and said they needed the boxes."

"The D.A.? Do you remember who you spoke with?"

"No."

Claire's heart fell.

"Hold on a minute." Claire heard the phone being put down. Then a long minute later, Mrs. Krause came back on the phone. "I found it. The receipt."

"Receipt for the material?"

"Yes. I remembered that a police officer came by and picked up the boxes." She paused.

"What was his name?"

"It's not on the receipt. Just an illegible signature. It's on Sacramento County Superior Court letterhead, though. Received three boxes, personal possessions D.D.A. Taverton."

"When?"

"January 21. It was the third Monday, I remember, because I was running late to my bunco game."

Claire thanked her and hung up. That was no coincidence.

Oliver Maddox had a copy of Chase Taverton's personal calendar, and he died on January 20. Less than twenty-four hours later, Mrs. Krause gave the calendar—and all of Taverton's material—to someone with the court. Or someone who *said* they were from the court. It was easy to fake letterhead and identification.

Claire rushed home, eager to go over the reports she'd received from Bill.

She was onto something.

TWENTY-TWO

Claire sat at her desk reading the police records on Frank Lowe.

Lowe had been a petty thief for most of his life. He had a sealed juvenile record, but Claire suspected it was more of the same. He broke into homes when the owners were away and stole small items—cash and jewelry. Never big-ticket stuff. But he was caught a half-dozen times, ended up with nine months jail time. After that he landed the part-time bartending job at Tip's Blarney and moved into the apartment above the bar. That was in 1988, and he'd been clean for those five years. At least, he hadn't been caught.

Until November 2, 1993. Two weeks before he died in the fire, he was arrested for a home invasion robbery. His statement was that he didn't know anyone was home, that he'd seen the owner leave and then broke in through an open window. That was part of his M.O.—he never forced entry. He found the easy marks, and his statement was consistent with his other arrests.

Except that there was a minor child, a six-year-old girl, alone in the home.

Claire didn't have time to dwell much on the idiocy of the mother leaving her young daughter alone—the mother claimed she was just going to the store for "a minute" and her daughter was sleeping. But the girl woke up and started screaming while Lowe was inside. Lowe fled and was apprehended by a neighbor who heard the girl.

He was arrested and booked. His arraignment was on November 4. Two weeks before he died. His trial was scheduled for six weeks later, right before Christmas, but he was dead by then.

Maybe this wasn't the Frank Lowe whom Oliver had told her father about. Except he'd asked Bill to pull *these* police records. And Bill had done it, though it was absolutely against the rules. Why was Bill helping Oliver? Because he *liked* him? Or because he believed him?

Did Bill know—or suspect—something else?

She rubbed her eyes. She was getting too tired. She hadn't been sleeping well, and though it was only six o'clock, she was exhausted. Isleton would have to wait until tomorrow. It was a dangerous road, and she didn't want to drive it when she was so obviously worn out.

She started at the beginning of the last case and glanced at the arresting officer. G. Abrahamson. Abrahamson . . . Greg. She didn't *know* him, but she'd heard the name. She needed to talk to him, find out if he remembered anything about that case.

Fifteen years. That was a lot of time in a petty theft case. Abrahamson wouldn't remember it. Or if he did, why would he share with her?

Because her dad had been on the job. And if that didn't do it, she would pull in Dave and Bill. It was worth a shot.

As she was about to track down Abrahamson's phone number, her bell rang.

Mitch.

She'd almost forgotten, but now that he was here she was happy. She needed a break. Just a couple minutes. She wanted to spill everything, but knew that would be dumb. Even if Mitch understood what she needed to do, she refused to put him on the line.

She looked through the peephole, then opened the door to Mitch. "Hi." She smiled.

He walked in. "Hi yourself."

Then he pulled her into his arms and kissed her. The stress of the day disappeared for one blissful moment.

She wrapped her arms around his neck and stood on her tiptoes, returning the kiss with the same force and passion, tilting her head slightly to get the best angle.

Mitch kicked the door shut with his foot and leaned her up against the wall, his body hard against hers.

"I missed you," he whispered.

"Same here," she said, breathless.

He leaned back, rubbed her shoulders. "You feel tense."

"It was a busy day." Busy was an understatement. She'd been moving nonstop for almost twelve hours. Her head was reeling with all the information she'd collected.

"Have you eaten?"

"Um, a little." She'd had a scone with her Starbucks coffee at seven, then the muffin and milk at Bill's.

"Let me take you out."

"I don't want to go anywhere right now. I'm beat." She smiled slyly. "You wore me out last night."

He laughed, kissed her temple. "That goes both ways, sweetness." Mitch led her to the couch. "Lie down."

"I'll fall asleep, and I have a lot of work to do."

"It can wait. Lie down."

He sat at one end and put Claire's head in his lap. He slowly rubbed her temples, putting an exquisite pressure on them. Her tension began to fade and she was lulled into a half sleep.

Mitch watched Claire as her eyes fluttered closed and she breathed easier. She relaxed so completely, her skin so fair, her hair so dark, he thought of Snow White lying in the glass coffin.

The thought made him shiver involuntarily.

She opened her rich blue eyes. "Something wrong?"

Beautiful and perceptive.

"You're beautiful, Claire."

"So are you," she murmured, eyes closing again.

She trusted him. He saw it for the first time. In bed the night before, she'd trusted him then, too, but this was different. The massage, though fully clothed, was intimate. Comfortable. Easy. She fit here with him.

And he was going to betray her.

He hated himself. It didn't matter that it was for the right reasons, he was worried about her safety, and worried about losing her. He had no right. He could hardly expect that when she learned he was an FBI agent she would forgive him, but he couldn't help but hope she'd understand. Eventually.

Where was her private investigation leading? Oliver Maddox had been murdered because he knew something. Mitch wasn't about to let anything happen to Claire. He ran his fingers through her hair, marveling at how right it felt to be here. He'd been directionless for so long. Most of his life, really. Trying to please his dead father while at the same time despising the man for what he'd been. Mitch was a good cop. One of his instructors had told him he was a natural, that his blood ran blue. But Mitch hadn't wanted this life. He'd taken it because it was a noble profession, something his father would have been proud of. That he was good at it was beside the point. He hadn't been truly satisfied or content with his life since he'd joined the military. He'd always felt like he was in limbo, without any clear sense of direction. He lived day by day, preferring fugitive apprehension because he could be out of the office ninety-five percent of the time, walking the streets, talking to people, catching bad guys. Criminals who were evading punishment. Who were *clearly* bad guys.

Until Tom O'Brien, who shouldn't have been one of them. And who reminded Mitch of the unaddressed crimes of his father.

Anyone can prosecute a guilty man.

"Mitch?" Claire whispered.

He looked at her. She was studying him. He leaned over and kissed her on her red, red lips. She tasted like home and hearth and everything he thought he never wanted until he met her. He couldn't help but smile. Claire was the last woman who would be content cooking and cleaning. That was one of the reasons he loved her. She could hold her own on the racquetball court, the gun range, and in bed, while still looking like a sexy siren dancing at a club, or beautiful and sweet lying here in his lap.

"What are you smiling about? One minute serious, the next like you heard a dirty joke."

"It wasn't a dirty joke," he said. "I was thinking about you and how much I enjoy having you here like this." He smoothed back her hair, needing the connection with her now, knowing what was about to come.

"My life is a mess."

"Why would you say that?"

"It's true. I haven't been truly happy in years. Except when I'm with you. You make me put aside everything else. You make me want a happily-ever-after I never believed I deserved."

"How can you say that? You deserve happiness. Maybe more than most."

"You make me believe that." She reached up and touched his face. So gently, so lightly, but it ignited a deep passion inside. A turning point.

She brought his head down to hers, kissed him with a quiet intimacy that stirred his soul. "You're the only thing in my messy life that gives me hope for the future. I have some things I need to do, and I wouldn't blame you for not understanding when it all comes out. But I hope you'll be here."

"I'll be here, Claire. There's nothing you can do that could change the way I feel about you." He wished he could say the same for his own deception.

She smiled, her eyes still sad and troubled. "I love you, Mitch. I've never said that before. I never believed in love. But I watched you sleep last night. And it just clicked and I knew. Life is too short. I had to tell you."

"Sweetheart, I feel the same way." He did. Why couldn't he tell her? Why couldn't he say the words he knew in his heart?

Because they would be coming from a liar, a man he pretended to be. He needed to tell her he loved her after she knew the truth about him, when there were no secrets between them. When she hated him.

He kissed her, pulling her into his arms to get a better angle at those perfect lips. Her arms went around him, her fingers holding his head to hers, her heart beating as fast as his.

The doorbell rang. Mitch tensed. It was time.

"I don't want to get up," Claire moaned, then sighed and extricated herself from their embrace.

She slid off the couch, kissing Mitch again before walking to the door. She looked through the peephole and said, "Company."

Mitch straightened, resisting the urge to stand. Claire didn't sound . . . angry. Or surprised.

She opened the door and a familiar stranger stood on the other side. Where did Mitch know him from?

"Dave, I didn't expect you tonight."

Dave. Dave Kamanski. His father, Bill Kamanski, had been Claire's guardian when Tom was convicted. Claire had talked about him, said he was the brother she never had. Kamanski was a good two inches shorter than Mitch, but broader, built like a linebacker. He was a cop, Mitch would have him pegged even if he didn't already know it. He had cop eyes, a cop stance, and he wore two weapons—a 9mm in a holster in the small of his back—Mitch had only a glimpse of it when he entered, but Mitch was good with guns. And he also wore an ankle holster with a smaller firearm. Probably a slim .25. It wasn't obvious unless you knew what to look for.

Mitch did.

And so did Claire, which is why Mitch never carried when he was with her. He hated it, because it potentially put him and Claire in danger. But protecting his cover at this point was more important.

Dave glared at Mitch. "Claire, we need to talk."

"It must be important if you came all this way."

Claire led Dave into the living room. "Dave, this is Mitch Bianchi. I told you about him. Mitch, Dave Kamanski." She plastered on an uneasy smile. "I told you about him as well. No secrets."

Mitch stared at Dave, who returned the glare. Mitch was trying to sit casually, but he had to stand. He tried to stand casually, but knew he failed. Dave was in attack stance and Mitch was on full alert. Something was wrong. Against his better judgment, he extended his hand. Dave didn't move.

Claire frowned and said to Dave, "We can go to the kitchen if you want privacy."

"No. No secrets, right?"

There was a knock at the door.

"Damn," Claire muttered. "I thought I was going to have a relaxing evening." She caught Mitch's eye. He saw the worry, the frustration, and the affection. Then her face cleared and she was in business, defensive mode as she turned to the door.

Claire walked to the door, shaking her head. Something was up with Dave, and she wished she could get him alone for five minutes. Then get him out of here. She needed time to unwind with Mitch, to clear her head and figure out what her next step would be.

But maybe Dave knew something about her dad . . . that worried her. What if there was a sting in progress? What if they were tracking her father right now? And Dave wanted to warn her, but Mitch was here . . .

She glanced through the peephole again. Agent Steve Donovan. She pounded her fist on the wall. "I don't believe this!" She flung open the door. "What are you doing here? Harassing me again?"

"We can do this easy or hard, whatever you like," Agent Donovan said, then saw Dave and Mitch in the living room. "You might want to get rid of your company. We don't need to bring anyone else into this business."

"No." She crossed her arms, anger and hurt building inside. She didn't want to do this. Why did Agent Donovan have to come by *now*? Why did he have to mentally torture her this way? How could she throw him off without outright lying to him?

Donovan started to step inside, but Claire put up her hand. She'd never let the Fed into her house before, and she wasn't about to now. "Stand there. Talk."

"The hard way? I can bring you in for questioning."

Dave crossed over and stood next to her. "I'm Sergeant David Kamanski with the Sacramento Police Department. Is Ms. O'Brien under arrest?"

"I don't have to arrest her to bring her in for questioning."

"And she doesn't have to come in unless you arrest her."

"Dave," Claire said, putting up her hand. "I've handled Agent Donovan before. This is nothing new."

"I'm afraid this is something new," Donovan said. "You're interfering with a federal investigation. Give me ten minutes and I'll have the U.S. Attorney's office draft up a warrant for your arrest. I'm giving you the benefit of the doubt right now, but you have some questions to answer or I *will* bring you in."

"I'm not interfering with anything."

Donovan looked at a slip of paper in his hand. "This morning, you spoke with Detective Theo Barker with the Davis Police Department and obtained a copy of

Oliver Maddox's missing person's report under the pretense of being a private investigator working on an insurance claim."

"I am a private investigator and I do work insurance claims," Claire said, her heart pounding. Why now? Why in front of Dave? God, why in front of Mitch? She didn't want to drag either of them into this. But she couldn't back down. Backing down was a sign of weakness.

"You also spoke with Tammy Amunson yesterday on the UCD campus regarding what she knew of her boyfriend Oliver Maddox's disappearance and the thesis he was working on. Then this morning you had a verbal argument with Professor Don Collier, said individual's advisor. Collier canceled his classes and no one has seen him since. You need to come clean, Claire. What did you and Collier argue about?"

"He canceled his classes?" She'd suspected he was hiding something. Now she knew. She had to talk again to Sizemore, the head of the Western Innocence Project. Something was strange with that operation, or at least about how her father's case had been handled. It reminded her that she needed to do a more thorough background check on Collier, and for that she'd need to go back to the Rogan-Caruso offices.

"Well?"

"I didn't break any laws," she said, distracted. "You can leave now."

"I think you've been in contact with your father, Claire," Donovan said suddenly, shocking her into a double take.

"What?"

"We know he's in town. We have surveillance footage of him at a diner off the interstate headed for Sacramento."

"I don't know where my father is," she said firmly. "You can go now."

Dave stepped forward. "You heard her."

"I believe you," Donovan said.

"Good," Dave said.

Claire looked at the Fed oddly.

Donovan said, "I believe you don't know where he is. I'm asking have you been *'in contact'* with your father."

She shook her head. She was shaking. This was all coming to a head too fast. She hadn't finished pursuing all possibilities. And there were so many. She felt the weight of doing this all alone, but she stood straighter and looked Donovan in the eye. "Get off my property."

Two strong hands rested firmly on her shoulders. She glanced up and saw Mitch behind her. He hadn't said anything since the Fed walked in, but his stalwart, quiet presence comforted her.

There was too much riding on this. She had to follow up on Frank Lowe and Taverton's personal papers. She had to talk to Lowe's former boss in Isleton.

Mitch said, "You need to back down. This is Claire's home." He squeezed her shoulders, and she leaned back against him. She was independent to a fault, she knew that, but having Mitch behind her—literally and figuratively—renewed her inner strength.

"Like I told you last night, Mr. Bianchi, aiding and abetting is a—"

"That's enough!" Dave exclaimed.

Claire frowned at him. "Dave, I—"

"They're playing you, Claire. Good cop, bad cop. Classic game."

Claire didn't know what Dave was talking about, but her head began to pound. "This isn't a game. This is just the Feds going after my dad. We talked about this, and there's—"

"No, Claire, it's more than that."

Mitch's hands fell from her shoulders. She almost didn't register it, until she felt chilled.

Her brain registered the deception before her heart felt it. Then, like a knife cutting through her skin, she bled inside.

She stared at Dave. Everyone was silent. She felt like a child, the last person in the room who still believed in Santa Claus, until his beard was pulled off.

"Agent Donovan, you need to leave," she said, her voice shaky.

"We'll talk tomorrow," Donovan said, stepping back.

"Bianchi?" Dave said.

Mitch didn't say anything.

"Or should I say *Special Agent* Bianchi?"

Claire faced Mitch. He stood only a foot behind her. Santa Claus wasn't real. And neither was Mitch.

When she looked in Mitch's eyes she knew Dave spoke the truth. The blood drained from her face and her heart emptied, leaving her with a sick, hollow feeling in the pit of her stomach.

"Claire—" Mitch reached out to touch her face.

She turned from him, biting her cheek to keep from yelling or crying or coming out swinging. She wanted to do all three. Instead, she found her voice for one word.

"Leave."

The unbearably long time—twenty-five seconds—it

took for Mitch to join Agent Donovan on the porch tested Claire's resolve. But she stood firm.

She slammed the door behind them, dry heaving.

Dave stepped toward her, touched her lightly on the back. "Claire, sweetheart, I'm so sorry—"

She turned and pushed him in the chest so hard he took a step back. "You asshole! You did a background check on him when I told you not to! I've told you over and over to leave my boyfriends alone!"

"I wanted to protect you. I wasn't going to say anything, but then I didn't know he was an FBI agent until . . ."

"Just go. Just leave. *Leave me alone!*"

"Please don't . . ."

"Now." She didn't want Dave to see her fall apart. She didn't want anyone to witness her pain.

Reluctantly, he left. Claire bolted the door behind him, her body sliding bonelessly to the hardwood floor. She hugged her knees tightly to her chest and sobbed uncontrollably.

TWENTY-THREE

Mitch sat in the Fox & Goose drinking Guinness while Steve talked at him—*at* him, because Mitch wasn't listening. He couldn't get Claire's stricken expression out of his mind. The strong beer did nothing to diminish the awful memory.

"Mitch, listen up," Steve said. "We have to come up with another plan."

"Plan. Right. Bring Nolan back to town and have him sidle up to Claire. Word from the single women around the watercooler is that he's good-looking." Mitch drained his first pint and motioned to the bartender to bring him another.

Mitch had never drunk Guinness before meeting Claire; the rich brew had ruined all other beers for him. Worse, the dark stout and Claire were a joint memory.

"Get serious, Mitch. I know it's a blow, and I know you like the girl, but we have an overriding issue: finding O'Brien. Because we're confident he's in town, we need to stake out Claire's house. We'll bring in another team since we're too recognizable."

"Claire will spot a tail."

"We don't have a choice. We can ask for Lexie—

being a woman might provide a bit of cover, and she's one of the best at discretion."

"Lexie's good. And she doesn't look like a Fed."

"And we do?"

Mitch looked at Steve. "You more than me, but yeah, we do."

Claire was never going to forgive him.

"Spill it," Steve said. "Something's different. I know you're hung up on O'Brien's daughter, but this—I'm sorry she had to find out like she did, but you knew it was going to happen sooner or later. Get over it. It's just a job."

Mitch slammed the pint on the table with more force than he intended. Beer sloshed over the sides. "It was more than the job."

Mitch wiped up the spill with cocktail napkins and drained a third of the glass.

"You're in love with her," said Steve.

What did Mitch know about love? You don't lie to those you love. You don't manipulate them, use them, hurt them.

"You'll get through this, Mitch. Focus on the job. Hell, that's the only way I can go home to an empty house some nights."

Steve motioned for another pint. What a pity party, Mitch thought. Steve hadn't had it easy in the relationship department. He'd married his high school sweetheart, had a kid, then left, ostensibly because of his job. Steve, like Mitch, took risks. To save lives, sometimes you had to risk your own. Now his ex was remarried to a doctor—same long hours, but less risk of being killed. Steve saw his son every other weekend.

"I'll take you back to Nolan's. First thing tomorrow

we head down to Isleton and canvass for information about Oliver Maddox. He met someone there. That someone may know more about whatever got Maddox killed."

"Maybe he met his killer down there," said Mitch.

"I don't follow."

"He goes down there, starts questioning the wrong person. That individual follows him, runs him off the road." Mitch frowned.

"Sounds plausible. You don't think so?"

"But if he was being chased down River Road he'd have both hands on the wheel. Would he think of swallowing the flash drive? Either he was nervous when he left his house in Davis and swallowed it as protection, or he saw someone he recognized who was a threat, and swallowed it to protect the information."

"And then was run off the road."

Mitch shook his head. "There was no damage to his Explorer to suggest that he was run off the road."

"You just said you thought he was run off the road. And someone can be run off the road without their car being hit."

"I was thinking out loud. Maybe he *was* but that doesn't explain the contusion on the back of Maddox's head. You know what I think?"

"No."

Mitch visualized a probable scenario. "I think he stopped his car for some reason on Delta Road after leaving Isleton. Maybe to let a car pass. Maybe to help a stranded driver. Maybe someone set a blockade and he had to stop, or he felt sick or needed to take a leak. Whatever, he stopped. He got out of the car and someone attacked him from behind."

"Why would he turn his back on someone he didn't know?"

"He must not have thought the person was a threat."

"So when did he swallow the flash drive?"

"I don't know." Mitch rubbed his face. "But he had to have had a reason, unless swallowing computer chips is the nerd equivalent to frat boys swallowing live goldfish."

"Okay. It's plausible. So then you're thinking the killer somehow got Maddox to stop his car and clocked him. The killer puts him back in the car and pushes it into the river?"

Mitch nodded. "That week in January was wet. The river was running high. It wouldn't have been too difficult. The Explorer was in neutral, making it easier to push."

"But wouldn't it have gotten stuck in mud? Wouldn't there have been tracks of some sort? We didn't find anything."

"Four months ago?" Mitch shook his head. "Not a chance. Between the rain, sleet, heat, and ebb and flow of the river, any sign of major disturbance would be long gone after four months. If we had gotten there a couple days after Maddox went in? Yes, there could have been tire marks and other signs in the mud. But remember, most of the shoulder on River Road is gravel."

"I say I take you to Nolan's and we both get a good night's sleep. It's nine o'clock and we've had two full days. I'll pick you up at seven, okay?"

Mitch relented, though there was nothing more that he wanted to do except sit here and drink away his guilt. But he had to be sharp in the morning. Having a hangover wouldn't help anyone—him, Claire, O'Brien, or Maddox.

He paid for the beers they'd drunk and left. If he hadn't had two pints, he would have seen the sucker punch coming.

Dave Kamanski's fist connected dead-on with Mitch's jaw. Mitch's head twisted around and slammed into the brick wall.

"You fucking bastard!"

Steve pushed in between them, a hand on Dave. "Cool off, Kamanski."

"You're no better. You knew he was lying to her. You two give law enforcement a bad name. Would you do anything to close a case? Including destroying a fragile woman?"

"Claire is anything but fragile," Steve said.

Mitch wanted to tell him to shut up. Claire was tough on the outside and braver than most anyone Mitch knew, but inside? Kamanski was right. She *was* fragile. She harbored pain and guilt and regret and grief so powerful it controlled her life.

"Back off, Dave," Mitch said.

"*Me?* You set her up. You couldn't just keep an eye on her, you had to date her? Lead her on? And it's been going on for months. *Months!* You think you can just throw her dad back in prison and walk away and she won't care?"

Kamanski looked like he was going to hit Mitch again and Steve stepped forward. Mitch straightened and said, "If you care about Claire, you'll keep an eye out for her. She's in the middle of a dangerous situation."

"Tom killed his wife under extreme emotional duress. He wouldn't hurt Claire for the world."

"That's not what I'm talking about." Mitch moved his jaw back and forth, spit out blood-tinged saliva. It hurt, but there was no permanent damage.

"Are you threatening me? Are you threatening Claire?"

Kamanski made a move toward Mitch, and Steve put a firm hand on his chest. "You got one freebie. Next time I'll arrest you for assaulting a federal officer."

Kamanski barked out a laugh. "That's rich. You fucking Feds."

A group of patrons walked out of the club and suspiciously eyed the three men before quickly crossing the parking lot.

"Claire is investigating Oliver Maddox's death. He was murdered, Dave," Mitch said quietly. "That puts her at risk."

Kamanski glared. "That's none of your concern. I'll keep my eye on Claire. You stay the hell away or I'll file charges." As he said it, he realized it was a dumb thing to say. "Just stay away from her."

Mitch knew Kamanski was right. Claire was none of his concern. He'd lied to her, and she'd found out in the worst way possible. If only he could take it back. If only he could have told her himself. But what good would that have done? The truth was still the truth, and Claire wasn't going to forgive him.

Mitch couldn't forgive himself. The pain of losing Claire, from *I love you* to the betrayal on her face . . . Mitch wouldn't sleep well tonight, or any other night.

Steve said, "O'Brien is in Sacramento."

When Kamanski didn't say anything, Mitch knew the

cop suspected the same. "Have you heard from him?" Mitch asked.

"No. If I did you know damn well I'd bring him in. I'm not harboring a fugitive, or helping him, and neither is Claire. You obviously don't know her as well as you thought."

Mitch shook his head. "You don't know her as well as *you* thought."

"Stay away from her."

"You need to go now," Steve said seriously.

Kamanski turned and stormed off. Mitch watched him drive away. Was his rage justified? Was it brotherly love . . . or something more? Mitch squeezed his eyes closed and rubbed his temples.

Steve slapped him on the back. "Let's get out of here. We have a lot to do tomorrow."

Claire pulled herself up from the floor and staggered like a drunken old woman to her bathroom. Her entire body felt bruised and sore, as if she'd had the toughest workout in her life, but without the adrenaline of a good hour at the gym.

The physical pain of Mitch's betrayal stayed with her as she turned on the shower. She looked at her pitiful reflection in the mirror. Her eyes were swollen and red. When was the last time she'd cried over a man? She couldn't remember when . . .

Yes, she did. Her father. When she believed he'd killed her mother. She'd cried then, too.

But none of her boyfriends until now were worth crying over. Claire might have been angry, upset, or relieved when a relationship didn't work out, but she'd never been so shattered.

You fell in love with him. You fell in love with a lie.

The tears flowed again and Claire clenched her fists, slamming them on the vanity. She didn't want to cry. She didn't want to feel anything. She wanted to forget she'd ever met Mitch Bianchi. She wanted to harden her heart and keep the pain out.

"Dammit, Claire! Get a grip. So he lied to you, manipulated you. He fucked you."

She'd slept with him. God, she'd slept with him and remembered feeling over the moon about it. She'd thought they'd had a connection, that they'd taken an invisible step toward something real and permanent.

You told him you loved him.

Her mirror steamed in the heat of the shower and she could no longer see her reflection. Good. She didn't want to look at her pitiful self. She'd prided herself for years on being able to detect liars and frauds, but she was only deluding herself.

Stripping off her clothes, she stepped under the hot, pulsing spray. A flash of her and Mitch in this shower last night hit her and she gave into the hurt one last time. Here, in the shower, alone. She let it out. She had to finish with it. She had a job to do. Prove that her father was innocent. That's all that mattered now.

Forget everything else.

She had to. For herself, and her dad. Later there'd be plenty of time to deal with her hurt feelings about Mitch.

By the time she stepped out of the shower, she'd put on her armor. She remembered an old Bible verse from catechism. *Putting on the armor of God.* She didn't know where God was in her life, but the armor was useful. She mentally brought up her shield, donned a helmet, held her sword.

Not to attack, but to protect herself.

On autopilot, she dried her hair. She stared at her body, saw a faint hickey Mitch had left on her left breast. Stared at it. Remembered how it felt when he kissed her. Remembered how he looked at her.

She closed her eyes and bent over the sink, nauseated. She was normally so good at controlling her emotions, blocking out the pain, why was it so hard to do it now?

Put on the armor, Claire. Dammit, he can only hurt you if you let him!

So not true.

She brushed her damp hair and went through the comfortable ritual of cleansing her face and rubbing in moisturizer. Circular motions. Over and over. Forget Mitch. Forget him. Focus on Oliver. Her dad. The truth. Mitch had nothing to do with any of that.

Claire left the bathroom and pulled on panties and an oversize Stanford T-shirt that fell nearly to her knees. She should go to Isleton . . . but it was already nine.

Neelix wound himself around her feet until she picked him up. He purred against her face and she breathed in his clean, soft fur. "Sorry, kitty. I know what's important. You and the boys."

Animals didn't lie. When they were hungry, they jumped on you and whined. When they were happy, they wagged their tails or purred. When they were startled, they barked or hissed. They were innocent as children, and gave affection freely. No strings.

Yoda started barking and Claire turned toward the back door, when the front bell rang.

"Who now?"

She didn't want to answer the door. The idea of pretending no one was home came and went. She walked to the front door and through the peephole spied an unfamiliar tall woman in her forties. A neighbor? Claire wasn't sure.

She opened the door without taking off the chain. "Can I help you?"

"Claire."

She frowned. She didn't know this woman. Yoda had gotten Chewy and the stray dogs barking up a frenzy. She didn't want her neighbors to complain. "What can I do for you?"

"My name is Nelia Kincaid. I know your father."

Nothing could have surprised her more. She didn't know what to say.

"Can I come in? I promise I won't stay long."

Claire was reluctant to let the stranger in, but she was intrigued. She closed the door, undid the chain, and reopened the door. "We haven't met."

Nelia Kincaid shook her head. "But I feel like I know you. Your father has told me a lot."

"I don't know how. He doesn't know me."

"Yes, I do."

She whirled around. Her father was standing right behind her. She felt trapped and scared and hated that feeling. She backed down the hall two steps, then stopped. "What are you doing?"

"We have to talk, Claire."

"You can't be here. The FBI could be watching the house. They could—"

"They're not. Believe me, I've become very good at spotting surveillance."

She remembered when he'd told her yesterday morning that the Feds were watching her. He'd been right, and she'd thought he was being paranoid.

Her dad looked tired. Worn down. Defeated. She glanced at the woman. Who was she?

"I heard about Oliver on the news tonight," he said, his voice thick and troubled. "I had to see you. One last time."

"I don't understand. I'm getting close, Dad. I can feel it."

"Close?"

She swallowed her emotion. She'd spent all her tears on Mitch, and she wished she hadn't. Her father deserved more of her pain than a lying FBI agent.

"I am so s-sorry." She stuttered and swallowed. "I should have believed you. Then. But I know you didn't kill Mom."

His face twisted in surprise and hope. "Who did?"

"I don't know."

"But you know I didn't?" He sounded skeptical.

"Yes. If I had only listened to Oliver Maddox when he came to me in January, he might still be alive, and you would be truly a free man. I should have known in my heart that you were innocent. And now . . . I'm sorry I needed something more than your word. I don't know why, I don't know how I let it come to this, but—"

He stepped toward her and she stumbled into his arms. "Daddy."

He held her for the first time in fifteen years. Her father. She felt like a little girl again. She clung to him. "Please forgive me."

He stroked her hair. "There's nothing to forgive, Claire."

He held her and Claire breathed in the familiar—and unfamiliar—scent. He was her father, but time had wedged between them. She stepped back. Looked at Nelia Kincaid again.

"Nelia saved my life. She found me in Idaho after Aaron Doherty—another escaped convict—shot me and left me for dead."

Claire didn't know what she could say.

"I've been in Idaho for the better part of four months. I was in no condition to come back here. In some ways, I wish I hadn't, but I'm glad I did—just to see you again." He touched her face. "To know that you believe I'm innocent. You've given me my life back, Claire. And I mean that. I came back to Sacramento for you. I couldn't face my own death with you believing I was guilty."

Tears welled in her eyes. "Don't talk that way."

"I'm surrendering tomorrow."

"No! Why?"

"When I heard that Oliver Maddox was dead and had been for months, I realized he had to have been killed because he was helping me. Helping prove I was innocent. When he first visited me in Quentin, I—"

"Why were you even at San Quentin in the first place?" she asked. "You were supposed to be at Folsom."

"I wrote to Bill about it."

"Bill?"

"Bill and I corresponded regularly. He told me everything about you. Everything that I wished I'd seen for myself."

"Bill?" she repeated. He'd never let on. How could Bill have kept something so important from Claire?

"I told him not to tell you. You didn't want to hear from me. I understood that. Hated it, but understood it.

I guess I'd hoped that Bill would find a way through that thick head of yours." He laughed, but the joke fell flat.

"You're like me, Claire," Tom said. "I was so certain of everything back then. I was positive that I would be exonerated. Because I was innocent. I was cocky for the longest time, worried more about how I was going to get my job back and take care of you. It took me a long time to realize that I was going to stay in prison until they killed me."

He looked around, motioned toward the couch. "Let's sit."

Nelia said, "I'll make some coffee."

"Tea," Claire and her father said simultaneously.

Nelia smiled. "Tea." She went to the kitchen.

"Who is she?" Claire asked quietly.

"The woman I love. She saved me in more ways than one, Claire. I want to live now. But I don't know that it will happen. But what I won't do is be gunned down in the street like a criminal. This has to end. I didn't realize until yesterday that I was putting you in danger. Risk, yes, of being prosecuted as an accessory, but I figured that with the backing of Rogan-Caruso and the sensitive situation of you being my daughter, you'd get off with a slap on the wrist. But I never imagined that you would be in physical danger."

"I'm not—"

He ran his fingers through the ends of her hair. "Yes you are. Please. No more about it, okay?"

She took a deep breath. "Okay."

"Nelia is an attorney. She's going to arrange for my surrender. I'm going to turn myself over to the FBI."

"The FBI? Why them?"

"I believe that if I go into state custody my days are

numbered. Someone wants me dead. I'm hoping that the FBI will listen to what I know."

"You can't trust them. You can't trust anyone, Dad. Except me. I'm working on this. I already know so much more than you did yesterday morning. Stay away. I'll figure it out, I promise."

Nelia came in with a tray of teacups. She put it down and sat on the armrest of the chair Tom was sitting in. He absently took her hand. The simple sign of affection wasn't lost on Claire.

"Frank Lowe died in a fire the night after Mom was killed," Claire said.

"That's not possible. Oliver said he'd tracked down Frank Lowe and that he had the key to what happened."

"Lowe died in a fire, but Oliver told Bill that he thought he was alive. I don't see how—it's actually hard to fake your own death. Disappear? Much easier."

"Oliver must have had a reason to think Lowe wasn't dead."

She frowned. "Maybe. I do know that Lowe's boss at the time now owns a bar in Isleton. Oliver was returning from Isleton when he went into the river."

"Stop. Stop looking into this right now," her dad said.

"I'm going to find out who killed Mom and Chase Taverton."

"Dammit, Claire!" He took a deep breath and turned to Nelia.

"Claire," Nelia said, "if anything happened to you, Tom wouldn't be able to live with it. You have to step back."

Claire shook her head and looked at the ceiling. "You

might think you know me, but you don't." She looked from Nelia to her father. "I'm not the naïve fourteen-year-old who was in shock during your trial. I'm a trained private investigator. Oliver Maddox found Chase Taverton's personal day planner. He had a copy of it. That disappeared, and so did the original. Taverton's sister gave it to a cop who claimed he was from the Sacramento County Superior Court.

"A friend of mine at the morgue told me Oliver swallowed a flash drive. The FBI has it. Something important was on there. Something that *might* prove you're innocent. And there are other things. Like your transcripts are missing from the county archives. There are no coroner's reports on the murders."

Her dad leaned forward, a stern look on his face. "Don't you see? Someone powerful is calling the shots."

"What powerful person would want Chase Taverton dead? To the extent that he would frame an innocent man, destroy government records, and kill a law student?"

"Someone with a lot to hide, and even more to protect," Nelia said softly.

Tom and Claire turned to her.

Nelia said, "You two are so much alike. If the situation weren't so dire, I would laugh. Stubborn. Determined. Smart. Temperamental. But we know that Tom is innocent. That he was framed. That someone else killed two people, but we don't know the motive."

"It was about Taverton," Claire said.

Nelia nodded. "Prosecutors make enemies, but usually they leave a paper trail. Something to follow that shows what they were working on."

"Wouldn't they be working only after an arrest?"

Claire asked. "I mean, isn't their job to prosecute those arrested for a crime?"

"Usually," Nelia said, "but sometimes they are involved in sting operations. Or they arraign a petty criminal who has information to take down a bigger fish."

"Frank Lowe," Claire said. "He was a petty thief. He was arrested two weeks before he died in a fire. It's too big a coincidence that Lowe died about the same time Taverton did. What happens after someone is arraigned?" she asked Nelia, who seemed to know more about legal issues than she did.

"He's a thief? So he was caught robbing someone. He was arrested, put in jail, and then arraigned within seventy-two hours—that's usually the case. Could have been out on bail pending trial. An investigation would continue. That's when the district attorney would go through the case, making sure he had everything he needed for a conviction. There could be a plea agreement between the D.A.'s office and the defense. Often for a lesser charge or lighter prison term."

"Are you a prosecutor?" Claire asked, suspicious.

Nelia shook her head. "I used to be a corporate attorney. My ex-husband is a D.A."

Claire glanced at her dad, but he wasn't concerned. He looked at Nelia as if she were a goddess.

Claire pulled her gaze away. "What if Tip Barney, Lowe's old boss, knew what Lowe and Taverton knew?"

"Then why is he still alive?" Nelia asked. "If Barney had information that would have hurt someone, he would have been killed. That follows this pattern."

"He could be part of it, Claire," her father warned. "I don't want you going down there. Leave it to the FBI."

She jumped up. "They're not going to even try and

prove your innocence. All they care about is putting you back in prison!"

When neither of them said anything, Claire knew she was right—and so did they.

"I have to do this."

"It's okay, Claire. I can die now."

"No! Dammit, what's with this fatalistic attitude? You escaped during the earthquake, why? To go back and die?"

"I escaped so that I could have a chance to convince you I didn't kill your mom."

"No. No! You escaped to prove you're innocent. Fifteen years was stolen from us. Half my life I hated you. Hated myself. It was a lie. We can't get the time back, but we can find out who took it away from us."

"I'm turning myself in."

"Please don't—"

Nelia said, "Claire, he has to. He can't live the rest of his life running. And—" She glanced at Tom, worry crossing her face.

"What?" She looked from Nelia to her dad, fear making her heart beat faster.

"There's a bullet in me. Nelia patched me up, but she couldn't remove the bullet. It's been bothering me the last few weeks. We think it's shifted."

"Bothering." Nelia shook her head. "Your dad has been in severe pain. His legs are weak, and he's experienced numbness during the last few days. He needs medical attention."

Claire stared at them in disbelief. "They're not going to do anything to save you when they plan to execute you in six weeks."

"I'll take my chances. If I keep running I doubt I have six days, let alone six weeks."

This was not happening. Claire closed her eyes, tried to change it, but when she opened them Nelia and her father stared at her.

"I'm going to do everything I can, Claire, to make surgery a term of his voluntary surrender," Nelia said with passion. "Your father saved lives these last four months. He was responsible for apprehending nearly every one of the escaped fugitives. They owe him."

"They won't see it like that."

"I'll convince them."

Claire desperately wanted to believe Nelia. But she also feared this would be the last time she saw her dad. She believed him, believed *in* him, and now he tells her he's dying?

"Dad."

He held her tight and she clung to him like a little girl awakened by a nightmare. Her daddy. Her protector.

Now it was up to her to save him.

TWENTY-FOUR

The assassin watched the GPS tracking program on his computer. Claire was still at home. Good. He glanced at the clock. Nine thirty. It was getting late and he still had many chores to complete.

First things first. He learned long ago that he couldn't keep the girls alive indefinitely. The first time, he'd had a warped idea that he could convince the young runaway to stay with him, to be his forever, and she had played along. *Played* with him. But the first opportunity she had, she ran.

He'd caught her, but it had been close. Too close. He wouldn't trust another one, no matter what they said or promised.

His mother had promised she wasn't going to die, and she died.

Bridget had promised he was her special man, and she lied.

He'd hoped someday Claire would come to him, stay with him, on her own, but that wasn't going to happen. He could dream about it with the heart that loved her, but in his calculating mind he knew she'd never feel for him what he felt for her.

He could protect her from himself for only so long.

With the discovery of Oliver Maddox's body, there was a chance he could be exposed. He listened for the telltale police cars in his driveway, one ear cocked to the police scanner.

There was no way he would go to prison and leave Claire to someone else. It physically hurt knowing other men had slept with her, but he'd allowed it because he hadn't been ready yet. Self-preservation drove his actions for years.

But if decades of secrets leaked out, he would have to kill her. Better to have her dead and buried than for him to be locked behind bars knowing another man had her body and her heart.

There was all the difference in the world between killing the runaways and killing Claire. First, no one missed the runaways. Claire had people who would look for her if she disappeared. Her employer, her friends. That made taking her dangerous.

But with Tom O'Brien on the run and the stress of these last months on her, coupled with the newly discovered information about her boyfriend, taking her now and making it look like she'd killed herself . . . or run away . . . was tempting.

He'd think about that.

For now, he needed to take care of the girl in the shed.

He left his house and crossed to the back of his property, protected by rows of trees that were a windbreak, as well as a sound barrier. Even if the girl screamed, no one would hear unless the wind was just right.

The evening was still warm after the hot day. Another reason he couldn't leave the girl for long. Without food and water in this heat, she'd die and start to decompose.

Flies would lay eggs and maggots would infest her orifices and her skin would get slimy and start sliding off.

He hated the dead.

He unlocked the shed. If it hadn't been shaded by the trees, the girl would likely have died from the heat. She was kneeling where he'd left her early this morning chained to the wall. The white gown he'd put on her was dirty from sweat and the dust in the shed. He cleaned the place weekly, but still dirt accumulated. Her arms were bolted to the wall, body sagging to the floor. He had no desire to torture the girls, but he found that if he restrained them in a prone position they regained some of their strength. He didn't want to have to explain any scratches or bruises she might inflict, and he couldn't take sick time now.

"Hi, Claire," he said. He never knew the names of the girls. They may have told him, but he never remembered. In his mind they were all Claire.

She whimpered, straining against the tape secured across her mouth. Her chest and neck were bruised. He felt bad about that. He hadn't wanted to hurt her, but it was inevitable when they had sex that she'd get hurt. It was something he was working on; he didn't want to hurt Claire when he made love to her.

But if he wanted to feel anything, he had to hold them tight. Squeeze them. And like a treasured insect in a young boy's hand, sometimes the life got squeezed out of them. It wasn't his fault they were too fragile.

He touched her black hair. Longer than Claire's, the way Claire used to wear it. Long and flowing.

He took scissors and cut it off. Held it to his face. He'd washed the girl's hair in the same rich shampoo Claire used. He walked across the large shed and tied a pink ribbon around the thick lock of hair, then placed it in a drawer next to more than a dozen others.

He unlocked the restraints and brought the girl to her feet. "Claire, I'm sorry, but this is good-bye. I promise, you won't suffer."

He had wanted to bury her last night, but he'd kept her in his bed too long, until dawn, and he didn't trust that he wouldn't be seen. Even on his large property, it was better to do this task under the cover of darkness.

Her grave had already been dug.

His aversion to dead things held true. He had, two or three times, accidentally killed his girls while they were in his bed. He'd had to dispose of them immediately, and he couldn't touch their flesh when he did it. Those times were the worst. He still had bad dreams. But he'd practiced and learned, and now he could make love without choking the life out of them.

He didn't want them to suffer. He didn't want Claire to suffer.

He put a blindfold over her eyes. She had the dark hair that Claire had, but not the blue eyes. He'd been in a rush, needing someone, and this one was close enough that he could pretend.

He was good at pretending. And he had the disks to play in the background. As a reminder.

But the blindfold wasn't just to cover her eyes so he didn't see them. He didn't want her to see her fate. The first time . . . he still heard the first Claire's screams, every day, and that was fourteen years ago . . .

He led the girl, naked under her white gown, to his garden. He breathed in the scent of roses. All white roses, because those were the flowers Claire loved best.

He'd excavated the grave with his backhoe. He'd gotten quite proficient with it over the years. It hadn't taken him long. The smell of fresh dirt mixed with the floral aroma and he smiled. This was his favorite place on earth. In his garden. Surrounded by Claires.

"Good-bye, Claire."

He pushed her into the freshly dug grave, a scream coming from her chest, but without the power to project beyond the dirt walls of her eternal prison.

He walked over to the backhoe and turned the ignition. He refilled the grave.

It was better this way. They died quickly, within minutes he was pretty certain. And he didn't have to touch or see their dead bodies.

He drove the backhoe back to its place next to the shed. With a hoe, he returned to the fresh dirt and smoothed it out. Then he planted a new rosebush at the head of Claire's grave. Finally, he spread the rocks out so no one at a glance could tell that there were fourteen graves in his rose garden.

By the time he was done, he was physically tired but mentally alive. He returned to his house and checked the status of Claire's Jeep. Still at her house. Good. It was late, he doubted she'd be going anywhere tonight.

He showered under scalding water, scrubbing the dirt from his pores. Then he turned the water icy cold, before stepping out. He dried off and walked downstairs, naked. Poured a glass of dark, rich cabernet. Then he went back to his bedroom and lay naked on his bed, the air moved by the ceiling fan caressing his body. He turned on his special disk. Claire filled the screen. A teenage Claire nude in her old bedroom, standing in front of the closet trying to decide what to wear. He watched her dress and undress for hours, working himself up into a frenzy.

"You're mine, Claire. I protected you. You'd be dead if it weren't for me. Dead!"

That's why he knew he could kill her now without remorse. She should have died fifteen years ago. But when he saw her photograph, he knew he couldn't kill her.

All these years, she had been living on borrowed time. Time he'd given her.

He was ready to take it back.

TWENTY-FIVE

Mitch's cell phone woke him. 1:00 a.m. Good news never came after midnight.

It was a blocked number. "Bianchi."

"This is Tom O'Brien."

Mitch swung his legs over his bed, wide awake, and grabbed a pencil from the nightstand. Where was the paper? He'd put it there . . . he picked the pad off the floor.

"Where are you?"

"I'm surrendering tomorrow. I have a new attorney and she's going to meet with the Sacramento district attorney in the morning. I was hoping you might be able to help."

"I'll do what I can. I can pick you up now—"

"No. I need a few things before I come in."

"I can help—"

"I saw you watching Claire's house the other morning."

Shit. Tom O'Brien had been that close and Mitch hadn't seen him! Hadn't even *felt* him. Was he losing his touch? Or maybe he was just too preoccupied with Claire.

"It's my job. To find you."

"You almost had me a couple times. After the warehouse shoot-out you were right on my heels most of the way north. Sheer luck had you looking the wrong way in Salt Lake City."

"Why didn't you tell me where Doherty and Chapman were?"

"I didn't know exactly where they would be, and if they thought the Feds were on their tail, they would have gone under. I had to find them first, then it all went to hell. Believe me, Bianchi, if I could have changed things I would have. I wish people didn't have to die."

"I wish you'd let me pick you up right now. There's a lot of new information we're trying to get a handle on. Oliver Maddox was murdered—"

"I know. That's the reason I'm calling you. I made a huge mistake. I wrote to my daughter and told her everything I knew about Maddox's investigation. I didn't know he was dead. I was transferred from North Seg the day after he was supposed to meet me, and I couldn't get phone access to find out why. Then the earthquake hit, and I didn't try to approach Maddox, fearing he'd be under surveillance. If I'd thought for a minute he was dead, I'd never have given Claire the information I did."

"What did you tell her?"

"Oliver believed that Taverton was the target and a man named Frank Lowe was the key. I asked her to find Maddox so he could convince her he had something to prove I was innocent. I thought with her knowledge and resources at Rogan-Caruso she could help him, then I could come in free and clear. But Claire told me— through my attorney," he quickly added, "that Lowe was dead, killed in a fire the night after Taverton and

Lydia. And their coroner's reports are missing. There's more, but I don't have time."

Mitch wrote it all down. "Of course you have time, I'm not going anywhere."

"Bianchi, we're on opposite sides right now."

"I believe you're innocent."

O'Brien continued, "My attorney told Claire that I plan to surrender tomorrow after we make arrangements with the D.A. I told Claire—my attorney told her—to leave it alone. If Maddox's killer knows Claire is retracing his footsteps, she's in danger. Protect her, Bianchi. You have to keep her safe. She's not going to let this go."

Mitch's heart pounded in rhythm with his growing headache. "I'll try, but—"

"You have to do better than *try*! Put her in protective custody. Arrest her for, for—hell, you can come up with something! Tell her to back off. Anything to keep her safe."

Mitch wasn't surprised that Claire had made progress on the investigation. She had additional information that could help them track Maddox's killer. "I'll bring her in for questioning. Find out what she knows and go from there."

"Thank you. I'm counting on you to keep Claire safe."

Click.

Jeffrey Riordan woke up before dawn in the San Francisco hotel room he'd been living out of for the last three days while he met with every major donor in the area. He hadn't planned on returning to Sacramento until Sunday, but his meetings were over and the situation at home was dire.

Damn Hamilton and Richie. Hamilton was supposed to have made sure that Tom O'Brien died in prison so no one would be interested in pursuing his cause. If he didn't die, there was always the possibility that someone would dig into the files. Between appeals and do-gooders like the Western Innocence Project, they couldn't be certain that the case was dead unless O'Brien himself was dead. They'd done a damn good job of covering their tracks, but nothing was foolproof.

Too many people were involved. Someone was going to talk. It was just a matter of time. And it wasn't like they could kill *everyone* who had a piece of the puzzle.

Jeffrey didn't think the authorities could trace Taverton's murder—or any of the others—to him. That bastard law student had been too close, knew too much. But he was dead and he should have *stayed* buried.

Less than four weeks! Three weeks from Tuesday was the primary, and then he could focus on the general election, where he was a shoo-in. No Republican had won a U.S. Senate seat in California in more than twenty years, so Jeffrey wasn't worried about his right-wing competition. All Jeffrey had to do was win this primary and it was smooth sailing.

He slid out of bed and started packing, fuming that the primary wasn't in the bag. Everyone had some skeletons in their closet. Sheryl Browne couldn't possibly be as squeaky clean as she came off. She had been in college during the sixties, for shit's sake. While long-ago drug use wouldn't damage her, if she had hit someone while drunk driving or high . . . or had an affair with a married man . . . and what about her ex-husband? What had happened there? And if not that, what about her current husband? He'd made his money in the dot-com boom and sold out before it fell apart. He was ten years younger than the bitch. What was up with that? If Harper found out he was cheating on the bitch . . . no, that might generate sympathy for her. What about her public record? She'd been on the board of supervisors of some small central valley county, and Jeffrey knew there were many opportunities to put your hand in the wrong · pies. He'd done it. It was just a matter of being careful and finding the right people . . .

Dammit. He'd paid for an opposition report and nothing juicy was in it. They hadn't looked deep enough. *Everyone* had a scandal in the past. Even that perfect bitch.

Barring that, there was always the October Surprise technique. Or, in this case, the May Surprise.

He would have someone come forward against Sheryl Browne. Tell the voters she was a two-faced corrupt bitch. It didn't have to be true, it would only need to generate enough doubt about her. It would leak late on the Friday before election day so Browne didn't have time to respond. It would be all over the Sunday papers, the Internet, the news.

Now that Jeffrey had a plan, he felt much better.

He also needed a plan to deal with the crap going on back home in Sacramento.

Jeffrey had been the one to come up with the blackmail plan so that he, Hamilton, and Richie wouldn't get their hands dirty. It had also been his idea to take Chase Taverton out, and who had thought about the court archives? Jeffrey, of course. Not that there was anything incriminating in the transcripts. But if someone dug deep enough, they might connect Hamilton to the mole in O'Brien's legal team, which would open up scrutiny regarding the pretrial motions. And if the case was under serious investigation, the falsified coroner's report would be discovered, and the lab tech Harper black-mailed might decide the fact that he solicited underage prostitutes wasn't worth keeping secret any longer.

Maddox was settled, and now Claire O'Brien needed to be dealt with. Just like Jeffrey had dealt with Rose Van Alden, which had unfortunately led to Chase Taverton needing to die ten years later.

Jeffrey had been to her house before, using his charm to entice her to sell. Richie called her the psycho cat lady. Hamilton was disgusted by the clutter and stacks of newspapers and magazines along every wall. Jeffrey just wanted the deal to go through. They needed the money from this development, and the old bitch wouldn't sell.

Without the Van Alden property, the entire deal would fall apart and they'd be out millions. They wouldn't recover for years. And some of the investors would take it out on them. But with the property, they were set for good. The money they'd make would launch their careers.

He'd attempted to charm, plead with, cajole Van Alden into selling. He hadn't wanted to kill her. He'd always gotten what he wanted when he wanted it because of his charisma and good looks. None of it worked on the old lady. Jeffrey hated to fail. Failure was, simply, never an option.

So she had to die.

Rose Van Alden was a small woman. She looked like a gray, wrinkled child when she slept. Her mouth was open and she snored lightly. She slept on her back, which made the job easier. They didn't want a struggle that could potentially leave suspicious marks on the body.

Jeffrey had the clear plastic garbage bag in his hands. Hamilton had come with him to hold the blankets down in case she tried to fight. Fighting would leave marks that might lead the police down the wrong path.

Jeffrey leaned over the body and placed the plastic over her face, holding it tight on both sides by pressing into the pillow, not her body.

Her eyes flashed open and in the black gloom of the bedroom her white pupils seemed to glow. Swallowing uneasily, he didn't flinch as Rose Van Alden's body twitched. He didn't flinch when she reached up and hit his arm, her pitiful attempts unsuccessful. When she tried to grab his hand, Hamilton reached over to stop her, but Jeffrey whispered, "Don't! You'll leave a bruise."

She never got ahold of any part of him. Just flailed about. Her eyes rolled oddly, and then closed. They briefly opened and he stared at death. His heart thudded, his blood pumped hot, but he saw everything with shocking clarity. The moisture on the plastic where her mouth and nose couldn't draw breath; the knowledge of death in her blue eyes. Her skin, flattened by the plastic, distorted. In the moment of his first kill, he had never felt more alive.

Jeffrey had never told Hamilton and Richie how he felt killing Rose Van Alden. For them, it was a necessary evil. It was about money, not murder.

For Jeffrey, it was about both.

Hamilton was in private practice then. A new attorney with a new law firm, given a handful of clients, including Rose Van Alden. It wasn't difficult to create a *fake will that indicated that upon her death, she intended to sell her property for fair market value and give the proceeds to the Delta Conservancy.*

It had been Richie's idea to create the Delta Conservancy. It was a great place to launder money. Their investor group, solely controlled by himself, Hamilton, and Richie, bought the Van Alden property. The money that went to the estate was then turned over to the Delta Conservancy—secretly controlled by the three of them. They were able to build a sizable war chest, which then catapulted Jeffrey onto the Board of Supervisors. After that, the state house, then Congress. And now his chance at the U.S. Senate.

Brilliant.

His rise had been temporarily endangered when Chase Taverton made a plea agreement with Frank Lowe. How were any of them to know someone had seen them that night?

They'd taken care of those two.

And then came Oliver Maddox.

Also dealt with.

Now Claire O'Brien.

Jeffrey was not going to lose this election, his money, his stature, everything he'd built. He was on the brink of greatness. It was his turn!

Flushed, he leaned forward and put his hands on the dresser.

"Jeffrey?"

He'd almost forgotten that Julie was in his hotel bed. He didn't make it a habit of keeping his women in bed all night. But they'd dropped Ecstasy last night and fucked like rabbits.

"I have to go."

"Okay."

"But first things first."

"I'm kind of sore this morning."

"I really don't care. You want the room all weekend? It's yours. Spread your legs or I'll do it for you."

She complied, because she was a good slut. The drugs messed with his performance. He was hard as a rock but couldn't get relief. He pummeled her over and over. She begged him through tears to stop, that it hurt. Finally, he withdrew.

"I'm sorry," she whimpered. "I want to, but—"

He flipped her over and held her mouth shut with one hand. He took her from behind, sweat pouring off his body, wanting, needing, release. He knew better than to fuck around with drugs. This had happened before. But the high had been so good . . .

She bit his hand and he pulled her ear, growling, "Don't. Or the only job you'll get is on your back."

Women should do what they're told. He remembered Niki in the middle of the woods. The one who tried to screw him over. He remembered taking her against her will. The thrill, power flooding his senses.

When it was over, Julie was crying. Jeffrey rose. He was surprised to see blood on his cock and between her legs.

"Don't say a word, Julie, or not only will you be out of a job, I'll send the disk of you sucking my cock to your dad."

He went into the bathroom and showered. He wanted to be on the road before the sun rose.

Time to take care of another bitch.

TWENTY-SIX

Mitch called Lexie on her cell phone. "Is Claire still at home?"

"This is the third time you've called since two in the morning. She's still there."

"You might have fallen asleep, or—"

"I'm going to forget you said that, Bianchi. She walked her dogs at seven this morning, stopped at Starbucks, brought back something in a Venti cup, and went inside. She hasn't moved since."

"Call me—"

"—when she leaves, follow her—but discreetly because she's a PI and can spot a tail. Your concern is wearing thin. Let me do my job and you do yours."

She hung up before Mitch could thank her.

Steve shook his head as he drove south on I-5 toward Isleton. "Lexie is going to explode if you call her one more time."

"I promised Tom O'Brien that I would keep Claire safe."

"And we're doing everything we can, you know that."

Mitch had called first Meg, then Steve, with the information from O'Brien's phone call. He tried to sleep, but ended up watching Claire's house until Lexie showed up. He managed a couple hours of shut eye before Steve picked him up.

Steve said, "Meg said she'd call with the terms of the surrender when she hears from the D.A. We can be back in thirty minutes."

Steve turned off the interstate and drove along River Road, and Mitch called Meg. "Did you run Frank Lowe? The one who died in the fire at Tip's Blarney the night after Taverton?" he asked her.

"Yes, Mitch. There's nothing here. Petty thief, arrested for a home invasion robbery two weeks before the fire. I read the arson report. The final report said faulty wiring with a possibility it could have been intentional. Maybe Lowe preferred suicide to prison."

"How much time was he facing?"

"I'm only guessing, based on his record, three to five."

"Would you kill yourself instead of sitting in jail for three years?"

"You can't think of it like that. Maybe he had more secrets. We don't always understand human nature."

"Self-preservation is usually at play in most decisions."

"When did you get your psychiatric license?"

"Motivation is behind everything. Why would he kill himself?"

"Maybe it was just a coincidental accident. They're known to happen."

"Did you get his next of kin? Previous addresses?"

"I'll send the report through to your BlackBerry, if that'll satisfy you."

"Thanks, doll."

"Don't call me that. Are you on your way to Isleton?"

"Yes. We're going to the Rabbit Hole to flash Maddox's picture around, see if anyone remembers seeing him. Call as soon as you find out if Menlo Park was able to get anything off the flash drive."

"I will. By the way, I talked to Matt after you woke me last night."

District Attorney Matt Elliott was Meg's brother. Small world, but it came in handy when working joint jurisdictional cases. Six years ago, Meg had selected the Sacramento post out of three offered so that she could be close to her only family, which consisted of Matt and their younger half-sister, Margo. Mitch had always gotten along with his ex-brother-in-law, who was solid in every meaning of the word.

"And?"

"He said he'd call me as soon as he spoke to O'Brien's attorney and found out what he wants. Matt isn't inclined to give him anything. He's a fugitive."

"He helped us capture virtually every escapee."

"He's a killer."

"Meg—"

"I know you think he was framed. But that's neither here nor there. The facts as we know them are that he was convicted of a double homicide, sentenced to the death penalty, and escaped from prison. He's ready to surrender, great, but we're not going to negotiate with a fugitive. What kind of example does that set for other convicts? Besides, we can't remand his death sentence, or reopen his case. That's outside our jurisdiction."

"But it *is* Matt's."

Meg sighed. "We're talking about it. Matt wants to be here when you debrief Claire O'Brien this afternoon.

He's going to listen carefully to any evidence she might have. You're not going to find any D.A. more fair—or more resolute—than Matt."

"I know. I appreciate it, Meg."

"One more thing. Stop calling Lexie. She's had it with you questioning her competence."

"I wasn't. I'm just—"

"I know. You promised O'Brien you'd keep his daughter safe. Got it. Lexie will bring Ms. O'Brien in at two p.m. for debriefing. Leave her alone until then. Don't think for a minute that I'm unaware of what's going on."

Mitch glanced at Steve. Had he said anything? He didn't think so . . .

"I know you better than you think," Meg said. "Remember, we used to be friends."

"I thought we still were."

"We're getting there. Be careful."

Mitch and Steve parked in front of the Rabbit Hole just before nine that morning. The sign said CLOSED, but the posted hours were 9 a.m. to midnight, Tuesday through Saturday; noon to ten on Sunday.

"Maddox called the Rabbit Hole at 9:45 p.m. on Sunday. Near closing," Mitch said.

"Yet he left Davis about 5:30 that afternoon," Steve said. "Where was he for those four hours?"

"Without anyone coming forward, we may never know. But we do know that he was alive at 9:45 p.m. since we recovered his cell phone, which was attached to a charger in his car. Maybe he called the Rabbit Hole because he was running late and knew they closed at ten, and wanted to make sure that whoever he had planned to meet was still there."

Mitch checked his BlackBerry for the report Meg promised to send.

The e-mail was there. Mitch scanned it. "There's nothing unusual. Born in Sacramento County at Mercy Hospital in 1967. Hmm, younger than I thought. That makes him about forty-one. He joined the military in 1985 when he turned eighteen, out in three years—communications. Honorable discharge but nothing else noted. Didn't take the GI Bill. First arrest in 1989 for theft. Again in 1989. Pled, community service . . . same, same, six months for theft in early 1990. Then he started working at Tip's Blarney, no arrests. Clean for a couple of years, or just a better thief."

"Maybe we're barking up the wrong tree."

"Get this—he became an emancipated minor at the age of sixteen. Why?"

"Maybe his parents were dead."

"Not his mother. She lives in Elk Grove. That's on the way back to Sacramento."

"Fine, we'll make the stop. But again, maybe Maddox took the coincidence and built it up in his head as something more than it was."

"Then who killed him? This is the only thread he gave O'Brien other than Taverton was the target. The Rabbit Hole is owned by Lowe's former boss," Mitch continued, his voice lowering in his excitement that the final pieces of a complex puzzle were within reach. "That must be the connection Maddox made. Why he came down here in January."

"You think this guy killed Maddox? That's a stretch."

"Unless he burned down his own bar fifteen years ago for the insurance money."

"Getting away with arson—and murder—is rare, especially when there's a profit motive."

Mitch picked up his phone and dialed Meg's direct line. "Agent Elliott," she answered.

"Meg, it's me. Can you also run a background check on Tip Barney? The owner of the bar where Frank Lowe died. I see here that Barney got a nice insurance settlement. He now owns the Rabbit Hole in Isleton."

"Got it. I have to go." She hung up.

The Rabbit Hole looked like a dive from the outside—a narrow corner entrance, no windows, and a plain wooden sign with a white rabbit painted on it nailed above the door.

As they watched from across the street, two old, slow-moving men—one large, one small—approached the door. They stood there after trying the door and finding it locked.

A minute or so later, a slender, fit man in his forties—judging by the graying hair—came out of an opening that Mitch hadn't noticed. He glanced up and saw that there were windows above the bar. An upstairs apartment? Likely.

The man smiled at his patrons and opened the door. They entered together and the door closed.

"Ready?" Steve asked.

"Oh, yeah."

When they entered the bar Mitch expected a stench of stale beer and burned popcorn. Instead, the ventilation was surprisingly good and the bar smelled fresh and clean. A jukebox stood prominently next to the bar, but no music played. Probably too much external stimulation for the morning drinkers.

A smattering of cocktail tables with two or three

chairs each were grouped to one side; a small, worn wood dance floor was on the other. The bar itself was old but polished, with a full-length antique bar mirror mounted behind. The two old men sat on stools next to each other, their eyes following Mitch and Steve in the mirror.

The bartender was going about morning duties— checking stock, filling the cooler with ice from a machine Mitch couldn't see but heard churning around the corner, on the other side of a neon sign that proclaimed RESTROOMS.

They'd decided on the direct approach. Steve flashed his badge at the bartender and said, "Special Agent Steve Donovan, Federal Bureau of Investigation. My partner, Special Agent Mitch Bianchi. We're investigating the car that went into the river about two miles up the road. Did you hear about that on the news?"

The bartender walked over to them, leaned against the back bar. "The news? Sure. Heard about it from everyone who came in here the last couple of days. Your people were all over the river, hard to miss what happened."

"And your name?"

"Tip Barney."

"This your place?"

"Yep."

Mitch didn't reveal that he already had that information and held up a recent picture of Oliver Maddox. "Do you recognize this man?"

Barney took a good look. Shook his head. "Not familiar. He the one who went under?" Barney glared at them. "It wasn't a drunk driving thing, was it? I don't let anyone leave here with his keys if he's drunk."

"That's right," one of the two early morning regulars at the bar piped up. "That's why I walk here."

"You only live two blocks away. You need the exercise," Barney responded.

"We have no evidence that it was a drunk driving accident," Steve said. "We believe Mr. Maddox was on his way to meet someone here on Sunday, January 20."

"January? That was awhile back," Barney said.

Mitch had been watching the bartender closely while Steve asked·the questions. When Steve mentioned Maddox's name, Barney tensed. It was a minor physical reaction, unconscious for the most part. His face didn't change, but his neck muscles tightened, and he straightened just a fraction.

"Mr. Maddox has been in the river since," Mitch said.

"I have no objection if you want to flash the picture around, or leave it with me."

"We know that Mr. Maddox was here that Sunday night near closing. He was likely meeting with someone."

"I'm really sorry. I wish I could help, but I just don't remember. Except for a gal who comes in to help me on the weekends, I'm the only one here. Most everyone are locals, but we get a good tourist crowd on the weekends and summertime. People coming in for a beer after a long day on the river."

"In January? When it's raining?"

"The fish bite in the rain," one of the drunks said.

Mitch was on the verge of losing his temper. Something was odd here, but he couldn't put his finger on it. He pulled out his ace and hoped he wasn't playing his hand too soon.

"Mr. Maddox was looking into the death of one of your former employees," he said to Barney. "Frank Lowe."

Barney glanced at Steve, then at the bar. He crossed his arms. "I told the police everything fifteen years ago, and the arson investigator, and the insurance company. They said I had nothing to do with the fire. Hell, it may not have even been arson! The owner of the building put in substandard wiring, that could have done it. Probably was the cause."

"I didn't say we were looking into the cause of the fire," Mitch said. Barney was talking too fast. Something was definitely odd. "Did Maddox talk to you about Lowe?"

"No. If he did, I don't remember. That was months ago. I don't even remember the kid coming in here."

This was going nowhere. Mitch left a copy of Maddox's picture. "I'd like a list of your regulars."

Barney laughed. "Just about everyone in town. I'm the only bar."

The small drunk piped up. "Lora. She's here every night, till closing." He winked at Barney. "I think she has a thing for you, Tip."

Tip turned red. Mitch had never seen a man blush before.

"Don't go bothering Lora," he said.

Steve approached the men at the end of the bar, notepad in hand. "Lora?"

"Lora Lane. Nice name, eh? Lora Lane. Yep. She's the daughter of the chief of police. A bit slow, but sweet as all get-out. Sits at the bar every night nursing her rum and Diet Coke after getting off work from the tackle shop. Her daddy owns that, too."

"Does she live around here?"

"Course. With her mom and dad. In that big yellow Victorian on the corner of C and 4th. Can't miss it."

Claire spotted the Fed before she left the house with the dogs for her morning walk. She'd suspected that Agent Donovan would have someone sit on her after last night. Her dad was lucky that the Feds were slow to react. He might have been caught last night, and then there'd be no reason for the prison authority to give him the surgery he needed.

He was a walking dead man either way.

She confirmed the Fed—a female—when she went out with Chewy and Yoda. While sipping her coffee coming back from Starbucks, she knew that no matter what she did, the FBI would follow.

Screw that. She wasn't going to lead them to her father. She considered driving up to Lake Tahoe just for the hell of it, make the Fed wonder what was going on. Might be fun . . . but she had too much work to do. She had to track down Greg Abrahamson and find out about Frank Lowe's arrest. And then there was Tip Barney down in Isleton. It wouldn't hurt to have the Fed follow her around town, but it was the principle of the thing: She didn't like being followed. Or manipulated. Or treated like a fragile little girl.

Her dad was turning himself in because he was dying. She needed to prove he was innocent before . . . no. He wasn't going to die. Nelia Kincaid, his attorney—or whatever she was—wasn't going to let him surrender without an assurance that he'd be given the medical attention he needed.

With that belief firmly in place, Claire showered,

dressed in jeans and a T-shirt, and threw on a loose-fitting blazer. She holstered her 9mm as well as her Taser, then strapped on her ankle gun, a Kahr P40, and picked up her house phone. Were they listening in? She put down her phone, pulled out her cell phone. The cell phone was owned by Rogan-Caruso. If it was tapped, they'd know. And if they knew and condoned it, then she was already up the creek. She hoped her employer would talk to her before cooperating with the FBI.

She called a local taxi service and sent a car to the corner of 40th and H Streets.

Claire went out the back door, hopped over two fences, and ended up on the street parallel to hers. She took the long way to the meeting place, making sure the Fed wasn't driving up and down the streets looking for her. She had the car pegged—not what she thought of as a typical FBI sedan. A small, sporty black Honda. Must be the agent's personal car, or the Feds had gotten more discreet in surveillance.

She called Bill as she neared her destination. "Hi, Bill. Can I borrow your truck? My Jeep isn't starting. No, don't pick me up, I'm already in a taxi. I'll be there in twenty minutes."

TWENTY-SEVEN

Mitch and Steve didn't find Lora at the Victorian house on the corner, but she was at the tackle shop on the main dock in Isleton.

She was a stick of a thing, with dyed blond hair and huge fake diamond earrings that made her lobes sag with their weight. She smiled when she saw them, but it wasn't until she spoke that Mitch realized the man at the bar was right: Lora Lane was on the slow side.

She was making lures behind the counter. There were no customers in the shop, but Mitch saw several boats on the river through the windows behind the counter.

"Ms. Lane?"

She looked up, smiled, and said brightly, "Hi. Welcome to Isleton Bait and Tackle."

They identified themselves and showed their badges. Mitch said, "I think you can help us in an ongoing investigation."

"Sure!"

"We're trying to trace the last steps of a law student who was found dead in the river near here. You might have heard about it. His body was found on Wednesday."

She bobbed her head several times. "Everyone who comes in is talking about it."

"We know that he was at the Rabbit Hole the night he disappeared. We were told that you're a regular." Mitch held up Maddox's photograph. "Do you recognize this man?"

She stared at the picture and bit her lip. "I haven't seen him recently. I'd remember, because he has nice glasses."

"In January. It was a Sunday night and it was raining pretty badly."

She brightened and nodded. "Oh, yes! I remember. I think." She bit her lip again. "I think so. But it was a long time ago. But I have a good memory."

"You think you might have seen this man in the bar?"

"Yes," she said cautiously. "I think he came in late, after dark."

That didn't help—in January it was dark before six in the evening.

"Do you know if he met with anyone? Maybe had an argument?"

She shook her head, her eyes wide. "I just remember what he looks like. I'm good with faces. And he was sitting in his car a long time after he left."

"His car? Do you remember what kind of car?"

She shrugged. "Not really. Tip was walking me home. It was raining pretty hard and we were walking really fast. I thought maybe he didn't want to drive in the rain."

Steve asked, "Did Tip see the man in the car?"

"I don't know. Maybe. Maybe not."

Mitch retraced the conversation. "This man came in

after dark, and how long do you think he stayed in the bar?"

"I don't know. Long enough to have a drink."

"Did he seem nervous? Agitated? Angry?"

Lora Lane frowned, her eyes worried and confused. Mitch backtracked. "Did this man act strange?"

"I don't remember."

"But you remember him having a drink?"

She blinked in confusion. "I got to bring him his beer. Tip lets me do that sometimes, especially when it's slow, and I like to help."

"Were there any other strangers in the bar that night?"

She looked worried. "I don't know. Should I know that?"

"No, not necessarily."

"If you have a picture I might be able to remember. I'm very good with faces," she repeated.

"You've been a big help already, Ms. Lane."

"I have?"

"Yes. Thank you for your time."

They left.

"Who did Maddox call at the Rabbit Hole?" Mitch asked. "Directions? And why the second call?"

"Maybe it was a mistake, a misdial," Steve suggested.

"A rainy Sunday night. No other strangers. Barney has the only connection to Maddox through Frank Lowe. But why?"

"Maybe he followed Maddox out of town. Ran him off the road."

"Maybe. But why was Maddox sitting in his car?"

"Waiting for Barney to leave, maybe. Want to go back and push him?"

"We need something else. Lora Lane is not a reliable witness. Something definitive, otherwise we're just fishing and if he *is* guilty, then we've tipped our hand."

"No pun intended," Steve said as he unlocked the car.

Mitch rolled his eyes and slid into the passenger seat. "Let's get the background check on Mr. Barney and see what we can find. We can always come back."

"Great," Steve said sarcastically as he turned onto River Road. "I hate driving this road."

"Could be worse."

"How?"

"It could be dark and raining."

Lora Lane liked pretty things.

Ribbons for her hair. Shiny jewelry for her fingers and ears. Manicures and pedicures and keeping her boring brown hair blond.

She didn't like working in the dirty tackle shop, but she liked the money she earned every Friday. Her mama always said she was a pretty little girl without an ounce of common sense. Daddy let her live at home because she wasn't very good with her money and he said people would take advantage of her.

She knew she wasn't a smart girl, but she was smart enough to know that people thought she was a retard. She'd heard them talking. Her daddy shut them up right quick, but she heard them sometimes. She ran the tackle shop almost all by herself, knew the difference between a night crawler and a butterworm, and made the world's finest lures. Her daddy said so himself, and everyone came into the shop to buy them because they worked.

She wasn't stupid. She knew how to mind her mouth. She didn't tell those nice men about her agreement, did she? No, she didn't. She kept it to herself like she'd sworn on the grave of her grandmama that she would.

For two years, Lora had watched Tip Barney like she was told. Every night she went to the Rabbit Hole and watched him. She kind of liked him, he was nice to her and didn't treat her like she was dumb. He talked to her like she had something important to say, even when she didn't say anything. He was nice-looking, too. Had nice blue eyes and a pretty smile.

When the men came to her house, Daddy wasn't home. He was working. He had an important job, just like she did. He was a policeman. The chief policeman in Isleton. At first she was scared, but then the pretty man smiled at her and she felt all fluttery inside.

She had a job. And it was as important as her daddy's job. She was *undercover* for the Department of Homeland Security. She reported back to Agents Smith and Jones everything that happened at the Rabbit Hole. *Everything*. She took very good notes.

She liked Tip, but he was a terrorist. As Agent Smith said, not all terrorists look like terrorists.

She was protecting her friends and neighbors from being killed like those poor people in New York. Lora was important.

When the two nice men left her tackle shop, she called the special number she was given for emergencies. *Only* to be used if someone was asking questions about Tip's Blarney.

"Harper."

She frowned. "Agent Smith or Agent Jones, please."

There was silence, then several minutes later there was a click. "This is Agent Jones."

"Two men came to my shop today. They were asking questions about Tip and another man."

"Who?"

"That man you told me about. Mr. Maddox. The terrorist who was going to poison the river and kill all the fish."

"Do you remember their names?"

"Of course. I got their business cards, too. They *said* they were from the FBI. Agent Mitch Bianchi and Agent Steven Donovan."

Agent Smith had told her that a lot of people lie. She knew that. Her mama lied about a lot of things to her daddy. Mama didn't think Lora knew, because she thought Lora was stupid, but Lora was smarter than that. She knew that her mama wasn't at Book Club on Thursday nights.

"What did they say?"

"They asked if I remembered Mr. Maddox. I told them yes. He was in the bar. I told them the entire truth, except about the poison."

"You did very good."

"I did?"

"Yes. Lora, this is very important. If a woman comes to the bar who you don't know, and starts asking about Mr. Maddox or a man named Frank Lowe, I want you to do the same thing to her that you did to Mr. Maddox. Can you do that for me?"

"Is she a terrorist too?"

"Yes. Her name is Claire O'Brien and she is very dangerous."

"I promise. I can do that."

"Thank you, Lora. There's no one else we can trust with this very important assignment."

She hung up and smiled, went upstairs, and closed her bedroom door. She locked it, even though she knew her daddy wouldn't be home for a long time. She went to her closet, into the far back, behind all her shoeboxes. She pulled out the secret box where she kept things she didn't want her daddy to find. She used to keep candy and the weekly magazines her daddy hated in the locked box. Now, the only thing inside was a large vial of poison.

Terrorists needed to die. And Lora knew how to do it.

TWENTY-EIGHT

Greg Abrahamson was much harder to get an audience with than Claire thought. He was now a detective, and she left several messages trying to track him down.

She didn't want to talk to him on the phone. She needed ten minutes in person. People were more forthright in person.

Claire took the opportunity while waiting for Abrahamson to return her call to stop by Rogan-Caruso and do more research, this time on Don Collier. He'd canceled his classes and seemed to have disappeared, according to Agent Donovan.

She typed in search parameters and pulled up far more detailed records of Collier than she could from home.

He'd earned tenure last year at Davis. Now eleven years as a professor, took pro bono cases, yada yada. Big do-gooder on the surface. His affiliation with the Western Innocence Project was noteworthy. He'd been written up in the paper many times. Philanthropist this, noble that. Blah, blah. But the more she read about his good work, the more she wondered if she was wrong about him. She dug deeper, using her PI license to do an employment background check.

Confirmed his tenure with UC Davis.

Six years with Madison, Bergstrom, Truedell & Smith. Three years with Johnson & Mather. One-year internship with Young, Blaine, Forsyth & Associates. Graduate USC law school, 1990. Graduate UNLV, 1987. Born 1964 in Phoenix, Arizona.

Her eye went back to Johnson & Mather. She recognized all three law firms, but that one . . .

Her hand started shaking as she typed in another search.

George Prescott with Johnson & Mather was her father's defense counsel. During the same time that Don Collier was on staff.

Don Collier had been responsible for reviewing her father's case file for the Project, and rejected looking into it. Don Collier had been Oliver Maddox's advisor. Had Maddox known that Collier had been with the same law firm that represented her father at trial? Claire had to assume he did . . . he was a law student. He would definitely have known who represented her father. And if he was doing research, he would have figured out that Collier was there at the same time. That there was a huge conflict of interest. Collier knew more about the case than he'd admitted.

She dialed Randy Sizemore at the Western Innocence Project. It took several minutes, and a threat to come by and sit in the office until closing, before he came on the phone. "Ms. O'Brien, I don't see how I can help you any more than I already have."

"One question. Please."

"One."

"Do you allow the attorneys reviewing case files to

assess cases they've worked on, or where one of their colleagues worked on it?"

"Of course not. That would defeat the purpose of our checks and balances system."

"Do the attorneys know this?"

"Of course they do. They simply recuse themselves from reviewing the file. It's not a problem. I have dozens of attorneys who review files for me."

"Thank you."

"May I ask why?"

"You told me that Don Collier reviewed *State of California v. O'Brien* and deemed it a just conviction."

"Yes."

"Collier worked for the same law firm as my father's attorney. Johnson & Mather."

"That's not possible."

"It's not? Why?"

"Don would have told me." Randy Sizemore didn't sound so sure of himself.

"So you didn't know."

"Ms. O'Brien, I don't know what you've found, but there must be a logical explanation."

"Thank you for your time." She hung up. She didn't think that Sizemore had known about Collier, but since they were friends, she didn't want him to tip Collier off that she was onto him.

"Claire?"

She jumped, turned, and saw her friend Jayne standing in the doorway.

"You scared the hell out of me."

"What are you doing?"

"Background check."

Jayne frowned. "J.T. called me this morning about

you. Asked me to monitor your database usage. He's a little worried."

Claire straightened. J. T. Caruso was one of the principals of her firm. "Worried? Why?"

"He didn't say, but, well, I did a little research and I think he found out your dad is in Sacramento."

Claire's stomach dropped. "How could he know that? How did you know?"

"The FBI has a surveillance tape of your dad in Redding. And then there's the buzz around the D.A.'s office that he's surrendering today. J.T. knows people there. And in the FBI."

"I'm not doing anything illegal," Claire said.

"Just watch yourself, okay?"

Claire didn't want to be fired, she loved her job, but her father's innocence and safety were more important than her career.

"I'll be careful."

Jayne nodded. "If you need me for anything, you know how to reach me."

"I have a question. A computer question."

Jayne sat down on the corner of Claire's desk. "What?"

"How could a digital file disappear?"

"You need to be more specific."

"Don't ask me why."

"All right."

"There're two missing coroner's reports. They are archived digitally and kept in a data warehouse. They are in the log, but not on the tape."

"Is there other data on the tape?"

"I think so."

"Well, if there *isn't,* the tape was corrupted. Someone

didn't check once they burned the tape or the disk that the data was readable or even there. It happens *all* the time because people are lazy. But if there's other data on the tape, then those files were never copied over."

"You can't just delete them?"

"Most data warehouses store data on unrewritable software, to prevent accidental deletion of data. There are a lot of protections in place. Climate controls, backups of all data, and—"

"Backups? Why would they need a backup?"

"Most good archive systems have a searchable system, then a condensed data file that has everything they have in the searchable system. So if there's some big catastrophe, they can re-create the data files."

"Is there a way to erase some files and not the others?"

"There's a way to do everything, Claire. But it wouldn't be easy. They'd need access and everything leaves a trail. It's easier to leave a false trail than no trail. Unless you're really good."

"Like you."

Jayne smiled.

"But if it was never there . . ."

"If it was never there, you can't do anything about it, but then there shouldn't be a record of the data in the log. Unless the log was manually created, which sort of defeats the purpose of eliminating human error. If there's a log of the files, and they're just gone, then they're still there."

"Stop. You've confused me."

"Anything deleted isn't really deleted. Unless the tape is completely wiped—and there're ways of doing that—then the data is still there. It's just hidden."

"Could you find it?"

"If it's there, I can find it."

"Would you do me a favor?"

"Depends."

"I have a friend in the coroner's office. He has access to the archives. He's the one who discovered the files were missing. If I clear it with him, can you help him find the hidden files?"

"Between you and me, right?"

Claire pretended to zip her lip and toss away the key. Jayne nodded. "Okay."

Jeffrey Riordan arrived in Sacramento just after ten that morning. He'd had to suffer through traffic almost the entire drive from San Francisco—it had taken *three hours* when it should have taken two. He drove directly to Richie's house. Chad Harper answered the door.

"Clue me in, Harper. What the fuck is going on? Hamilton has called me a half-dozen times in the last two days. It's usually Richie who panics, not Judge Prozac."

"You know everything, except the latest news. Hamilton is on the phone with Richie. The district attorney is meeting right now with O'Brien's attorney to arrange terms of surrender."

"Good! Get him back into custody. Take care of him once and for all."

"There's a little problem."

"What?"

"The FBI is involved."

"Shit."

They didn't have a mole in the FBI office. Local government, local law enforcement, D.A.'s office—within reach, they had at least one person under their thumb. But the FBI? None. And it irked Jeffrey. He had *one,* but only in Washington. That sure as hell wouldn't help him here in Sacramento.

He started up the stairs, but Harper called him back. "I had a call from Isleton."

"Isleton? Who the fuck cares about—" He stopped. "Dammit, I knew we should have offed Barney when he moved back to Sacramento."

"Jeffrey, sometimes murder isn't the best solution. Barney knew nothing of Lowe's arrangement with Taverton. He went to L.A., bought a bar, lost a bunch of money, returned to his hometown. Nothing strange there. Killing him? No. Maddox didn't learn anything from him. He's not talking because he knows shit. If he knew anything, our snitch would have heard."

"That retard?" Jeffrey snorted.

"At least she follows orders and keeps her mouth shut."

"So who's down there snooping this time?"

"Two federal agents."

"Shit."

"They're only following up on Maddox's death. I don't think they will be a problem."

"You don't know that! This is spiraling out of control again, just like with Maddox. If we'd taken Barney out of the picture with Lowe, or even two years ago, I'd be far more comfortable."

"Barney knows nothing. It's too late to do anything— killing Barney would only raise suspicions, and *if* he knew what Frank Lowe did, he would have talked or asked for money."

"Maybe, but somebody tipped off Maddox about Tip Barney being back in Sacramento." Jeffrey hated not being in control.

"Maddox found out about Lowe and Barney from Taverton's personal files, but we have those now—both the copies and the original—so there's no threat. And if Claire O'Brien starts asking questions, she'll be taken care of."

"She's far too nosy. Let's keep this tidbit from the others. They are already too paranoid, and paranoia makes people act stupid."

"Agreed."

Jeffrey went to the top of the stairs and opened the double doors into Richie's plush office. "Put Hamilton on speaker," he demanded.

Richie said into the phone, "Jeffrey's here. You're now on speaker, Hamilton."

"O'Brien is surrendering to the FBI today at six," he said.

"The FBI? Why?"

"Safety issues. I didn't get much out of the D.A., but the word is out that Matt Elliott is quietly reopening the case."

"That's it. We're done for," Richie said.

"No we're not." Jeffrey slammed his fist on the desk. "Keep your cool. It's not over. It's never going to be over. They can't connect anything to us."

"You're the one all hot and heavy to kill people!" Richie said.

"Only if it has to be done. Maddox had to go. He made too many connections." Jeffrey started giving orders. "Richie, you make sure there is no paper trail."

"There isn't—"

"Double check. Triple check! And Hamilton, you keep your ear to the D.A.'s office. We need to know *everything* Matt Elliott is up to."

"I'm already on it, but I have a bad feeling about this."

"It's not over," Jeffrey reiterated.

Lexie Santana hated surveillance. She'd much rather be in the thick of things, like bringing in the fugitive, Thomas O'Brien.

But maybe she'd get lucky. Maybe the daughter would lead her to O'Brien and Lexie wouldn't be so bored just *sitting* here.

She watched as a car pulled up in front of Claire O'Brien's house. Maybe this was it . . . A man got out— late thirties, a bit overweight, dressed business casual. A kid got out of the passenger side. Boy, ten or eleven. The man put his arm around the kid's shoulders, squeezed, then dropped the arm as they approached the front door.

Not O'Brien. Damn. The dogs in Claire's backyard started barking. They continued to bark. No one answered the door. The man stood there a few minutes, then walked away. They sat in the car for about five minutes, then drove off.

Lexie left her surveillance post and ran across the street to the house. She knocked on the door. The dogs barked. There was no answer.

Did she have probable cause to enter O'Brien's house? No one had left or entered. Yet . . .

She called Meg. "I think Claire O'Brien has given me the slip. She didn't answer her door to a visitor, and now I'm looking in all the windows and it doesn't look like she's here. Her Jeep is, she isn't."

*   *   *

Mitch and Steve walked into FBI headquarters at noon. They'd stopped by Frank Lowe's mother's apartment, but she wasn't home. Her neighbor said she worked for the postal service and usually came home between four thirty and five.

"Mitch. Steve." Meg waved them into her office. "Good news, we got the contents off the flash drive."

"What do we have?" asked Mitch as he sat down in front of Meg's desk.

"That's the problem. I'm not quite sure." Meg slid over a small stack of papers. The top was the cover page from their Menlo Park facilities verifying they were able to retrieve all data from the flash drive. The second page was a print of a JPEG, a beautiful young woman. "There's nothing about her on the drive, but we ran her photo. Jessica White. Missing since 1978. She was a student at Stanford University and disappeared her sophomore year. No evidence of foul play, no anything. The police felt there were some shenanigans at one of the fraternity parties, but the girl was seen at three different parties the night she disappeared. They interviewed everyone at the fraternities and Jessica's sorority; nothing solid. I've requested the files, but I don't know how that's going to help us. Except I did learn one thing—Oliver Maddox requested the files as well."

"Did they send them?" Steve asked.

"Maddox picked them up in person on Friday, January 18," she answered.

"We didn't find anything like that in his town house," said Mitch.

"And they aren't on the flash drive, either," said Meg.

Mitch turned the pages. There was a series of articles

related to the Delta Conservancy, Elk Grove, the Waterstone Development Corporation, and probably a half-dozen more. They were all LexisNexis files that had been saved to the drive.

"Did you contact LexisNexis to retrieve any other searches Maddox might have done?" Mitch asked.

Meg frowned. "The U.S. Attorney's office is working on it, but there are huge privacy issues. We won't have anything today."

"These are all old stories. Twenty, twenty-five years." He turned pages and found an obituary. "Rose Van Alden. Died at ninety-one, in her sleep." Mitch read the article. She was a lifelong resident of Elk Grove and left her money to the Delta Conservancy. "Is there anything important here?"

"I don't know. They're old articles, and normally I wouldn't waste my time, but Maddox swallowed the flash drive for a reason, so I'm thinking there's a connection we don't see. I've sent everything to analysts at Quantico and asked for a rush. But one thing seems pretty obvious: Keep going," she said.

Mitch flipped through the articles, then started to see another pattern—a series of stories about Judge Hamilton Drake.

Steve looked over Mitch's shoulder. "A judge? Why's that important?"

"If you read the articles, you'd learn that Drake is one of the original partners in Waterstone Development," said Meg. "Maddox was digging into something. The analysts are doing a complete background check on Drake and seeing if there is any crossover to Maddox's other articles. Even if there is something here, that doesn't mean it's related to O'Brien. In fact, I don't see

how any of this relates to the O'Brien case. Maybe Maddox was killed for a completely different reason."

Mitch didn't yet see the connection either, but he
sensed it was there. "Did Matt call?" he asked Meg as
he handed back the file.

"Yes. He met with O'Brien's attorney. She happens to
be the ex-wife of the district attorney in San Diego, so
there's apparently some clout there. Matt didn't get into
all the details, but O'Brien will surrender here, at headquarters, at six p.m. today. There's one major conces-
sion that Matt agreed to. We're transporting O'Brien
directly to Sutter Memorial Hospital."

"Why?"

"In your report from Montana, you said that O'Brien
had been shot, but was presumed alive because of his
call to the Beaverhead County sheriff several hours
later."

Mitch nodded.

"He never got medical attention," said Meg. "It's
probably a miracle he survived. The bullet is still in him,
and according to his attorney there is a serious medical
problem that has come up in the last few weeks. I'm not
a doctor, I have no idea what's wrong, but he'll be given
a complete exam and surgery if necessary. We'll be responsible for a guard on his room at all times."

"I'm glad this is nearly over," Steve said, his hand on
the door. "Now we just need to find Maddox's killer."

"One more thing," Meg said. "Lexie called right before you walked in. You were right, Mitch. Claire is
good. She slipped out sometime this morning. Took a
taxi, which we tracked down to Elk Grove and the residence of a retired sheriff deputy, Bill Kamanski."

"Her former guardian. Was she there?"

"No. Kamanski loaned her a vehicle. She said her Jeep wouldn't start."

"Shit! Where is she?"

"We have a BOLO on her," said Meg, "but I'm not going to put her under arrest. We want her to cooperate with us, and it's in her best interest to do so, but the truth is O'Brien is coming in. She wasn't involved in Maddox's homicide. For all we know, she convinced her father to surrender. Hard to arrest her for that."

"She's working the Maddox case on her own. She's in danger."

"So I should arrest her? Mitch, she's a professional, a licensed private investigator. Researching a missing, now dead, person. She hasn't interfered with or stymied your investigation."

"She knows stuff we don't know."

"Why is that?"

Mitch ran a hand through his hair. "Dammit, Megan! We have to bring her in for her own safety."

"When—or if—we track down Claire O'Brien, you talk to her and convince her to come in. But unless she has information about the Maddox homicide I don't see how she can help."

"Do you want us here for the surrender?" Steve asked.

"No. I've assigned Davidson and Kinsley to handle transport to the hospital and guard duty."

"Then we're going to follow up on some information related to Frank Lowe down in Elk Grove."

"Go ahead. I'll call when I get the analysis back."

"If it's today. I'm not holding my breath to get a report on Friday afternoon," Mitch said.

Meg smiled. "You might be surprised."

TWENTY-NINE

When Greg Abrahamson finally called back, he agreed to give her a few minutes if she could meet him at 12:30 outside the Crest Theater on the K Street Mall.

She was early and he was late. She sat on the bench across from the theater as he'd instructed.

A homeless man shuffled up the street past her, so filthy he smelled like he'd slept inside a Dumpster. He wore three layers of long-sleeved shirts, though it was ninety degrees out. He looked in the garbage and Claire was both revolted and filled with compassion.

"Loaves and Fishes is only a couple blocks that way." She pointed north.

He sat down next to her. Why had she said anything?

"Look, I have no money for you."

"Claire."

He spoke under his breath. When Greg Abrahamson said he was undercover, he was *really* undercover.

"What are you working on that you have to smell like that?"

He responded, "What are you working on that is so important that I have to risk my cover?"

"I'm sorry—it's about my father."

"Which is the only reason I'm here."

She got to the point. "You arrested a man named Frank Lowe fifteen years ago. In November of 1993. The charge was home invasion robbery—I don't remember the specific penal code. But he was about twenty-five, a petty thief, broke into a house where a little girl was sleeping after her mother left."

"I remember."

"After fifteen years you remember?"

"I don't remember the name, but I remember the arrest. Girl's dead now."

"What?" She frowned at the non sequitur.

"Mother was a piece of work. Left the girl every night. I didn't buy for a minute that she was running to the store for five minutes. So I added that house to my regular drive-bys. Mother brings a guy home, he moves in, beats both the mom and the kid. I get two domestic calls in three months. Mom won't press charges, third call is a homicide. Guy was beating up on the mom, the kid walks in and tries to stop him, gets shoved aside, and cracks her head open on the fireplace."

"That's awful."

"Yeah, so I remember that call. Hate the fact I could do nothing to protect the kid. What can we do? The system is fucked."

"If it is so fucked why are you sitting here dressed as a bum and smelling like ripe garbage?"

He stared at her. "You trying to help your dad?"

"He's innocent."

He raised an eyebrow.

Claire continued, "Taverton was assigned to the Lowe case. Arraigned, then there's evidence that maybe there was a plea agreement. All hush-hush. Taverton's records disappear, he's killed, Lowe dies in a fire, and my dad is framed for murder."

Abrahamson didn't respond for a long minute. "I honestly don't remember much about what happened after the D.A.'s office took the case. I would have testified at trial, but then Taverton called me and said he was working a plea. I probably said something to tick him off—I have no tolerance for prosecutors who let repeat offenders off. But because it was so unusual I do remember what he said to me before slamming down the phone."

"Which was?"

"He said, 'Sometimes you have to put a little fish on the hook to bait the bigger fish. And when I'm done with this case, you'll be hearing about it for years to come.'"

"That's it?" Claire was heartbroken. She'd hoped he knew something more. A name, perhaps, or at least something more to follow up on.

"That's it. At least what I remember. It was a long time ago, and I've arrested easily a thousand perps since." He stood, began shuffling away.

"Thanks."

"Drake."

"Excuse me?"

"Judge Drake. Might want to ask him. He was the judge at Lowe's arraignment. If there was some big plea deal, he might know what it was about. He's still on the bench."

Claire sat there for a few more minutes, thinking. She wanted to get down to Isleton and talk to Lowe's old boss, Tip Barney, but this was a hot lead, and the courthouse was only a few blocks away.

She pulled out her cell phone, looked up the courthouse number, and dialed. After several transfers, she was talking to Judge Drake's secretary. She told her why she wanted to speak to the judge.

"He's on the bench right now," the secretary said. "I'll give him your message when he returns."

"Is there any way you can look up the file?"

"No," she said haughtily. "Plea agreement details are not always public record."

Claire left her cell phone number and hung up. It was after one in the afternoon; she didn't want to wait. Chances were the judge wouldn't be done until late that afternoon. Time to hit Isleton and maybe when she returned the judge would be free.

Frank Lowe's mother lived in a run-down row house in an old Elk Grove neighborhood surrounded by four-unit apartments built in the seventies.

Mitch knocked on the locked screen, then glanced at Steve and rolled his eyes. There was no doubt she was home. The sound of game shows rang loud and clear through the open windows. A wall air-conditioning unit rumbled loudly in the background. No wonder her television was on full volume—Mitch couldn't hear himself think. He rang the bell, holding the buzzer down for three full seconds.

The woman may not have heard the bell, but the small dogs did. Three of them began barking in earnest.

"Down, boys! Down. Stop it!" A moment later she opened the door. "Yeah?"

"Ms. Betty Lowe?"

"Yeah? You selling something I don't want?" Ms. Lowe was a short, skinny woman. Dyed red hair with gray roots. Leathery skin from long-term sun exposure.

Mitch and Steve flashed their badges. "FBI Special Agents Bianchi and Donovan, ma'am. We have a couple questions about your son if you don't mind."

"Who? Frank? He's dead. Can't get into any trouble from the grave."

"Yes, ma'am, but we're looking into his death."

"The fire?"

"Yes."

She opened her screen and they stepped across the threshold. Three fluffy dogs barked and turned in circles at Mitch's feet. They ignored Steve.

"You must have a dog at home," Ms. Lowe said. "That's why they're acting up." She herded the dogs down the hall and shut the door behind them. They barked a minute, then calmed down.

Mitch didn't have a dog, but he had been around them a lot lately. He put Claire out of his mind—and the question of where she might be right now—and focused on finding out if Betty Lowe knew anything about her son's activities prior to his death.

Steve asked, "Just for the record, are you Frank's only living relative?"

"I have two sisters, both live out of state. Never see them. My parents are dead. They didn't much care for me after I got pregnant with Frank and didn't want to get married."

"Frank's father isn't in the picture?"

"He was, on and off. More off, really, until Frank was grown. I think if Tip was around more, Frank wouldn't have been so wild growing up. Though the military was good for him, very good."

"Frank's father is Tip Barney?"

Mitch couldn't restrain his surprise, and Ms. Lowe

turned to him. "Is there a problem? Tip and I never married, and he never paid child support, but we settled that after Frank died. Tip felt awful about that, sent me half the insurance money from the fire and moved to Los Angeles."

"Did Frank know that Tip was his father?"

"Know? Of course he knew. Tip came 'round every so often, gave Frank that job in the bar when he got out of prison. Why is this important?"

"We're just trying to put the pieces together of what happened during the two weeks prior to the fire," Steve said.

"Frank always had sticky fingers. It's why I kicked him out of the house when he was a teenager. He started stealing from friends, and I was having none of that. He went to live with his great-aunt after living on the streets didn't sit well with him. Aunt Rose and Frank seemed to get along all right, though I think Frank was the only person she didn't hate. Frank was a nice kid. Just couldn't keep his hands off other people's stuff."

"Is that why Frank got emancipated?" Steve asked.

Regret crossed Ms. Lowe's face. "Aunt Rose died and Frank thought she was leaving her house to him—he liked it out at her ranch. He'd been living there on and off about a year, in the apartment above the garage. Had a part-time job. Helped her when she needed it. Then she ended up having her house sold to some developer and giving the money to a conservancy group. Not that I'm knocking the need to help the environment, mind you, but it wasn't like her. She was stingy. I expected her to want to be buried with her money. Giving it to a liberal charity? Naw."

Her voice softened. "I was a bit of a free spirit back

then. I let Frank do what he wanted. In hindsight, that wasn't such a good idea. I didn't discipline him enough, but see, my daddy always used a paddle on my butt, and I didn't want Frank growing up being hit to stay in line. And he was a good kid, but for those sticky fingers. We'd just started getting things back on track when he died."

"We're sorry for your loss," Steve said.

She sighed. "I miss them."

"Them?"

"Frank and Tip. Tip moved to L.A. after the fire—I think he blamed himself in some ways—and he died of cancer two years ago."

Mitch straightened, exchanged glances with Steve. "Do you know what Frank was offered as a plea agreement before he died?"

She was confused. "I don't know what you're talking about."

"You know he was arrested for home invasion robbery two weeks before the fire."

"Of course, but he told me they gave him probation. Community service."

So she didn't know anything. "Do you have any of Frank's personal effects?"

She shook her head. "No. Frank hadn't lived with me since he was fifteen, I didn't see any reason to keep anything, and he took what he wanted."

"Do you have a picture of Tip Barney?"

"Why?"

"For our report," Steve said.

She rose, crossed to a bookshelf, and took out a photo album. She sat back down, flipped through it.

Near the back she pulled out a picture. "This was Frank and Tip at the bar about a year before the fire."

She handed the picture to Mitch.

He stared. Showed it to Steve. Everything clicked into place. "May we borrow this?"

"Sure. I probably have the negatives somewhere."

"We'll return it," Mitch promised.

They thanked Ms. Lowe for her time, then walked out.

"It all makes sense now," Steve said.

"Frank survived the fire—or faked his own death—because he feared for his life," Mitch said, holding up the picture. "Think he and his father went to L.A. together?"

"And when his dad died, he took his identity and moved back, close to home."

"Now we just have to figure out why."

"Back to Isleton."

THIRTY

Claire parked down the street from the Rabbit Hole in Isleton.

She'd just gotten off the phone with Nelia Kincaid. Less than three hours from now Tom O'Brien would surrender at FBI headquarters and be taken to Sutter Memorial Hospital for evaluation and possible surgery.

She wanted to see her dad before he went into surgery. What if he didn't survive? She shook her head. Right now figuring out who killed her mother and Chase Taverton was the single most important thing. She'd call Nelia when she was back in Sacramento and see if the attorney could get her in to visit her dad.

She took a deep breath and put her forehead on the steering wheel. She hadn't slept much last night after her father and Nelia left. She worked on the case, putting together all the information she had and what she needed to check out, telling herself it was for her dad. And all that was important, but it was all rehashing the same stuff.

The truth was, as soon as she went to bed, she couldn't get Mitch out of her mind.

She wanted to be angry with him. She wanted to hate him. He'd used her, manipulated her. She'd always prided herself on reading people, and yet Mitch hid himself, created a false identity. And she'd fallen in love. He'd been exactly who she wanted him to be, as if the FBI agent had been able to read her subconscious and identify the perfect man for her. He became that man, and she fell for it. She'd exposed so much to him, not just her body, but her heart. She'd wanted to share more with him than with anyone.

Claire had dated more than a dozen guys, more or less seriously, over the years, but it never hurt—physically hurt—when they split. Nothing like this.

She almost wished she could cry over it again, but the tears had dried up last night.

Taking another deep breath, she got out of Bill's truck. Time to focus on what was most important right now: proving her father's innocence. She double-checked the Kahr P40 she had strapped in her ankle holster. She opted to leave her blazer in the truck, knowing full well that men were more forthcoming with information if you gave them something to look at. Anyway, her blazer made her look too much like a cop or a PI. She unbuttoned one of the buttons of her black shirt, just enough so her lacy pink bra could be seen if she turned the right way.

She retrieved her Taser C2 from her tactical bag in the back. She loved the new design—she'd bought the metallic pink version—as well as the intense voltage in a compact six inches. She could hit someone up to fifteen feet away. If Claire were being attacked, she'd rather take them down safely without having to touch or shoot them.

She stuffed it in her small purse, an image of hitting

Mitch Bianchi below the belt with the two electric probes making her smile. *Zap!*

Much better. Focus on the anger, not the pain. Toughen up.

Claire surveyed the building. The Rabbit Hole was not much of anything to look at, but then again, at night Isleton pretty much rolled up the sidewalks unless it was their annual summer Crawdad Festival.

Downtown Isleton was quaint with restored buildings, a few gift stores, an old-fashioned ice cream "shoppe," and a video arcade. A must, Claire thought, for a small town. A sporting goods store took up half the block across from the Rabbit Hole. No surprise there, fishing and boating were big here in the delta.

Though it was the middle of the day, there was little sign of life on the street. Three young teens were walking around with nothing to do. A mother with two young children exited the ice cream shoppe. There were no windows in the bar, but a red neon sign declared they were OPEN.

She crossed the street and walked in. The bar was a third full—almost all of the men over sixty—and the music greeted her warmly. She didn't particularly like country music, but it fit the atmosphere, and the sound was definitely more pop-country than the soulful my-dog-died-and-my-wife-ran-away-with-the-sheriff ballads. Two men played chess in one corner, and a larger table had a quarter poker game going on.

"Hey, Tip!" one of the old guys at the bar shouted loud enough for her to hear, "you're really bringing in the lookers with that snazzy new sign you put up."

Claire had seen the sign—it looked neither snazzy nor new—but she turned her attention to the bar.

"Told you it would help," a man behind the bar said. Claire couldn't see him behind the heads of the patrons. She approached and sat on an empty stool next to a man who wore a military hat from WWII with SANDERSON sewn on the edge. He looked old enough to have fought nearly seventy years ago.

"Told you classy chicks like men in uniform," Sanderson said. "I'd buy you a drink, sweet thing, but my military pension only covers two drafts a day and I'm already on my third." He laughed at his joke.

She smiled. She liked this place. It had a good feeling about it, small-town folks of modest means coming together for a beer to keep each other from getting too lonely. She'd bet every one of the five men sitting at the bar was a widower.

Claire smiled at the bartender. He wasn't exactly what she expected, but she didn't have a description of Tip Barney. The bartender was in his mid-forties with an average build and average features. Pleasant looking.

"What can I get for you, pretty lady?" the bartender said, putting a cocktail napkin on the bar in front of her.

"Whatever you have on tap is fine." Claire didn't particularly like draft beer, but fitting in was important when you were looking for information.

There was an older couple sitting at a table near the bar, and the only other woman was two stools over from Claire. She leaned over. "Hi, I'm Lora. Who are you?"

The woman had a bright appearance and subtle manner that told Claire she might be developmentally disabled. She was very pretty even though she wore too much makeup.

"Hi, Lora. Claire." She smiled.

The bartender put the beer in front of Claire. She

sipped. Smiled. Ugh. She'd been spoiled after drinking Guinness for so long. "I'm looking for Tip Barney."

The bartender crossed his arms and leaned against the back bar. "That's me."

Claire didn't know what she was expecting, but he looked much younger than she thought he would. By the looks of it, he'd have been in his twenties when he'd owned Tip's Blarney. Not impossible, she supposed, but odd enough that she made a mental note to check into the history of the previous bar.

"Popular guy today," one of the guys at the end of the bar said.

Tip smiled and shook his head. "Ignore them. What can I help you with?"

She'd already decided that honesty would work best with Frank Lowe's old boss.

"My name is Claire O'Brien." She took a sip of beer. "I work for Rogan-Caruso Protective Services, and I have some questions about one of your employees."

He knew exactly who she was. She saw the recognition in his eyes when she said her name.

"I don't have any employees."

"Frank Lowe. He died in a fire in your bar fifteen years ago."

"Frank." He nodded. "Poor Frank."

"You've never talked about him," one of the guys at the bar said. Claire wished she could have this conversation in private.

"He was a good guy. A friend, though he had some problems. A couple arrests, petty theft mostly, but I told him if it happened again I'd have to let him go." Tip shook his head and reached for a half-empty water bottle on the back of the bar, took a long swallow. "It was a tragedy, really. The police thought that some gang-bangers burned down the bar for fun, not knowing Frank lived upstairs. It was an old building, burned down quick."

"That's sad." Lora had moved to the stool next to Claire, elbows on the bar and chin in her hands.

"What do you want to know about Frank?" Tip asked her.

"Fifteen years ago, my father was convicted of killing two people. You probably remember it, if not then, perhaps because it was all over the news after the San Quentin earthquake."

"Of course I've heard of it."

"Hey," Sanderson said, "O'Brien. Isn't he the guy Channel 3 did that report on a couple months ago? That he was capturing the other prisoners? I remember that. He'd been a cop, right?"

Claire nodded. She needed to get the conversation back to Frank. "As a favor to me, Rogan-Caruso is looking into the conviction." She had no qualms about lying on this point. Rogan-Caruso's reputation was such that everyone would take their involvement seriously, which gave everything she said credibility. In addition, if Tip Barney—or anyone else in this bar—had killed Oliver, they would think twice about attacking her if they believed that Rogan-Caruso had the same information she had.

She continued, "When Oliver Maddox turned up dead, I approached my boss and asked if he would look into what happened. I never believed Oliver when he told me my father was innocent and he felt he could prove it. But with Oliver being murdered, it looks like he was right."

"I don't understand what any of this has to do with me or Frank."

"Rogan-Caruso uncovered information about Chase Taverton, the prosecutor who was murdered, that leads us to believe that he had a plea agreement with Frank Lowe regarding a capital offense that Mr. Lowe could testify to." Claire remembered what Abrahamson said about big fish and little fish. "Mr. Lowe was a petty thief. I'm sure you know he was arrested several times. He always got off with a slap on the wrist or minimal jail time. But after the last time with the little girl in the house he graduated to the big—"

Tip interrupted. "I knew Frank very well, and he didn't hurt kids. He never hurt anyone. He only broke into places where no one was home."

She nodded. "Right. That's what the records say. Until the last time."

"What do you want?"

"Do you know what Frank told Chase Taverton? I know there was a plea deal. It might not have been signed, sealed, and delivered, but it existed."

"I don't know anything about that." He picked up a rag and started wiping down the clean bar.

"The fact that both men were killed within twenty-four hours has us suspicious. Both of them. Murdered."

"Those kids didn't know Frank was inside."

"And you believe that?"

Claire had almost forgotten Lora was sitting next to her until she leaned over and, practically right in Claire's face, said, "Why are you being so mean to Tip?"

Claire *really* wished she had Tip Barney alone. He knew something important. She ignored Lora and said,

"Tip, please. An innocent man will die if you don't tell me what you know."

He shook his head back and forth. "You're barking up the wrong tree, girl. I'm sorry about your dad, but there's nothing I can help you with. Nothing."

"Frank could have been killed before the fire even started, and the arson was to cover it up."

"You have an overactive imagination, missy. Look. I'm sorry about your father, really, but there's nothing I can do for you. Frank didn't tell me anything. And it doesn't matter anymore because he's dead."

"It does matter. It matters to my dad. To me." Her voice caught. She'd planned on appealing to his humanity to talk, but the emotion wasn't planned. This whole miserable situation was getting to her.

Her cell phone rang and she grabbed it. It was Phineas. Lora was staring at her with a frown on her face. Claire swiveled in the seat and put her finger in one ear as she answered the phone. "Hey, can I call you back?"

"I think I found something important."

"Okay. Shoot."

"Your friend Jayne came by and we went out to the data warehouse. She's damn brilliant."

"She is. And?"

"Nothing was deleted. When the reports were scanned, blank sheets were scanned in place of the two reports you asked about. So the right log was generated, but unless someone had rechecked the data, they wouldn't have known the reports were blank."

"Damn."

"I thought that would help."

"I need to see those reports, Phin. What about hard copies?"

"We only keep hard copies for three years, then they're preserved at the data warehouse and destroyed."

Shit! "So we don't have them at all. Anywhere."

"If they're not in the court file, I don't know where they would be. Unless the prosecutor kept a copy for some reason. And I'm sure the D.A.'s office has their own archive system."

"Thanks. I'll think on it."

"I do have one more thing, though. I have the name of the head tech who performed the autopsies and filed the reports. The employee number is in the log as part of the file. Reny Willis. He's not here anymore, he went to Contra Costa County in 1994, according to his employee file."

1994. The year of the trial. "When in 1994?"

"His last day here was August 31, 1994."

Her father was sentenced the week before that. The trial had ended two weeks earlier. Coincidence? "Phin, is Jayne still with you? I need to talk to her."

"Here she is."

Jayne got on the phone. "What—"

"Find Reny Willis. Phin has his personnel file. I need to find out exactly where he is, preferably an address. I think he knows exactly why those two coroner's reports are missing."

"I'll do it for you, Claire, but promise me you won't confront him alone."

Who was she supposed to bring? Call up the FBI and ask Agents Bianchi and Donovan to join her? But . . . Bill would do it. Or Dave. She felt bad about throwing him out last night, but at the same time she was still furious that he continued to dig into her personal life when he promised he wouldn't.

"I promise," she said and hung up.

Tip Barney had moved to the opposite side of the bar, serving up drafts to the men at that end. Lora had migrated to that end of the bar as well. Good, the woman was a bit freaky. Since she'd arrived, more people had come in. It was nearing five o'clock. People getting off work. Tip was avoiding her, Claire could tell. What more could she get out of him? She was certain he knew more than he was telling her. She sipped her beer. She'd pushed him hard, appealed to his sense of humanity and justice, and he hadn't budged. Maybe he knew Frank had been murdered and he was scared. He had left Sacramento shortly after the fire, for Los Angeles. A big place. She'd need to go back to the Rogan-Caruso offices and run a more detailed search on Tip Barney, focus on L.A., see if she could find a pattern to anything. Maybe he'd been paid off. No, that didn't fit. He seemed genuinely upset that Frank was dead. Upset and scared.

Tip lived upstairs, and he was working down here in the bar.

Claire drained half her beer, put a five-dollar bill under the glass, and walked out.

Out of the corner of his eye, Frank Lowe watched Claire O'Brien leave the bar. When she was gone, he was still tense.

First the law student, then the Feds, now Tom O'Brien's daughter.

For fifteen years Frank Lowe had led a quiet life off the grid. And now it was over. He should never have come back to Sacramento. But after his dad died, he had nothing left in L.A. And even though his mother thought he was dead, he felt better being here than there. Isleton was perfect. No one should have been able to find him. He'd taken Tip's identity—it had been his dad's idea in the first place—and he thought he could simply run the bar here until he was as old as Sanderson.

But for the first time in fifteen years, he feared his days were numbered. In the single digits.

"Tip? You okay?"

He smiled brightly at Lora. The dim woman was really a sweetheart, but sometimes she was too nosy. Because her father was the chief of police, Frank made sure Lora was well taken care of. He didn't need Henry Lane looking too hard at his past. He might find out that Tip Barney was supposed to be sixty-one years old.

"Just fine, Lora."

"That woman was mean."

"She was just doing her job."

"I don't understand."

"She's a private investigator. I just didn't have the information she wanted."

What he knew would get him killed. If they knew he was still alive, they would burn down this bar with everyone in it. Frank didn't want anyone else getting hurt. It was bad enough that the woman Taverton was having an affair with had been killed, but . . .

Claire O'Brien was that woman's daughter. Guilt washed over Frank. While he didn't know for certain that the husband wasn't guilty of murder, he knew in his gut that Jeffrey Riordan and his partners were responsible for Taverton's death and the fire that killed Buddy, the poor bum whom Frank and Tip had let sleep in the

storeroom on those nights when the temperature dipped
below thirty-two.

It was sheer luck that Frank had been able to climb
out the window and into a tree; then he'd hopped a
fence and gotten out into the neighborhood. He'd
walked the twenty-seven blocks to Tip's small house and
told him what happened.

"It was Riordan's people, I know it."

"Did you see them?"

*"No, but on the news they said D.D.A. Taverton was
killed today. He knew. Somehow, Riordan knew I was
turning state's evidence. I couldn't get to Buddy—he's
dead, I'm certain. I don't want to die, Pop."*

"I'll figure something out."

What Tip decided was to let everyone think Frank
was dead—including Frank's mother. Frank felt bad
about that, but he'd never been close to his mom. Always wrapped up in her own life, she had never really
cared what he did or who he did it with. She had sent
him to live with Aunt Rose, who was ancient.

Which was what put him in this miserable situation
in the first place.

*Aunt Rose had kicked him off her property because
he'd pawned one of her two hundred fifty-seven brooches.
He didn't think she'd miss it—he didn't realize she
counted them every Sunday. She threatened to call the
police if he ever showed up again, until he brought back
the brooch.*

*Frank had no place to go. He didn't want to go home,
and doubted his mother would welcome him. His dad*

was living in L.A., and he'd worn out the welcome at his few friends' houses. He stole money by picking pockets on the K Street Mall to buy back the brooch. Three days later, he went in with the cash, but the brooch was gone. "You said I had thirty days!"

"I didn't think you'd show up for it. Sue me."

He didn't doubt Aunt Rose's threat to call the police. He snuck onto the property at night and hid out in the apartment above her garage. She didn't handle stairs very well anymore, so it was fairly safe. When he was certain she was asleep, he'd walk right into the house—she never locked the door—and nibble on her leftovers, or quietly make a sandwich. She was ninety-one—her hearing was going, but not her mind. He made sure he never took the last of anything. That she'd notice.

It was on one of those midnight kitchen runs that he heard two men enter the house.

They didn't speak. He didn't know who they were, though he got a good look at one of them. He heard a third man pacing on the front porch. Frank was trapped.

Ten minutes later, the two men came downstairs. One man held a sheet of plastic in his hands. They left.

Frank walked upstairs and saw his aunt in her bed. And knew she was dead.

He left and went back to his apartment. It would be dumb to disappear. The police might think he had something to do with his aunt's death. He considered calling the police, but he wasn't supposed to be here. And why would they believe him? Especially since his aunt was leaving her entire property to him. She'd told him that many times before he swiped the brooch. She had a son, but she didn't like him. "I like you more, Frankie." She may have changed her will. But he'd only been on the outs with her for a couple weeks.

The police should be able to figure it out, right? Without him saying anything?

Except when her neighbor came by the next day when Aunt Rose missed her bridge game, her doctor said she'd died in her sleep of a heart attack. She had a bad heart and high blood pressure. There wasn't even an autopsy. Frank still didn't say anything. After all, he didn't know who the men were. He wasn't even sure he could identify them.

But when his aunt's will was read, Frank got nothing. Her property was sold to Waterstone Development, and the money given to the Delta Conservancy. It made no sense. But Frank didn't know then what he learned ten years later when he saw Jeffrey Riordan on television running for Congress.

He was the man with the plastic in his aunt's house.

The only person Frank had told the entire story to was Chase Taverton—not out of the goodness of his heart, but because Frank didn't want to go to prison— and look where that got the prosecutor. And Frank.

Riordan would kill him in a heartbeat if he knew Frank was alive. Frank didn't know who Taverton told, who had connections to Riordan so strong that they would kill to keep the secrets.

When Oliver Maddox had called, Frank told him he knew nothing, but the kid came down anyway. Frank denied everything, but Maddox kept pushing. The kid had been scared. Then he whispered, "I know who you are, Frank. You can save a man from dying for a murder he didn't commit if you just come forward."

Frank continued to deny everything. He thought Maddox had given up. It wasn't until two days ago when his body was brought up from the river that Frank realized he may have gotten the kid killed.

He didn't want anything to happen to Claire O'Brien.

More important, he didn't want to die.

The bar door opened and Frank turned his head to see what drink he needed to pour, based on who was coming in.

He might as well lace his own soda with hemlock. The Feds were back, and Frank knew damn well they wouldn't be able to protect him.

THIRTY-ONE

Claire didn't know exactly what she was looking for, but figured she'd know it when she saw it.

Tip Barney was a tidy bachelor. Rather minimalist with one old, clean sofa; a recliner; a tiny table and two chairs in the kitchenette; and a small desk with an old IBM computer. So old that the monitor was black and white. The only expensive item was a wide-screen television centered to face the worn leather recliner. His small bathroom smelled like Old Spice and the bedroom barely fit a double bed and dresser. His tastes in art were simple as well: scenic rural photographs.

Even his paperwork was filed away neatly in the desk drawers.

She searched the desk and quickly learned that it was all business. No personal papers. Insurance documents, but all business-related. The bedroom had less interesting items in the solitary dresser—socks, boxers, T-shirts. The guy hung up his pants and a couple dress shirts. Tip certainly lived modestly enough. The insurance settlement must not have been that great, or he'd spent it all in L.A.

She felt uneasy, and hot, and a bit sick to her stomach. Served her right drinking half a beer without eating.

What did she want here? What did she expect? A connection to Oliver Maddox? Did she honestly think that Tip Barney had anything to do with Maddox's murder? He didn't seem the killer type, but then again there wasn't really a *type*.

She walked the small apartment twice, found nothing, and turned to leave. Her head hurt and she just wanted to get home. Lack of food, lack of sleep, too much caffeine was catching up to her. Her hand was on the knob when she saw a picture of Tip and an older man. They looked a lot alike. Must be Tip's dad. But something seemed . . . off.

She took the picture off the wall. There was no writing on the back. She used her key to slip off the cardboard backing.

On the back of the photograph was written:

Dad and me, March '06.

Stamped in the lower right corner was: STILLMAN PHOTOGRAPHY, MANHATTAN BEACH, CA.

She put the picture back on the wall and quickly texted Jayne to find out about Stillman Photography and anything about Tip Barney living or working in Manhattan Beach.

Maybe Tip's dad could be gotten to. If Tip had been living near him while in L.A., maybe he said something. It was worth a shot. Hell, Claire was willing to try anything at this point.

She glanced at her watch. Quarter to six. Her dad was surrendering in fifteen minutes. She wouldn't make it to FBI headquarters, but she could make it to the hospital by the time he got there.

She quietly left the apartment and walked down the

back stairs in time to see Mitch Bianchi and Steve Donovan enter the bar.

Mitch approached the bar and flashed his badge, even though they'd been here earlier in the day. He and Steve had discussed how to approach Frank Lowe, and they decided to just bring him in. He'd faked his own death. That wasn't a felony unless he profited from it, but since there had been an outstanding charge against him at the time, he was a fugitive: unlawful flight to avoid prosecution.

Steve walked up to the bar. Frank approached him. "Back so soon?"

Steve clicked a cuff on Frank's wrist before he realized what had happened. He put the other side around his own wrist. "Frank Lowe, you're under arrest. You have—"

"I don't know what you're talking about. My name is Tip Barney. Real name's George, but no one calls me that."

"We were just at your mother's house. Betty has a whole photo album of you and your dad."

Frank paled. "You're making a mistake. You're going to get me killed. Please don't do this!"

"If you talk now, there'll be no reason why anyone would kill you. Spill the beans and you'll be safe."

"You don't know what you're talking about!"

Mitch said, "What was the plea agreement between you and Chase Taverton?"

"I'm not talking."

"Fine." Steve yanked Frank's arm to force him to follow around the end of the bar.

Mitch announced, "Okay, folks, go home."

Lora Lane, the woman they'd spoken to earlier, frowned. "I don't understand. Did you catch him doing something?"

"Ma'am, this isn't your concern," Steve told her.

"But you can't arrest him."

"Ma'am, please leave."

The patrons were leaving, murmuring among themselves. "Lock up, Frank," Steve said.

The door opened, and Mitch was about to tell the customer the bar was closed when he saw Claire standing there.

She was pale, much too pale. She glared at him, hurt and anger in her expression. But Mitch was so relieved to see her—to know that she was okay.

"Did you follow me here?" she asked, one hand on her hip.

"No, we're following up on Oliver Maddox's murder. I had no idea you were here."

She grinned without humor. "You had someone sit on me."

"Didn't last long."

"I'm too smart for you."

"How did you end up here?"

"I'm not telling you anything."

"Claire, we need to talk. About your father and what you've learned about Maddox."

Frank Lowe said, "I didn't kill anyone!"

"No one said you did, Mr. Lowe."

Claire blinked and rubbed her temples. "Lowe?" She turned to him. "You're Frank Lowe?"

"No," he said while both Mitch and Steve said, "Yes."

Claire stared at Lowe. "You can clear my father. You bastard, why did you lie to me?"

"You're going to get me killed! Don't you understand, this is way above you. I'm going to *die*."

"If you don't talk, my father is going to die!"

Mitch watched the exchange, wondering if Frank was going to crack. He was clearly between a rock and a hard place.

"I can't clear your father," said Frank. "I swear, I don't know what happened that day."

"But you know why Chase Taverton was killed."

"I'm not saying a word."

"You're still under arrest," Steve said.

Mitch walked over to Claire. "I will find out the truth. I promise."

She stared at him, arms crossed.

He continued, "Your father called me a few days after the earthquake and tipped me off to where Blackie Goethe's gang was. We took down the gang and your father risked his life to save mine. He told me he was innocent. I didn't believe him, but I owed him. Out of curiosity I looked into his case. Saw some things that made me question whether he was even guilty. I befriended you because I wanted to bring him in safely and knew he'd be in danger if he went into state custody."

He stepped toward her, reaching out and touching her cheek. Claire flinched. Her mouth trembled.

"I never expected to fall in love with you, Claire."

She whispered, "I don't believe anything you say."

"I'm not sorry I met you, but I'm sorry I had to lie. I did it for the right reasons."

"And what right reason did you sleep with me for?"

"I'd do anything to prove to you that I care."

She turned and left.

"Ready?" Steve asked quietly.

"Let's get Lowe to headquarters," said Mitch.

Mitch stared at the door. Claire didn't look herself. More than because he'd hurt her. He wondered if she was sick. She'd rubbed her head like it hurt.

Or maybe it was all because of him.

THIRTY-TWO

Claire's stomach was queasy. Damn Mitch. Why'd he have to say anything to her? It would have been easier if he just acted like a damn FBI agent. Why'd he have to tell her he'd fallen in love with her? Was it another game? Why?

She was going to puke. No, no. She had nothing to throw up. She turned the ignition of Bill's truck and started toward River Road. Just get home. No, the hospital. See her dad.

She couldn't even think straight, Mitch had upset her so much. She slowed to focus on driving. She hadn't even drunk half the beer at the Rabbit Hole. She wasn't drunk or even slightly impaired. But she felt . . . impaired.

Had Frank Lowe drugged her? That didn't make sense. She'd ordered her beer before he knew who she was. Could he have done it without her seeing? Maybe. Maybe when she was talking to Phin and turned away for a minute. But why?

Maybe that's what he'd done to Oliver Maddox. Drugged him at the bar so he crashed into the river and drowned. Again, why?

She focused on the reflective markers in the middle of

the winding road. The lines were blurry. She slowed down. *Stop driving.* Her foot was so heavy. She couldn't move it.

Bump bump bump.

She jerked her head up, eyes wide, turning the wheel to the right. She'd gone over the line. She thought she heard ringing. It was her cell phone.

Stop the car!

She tried to lift her left foot up to push down on the emergency brake. Her foot wouldn't move, like a pile of bricks weighted it down.

She stared at her hands gripping the steering wheel as she swerved again. Weaving. Over, under, around, through. There were six hands. Did she have six hands? Now eight.

She focused on the white lines. Bright. Bright lines. Yellow. Red. Orange. Purple. Sparkling.

Stop!

She was hallucinating. Drugged. She knew it, but her mind couldn't order her body to behave. Her eyes saw things she knew in her head couldn't be there.

Her foot slipped off the gas, but she had no strength to lift it to the brake. But she was slowing down. Good.

So tired.

Mitch was quiet as Steve drove toward Sacramento. Frank Lowe was silent in the back, cuffed to the door. Mitch was turned slightly to watch the prisoner as Steve drove.

Steve said, "Your love life notwithstanding, this is turning out pretty good. O'Brien is turning himself in and we have a major lead in the Maddox homicide." He jerked his head toward Lowe.

"I swear, I didn't know the kid was dead until his body was pulled out of the river."

"But you knew it was Maddox when he came into the bar in January."

Lowe stayed quiet.

Steve said, "Frank, we have enough to arrest you, and you'll have to answer to the Sacramento PD about who really died in that fire fifteen years ago."

"No. As soon as my name gets out, I'll be dead."

"I don't buy it."

"Don't you see? The only person I told was Taverton, and a week later he was dead and someone tried to kill me. I don't know who Taverton told, but it couldn't have been many people. It was someone inside. So I'm not talking."

"You're still wanted on the home invasion robbery from fifteen years ago, plus I'm sure there are a whole host of tax laws you've broken. And identity theft, lying to federal—"

"Stop. Please don't do this." Lowe was scared shitless, and that was fine with Mitch. It just might make him talk.

"Look," Mitch said, feigning disinterest, "talk to my boss, okay? She might be interested in cutting a deal. Or not. I don't know. What do you think, Steve?"

"Elliott's a hard-ass," Steve said. "And it's Friday. She might not even want to talk until Monday morning."

"Right. You can cool your heels in county lockup."

"No." Lowe blanched. "Please don't."

"Steve, don't you think it's interesting that Maddox found out about Waterstone and the Delta Conservancy? The same two companies that Frank's aunt gave all her money to. It must have been important to him if he swallowed a computer flash drive with the information. Might take us longer to put it together, but—"

"I didn't do anything. I didn't *do* anything wrong. I swear to you, please let me go. I'll disappear—"

"You're a suspect in a homicide," Mitch said, hardening his voice.

"I didn't kill the kid! I swear on my dad's grave, I didn't do it, I had nothing to do with it. Do you swear you can protect me?"

Steve and Mitch glanced at each other. "If your information is good, we'll take care of you."

"What's that?" Mitch leaned forward in his seat. "A drunk driver on this road? He's going—wait!" Green Ford 150. That was Bill Kamanski's truck, the one Claire was driving.

"It's Claire," he said.

"Something's wrong." Steve accelerated.

"Hurry." Mitch's heart thudded painfully. He glared at Lowe in the back. "Did you drug her or—"

"I didn't do anything to her! I swear!"

Claire's truck was moving slowly but steadily toward the river.

Mitch knew the second before the front wheel went off the edge that they wouldn't make it in time. He pulled off his holster and kicked off his shoes while Steve sped up until they were right next to where Claire's car had rolled into the river.

Cars sank fast, but this section of the river had a slight slope and the current was weaker on the curve. Still, the truck was front-heavy. Claire's front wheels were in the water. It continued to roll forward as Mitch slid down the ten-foot slope and grabbed the door handle.

Claire was unconscious in the driver's seat, her head

forward on the steering wheel. Mitch had no time to think about what had happened to her; he pulled at the handle.

Locked.

"Claire!" he shouted and pounded on the window. She didn't move. The front of the truck was fully submerged up to the tires, tilting at a steep angle, and the car kept sliding.

Mitch shouted at Steve, "I need the spring punch from the emergency kit. Now!" Steve turned to the car.

"Claire, come on!" He pounded on the window. She rolled her head back, her eyes fluttered open, then closed. Her mouth was moving, but he couldn't hear what she was saying. He kept pounding the window and pulling on the door as the truck continued its descent. His feet sank into the silt, he was wet to his knees. The only thing slowing the Ford was shrubbery.

Steve came as fast as he dared down the slope and handed Mitch the spring punch. Without hesitation, Mitch snapped it on the window, putting a hole in the safety glass. He tapped it again, again, pulling away the shattered glass in chunks. The water reached his waist.

The truck broke free of the bushes and sank faster, the angle increasing to sixty degrees. Mitch feared the suction would pull him down or make him lose his balance. He reached inside the door and pulled on the handle.

The water rushed in to fill the car as Mitch reached over and clicked Claire's seat belt.

Claire was awake, her eyes wide and unfocused. She was talking but it made no sense.

"Got her!" Mitch shouted, grabbing Claire by the underarms and pulling her from the truck. Instead of fighting the car as it fully submerged, which could have drowned them both, Mitch took a deep breath and they both went underwater for a few seconds. It felt like minutes. Claire started kicking frantically, and for a moment Mitch feared she was fighting him, then he realized she was trying to get to the surface in a panic.

Two strong strokes and he pulled himself and Claire to the surface of the river.

The truck settled on the river's bottom.

Mitch pulled Claire out of the water and he and Steve carried her to the road. Mitch laid her down, checked her all over. Her eyes were open, terrified, her hands like claws as if defending herself from a dragon. She was shivering uncontrollably.

"Get the med kit and a blanket," Mitch told Steve. "Claire, it's okay. It's me. Mitch. I'm here. You're okay. You're safe."

"What's wrong with her?" Steve asked as Mitch wrapped Claire in the wool blanket.

Mitch checked her eyes. Her pupils were dilated and unresponsive. "Some sort of drug."

"Does she use drugs?"

"No. I've never seen any. Lowe!"

Mitch jumped up and took three strides to the car. He flung open the rear door, unlocked Lowe's cuff from the handle, and pulled him out. Grabbing his shirt with his fists, Mitch jerked Lowe and said, "What did you give her? If anything happens to her, I'll kill you, Lowe. What did you do to her back at the bar?"

"I didn't do anything, I swear to God, I didn't. I don't know what happened. She was asking me questions about me—asking Tip questions about me, and I played Tip, told her Frank was dead, and I didn't know anything about a plea agreement. I swear, I didn't hurt her. I wouldn't."

Mitch pushed him against the car. "If you're lying to me—"

"I'm not. I swear I'm not."

Mitch believed him.

"Mitch," Steve said, carrying Claire over to the car, "lock him back up. Let's get her to a hospital and send ERT back down here to inspect the bar. If he drugged her, something will be there."

"I didn't do anything," Lowe said. "She came in. She only drank half her beer."

"What time?" Mitch asked as he locked Lowe back into the rear seat."

"About four. She was there an hour maybe. Then she left. I thought she was gone. Thirty minutes passed, you came in, then she came back."

"We can search the bar for drugs, talk to the customers," Steve said. "Get in, I'll slide her over to you."

Mitch went around to the passenger side and got in. Steve gently laid Claire down, and Mitch pulled her into his lap. Steve got in and called in the accident.

Mitch couldn't help but think that only a mile south, Oliver Maddox had drowned in this same river.

Mitch resisted the urge to snap at Steve for moving too slowly along the dangerous delta road. Claire was shaking uncontrollably in his arms. She held on to him as if she were drowning, her face buried in his chest. She was having a hard time catching her breath, and her skin was cold and clammy.

"Turn on the heater," he told Steve. "She's freezing."

Steve did, but Claire still shivered. "Meg said to take her directly to Sutter Memorial, where O'Brien is."

"He's already there? Isn't it early?"

"O'Brien is going in for emergency surgery in less than an hour. He surrendered early when he found blood in his urine. Meg's at the hospital talking to him right now with the D.A. and O'Brien's attorney to get a statement regarding the prison break and his activities since."

Meg could be a hard-ass, Mitch knew, but she had a deep, quiet compassionate streak.

Steve spoke to the sheriff, told him about the truck and asked him to send a deputy to secure the Rabbit Hole, that they'd be sending an FBI forensic unit to process the evidence because this was now a federal crime. When he hung up, Mitch asked, "What federal crime?"

"Tax evasion," Steve said, glancing in the rearview mirror at Lowe.

Mitch doubted Claire even knew it was him she was clinging to. But he would take it. What could he do to make it up to Claire, lying to her about who and what he was? Claire wasn't a forgiving soul, but even if she were what he'd done was unforgivable.

"How long?" he asked Steve when they finally reached the main highway.

"Twenty minutes."

Mitch kissed her forehead. She was conscious but unfocused; shaking and confused. "Stay with me, Claire."

Forgive me, Claire. Stay with me.

Lora was alone in the house. Her mother was still at the mall, had been gone most of the day, and her father had been called to The Rabbit Hole. He'd ordered her to stay inside. Daddy had been furious and worried—she'd befriended Tip, and now Tip had been arrested.

Lora didn't know what exactly was going on and she sat in her bedroom writing everything in her diary.

The men said his name wasn't Tip, but Frank Lowe. They can't be right. Agent Smith and Agent Jones called him Tip. Wouldn't they all know the same thing? I don't understand what's going on. I called Agent Jones as soon as I left the bar and told him everything. Maybe the men weren't real FBI agents. Maybe they kidnapped Tip. They knew the terrorist girl who came in.

Agent Jones was very mad, and I wish I didn't call him. I wish I'd just kept the information to myself, because I don't want to make him mad. He's so pretty and nice.

The doorbell rang. Lora went down to answer it, certain it was someone else coming by to find out what had happened. Three neighbors had already called on them to ask what was going on at the Rabbit Hole.

It was Agent Smith and Agent Jones.

"Is your father here?"

"No, he's at the Rabbit Hole if you need to talk to him."

They stepped in and closed the door. She noticed they were wearing gloves, which seemed strange because it was so warm outside. Agent Jones wore a nice suit and his shoes were polished. He was so pretty, Lora could stare at him all day.

"I'm sorry," she said. "I called you as soon as I could."

"You did the right thing."

She smiled and relaxed. He wasn't mad at her anymore. Agent Smith walked around the living room, but she focused on Agent Jones.

"What happened to Tip?"

"He was arrested. He'll be dealt with appropriately."

"So you proved he was a terrorist? Did I help?"

"Unfortunately, not as much as I had hoped."

She frowned.

"You did write down everything, right?"

"Yes, of course."

"Will you show me? Please?"

"You need it for evidence, right?"

"Exactly."

She smiled and started up the stairs. Agent Jones followed. "Will you need me to testify? I can do that, you know. I have a very good memory."

"I know you do. I'm sure I'll be in contact once we have what we need."

"Oh, good! Isn't this exciting? Maybe not for you, you do it all the time, but for me. I've never had something so exciting happen."

She turned into her bedroom and went to the closet. She pulled out the shoebox with her most current notes and handed it to him.

"Is this all?"

"No, just the last two months."

She opened her closet and pointed to all her pretty shoeboxes. "I labeled them in code, so no one would figure it out. Did I do good?"

Jeffrey Riordan, aka Agent Jones, stared at the shelves of shoeboxes in the retard's closet. Fuck. They couldn't haul all this crap out of here! But they couldn't leave it, either.

"Jones!" Harper called from downstairs. "It's getting late."

"We need it all, Ms. Lane."

"Oh. I see." She bit her lip and looked at the boxes. "I guess twenty-six boxes is a lot, isn't it?"

"You've been very diligent." Too fucking diligent. "Would you please pull them down for me? I'll ask my partner to help transport them to the car."

"Oh, yes, certainly." She began pulling them off the shelves. Slowly.

"We have another appointment, we need to rush a bit."

"I'm sorry. Of course." She was flustered, but she pulled them down faster.

Jeffrey went downstairs. "There's twenty-six boxes of crap," he whispered to Harper.

"We need to get out of here."

"You get the boxes to the car, I'll take care of her."

Ten minutes later, the boxes detailing every night Lora Lane had spent at the Rabbit Hole were stored in Riordan's trunk. Including, Jeffrey was certain, her "orders" to poison Oliver Maddox, who'd been far too close to figuring out what had happened to Rose Van Alden's estate. And that would have led to even more secrets that Jeffrey couldn't have come out—ever—especially in an election year.

"Thank you, Ms. Lane," he said.

"Will you be by again?"

"Very likely. I like you a lot." He leaned forward as if to kiss her.

She blushed, but her eyes were bright and excited and focused on his eyes. Better his eyes than his hand that now held a knife.

He placed one hand on her shoulder, dipped his head, then shoved his fist forward, the knife cutting through her. He'd never stabbed anyone before, and it felt strange and exhilarating. Her eyes were innocent and surprised. She hadn't registered what happened. She gasped.

He pulled the knife up until it hit bone, then pulled it out and she dropped to the floor, mouth open, eyes wide and fading.

He stared at her. The incision was deep and long. There was a lot of blood. Shit, all over his hands and his favorite jacket.

"Let's go before anyone comes," Harper said. "We'll burn your clothes with the shoeboxes."

He turned and followed Harper out.

"Our guy had better take care of Lowe before he opens his mouth," Riordan told Harper. "Why the fuck didn't we know Lowe changed his identity?"

"Hamilton was the only one who ever saw Lowe in person, and he never came down here."

"We should have followed up."

"We had the girl watching Barney as soon as he returned from L.A."

"You mean Lowe," Jeffrey snapped.

"After all these years, he didn't say anything—and I don't think he ever would have. He didn't say anything to Maddox, and Lora said he didn't say anything to Claire O'Brien. It was the Feds who learned—"

"Exactly! The Feds learned, and now we're screwed."

"Lowe's too scared to talk. He'll be dead first."

"He'd better be. I'm sick and tired of this crap. I have an election to win, I can't go clean up after everyone.

Where the fuck is Collier? I don't like that he's running around. I never trusted him."

"We're looking for him, but he's gone to ground. He has everything to lose. He won't talk."

"That's bullshit. He'll sing like a canary if they cut him a deal. We need to find him before the Feds. If he hadn't panicked and left town, the Feds wouldn't be so damn suspicious."

Everything would work out, Jeffrey told himself. Problems like Lora Lane and Frank Lowe and Claire O'Brien were bumps in the road. They happened every once in a while. He would control this situation, win the primary, and everything would be just fine.

THIRTY-THREE

Mitch rushed through the emergency room doors carrying Claire. Steve was driving Lowe to FBI headquarters in order to print and interview him. Lowe wanted a written guarantee of protection before he talked, and Meg was already working on it.

Mitch went to the nurse's station and said, "I have an emergency. This woman was drugged and crashed into the river."

"Are you her significant other?"

He couldn't reach his badge. "Special Agent Mitch Bianchi, Federal Bureau of Investigation. My badge is in my wallet."

"I'll take your word for it." The triage nurse walked around to Mitch, bringing a gurney with her. "Put her down here. I have some paperwork for you to fill out."

"Can't you just see what's wrong with her?"

"We will, but I still need to know her name, any medications she's allergic to, health insurance."

"She lost her identification in the river," he said. "Her name is Claire O'Brien. She works for Rogan-Caruso Protective Services, I'm sure she has insurance through them. She's twenty-nine. I don't know if she's allergic to anything."

"What kind of drugs was she taking?" the nurse asked, shining a light into Claire's pupils.

"Stop that!" Claire exclaimed and batted at the nurse's arms.

The nurse said, "I'll need to restrain her. If she's on PCP or—"

"She wasn't taking any drugs," Mitch said, taking Claire's hands in his. "Claire, honey, hold tight. This nurse wants to help find out what's wrong."

"Don't leave," Claire said, her eyes frantic. She looked like a trapped and frightened animal, ready to bolt.

"I'm not going anywhere. I promise." He said to the nurse, "Someone drugged her. I don't know what with—it was probably something slipped into a drink."

"Has she been drinking?"

"Half a beer, a couple hours ago." He thought back to their argument at the Rabbit Hole. "She was rubbing her head as if she had a headache, but I don't know if that means anything. She passed out while driving, has been alternately lethargic and intensely paranoid. Her muscles were stiff when we first brought her out of the river, her hands like this." He made his own hands into claws. "And she's been shaking the entire time."

While Mitch talked, the nurse examined Claire's vitals and eyes, then put an oxygen mask on. Claire had a bump the size of an egg on the front of her head, likely from when she hit the steering wheel, and small scrapes and cuts from Mitch pulling her from the car and hauling her up the slope. He took her hand. Claire was not a woman he ever expected to see in a hospital looking disorientated. Claire had far too much life and energy in her.

"You'll have to leave us—" the nurse began.

Claire shook her head back and forth and tried to talk, but the oxygen mask prevented it. She squeezed Mitch's hand, her eyes fearful and wild.

"Do a tox screen for psychotics, LSD, or Rohypnol. I think they're detectable in the urine," Mitch said.

The nurse eyed him suspiciously. "Do you know something more?"

"I've been in either the military or law enforcement for nearly twenty years. I've seen this kind of reaction before."

"I'll add the tests. I need to undress her to finish the preliminary exam and then send her to X-ray to make sure she doesn't have any internal injuries. If you could please step out—"

Claire moaned, "Noooo."

"Let me stay, please," Mitch said. "She had a terrifying experience in the river." So had he. Unwillingly, a picture of Claire, dead and bloated, trapped underwater in the truck, hit him and he became queasy. She'd been drugged, unable to fight back, unable to do anything but die . . . and she would have if they'd been five minutes later. The truck would have sunk and he would have passed by, unaware that Claire was drowning . . .

He pushed the image from his mind, stared at Claire's scared blue eyes, squeezing her hands. They were so cold. But she was alive.

The nurse handed him a stack of papers. "Fill this out while I get her ready for the doctor. You can do it in triage." She wheeled the gurney around a corner, then pulled a curtain around Claire.

"No wonder you're so cold, sweetie," the nurse said. "Your clothes are soaking wet."

Mitch scrawled the information he knew—Claire's name, address, birth date, employer . . . he skipped what he didn't know.

"There's a patient here about to go to surgery. It's her dad. They need to talk before he goes on the table."

"I'll see what I can do, but I can't promise anything," she said. "Where is he?"

"I don't know, wherever they prep someone for surgery."

"Name."

"Thomas O'Brien."

"I'll check."

The nurse had put Claire in a gown, and wrapped her in blankets from a warmer. "I'll be back."

Mitch sat next to Claire. "Do you remember what happened before you went into the river?"

"River?" she mumbled through the oxygen mask. She squinted, then pulled the mask off.

"You should—"

"I can breathe." She was still shaking, her skin ghostly. "Everything is too bright." She kept her eyes squeezed shut.

"You're in the hospital."

"I know." She took a deep breath. "It was strange. I knew something was wrong, but I couldn't do anything about it. I didn't even panic. It was like I was out of my body. That sounds so stupid."

"Did anyone have the opportunity to drug your drink?"

"Drink? I wasn't drinking. I didn't even have half the beer—" She stared at him and it was as if her memory returned and she remembered who he was and that he'd lied to her. Her entire expression changed, from worried and confused to guarded.

She averted her eyes. "I want to go home."

"The nurse is getting the doctor. We need to find out who drugged you and why. Why'd you go to Isleton in the first place?"

"You think I'm going to tell you?"

"We're on the same side."

"Are we?"

Sitting next to her, Mitch spoke softly. "I told you my father was a prosecutor. I had tried to please him, never did. And then—" Mitch took a deep breath. "When he died, I went home to help my mom clear out his office. I went through his private files. Found information that he knowingly prosecuted three innocent men." He remembered that weekend. Everything he'd believed about his father, a man of honor and truth and justice, vanished. He'd been trying his entire life to understand why he and his father were constantly at odds, feeling guilty that he didn't want to follow his dad into law. The arguments they used to have about everything!

"I got two of the men out of prison by turning over the information to the new D.A. But one of the men was already dead. He'd spent ten years in Corcoran for a murder he didn't commit, because, according to my father, 'I knew he was guilty of other felonies, but we didn't have the evidence.'" All the lectures about the Constitution and the rights of individuals and government, all destroyed after Mitch read that.

"I think your father is innocent. I don't know how, but everything doesn't add up. I think you have more information than we do. Why'd you go to Isleton today?"

"I was trying to find out what got Frank Lowe and

Taverton killed. I thought that would lead to their killer. Did you talk to Professor Collier?"

"We have agents working all airports, monitoring his passport and credit cards. We'll find him."

"Unless he's dead. I found out something else about Collier. He worked for the same law firm that represented my father fifteen years ago. Then, while doing pro bono work for the Western Innocence Project, he reviewed the case files and determined that the Project shouldn't get involved."

"That sounds like a conflict of interest."

"Not legally, but ethically, yes. Thing is, Randolph Sizemore didn't believe me at first. He said Collier would have recused himself."

Claire rubbed her forehead, closing her eyes. "Oh, God, my head hurts."

"I'll get the nurse—"

"I'll be okay."

She still looked like death warmed over, her hair damp around her face, but she was no longer shaking.

"I talked to the cop who arrested Lowe back then," Claire said. "I planned on talking to the judge who arraigned him, because Abrahamson thought he'd be most likely to have been privy to a plea agreement with the D.A.'s office. But the biggest puzzle so far is the missing coroner's reports."

"What missing coroner's reports?"

"Taverton and my mom. They're gone. No hard copies, no electronic copies. They were replaced by blank pages. And the tech who headed up the autopsy left right after the trial for another jurisdiction. I have a friend at Rogan-Caruso tracking him down."

"He's not going to confront him—"

"No. *She* isn't a PI or a cop. She's going to call me, and then—"

"You're not—"

Claire interrupted. "I'm giving you this information because I know my father's innocent, and if you're actually telling me the truth, and you also believe he's innocent, then you can help prove it. But don't tell me what I can or can't do, and don't pretend that you care."

His chest tightened. "Claire, you need to listen to me. Believe me. Befriending you started out as a job, but it became more than that. You know it. The way I feel—"

"I don't care how you feel, Mitch. You lied to me. I don't love *you*. I loved who I thought you were."

The nurse came in with a doctor. "Agent Bianchi, you'll have to leave for a while," the doctor said. "I need to examine my patient."

"I'm not staying here all night," Claire stated emphatically.

"Let's see what we have here before we decide that."

"You can't keep me against my will," she said. "I'm feeling much better."

Mitch reluctantly left. He leaned against the corridor wall and rubbed his eyes.

"Well, that was interesting," a familiar female voice said only feet away from him.

He looked at Meg. It was rare for him to see her like this, silky blond hair hanging loose down her back, devoid of makeup, looking young and beautiful and like the woman he'd fallen in love with all those years ago.

"You heard."

"Oh boy, I heard."

Mitch didn't even try to explain. "Can you fire me tomorrow? I'm really beat tonight."

"I'll take it under advisement. It's hard to fire someone whose instincts are dead-on ninety-nine percent of the time. Still, even you surprised me this time. Unless . . ."

"Just say it." He really was tired. Physically and emotionally. He felt like he could sleep for a week.

"You really did fall for her."

Mitch didn't answer. What could he say? He wasn't going to talk to his ex-wife about the woman he'd fallen in love with.

"Where's O'Brien?"

"Getting prepped for surgery. As soon as the doctor clears Claire, I'm bringing her up to see him."

"Did he say anything?"

"Pretty much everything you told me. He also filled us in on what the fugitives were doing after the earthquake, how they evaded authorities. He could teach a master's class on stupid law enforcement stunts, particularly in the twenty-four hours after the disaster."

"What do you think?"

"About?"

"His innocence."

"I don't think anything right now. Matt's trying to figure out what Taverton had been working on. He's on his way to meet Steve at headquarters to interview Frank Lowe. You think he drugged Claire?"

"He denied it. I honestly don't know. He sounded sincere, and he's not hiding the fact that he knows exactly why Taverton was killed. He just refuses to talk about it until he has something from us in writing."

"Why don't you head to headquarters and sit in?"

Mitch glanced at Claire's closed door. "What about a guard on Claire? Someone tried to kill her tonight."

"I'll call someone in."

"Until then—Steve and Matt are perfectly capable of handling Lowe."

The doctor opened the door. "I'm running tests to confirm, but I think I know what Ms. O'Brien was drugged with. Rohypnol."

Steve realized he had a tail as soon as he exited the Capital City Freeway at Auburn. He was less than two miles from headquarters.

"What's wrong?" Lowe asked from the back.

"Sit tight."

Steve floored the gas as he merged onto the bypass exit ramp, but it was too late. The tail swerved into the breakdown lane and drew parallel with them.

"Down!" Steve yelled at the same time as he saw the gun in the driver's hand.

The killer didn't hesitate, fired three shots into the back of Steve's car. Heart racing, Steve slammed on the brakes while turning the wheel. The killer fired at him through the windshield.

Steve ducked before the blast, but a bullet hit him in the upper shoulder. He overcompensated and went into a tailspin, stalling the car on the opposite side of the road.

"Frank!"

There was no answer from the backseat. Steve spared a glance in the rearview mirror. There was a lot of blood against the rear passenger side window.

"Shit, shit, shit!"

The killer did a 180 at the T-intersection and passed Steve as he escaped back onto the freeway.

Steve leapt from the car, gun out, blood pouring from his wound. Traffic had stopped on the major thoroughfare, and a scream pierced the air. From this angle, he couldn't see which of three possible directions the killer went.

The entire hit took seventy seconds.

Steve could smell gas leaking from his car. He crawled over to the door, opened it. Frank Lowe fell out, blood pouring from his chest and a head wound. Steve unlocked the handcuffs, pulled him away from the car. He stripped off Frank's shirt, assessed the damage. Two holes, one next to the other, in Frank's upper chest. The bullet to his head had taken off one ear and a chunk of his scalp.

"Come on, Frank!"

Frank was breathing too rapidly, his pulse racing. Steve applied pressure to the wounds, but blood seeped through his fingers. Frank was trying to talk, but couldn't. Then his body convulsed and he was gone.

Steve stared at the dead witness. *No, no, no!*

A car skidded behind his. Steve held his gun on the driver.

It was Matt Elliott, the county's district attorney.

"Donovan!" Elliott ran to the bloody scene and felt for Frank's pulse. His lips tightened, and he turned to Steve. "You need to lie down."

"He came out of nowhere."

"You've been shot."

"He's dead."

"Did you see the shooter?"

Steve ran through those seconds. "He wore a mask. Ski mask in the middle of May. Late-model Ford Tempo. Black. 5THH. I didn't catch the numbers. There was an 8, but I don't know in which spot."

"That's good. We'll find the car. Lie down."

Matt forced Steve to the pavement and applied pressure on his shoulder wound. Steve was fading. The last thing he heard was the D.A. calling for an ambulance and backup.

The last thing he thought was *I fucked up big time. I got a witness killed.*

THIRTY-FOUR

Tom looked at Nelia. "Is she coming?"

"She said she would be here."

He needed to see Claire. He might die tonight, and he wanted to see his little girl one more time.

"Nelia?"

"I'm right here."

"I love you."

"I know. I love you too, Tom. You're going to be fine."

"I don't know."

He'd been in more pain than he'd told her. He hadn't wanted her to worry, but this morning he couldn't walk. His right leg was nearly paralyzed. He could *feel* everything, but he couldn't move it. She'd been indignant that the FBI had interviewed him while he was being poked and prodded and subjected to X-rays and a multitude of tests. But Tom didn't mind. They were listening to him. Really *listening,* and that meant everything. Someone cared about the truth.

The doctor said the bullet had been lodged in muscle near the spine. It had slowly moved over the past few months until it impinged on the nerves to his right leg. If he didn't have surgery immediately, he'd be partially paralyzed, and in the coming weeks he'd be dead since, as the bullet shifted, it had moved precariously close to his liver.

"Tom."

He turned to Nelia. She stared down at him with love and compassion and worry.

"They believed you," she said.

A weight lifted off his chest. "You think so?" he whispered.

She nodded, ran a hand over his forehead as if he were a child. "They know you're innocent. Be strong in there. I need you."

He clasped her hand. "I love you. If—if it doesn't work, tell Claire I've never blamed her for any of this, that I love her."

Nelia's voice cracked. "I will."

"Mr. O'Brien?" The doctor came in. "We're ready."

"Five more minutes?" he asked.

"I'm afraid not."

"I'll be here when you're done," Nelia said.

The nurse injected something into his IV, shifted the bed he was on, and started rolling it out of the room, down the hall . . .

"Wait!"

That sounded like Agent Elliott, whom he'd spoken to for more than an hour earlier.

The gurney stopped. A moment later, Tom heard, "Daddy."

Claire.

Tom was fading as the drugs began to do their work.

"Daddy, oh God."

"Claire. I'm. Okay." He reached up, though the lights in the hall were beginning to fade.

Someone grabbed his hand. He felt moisture. Tears.

"Claire Beth, don't cry."

"I love you, Daddy. I'm sorry. I love you."

He tried to speak but couldn't. The light faded.

Claire watched the medical staff wheel her father down the hall and into surgery. "What happened? Why is this an emergency? Is he going to be okay?"

Nelia spoke. "The bullet shifted. He woke up and couldn't walk this morning. It was lodged in the muscle near the spinal cord and has disrupted the nerves. I don't know the medical jargon, but the more it shifts the more dangerous it becomes. There's a fifty-fifty chance he'll be partially paralyzed, even after the bullet is removed." Nelia looked both unsure of the situation and worried.

"You care about him?" Claire asked, tears in her eyes.

"I love him."

Claire reached out and hugged Nelia. The woman wrapped her arms tight around her. "He's going to be okay," Claire said, as much for herself as for Nelia.

"Hello?" From behind Claire, Agent Elliott, Claire's babysitter, spoke into her cell phone. Claire pulled apart from Nelia, both of them staring at the closed surgery doors.

Nelia asked Claire, "What happened to you?" She gestured to the hospital gowns Claire wore—one backward so she didn't expose her ass for all to see.

"Long story. But I'm okay. Just tired." The doctor had given her a shot to help counteract the effects of Rohypnol, even though the tests hadn't come back yet. All Claire wanted to do was go home and sleep the rest of the night in her own bed, but she now had this FBI agent babysitting her.

"Where?" Agent Elliott sounded angry. Claire turned and watched her. Meg's jaw was tight and she stared at the wall. "Mercy? Who's with him? . . . Okay. Good. And Lowe?" She closed her eyes and rested her fist against the wall. "Right. I'll call Grant. I want Lowe's business and residence gone over with a fine-tooth comb." Agent Elliott straightened, all business again. "Talk to everyone who even stepped through that bar. And—really? Get him on a plane ASAP. Protective custody or whatever the U.S. Attorney's office thinks we can do. Arrest him if we can. He might be the only one who knows what's going on."

"What happened?" Claire asked when Meg Elliott shut her phone.

Expression hard, she said, "Frank Lowe was killed twenty minutes ago. One of my agents was shot and is in critical condition at Mercy."

Claire involuntarily sucked in her breath. "Mitch?" she whispered.

"Steve Donovan. He's going into surgery. But the professor you scared away yesterday? We just intercepted him outside La Guardia Airport in New York. We're transporting him back. He'll be here in the morning. And that information stays here, got it? I don't want it leaking out that we have a witness in custody."

"Witness to what?"

Meg said, "Mitch thinks that Collier is the last person—now that Lowe's dead—who knows exactly what happened fifteen years ago. I want him alive."

THIRTY-FIVE

Claire hadn't realized she'd fallen asleep until urgent voices in the hall woke her. She opened her heavy eyes when the door *whooshed* open.

A federal agent stepped in. She didn't recognize him, but he had his badge and ID clipped to his belt.

"Ms. O'Brien, I'm Special Agent Cliff Warren. I'll be stationed outside your door clearing guests until you're discharged."

"That's not necessary—"

"Supervisory Special Agent Elliott thinks otherwise," he said.

Elliott. Right. The blonde. Claire's memory was fuzzy. "What time is it?"

He glanced at his watch. "Oh two hundred hours."

It was after midnight. She didn't want to be here all night!

She swung her legs over the bed. "I need my clothes."

"You're not supposed to leave until the doctor okays it, then I'll take you home."

"Then call the doctor. I want to leave now." She felt like shit, her head pounded, but she was thinking clearly. She couldn't remember exactly what had happened, though thoughts and images popped in and out of her mind. The river. Mitch. Nelia.

Daddy.

Agent Warren was almost out the door. "Wait," she said. "My dad."

"He's in surgery."

"How long has it been?"

Warren checked his notepad. "Meg said he went in at about twenty hundred hours last night."

"Six hours ago? Is that normal? Is something wrong?"

"I'll call for the nurse. I can't leave your door. Sit tight, I'll get someone to answer your questions."

When he left, Claire rose and paced the room. Her body felt beat up and bruised. The more she moved, the better she felt. She did some stretches, felt dizzy, and sat down on the edge of her bed until it passed.

Steve Donovan had been shot. Claire hadn't liked him, mostly because he'd hounded her about her father, but she didn't want him dead. And Frank Lowe— dammit. Wouldn't the fact that someone had killed Frank Lowe at least give credence to her father's claim of innocence?

Mitch believes him.

Claire wished that Mitch hadn't told her about his own father, or why he'd lied to her. She particularly didn't want to hear about how Mitch thought her father was innocent. How would she know if he lied to her again?

Agent Meg Elliott came into her room. "Cliff told me you were up. How are you feeling?"

"I want to go home."

"I know. As soon as the doctor clears you, Cliff will

take you home and stay with you until we figure out what's going on."

The agent was distracted and kept looking at her cell phone and typing messages to someone.

Claire asked, "How's my father?"

Meg looked up with sympathy. "He's still in surgery. So far, he's holding his own."

"I found out earlier that the coroner's reports are missing. From fifteen years ago. I have a friend at the morgue who tracked down the pathologist who worked on the bodies. He left right after sentencing, and he has to have been the one to mess with the records. I know who he is, and—"

Meg held up a finger, typed another message, then said, "You're going to have to leave this investigation to us, Ms. O'Brien."

"I'm sorry, but you don't care as much as I do about what happens to my father! With Frank Lowe dead, this might be the only way to prove someone else killed my mother. I have to follow up!"

"Someone tried to kill you tonight. Doesn't that mean something to you?"

"Someone tried to kill Steve Donovan tonight. Do you think he'd just give up if he were physically able to investigate?"

"He's a trained federal agent."

"I'm a trained private investigator."

"Who was interfering with a federal investigation."

"It's not a federal investigation, at least it wasn't *officially* a federal investigation. I have to do something, Agent Elliott. I have to find those reports—or can't you send someone?"

"I have no one to spare right now. We'll get to it,

Claire, but it's not our first priority. Finding who shot Steve is my number one concern."

"What about my dad? He's facing death."

"I'm not going to let him out of our custody until we know exactly what's been going on these last couple days."

"A lot of good your custody did for Frank Lowe!"

Meg tightened her lips. Claire had crossed a line. "You are not to interfere with my investigation, or I'll bring you into custody. Do we have an understanding?"

The door opened while Meg was speaking. Claire stared when J.T. Caruso walked in.

J.T. Caruso was one of the three principals who ran Rogan-Caruso Protective Services. Tall, dark, and dangerous in every sense of the word. Claire had only seen him a few times in the office. He worked in the field, usually outside the country. His specialty was rescuing rich kidnap victims from Mexico and other countries south of the border.

"Mr. Caruso," Claire said, straightening.

"How are you, Claire?"

"I'm fine."

Meg extended her hand. "J.T. Always a surprise."

J.T. gave a half smile to Meg, took her hand in both of his. "Megan Elliott. It's been awhile. If the Bureau has to be involved, I'm glad at least you're on it. Of course, you weren't serious about taking one of my employees into custody."

"If she crosses the line, damn straight I am."

J.T. raised an eyebrow. "What is the problem?"

Claire spoke. "We've tracked down the pathologist who deleted the coroner's reports on my mother and

Chase Taverton. There has to be something odd in the reports if someone went to all the trouble to make them disappear."

"Jayne told me about Mr. Willis." J.T. leaned against the wall. "Megan. Allow me to follow up on the pathologist."

"Dammit, J.T., your ways are not the Bureau's ways."

"I'm not a thug."

"You forget I've known you a long time."

"I forget nothing, Megan."

Claire would have been more interested in her boss's past if she wasn't so worried about what had gone on while she was drugged and sleeping. "Thank you," she said. "I'll be ready to go first thing in the morning—"

J.T. turned to her. "You're on leave."

Claire's stomach fell. She felt ill. She was going to lose her job. *It's okay,* she told herself. If anything she'd done in the last three days had helped her dad, then it was worth it.

J.T. turned to Meg. "I heard about Donovan. What else happened? Is the homicide in Isleton related to this?"

Meg shook her head. "I'm always shocked at how you seem to know confidential information as if it's idle party chatter."

"What?" Claire said. "What homicide?"

"The police chief's daughter was stabbed in her living room. No witnesses, nothing to indicate a struggle, but there were some odd findings. Her closet shelves were completely empty, for one. However, our evidence response team found drugs hidden in her bathroom. They couldn't identify them on-site, so they've been sent to the lab for priority testing."

"Since when do the Feds have jurisdiction over a local homicide?" J.T. asked.

"Since it's connected to this case. Do you realize that there've been no homicides in Isleton—aside from the possibility of Oliver Maddox—in more than a decade? Then tonight Ms. Lane was in the same bar where Frank Lowe most likely drugged Claire, Lowe was killed, and now Ms. Lane? It's connected somehow, and while the sheriff has technical jurisdiction, one of my men was shot and that makes this my case."

"I am sorry about Donovan."

"I know."

"Lane?" Claire asked. There were only two women in the bar when she was there, an older woman and Lora. "Lora?"

Meg whipped around. "You know her?"

"She sat right next to me at the bar. She told me I was being mean to Tip. Frank Lowe," Claire corrected. Why would anyone kill the woman? "When did this happen?"

"Between seven and nine p.m. tonight. Her mother was in Sacramento, and her father had secured the Rabbit Hole and was waiting for our forensic team to arrive. But the body wasn't discovered until after midnight when her father came home." Meg glanced at her phone, typed a message, and said, "I really have to go. We have a man on Claire, but if you want to take over you're welcome to."

J.T. said, "Warren? He's fine. I'll deliver the pathologist to you before noon. If you need my services, don't hesitate to call."

Meg just shook her head and walked out.

Claire said, "I'm sorry, Mr. Caruso."

J.T. sat on the end of her bed and said, "It's always been J.T. Let's not get too formal."

"I know I broke protocol, but—"

He put his hand up and said, "Stop. I know exactly what you did and why. You don't have to justify your actions. What you have to explain is why you didn't come to me or Henry for help from the beginning."

She frowned. "I don't understand. I was helping a fugitive."

"You asked Jayne for help."

"I—" What could she say?

"She's your friend."

Claire nodded.

"Let me make one thing perfectly clear, Claire. As an investigator for Rogan-Caruso, you need to understand that we are a family. I expect—I *demand*—to be asked for assistance, even in a personal matter such as yours."

"I was walking a fine line, J.T. I didn't want the FBI to have a reason to go after Rogan-Caruso."

J.T. threw back his head and laughed. Claire didn't understand the joke, and she tensed, angry, hating feeling like an idiot.

"Claire, the Bureau and I go way back. They're not going to interfere with my business. You are my business. You're one of mine. You should have told me your theory from the beginning. I could have given you resources and assistance, and had someone watching your back."

"Yes, sir."

"I want you to take time—not as a punishment. You need to reconnect with your father. Recuperate. Just a couple days. I will keep you informed. But if you find out anything—anything—you call me." He handed her a thick ivory business card with JTC and a toll-free number printed in bold black type. "I will get the message."

"Thank you."

J.T. stood. "You're one of my best investigators. I would have pulled you into far more interesting and challenging assignments long ago, except for one thing."

She hesitated, then couldn't help but ask, "What?"

"You were too rigid. Everything you did was because you were on the side of right, and your opponent was wrong. Black and white, Claire. The world is anything but." He opened the door, then looked back and said, "You finally see the shades of gray. Welcome to the real world, Claire."

Mitch hung up his cell phone. Lexie was at Mercy Hospital's ICU ward, where Steve Donovan had just been moved after surgery. Steve was going to make it. Thank God.

Mitch had talked to Lora Lane's neighbor, every Rabbit Hole regular, anyone he could think of about Lora and why someone would walk into her house and kill her.

The method was cruel and efficient. No sexual assault, no other physical marks on the body. She knew her killer. She'd let him in the house, turned to him, and he pushed a sharp knife into her navel, then pulled it up until it hit her sternum. The killer pulled the knife out, leaving a six-inch wound in her gut. She'd have bled out in minutes. Even if help had been immediate, nothing could have saved her. The knife sliced clean through her intestines and stomach and nicked her liver and lungs, the latter evidenced by the dried blood around her mouth.

Who would kill the handicapped woman? Had she seen something tonight? Had she seen who drugged Claire? If this was related to Claire, then Frank Lowe hadn't drugged her.

Mitch stood in the middle of Lora Lane's bedroom, staring at her open closet and the empty shelves. Her father wasn't able to give them much help. He was devastated after walking in to find his dead daughter. All he could remember was that Lora had "a lot of shoes" in her closet. But Lora's shoes were all under her bed. Dozens of shoes, lined up carefully under the bed skirt, out of sight.

He hoped the man could get it together and answer some more questions. *Something* had been on those shelves. The room was pristine. Even the clutter was neat as a pin. Except the closet doors were open and those shelves were empty. It didn't make sense.

Shoes.

Mitch crossed over to the shelves. They were all a foot high. Tall enough for shoes, neatly lined up.

Or *shoeboxes*. Which would explain why her father said there were shoes on the shelves, but all the shoes were actually under her bed.

Shoeboxes. Why would anyone kill Lora Lane for shoeboxes? What did she have in them that was so important?

Lora Lane was a young teenager in a forty-year-old body. Her room was pink and frilly, with shelves of horses, her dresser covered with small, ornate boxes containing single pieces of jewelry. Some of the jewelry appeared to be quite expensive, and Mitch would need her father to document where the pieces came from.

Perhaps Lora had a boyfriend. He killed her. Stole . . . what? Money? Drugs?

Mitch could see how a woman like Lora, with a young girl's mind, could be used by someone unscrupulous. She worked in a tackle shop at the marina. Drug smuggling? Possibly, especially since drugs had been found in her bathroom.

Grant Duncan, who was heading up the forensic investigation, approached Mitch. He held up an empty vial that looked like it would hold an ounce of fluid.

"What's that?"

"It tested positive for Rohypnol. It was found in Ms. Lane's purse."

"So she drugged Claire."

"It looks like it. I'm going to have the coroner run tests on Ms. Lane as well. She may have residue on her fingers."

"I just don't understand what's going on here." Mitch stared once again at the empty shelves. "The police chief's daughter drugged Claire . . . why? Because she was being mean to her boyfriend?" Mitch frowned. "Did Frank Lowe put her up to it?"

"Your guess is as good as mine."

One of the sheriff's deputies stepped into the room. "I found a witness, Agent Bianchi."

Finally.

Fifteen minutes later, Mitch was sitting at the police chief's desk in the small Isleton police station, walking distance from the police chief's house. He had Grant with him, and sitting across from him was a ten-year-old kid. It was two o'clock in the morning and Mitch felt every one of his thirty-eight years. The kid looked both wide awake and excited.

His name was Josh Frazier and he lived across the street from the Lanes.

"Where are your parents, Josh?" Mitch asked.

"My mom works late on Fridays and Saturdays. She's a waitress in Lodi."

The deputy who had found the kid watching the police activity with binoculars from his bedroom, concurred. "Nita Frazier. She's on her way."

"And she always leaves you alone at night?"

Josh glared at him. "Are you going to get my mom in trouble?"

"No, I—"

"Because I'm not going to help you if you're going to get my mom in trouble. I told her when I turned ten—*five months ago*—that I was old enough to stay by myself. Why pay Mrs. Fatzoid five dollars an hour to watch television? My mom only makes eight twenty-five an hour, plus tips."

"Mrs. Fatzoid?" Mitch questioned.

"Gretchen Flannigan," the deputy said. "She lives two blocks over."

Mitch shook his head. "Josh, I'm not going to get your mom in trouble."

"Promise?"

"I promise."

"Okay." He crossed his arms, still suspicious.

"Deputy Pierson says that you have information about who hurt Ms. Lane tonight."

"Lora's dead, isn't she?"

"Yes," Mitch said. "Was she a friend of yours?"

Josh shrugged. "She was weird, but nice. My mom said she wasn't right in the head, and to be nice to her.

So I was. But my mom also said that Lora was smarter than people thought she was."

"What did you see tonight?"

"The Mercedes."

"Mercedes?"

"Yeah, an S550. My dad was a mechanic. He knew everything about cars. I only know a little."

"Where's your dad now?"

"He died a long time ago. When I was eight."

Mitch assessed the kid. Ten? Yeah, he looked ten. He acted much older.

"Okay, Josh, tell me everything you saw or heard from the time your mom left for work, which was"—he checked his notes—"five thirty."

"Mom left. Um, she said no one could come over, but Andy down the street came by for an hour to play my new Wii game, Lego Indiana Jones. Did you see the movie? It was hot."

The movie. "I saw the first three." *When they were released.*

"Cool."

"When did Andy leave?"

"Six thirty. He had to be home for dinner. And then I played some more; later I heard voices outside so I looked. It was the gang of five."

"Gang?"

"Yeah. The vets. Two from World War Two, one from Korea, two from Vietnam. My mom and I make them cookies on the weekends, and they go to the Rabbit Hole almost every night. They never leave that early. They were talking loudly, and I didn't really hear anything accept that Tip was arrested for something. Then Lora walked by and crossed at the corner—it would be faster if she just cut through the street, but she always crosses at the crosswalk—and went home. I almost went over—Lora is real nice to me—but then the Mercedes drove up and the two men got out."

"Can you describe them?"

"Not really." He shrugged. "It was dark."

"Would you recognize them again if you saw them?"

"No. But I'd recognize the car. There're not a lot of S550s out there, and this one was custom."

"How could you tell?"

"The spoiler on the tail, for one. And there was a valance on the front, but I didn't get as good a look at it. The S550 doesn't come standard with spoilers."

"You have a good eye, Josh. Your dad would be proud."

He squirmed. "Thanks."

"Anything else? Do you know how long they were inside?" Mitch knew the kill had been quick.

"Like twenty minutes. Maybe more."

That surprised Mitch.

"They were taking boxes from the house. Lora was helping them. They were shoeboxes, I think. A bunch of them. They put them in the trunk of the car. Then they went back inside, came out a couple minutes later, and drove off."

"What time?"

"Before nine. That's when *Drake & Josh* comes on, and I never miss it." It was dark, but before nine. That put the killers' arrival at between 7:30 and 8:30.

Mitch asked the deputy to escort Josh to another office until his mother arrived. He turned to Grant. "How many Mercedes S550s are registered in Sacramento and surrounding counties?"

"I already sent Kent a query. He should have a list shortly."

"How does this connect to Frank Lowe? Or Tom O'Brien for that matter?"

"Maybe it doesn't," Grant said. "Could be a coincidence, and maybe they thought Claire was snooping around about their drug smuggling. Anytime you put illegal drugs into the mix, you have problems. But I've already talked to the DEA and they're calling in their regional agents to see if there's anything out there that ties Isleton or Lora Lane, Frank Lowe, or Tip Barney to drug smuggling, Rohypnol, or anything else."

Mitch didn't think this had anything to do with drugs. He closed his eyes and pinched the bridge of his nose. Meg had called him earlier, and Claire was awake and under guard. She would be going home in the morning. Mitch wished he could have been the one sitting at her door, but with Steve out of commission, he was the only one who knew the principals of the case. And Claire didn't want him around. It was more important to find out who tried to kill her, who'd killed Maddox, and who'd framed Tom O'Brien.

He glanced at his watch—3:30. He needed a couple hours' sleep before heading to Mather Field, where Don Collier was being brought in on a military transport plane at ten a.m.

"I'll drive," Grant said, as if reading Mitch's thoughts. "My team is here for the night, no one is getting into the Lane house or the Rabbit Hole. We'll sit tight and finish processing the evidence, but you need to sleep or you'll be a damn good target for the bastard who shot Donovan."

THIRTY-SIX

Claire dressed in jeans and a T-shirt Jayne had brought over for her late the night before. It was six in the morning and she was already antsy. Her doctor had promised he'd come by early, and she was ready to leave the hospital as soon as he signed the papers.

She'd tried to leave earlier, but Agent Warren had orders to keep her until she was cleared by the doctor. She considered just walking out, but decided to sit tight for a couple hours. Worried about her father, Claire felt like she'd been run over by a truck.

The door opened and Agent Warren said, "There's a Bill Kamanski and Sergeant Dave Kamanski to see you. Their IDs check out."

"Thanks."

Dave and Bill entered, both father and son wearing worried expressions. "I'm fine," Claire said automatically.

Dave crossed the room and gave her a hug. "When Dad told me about the accident—I don't know what I'd do if something happened to you, Claire. What were you thinking? What have you been doing?"

"I'm okay. And you probably know what I've been doing."

"Not really." Dave glanced at his father, his expression unreadable, but Claire feared that Bill helping her may have been a contentious issue between them.

Bill kissed Claire on the forehead. "I can't tell you how relieved I am that you're okay."

"I'm waiting for the doctor to sign me out of here. I just want to go home."

"Why didn't you tell us about Tom's surrender?" Dave asked.

"Dave, leave her be."

"It's okay, Bill." Claire took a deep breath. These two men had stood by her for the last fifteen years, and they deserved the truth. "I should have told you before, but the surrender was supposed to be secret and without fanfare, and so far the media hasn't found out. Dad's here for surgery. He was shot four months ago and the bullet is causing problems now."

Dave stared at her. "You never cared about your father before. You've never believed he was innocent. All the evidence points to—"

"The evidence was all circumstantial, Dave. And between what I've found and what the FBI has found, they believe my dad. They're going to prove it. I know it."

"What did they find?" Dave said. "What could they have found that no one else did? Claire, you're deluding yourself—"

"Dave, that's enough," Bill said.

"Dad—"

Bill motioned his son to be quiet. "I've thought for some time that Tom was framed. Ever since Oliver Maddox came to me and told me about Chase Taverton's plea agreement with Frank Lowe, and how both of them died within twenty-four hours. And before—well, Claire knows my thoughts on what happened then."

She squeezed Bill's hand. "I am so lucky to have both of you in my life. I've taken you for granted for too long."

"You didn't," Bill said. "Don't hold on to the past, Claire, no matter what's back there. It'll eat you up and you'll never be happy. There is now, and there is tomorrow."

"I love you." Her voice cracked, and she hugged Bill.

A moment later, Dave said, "After what happened last night, it's obvious you uncovered something important. Maybe you don't even know the importance. Otherwise, why would someone try to kill you? I'm relieved the FBI has a guard on you."

"Claire, honey, let the police handle it," Bill said. "The FBI is on top of things."

"I can't just step aside. The police were supposed to be on top of everything fifteen years ago, and what happened? I'm in this to the end."

"Claire—" Dave tried to argue, but she cut him off.

"I'm not going to be stupid—I have the FBI's bodyguard, and J.T. Caruso is helping with the missing coroner's reports."

"Missing coroner's reports? What does that mean? Whose?"

She explained about the blank coroner's reports on Taverton and her mother in the morgue archives.

"And when I get home, I'm going to follow up on some loose ends. I talked to a supervisor from the FBI last night, but they want to fully debrief me later today or tomorrow morning. You might be right, Dave, that I know something important but don't fully realize its relevance."

"Thank God you're all right," Dave said.

"God and Mitch."

"What?" Dave asked.

"Mitch Bianchi was in Isleton with his partner. After they arrested Frank Lowe they were driving behind me. When I went into the river, Mitch fished me out."

Claire hadn't thanked him. She'd been so hurt, so mad, so confused that she hadn't even thanked him for saving her life. She'd rectify that, then say good-bye.

Bill said, "We'll wait until the doctor clears you, then you can come home with us."

"Thank you, but I need to be home. My animals need to be fed and walked. I can't go anywhere."

"It would make us feel better to keep an eye on you," Dave said. "FBI bodyguard notwithstanding."

She softened, giving Dave a spontaneous hug. "I appreciate it, really, but I need to be in my own house. I'm sorry for getting so mad at you the other night. I'm okay about it. I know that you were just looking out for me, and I love you, Dave. Never do it again, promise?"

He nodded. "Fair enough."

She'd research her own boyfriends in the future . . . if she ever felt like dating again. She doubted it. There was a lot to be said for being alone. You didn't get your heart shredded.

"Can we stop by later?" Bill asked. "Maybe around lunchtime?"

"Sure," Claire said. "That would be nice."

"We'll bring the food," Dave said. "Phil, Eric, and Manny have been worried sick about you."

"But if that's too much company," Bill said, hitting Dave, "then we'll do it later."

"That's okay. It'll keep my mind off my dad's surgery."

Claire's doctor entered with a nurse. "Gentlemen, I need a few moments alone with my patient."

"Of course," Bill said. "We'll see you around noon." They left.

"Well?" Claire asked the doctor as she checked her vitals and wrote information into her chart.

"It was definitely Rohypnol. Your last urine test came back negative, so I'll release you. But take it easy for at least the next twenty-four hours."

"I will."

"Somehow, I don't believe that."

Judge Hamilton Drake felt the weight of the world on his shoulders Saturday morning while he watched the sun rise over downtown from his twenty-fourth-floor penthouse balcony. From here, he saw everything. The state capitol, the growing skyscape, of which he was a part. He could see the river and Tower Bridge from the opposite end. He had a 180-degree view of the city he partly owned.

It was over.

Jeffrey was walking around whistling Dixie, stating that everything was hunky-dory and everyone should stay calm, but Hamilton saw his entire world crashing around him. Jeffrey was delusional. Money and power bought a lot of things, but it couldn't buy some people, and it was those untouchables who had the information that would destroy them. Killing Frank Lowe yesterday had only bought them a little more time.

Which Hamilton was using to pull together his resources and disappear. He already had a false identity, a
false passport, and a house in South America. He'd suggested that Richie and Jeffrey pull the plug and put their
own escape plans in action. Richie was working on it,
but Jeffrey balked. And that's when Hamilton realized
he'd never *had* an escape plan. *Fool.*

Judge Drake had gotten a message at the courthouse
from Claire O'Brien yesterday, and it wasn't until late
last night that he'd heard about her swim in the river.
Why couldn't she have drowned like the other nosy kid?
But that wasn't the worst of it. Frank Lowe had been alive
all these years. What if he'd kept a journal? Told someone? What if he'd spilled his guts to the Feds in the car?

No, if that had happened, Hamilton would be in custody already. Hamilton was the only one who knew the
terms of the plea agreement because he'd been the one
to arraign Frank Lowe. To protect Jeffrey, Hamilton
had orchestrated the murders of Taverton and Lowe. It
had been perfect . . . until now.

Frank Lowe hadn't seen anyone except Jeffrey the
night they had killed Rose Van Alden, as he'd told
Taverton, and he hadn't recognized Jeffrey until the
handsome pol was running for Congress. When Lowe
got arrested for home invasion robbery, he didn't want
the jail time and squealed.

They would have paid Lowe enough money to disappear, but he'd already talked to Taverton. There was no
making him disappear because Taverton *knew* what had
happened, and could go back to the official records.
Find out that Hamilton had drafted Van Alden's will
and forged her signature. Find out that Hamilton had
profited from Waterstone Development. Find out that

they'd been so greedy, they'd set up the Delta Conservancy in order to keep her money—clean—for their political "housekeeping" activities—bribery, primarily.

Oliver Maddox had gotten close to the truth and had to die. But now too many people knew. They couldn't kill everyone.

Hamilton sensed before he heard someone behind him.

He turned. Fear clawed up his spine.

Not him. He was a psychopath. A cold-blooded killer. Judge Hamilton only had people killed when there was no other choice. This crazy bastard had fun when he killed.

"I told you: No one touches Claire."

"I'm leaving this afternoon," Hamilton said. "I didn't have anything to do with what happened to that girl."

"I don't care."

"I have plenty of money."

"I don't give a shit about the money."

Thirty years ago, Hamilton, Jeffrey, and Richie had followed their fraternity brother to the hills on the far side of Stanford's vast property. Jeffrey had been getting a blow job in his car when he saw someone pull a body out a first-floor bedroom window and into the trunk of a car.

They'd recognized their frat brother after following him into the hills near the Dish. It was Jeffrey's idea to dig up the grave and see who it was. It was Hamilton's idea to take her earring. Richie wanted to blackmail him, ask for two million. The killer's dad was one of the richest doctors in California. He'd invented some major artificial heart valve and was set for life.

Hamilton suggested they just keep the information to

themselves until they needed something. Even in college, the three of them had plans that weren't entirely legal.

And Bruce Langstrom had been the perfect person to bring in to kill Taverton and Lowe. He'd been living in L.A., could come in, take care of a couple people, then slip away.

Hamilton had never expected him to change his name and stick around.

"Please," Hamilton begged.

"No one touches Claire but me."

Hamilton tried to run, but there was nowhere to go. He tried to fight, but the effort was laughable. As soon as he raised his arm, he was in a headlock and bent over the railing of the balcony.

And then the judge was falling. Falling, arms flailing, trying to reach for something, anything to stop himself from hitting the pavement, terror of his imminent death filling his every cell.

Nine seconds later, Judge Hamilton Drake hit the street.

THIRTY-SEVEN

Mitch was waiting outside the hangar for the military cargo plane to land with his prisoner, Professor Donald Eugene Collier. Grant was with him, and while Mitch had a lot of respect for the young agent, he wished Steve were here.

Meg phoned. "Collier land yet?"

"The control tower says fifteen minutes."

"Judge Hamilton Drake fell from his balcony this morning. He's dead."

"Drake? He's the judge Oliver Maddox had all those articles on."

"Right. I turned a copy over to Matt, and that's why he called me when the judge hit the pavement. Twenty-four stories in downtown Sacramento."

"Suicide?"

"They don't know. Sacramento PD is working the case. I've asked to be kept in the loop, but the PD isn't as cooperative as the sheriff's department. Matt's trying to smooth things over. If nothing else, he'll let me know if there's something we need to look at. However, I ran a background check on Drake and something interesting popped up. He was at Stanford when Jessica White disappeared."

"Shit. How did Oliver Maddox stumble on that connection?" The kid should have been training to be a cop, not a lawyer.

"We don't know that Judge Drake had anything to do with White's disappearance," Meg warned, "so keep a lid on it until I get those files from Palo Alto. I sent Lexie down this morning to retrieve them in person."

"Why not call the San Francisco field office?"

"First, I'd have to get them up to speed on this, which would take time, and then there's the issue that I didn't bring them in when we agreed to O'Brien's terms of surrender. They technically have jurisdiction over the San Quentin fugitives and should have been consulted. Second, Lexie's beating herself up over Claire skipping out yesterday, blaming herself that Claire nearly got killed."

"It's not her fault," Mitch said. He shouldn't have ridden her so hard last night about watching Claire.

"We know that, but you know Lexie."

"You mean 'failure is not an option' Lexie?"

"Right. Now I have Matt and the U.S. attorney on board with the plan, and Matt will sit in on Collier's interview. The information Claire gave you about his background is accurate—he not only worked for the same law firm as O'Brien's attorney, but he was involved in the case."

"Then why wasn't his name on any of the files? Wait—Claire said many were missing."

"Matt is pulling together as much as he can from the courthouse and O'Brien's law firm. We'll be able to recreate the case files, it'll just take some time."

"Claire said the director of the Western Innocence Project had a complete set in his storage. Sizemore, I think his name is."

"We'll get in contact with him." Mitch heard her typing on her computer. "I also have an analyst working on comparing Collier's background with all the names that have popped up in this investigation, see if there's anything else that connects him to Drake or O'Brien or anyone else."

"Good thinking."

"I've been known to think on occasion."

"Meg—"

"I have to go."

"Thanks. For everything."

She sighed, but it wasn't her exasperated sound. "Be careful."

Mitch hung up, watched as the plane with Collier on board descended.

Grant said, "I have the list of S550s in the greater Sacramento area. There are 210, half of which are black or dark blue or green."

In a regular investigation, narrowing the list that much would be a major lead. But researching over two hundred owners would still take time and right now they didn't have that luxury.

"I just e-mailed Meg and asked for as many people as possible to start weeding through the list, starting with Sacramento County and working out."

"Good work, Grant."

After the plane landed, Mitch walked over to the tarmac and waited. The side door opened and two armed Marines stepped out. Next came Collier, handcuffed, followed by a familiar face.

Mitch smiled. "Hans Vigo! Meg didn't tell me you were bringing Collier back."

"She didn't know," he said. "I volunteered when I heard about the case."

Agent Hans Vigo, closing in on forty-five and on the stout side, was one of the top behavioral scientists at Quantico, though he'd opted to stay in the field rather than join the elite BSU. He'd been a longtime friend of both Mitch and Meg. Most recently, Mitch had worked with him in Montana tracking two of the San Quentin fugitives through a harsh blizzard.

"I'm glad you came. I'll put you to work. I'm still trying to figure out what motives are at play."

Hans said, "My specialty."

Mitch glared at Don Collier. "And I think this man will be instrumental to putting the pieces together."

Jeffrey knew something was wrong as soon as he couldn't reach either Chad Harper or Richie Mancini on any of their phones.

He was sitting in his car outside the gates of Richie's tacky mansion. Hamilton was in a panic earlier when Jeffrey had talked to him, and then an hour later Jeffrey heard the news that his longtime friend and partner had jumped or fallen from the balcony of his penthouse.

Fell, my ass, Jeffrey thought.

Hamilton was gutless. How could he have killed himself over this bump in the fucking road?

Hamilton had caused far more problems by killing himself than they had with the Feds and that bitchy little investigator from Rogan-Caruso. The police would be all over his penthouse and the courthouse. And no matter how careful Hamilton had been with the records, something was going to leak out.

Which meant damage control.

Jeffrey needed a good plan. When the police came calling, he and Richie would of course be *shocked* and *dismayed* over Judge Drake's secret life. They had *no idea* he was involved with anything illegal. The cops might not believe them, but they'd need proof. And right now, there was proof of nothing.

"Dammit, Richie, where are you?"

Jeffrey got out of his car and typed in the code to the gate. It swung open and he drove his car through. The gate closed behind him, and he circled around to the front door, stopping behind Richie's Escalade.

Damn them all, Richie was panicking, too. Was he going to skip town and leave Jeffrey alone to answer all the questions? They'd agreed last night that as long as they stuck together and gave the same story, they'd be able to ride out the storm. Jeffrey couldn't just walk out. He was a *public figure*. A congressman, and he was going to win the U.S. Senate seat. These problems were deterring him from his responsibilities and his job. He was a winner. This crap wasn't going to touch him.

Jeffrey jumped out of his car. He looked in the Escalade. Dammit, packed bags were in the back. Bastard.

He stormed up the front steps and pounded on the door.

It swung open.

Jeffrey stared at the bodies in the foyer. Richie was dead. Shot multiple times in the head and torso. His wife was lying in the living room, dead. And Harper. Harper had taken out his gun, had seen a threat, but he hadn't reacted fast enough.

Jeffrey knew only one person who had the ability to kill in cold blood like this. Ability, and a reason to do it.

Hamilton hadn't killed himself. He was pushed.

Jeffrey was next.

"Not on your life, fucking asshole. I'll nail your tough hide to the wall."

He needed to watch his back, because Jeffrey was certain that he was next on Bruce's hit list. But what if Jeffrey surprised him instead?

Jeffrey's entire life, his future, was in jeopardy. Everything he'd worked for, all the bribes, the lies, the manipulation, the hours he'd put into obtaining power and control. He was so close! The United States Senate! He'd had plans. Senate pro tem, and then who knew? President? He would have been the greatest of the twenty-first century.

His dreams shattered in front of him.

He would kill the bastard assassin Bruce and then Jeffrey would disappear. As much as he didn't want to give up everything he'd earned, everything he'd worked so hard for, self-preservation was the most important thing. He would have to change his name and alter his appearance and create a power base in some pathetic third-world country.

After all, he still had plenty of money. And with Richie and Hamilton dead, he now controlled it all.

THIRTY-EIGHT

Though Claire had told Bill and Dave that she didn't mind them bringing the rest of the gang, she felt overwhelmed within ten minutes, even though Manny was with Jill, who was at the hospital in labor.

Bill sensed her distress. He eased her out of the kitchen where the three cops were dishing up take-out Italian, and sat her in the living room. "One hour, kiddo. You look tired."

She smiled. "It's okay. I tried to sleep, but couldn't. Dad was supposed to go into surgery at eight last night, but the surgeon was concerned about some test results, so they ran more tests and took more X-rays and didn't even start until three this morning. And he's still there. It shouldn't take this long, should it? What if—"

Bill squeezed her hand. "Don't do that. He's still in surgery and that's positive. Trust the doctors."

Claire just wanted her dad back, her life settled. "I hate not being there. I talked to Nelia this morning, and she's worried, but I think my pacing made her nervous."

"Are you sure you don't want us to get out of here? We'll leave the food and let you—"

"I want you to stay." She kissed him on the cheek.

Dave came in. "Do you want me to serve you up?" he asked Claire.

"I'll eat in the kitchen," she said, standing.

"There's plenty," Dave told Agent Warren. "Help yourself."

"Save me some," he said. "Though a cold soda would be good."

"I'll get it."

Phil said, "I got it, Dave. Grab the bread out of the warmer."

Claire walked into the kitchen and saw the spread—and the accompanying mess. "I'll clean up," Dave assured her.

"You'd better," she said and smiled. Even though she'd have preferred to be alone, all she'd been doing this morning was sulking and worrying about her father's surgery. That was hardly working to prove her father's innocence. Though Agent Elliott told her that they were taking her father's claims seriously, as well as following up on everything Claire had uncovered, Claire wasn't there to know herself. She was tired, but she couldn't sleep if she tried.

"Thanks for coming by," she told Dave quietly.

He rubbed her shoulder. "I love you, kid."

Claire didn't feel much like eating, but to appease Dave and Bill, she ate a small plate of spaghetti. Agent Warren took his soda and stood guard, leaving her alone with her friends. She wondered what Mitch was doing. Following up on information? Leads? Was he interviewing Collier yet? She wished she could go down to FBI headquarters and find out exactly what was going on. The waiting game was going to kill her.

She excused herself and made a call. SSA Megan Elliott had given her a private number, and Claire didn't feel guilty about using it.

"Elliott."

"Agent Elliott, this is Claire O'Brien."

"Is something wrong?"

"No. But I wanted to know what was going on. No one has called, I don't know if you have Collier, or what happened to Lora Lane, or if—"

"Okay," the Fed interrupted. "I get it. I hate being out of the loop as well, but right now I can't give you the information you want."

"But—"

"We're swamped. I have a dead judge, Collier in custody but not talking, and the media has set up shop outside the building."

"Judge?" Claire remembered the news report, and it clicked. "Judge Drake—he's the one who arraigned Frank Lowe. Detective Abrahamson told me yesterday he was most likely to know the details of any plea agreement between Lowe and the D.A.'s office."

Agent Elliott asked quickly, "Did you say Drake? Judge Hamilton Drake?"

"Yes."

"I have to go."

"Why is that important?"

"I don't know yet."

"Will you keep me in the loop? Please?" Claire hated to beg, but she didn't want to make Megan Elliott so mad she wouldn't keep her informed.

"As much as I can, I will."

"I guess I'll take it."

"Thanks, Claire. If you want a recommendation to Quantico, let me know."

She laughed. The first laugh in far too long. "Thanks, but I like working for Rogan-Caruso."

"I can imagine." She hung up.

Claire felt better knowing that the FBI was working the case hard. The truth would come out. It had to.

Yawning, she returned to the living room. The guys were all sitting around, relaxing. She sat on the couch next to Bill. "Eat too much?"

"I didn't think so, but I sure feel like it." He put an arm around her. "You holding up?"

"Yeah. I just talked to Agent Elliott and I know they're on top of things. It's just I wish I was there. I hate not doing anything."

"You've already done more than enough," Bill said. "If not for you, I don't think they'd have half the info they have."

"Maybe not," she said. "I don't know." She yawned again.

"Claire, go ahead and go to bed. You've had a rough night."

"Thought you guys were going to clean up?" she teased Dave.

"Phil's doing the dishes," Dave said. "He drew the short straw."

She leaned her head against Bill's shoulder and closed her eyes. "I'm so glad I have my dad back, Bill. But you will always be special to me. I wouldn't have survived those years without you and Dave." She felt herself drifting off. Bill didn't say anything. She tried to open her eyes, but they felt thick.

"Claire?"

She heard a voice. *Agent Warren?* She thought she'd

spoken out loud, but her tongue felt thick. A sliver of fear ran up her spine when she heard a heavy thud.

Then she heard nothing.

Mitch was the bad cop and he was irritated enough to play the role to a T.

Don Collier, the bastard, was saying nothing. He'd requested a damn lawyer who still hadn't shown, and Mitch wanted to smash the defense-attorney-turned-law-professor's smug face.

"We should let him go," Hans said.

Mitch didn't know what Hans had planned, and his initial reaction was to curse. He trusted Hans enough to follow through on the lead-in. "Shit, Vigo, what are you thinking?"

A faint nod told him that Hans had a plan and Mitch was on track.

"We really don't have enough to keep him. Keep his passport, by all means, but let him go home."

"I'd rather keep him behind bars," Mitch said. "Lose him in the system."

Collier wanted to say something, Mitch saw his jaw working, but he kept his mouth shut.

"Mitch, I've told you before that you're going to keep going up before the OPR every time you let your temper run the investigation." Hans stood, tapped on the window, and Meg came in. "Is the media still out front?"

"Yeah," she said quietly. "Right outside the gate. I can't get rid of them."

"Is there a back door where Mr. Collier can leave?"

"Sure, but they're lining that street as well."

"Well, it doesn't matter. Why don't you make a statement that Professor Collier isn't under arrest, that he's only wanted for questioning. I'm sure that will alleviate his mind. He's probably worried about his position and tenure. I don't want him to fear his job security because of this situation, especially if nothing comes of it."

"No problem, I'll write up a statement and have the SAC read it—"

"No!" Collier pounded his fist on the table.

Hans turned to him. "Mr. Collier, I don't want to waste your time or mine. We can bring you in for a formal interview Monday morning. We simply want to make sure you can't leave the country, until we find the answers we need."

"Just—I'll wait for my attorney. I want to get this over with."

"So do we," Hans said. "But your attorney is late." He glanced at his watch. "It's one o'clock on a beautiful Saturday afternoon. No one wants to be here."

"I know what you're doing," Collier said. "You're trying to get me killed."

Mitch stared at him. "Give me a fucking break."

"You want me to lead you to who killed Oliver? I had nothing to do with that, I had nothing to do with *anything*, and I'm not going to let you get me killed."

Hans sat down. "I'm in a position to offer you immunity, Mr. Collier."

"You're not an attorney. You can offer me nothing."

"I have a lot more clout than you might think. I'm not simply a babysitter transporting criminals cross-country."

"I'm not a criminal," Collier said. "I'll stay here until my attorney arrives. And I'm going to sue you for false arrest, transport across country without my permission, and harassment."

Mitch's phone beeped and he frowned. He looked at the message. It was from Grant.

We found the S550. Registered to Chad Harper, we're at his residence. He lives in a guest house on the property of Richard and Tiffany Mancini. He's dead as well as the Mancinis. Call me ASAP.

Tom tried to open his eyes, but everything was too bright. His whole body felt bruised and heavy, but he wasn't in any acute pain.

"Tom?"

Nelia was still here. "Umm," he moaned.

"Thank God."

He felt something warm touching his hand. Was Nelia holding his hand? He couldn't tell. But he was alive.

"Claire came by early this morning," Nelia said.

She'd looked so tired last night, but she'd come to him. His daughter believed in him. He had her back. The overwhelming relief and joy settled his soul like nothing else could.

"Am I—" Every word was a chore.

"Shh, don't talk. Now that you're awake, you're going to be fine. Better than fine. The surgery lasted over eleven hours, but they got the bullet out and repaired the damage. You just need time to heal."

Time. Did he have time?

"I know what you're thinking," Nelia whispered close to his ear. "You're safe here. You're safe with me. I will do everything in my power to make sure you are cleared. Claire is working on it. The FBI believed you yesterday, they are following up on what you told them and everything Claire learned. Agent Elliott and Agent

Bianchi both came by to check on you. They have a man on the door, but I think it's more as protection for you at this point."

"Good." It was all he could say. Except, "Love you."

"I love you, Tom. We're going to get through this. You, me, Claire, all of us. There's no one who deserves peace more than you."

"Call Claire."

"And tell her you're awake?"

"Yes."

"I'll do it as soon as I find a nurse."

THIRTY-NINE

Mitch stared at the three dead bodies in the entry of the midtown mansion.

Richard Mancini was a wealthy and successful Sacramento area developer. His bodyguard—for lack of a better word—Chad Harper had drawn his gun. His wife was dead just over the threshold of the living room.

He saw how it played out. Someone came to the door—had to be buzzed through, unless they had the code—and Harper opened the door. Did he see the threat immediately and draw his weapon? Or were they having a conversation, and it wasn't until a few minutes later that he suspected a threat? Pulled his gun, but the shooter was faster. And accurate. Twice in the chest and once in head. *Bang bang bang.* Mancini must have been next, because there was no attempt to flee.

This was an experienced, professional, cold-blooded killer.

Mrs. Mancini, the least threatening, had been the last victim. She'd run toward the living room, perhaps toward a phone or just to get *away* from the shooter. She'd been shot in the back three times.

Why were they killed? Mitch looked around. There

was a secure gate at the entrance, secure locks at the doors, there had to be cameras and added security.

"Did you find any cameras?"

"Yes, all digital, all erased. I have an e-team coming down to see if there are backups anywhere, but we couldn't find anything."

"The killer knew there was digital security. He knew the victims."

"I'm guessing yes." Grant led Mitch back outside. "The Escalade is registered to Richard Mancini. It's packed with suitcases. His passport was in his pocket, Dina Mancini had a passport in her purse. They were going on a trip, and it hadn't been planned. We're calling the airports to learn their destination. The S550 is registered to Chad Harper. And guess what we found in the trunk?"

They walked over to the covered garage. The sheriff's deputy was guarding the car; the trunk had been popped. Inside were dozens of shoeboxes. "Lora Lane's shoebox collection," Mitch said. Stuffed behind the boxes were clothes stained with what Mitch knew was blood. Lora Lane's blood.

Grant reached down and took the lid off one box. Inside were several journals. He handed Mitch the one on top.

Mitch opened it. In perfect, frilly script:

December 10, 2007.

I arrived at the Rabbit Hole at 6:07 pm. I was late because Daddy had a special order for lures for his friend John Deynor, who likes sturgeon. I made two of my best lures, and they took me time because I wanted to make sure they were perfect.

Tip was behind the bar. He wore a white shirt and

black jeans. He got a haircut today. Also in the bar were . . .

"What's this? Her diaries? Why would someone kill her for her diaries?"

"I haven't looked at them all, but they're not diaries. They are notes on Tip Barney, but she also adds in her random thoughts and observations. They appear to go all the way back to when he first opened the bar in Isleton. The sheriff is letting us have the boxes, and I'm waiting for a team to transport them to the lab. We'll work on it until we have an answer."

Mitch glanced toward the house. "Why did Harper have them in his car? Why was Lora Lane . . . stalking Frank Lowe? Why would Harper care?"

"All good questions. I have no answers yet—"

Mitch shook his head. "Sorry. I was just thinking out loud."

Mitch looked around. This felt odd. There was obviously a connection, but it eluded him.

His first reaction had been that a distraught Police Chief Lane had learned who had killed his daughter and came here for vengeance. But Mitch knew Chief Lane hadn't left Isleton. Two agents were down there watching him and the Rabbit Hole.

Mancini. Developer. "Grant, do you know if Mancini was involved at all with Waterstone?"

"No idea. Meg was researching that."

Mitch called Meg. "Who are the principals of Waterstone Development, other than Judge Drake?"

"Hold a sec." A moment later, she said, "Jeffrey Riordan and Richard Mancini. Riordan is a congressman," she added. "He's running for Senate."

"And Mancini is dead. What if Judge Drake didn't fall or jump?"

"The Sac PD is all over the scene. I've spoken to the chief of police. He's treating this as a possible homicide and has pulled the security tapes. His people are canvassing the building and immediate area."

"If Drake was murdered, someone could be after Riordan now."

"I'll put an APB out on him. He shouldn't be hard to find. But why?"

"I wish I knew. The only thing that connects all the dead is Rose Van Alden."

"Van Alden? From Maddox's flash drive?"

"Yes. Van Alden was Frank Lowe's great-aunt. Van Alden's will instructed the sale of her property to Waterstone, which resulted in a huge planned community. Drake, Mancini, and Riordan were all principals in Waterstone. Now Lowe, Drake, and Mancini are dead. Assassinated?" Mitch ran through everything he knew. "What if that's what this was all about? What if Lowe tipped off Taverton about something to do with that original sale?"

"Big enough to kill a prosecutor to keep it a secret?"

"I'm not a finance guy, Meg. Can you put someone on it? Someone who understands land deals. And definitely get a warning to Riordan. He might want to come in for protective custody."

"Unless," Meg said, "he's somehow a part of this. Do we want to tip him off?"

"So don't. He's a sitting congressman, we're concerned about his safety and want him in protective custody until we find this assassin. I'm sure you'll come up with something good. Maybe just put a couple agents on him at his house. But if he's *not* involved, and he ends up dead, there'll be hell to pay from Washington."

"You got that right. I'll take care of it."

Mitch hung up. He'd brought Hans Vigo with him to the Mancini triple homicide. It was time for a fresh pair of eyes and ears. If he laid everything out for the senior agent, maybe Hans would see something new. If nothing else, he could help with motive. For a guy as laid-back and pleasant as Hans Vigo, his understanding of criminal psychology was eerie. "Hans, I need to run something by you."

Meg bypassed the bureaucracy and called a friend at Quantico to pull Congressman Riordan's private cell phone number. This was a matter of life or death, she could justify the intrusion into his privacy.

A man answered. "Hello."

"Jeffrey Riordan?"

"Yes. Who are you? I'm busy and this is a private number."

"Congressman, I'm Supervisory Special Agent Megan Elliott with the Federal Bureau of Investigation. I'm calling because we have reason to believe that your life is in danger and I'd like to send two agents to your location to bring you into protective custody."

There was a long silence, but he hadn't disconnected.

"Congressman?"

"Why do you think I'm in danger? Has there been a threat against me?"

"In the process of investigating an unrelated matter, we've pulled files on Waterstone Development. Today two of the principals of that company were murdered. You are the third principal, and therefore we feel that there is sufficient threat until we can determine that the cause was unrelated to your connection with Judge Drake and Mr. Mancini."

"I see. I'll keep my eyes open. Thank you for the warning."

He hung up.

Meg stared at the phone. That conversation was nothing like she expected. Rage, maybe—she'd dealt with assholes in Congress before. Fear, yeah—she'd had one congresswoman who'd been terrified over threatening letters she'd received. But complete dismissal?

She straightened as she realized that Riordan hadn't expressed any shock or asked questions about Richard Mancini's murder. While the media was all over Judge Drake's more public death, no one outside of law enforcement knew about Mancini. Grant had found the bodies less than an hour ago while following up on the lead from the Lora Lane murder.

Damn, Riordan was an elected official. That meant politics, and one reason she'd transferred from the Washington D.C. field office when this promotion came up in Sacramento was because she was sick and tired of politics.

She should have known it didn't matter—politics influenced everything. She called her boss and clued him in on the situation. "I'll handle the flack," he said. "Go ahead and put two agents on him 24/7. We'll use the protective custody argument to surveil him—we have ample cause there—and I'll contact the U.S. Attorney's office."

"We're already on thin ice with Collier. His attorney is foaming at the mouth that we didn't properly extradite him from New York."

"I'll handle the lawyers. I'll be there in thirty minutes. In the meantime, we need to protect our asses. If Riordan is innocent and ends up dead, we'll have just as many problems as if we didn't jump through the damn legal hoops."

Meg had just issued the surveillance order on Congressman Riordan when her cell phone rang. "Agent Elliott."

"This is Nelia Kincaid."

"Ms. Kincaid, this isn't a good time. I'm pleased Mr. O'Brien is out of surgery, and—"

"It's about Claire. I'm worried."

"What happened?"

"Tom woke up thirty minutes ago. Claire wanted to see him when he was awake, so I phoned her at her home. There was no answer. I called her office, because I know she wanted to work—she hasn't come in."

"I'm sure she's sleeping. There were heavy drugs in her system with harsh side effects. But I'll call my agent and have him check on her."

"I'd appreciate it."

Meg dialed Cliff Warren's cell phone, with a tingle of worry. She'd met Claire, and while she'd tried to appease Nelia Kincaid, Meg didn't think Claire would sleep through a ringing phone in the middle of an investigation where she had a vested interest.

Cliff didn't answer his phone.

Meg called out to her secretary. "Bonnie, call Sac PD and have them drive by Claire O'Brien's house and check in with her. Send two agents to follow up."

Meg dialed Mitch. "Mitch? Are you still in Midtown?"

"I'm at Mancini's, yes."

"Cliff Warren isn't answering his phone, and Claire isn't answering hers."

"I'm on my way."

Thirty years ago he'd made a mistake that had cost him his soul.

Fifteen years ago he'd made another. But when you knew you were going to hell, protecting the new life you'd so carefully built seemed crucial.

But he knew now that it was over.

He finished digging Claire's grave. Burying her was burying his past. He could start fresh. He'd have to leave the country; a new identity in America wasn't going to help him this time.

He couldn't go back to his true identity, or the new one he'd created. He'd be too easy to find. He'd taken the identity of a dead man to stay close to Claire, but it was only a matter of time before the FBI put it all together. Fifteen years of watching her, protecting her, loving her—all gone.

He was both angry and relieved.

Now he could kill her. Though he didn't completely understand it, he'd stopped trying to figure out Claire's deep connection to him. He'd known the day he'd seen her photograph before killing Taverton and Lydia O'Brien that Claire was his fate; but he also accepted that there was no rational explanation. Just like he knew the runaways he killed were all pale imitations of Claire.

And wasn't Claire just a pale imitation of Bridget?

He couldn't kill Bridget again. He wished he could. He dreamed of it, tried to re-create it, but her death had happened too fast, without thought. When he stood over her dead body he wanted to do it all over again. Experience every sensation again. And again. For everything Bridget had done to him, and everything she hadn't.

Killing Claire would satisfy him more than the runaways. Like Bridget, he'd loved and protected Claire for years. And like Bridget, Claire never returned his feelings. She never would. Just teased him, took other lovers and rubbed them in his face. The damn Fed was the worst, the way she was all over him at the Fox & Goose. Touching him. Kissing him. Sliding her body over his, her breasts rubbing against his chest.

He'd sacrificed everything for her, and she'd never give him what he needed most from her. But he could take it. He could take everything, including her last breath.

After she was dead, he'd disappear. He didn't have much time. It wouldn't take the FBI long to discover Claire was missing. The truth would come out.

Claire needed to die before then.

He had his police scanner on, listening for odd chatter. If they figured it out, they would demand radio silence—in case he was listening. Radio silence was as good as announcing they were coming for him.

The sound of an approaching car disturbed his work. He jumped off the backhoe and looked into the newly dug grave. It was deep enough. He walked quickly toward the house, rounding the corner at the same time Jeffrey Riordan stepped from his car.

"You fucking lunatic!" Riordan screamed at him. "You screwed up everything. You killed Hamilton and Richie. Now the cops are all over my ass."

What was Riordan thinking, coming out here to confront him? Bruce Langstrom was a hired assassin. Riordan knew that; he'd paid him enough money over the years. Did the idiot really think he was just another employee he could jerk around?

Riordan had a gun in his hand.

As if that would do him any good.

FORTY

Claire had the worst hangover of her life.

She couldn't open her eyes, her tongue was thick, her mouth dry. All she wanted was a gallon of water and sleep. In the back of her mind she imagined she'd heard a gunshot, but it was quiet now. She was alone.

As she became more alert, she dismissed the idea that she had a hangover. She hadn't been drinking. She'd been drugged.

The first sign that something was really, really wrong came from her sense of smell. She wasn't in her house. She breathed deeply, struggled to open her eyes—but every time she opened them, they closed, the strain too much. And everything was blurry and out of focus, all light and dark with no form.

Maybe she'd passed out and Dave had taken her to the hospital. She'd been sitting on the couch talking to Bill. They'd just had lunch . . .

There were no hospital sounds. Total silence. This place smelled clean—Pine-Sol and bleach and some other fruity fragrance that made Claire's stomach turn. But definitely not the antiseptic scent of the hospital.

When she tried to speak, only a moan escaped. Every limb felt heavy, but her mind awakened as a faint sense of panic pumped adrenaline through her body. She continued breathing deeply, trying to regain full use of her eyes and body. It seemed to be working. She still felt sluggish, but at least she could open her eyes and focus on her surroundings.

A bright pink wall. She'd had a bright pink wall when she was a kid. In the old house, the house where her mother was killed.

She turned her head and saw white furniture with pink and green flowers. Her heart raced. This was her furniture! Or it used to be hers. Hands fisting in the comforter, trying to push herself up, she saw the myriad brightly colored pillows on the bed.

And the bear.

As if in a trance, Claire sat up on the bed and struggled to stand. Unsteadily she crossed to the rocking chair and picked up the teddy bear. It was brown, a plain, ordinary stuffed bear, but she'd had one just like it growing up. She'd had it for as long as she could remember. It was well-worn, like this one. It was missing an eye. Like this bear.

She turned it over and stared at the embroidery on the paw. At one time, the thread had been bright pink. It was faded now.

She dropped the bear as if he burned her hands. It had been months after her mother had been killed when she realized Bill hadn't brought the bear when he packed up her old room. She'd asked him to go back and look for it; he did. He said there were no teddy bears in the house. She had cried over it, certain that someone who didn't like her dad was punishing her. Stupid to cry over a stuffed animal.

The entire room she now stood in had been designed

exactly like the room she'd lived in when she was fourteen. One pink and three blue walls. On the back of the door was a corkboard, but instead of the collage of photos she'd kept, there was only one.

It was of her. A snapshot that looked like the pictures she'd had in her old room. Her and her best friend, Amy, who'd been killed by a drunk driver when they were freshmen in college. Amy had been the only one of her childhood friends who'd supported her unconditionally all those hard years.

This wasn't right. Where was she? Who knew about her old life?

She turned the doorknob. Locked. She was locked in this room. Heart thudding painfully, she pulled and pushed and kicked and couldn't get out.

There was only one window. She ran to it, pushed open the blinds. The light had changed—it had to be five or six in the evening. How long had she been unconscious? How long had she been held captive? What had happened to her friends and the bodyguard?

The landscape was unfamiliar. She was on the second floor of a house in the country, but there were no other houses she could see, no landmark to tell her anything about her location. It was mostly flat, but with some small hills and large trees. Not the mountains, not quite the foothills.

She tried the window. Nailed shut. She pounded on the glass. She'd have to break it to escape.

She looked around the room for a weapon, for anything she could use to defend herself or break this window. There was nothing. While at first it looked just like her room, it was a fake.

The drawers didn't open on the dresser. The closet

was empty. Could she break the mirror and use the glass as a weapon? It wasn't thick enough; she wouldn't be able to wield the shards in her hands with enough force to hurt someone.

The door opened.

She swung around. A wave of relief rushed over her. She ran to Dave's partner and hugged him.

"Phil! Thank God. What happened? Where am I?"

He hugged her back, but he wasn't talking. She slowly pulled away.

"What's going on?" she asked, her voice cracking. She swallowed and took a step back. Her temporary relief was replaced by fear.

He stepped forward. "I'm sorry, Claire, but it's over."

She kept backing up until she was against the wall. He followed.

Phil put his hands on her shoulders, touched the ends of her hair. "Fate brought us together fifteen years ago, but it's time to move on."

Claire had no idea what Phil was talking about, what drugs he was on, why he was so creepy—

Fate brought us together fifteen years ago . . .

—but she knew she had to get out of here now.

She kneed him hard in the groin. Her lack of strength from whatever drugs she'd been fed prevented her from causing him debilitating pain, but she had the element of surprise on her side.

Hands clasped, she brought her arms up between them and hit him dead-on in the face as he stumbled back from the blow to his balls. Now she had the room and momentum to kick him in the stomach. She pivoted, kicked him again, and he staggered against the bed.

It all took only seconds, and then she was out the door. Running.

She heard the echo of the gunshot at the same time her calf burned in pain. She fell to her knees and tried to crawl.

Phil pulled her up by her hair. His eyes were narrow, furious. His face full of hate and rage. This couldn't be the Phil she'd gone to Kings games with, who had taught her to shoot at the police range with Dave and Eric. This couldn't be . . .

"What happened to Bill and Dave? The others? What did you do to them?"

"They'll be waking up soon enough, but they'll never find us. At least not until they find your grave."

She screamed at the top of her lungs. Phil didn't show any reaction. "No one can hear you, Claire. Not where we are. I'm sorry it has to end like this, but I have no choice." He pulled handcuffs from his rear pocket and cuffed one of her wrists. "I'll bandage your leg. I don't want you to bleed to death."

"Why not? You plan to kill me, right? Why? What did I ever do to you?" She tried to sound tough, but she was terrified. She didn't see a way out. She was injured and Phil was insane.

He didn't answer her question, instead grabbing her under the arms and dragging her into another bedroom. A larger room, all white and too clean. A large-screen television was on the wall. On the screen was a still shot of her from years ago. In her old bedroom at Bill's house, a shot from above.

A camera in the ceiling.

She whimpered, then swallowed her fear. She couldn't

let him know how scared she was. But she couldn't stop her body from shaking violently.

Focus, Claire! You have to get out of here. Dave will find you. Someone will find you. Get to a road, get anywhere away from this fucking lunatic!

Phil secured the handcuff to a post on the bed. She pulled, but it was locked tight.

"Don't do that, or it'll get tighter. You should know that."

"Bastard! Let me go."

Her eyes went from him to the picture of her on the television screen. It wasn't a photograph. It was a still shot from a tape.

He leaned over her and whispered in her ear, "I've been watching you for a long time." He pressed a button on a remote on the nightstand and the image moved.

He'd had a video camera on her. He'd taped her. Oh God, how long? He'd been watching her, filming her . . . On the screen she was undressing, oblivious that she was being recorded.

"You were so beautiful," Phil murmured as her bra came off. She tossed it in the laundry and pulled on a T-shirt that barely covered her butt.

Claire's face reddened; she was hot and embarrassed and angry.

But more than the anger, cold terror froze her body.

"I'll get the first aid kit." Phil left her restrained on the bed watching her younger self reading a book on her bed.

He was going to kill her. And Claire had no idea how she was going to stop him.

FORTY-ONE

Dave Kamanski was the first to regain consciousness.

Mitch insinuated himself between two paramedics working on the younger Kamanski. "Dave," he said. "Dave, come on, Claire needs your help."

Dave blinked, his eyes squeezing shut at the light. "Wh-what?" he asked, his mouth thick. He looked around at Claire's house.

"Who took Claire? Dave, come on, man, I'm counting on you. Who has Claire?"

"Claire?"

A paramedic said, "Sir, you'll have to—"

"This is a matter of life or death," Mitch said without budging. "Dave, snap out of it."

"Where's Claire?" Dave tried to sit up. He held his head.

"Sir, lie down—"

Mitch interrupted the medic. "Dave, someone kidnapped Claire. Did you get a good look at him? How were you all knocked out?"

Hans said from across the room, "Warren is the only victim with a visible injury."

"Then how—" Mitch paused. "Poison?"

Grant came in from the kitchen. "There's a lot of

food spread out on the table. We're bagging it for testing."

"Poison?" Dave squeezed his eyes shut, then opened them wide and looked around. They were still at Claire's house. "We all ate the same food. From Claire's favorite Italian place, just up the street."

"Who? Did you pick up the food?"

"Phil and Eric got it."

"Phil?" Mitch questioned. "There're only four of you here—you, your father, Agent Warren, and someone with an ID and badge named Eric Jordan."

"Phil—what happened to Phil?"

"That's a damn good question," Mitch said, jumping up. He remembered Claire talking about Phil Palmer being Dave's partner and closest friend. He dialed Meg. "I need everything on Philip Palmer. He's a cop with Sac PD. Start with his address."

"I can tell you that," Dave said, mouth tight. "He lives in South Land Park on Robertson. I'm going with you."

He tried to stand, then sat down heavily.

"I'll keep you informed," Mitch promised Dave and left.

Meg had told him to stand down until backup arrived, but if Phil Palmer had Claire inside, there was no way in hell that Mitch was going to give him one more minute alone with her.

He had Grant and Hans with him outside Phil Palmer's small post-WWII bungalow in an older, well-maintained Sacramento neighborhood. Grant motioned he would go around back, and held up two fingers.

Mitch painstakingly counted to one hundred and twenty to give Grant enough time to get into place.

Hans had his back, and Mitch knocked on the door.

No answer. Total silence inside.

He knocked again. "Officer Palmer?" he said, forcing his voice to be calm. "There's been an attack on your partner and we're concerned about your safety."

No answer, total silence.

No one was there.

Mitch pounded on the door. "Palmer! This is the FBI! Open up!"

Moments later, gun drawn, Mitch kicked the door twice and it swung in.

Grant came in from the rear entrance. They quickly searched the residence.

No one.

They went through the house again, methodically. It was obvious that Phil Palmer didn't actually live here. There was some food in the freezer and pantry, but only enough to provide a meal if he had to be here. The house was devoid of clutter, a file cabinet was empty, a computer on the desk had nothing saved to the hard drive.

The house was a front. Phil Palmer had created a public image and Sac PD bought it. So had his friends, partner, and Claire.

Mitch couldn't lose Claire now. She hated him, and he didn't blame her, but he would fight for her. He loved her, dammit, he wasn't going to lose her, to her own hurt feelings or to a psychopath.

Why had Palmer kidnapped Claire? What did he want from her? Was this related to O'Brien's conviction, or some sick obsession that had developed over the years? If it was related to O'Brien, that meant it was related to Taverton and the past.

"Collier," Mitch said.

Hans nodded as Grant stared. "Excuse me?"

"Collier knows what's going on. He has to. Because if he doesn't know where Phil Palmer took Claire, she's going to die." And if Claire died, Mitch wouldn't—

Don't. He couldn't think the worst. He wouldn't be able to do his job.

I'll find you, Claire.

On the drive back to headquarters, Mitch spoke to Meg and learned there was no other property owned or leased by Philip Palmer in Sacramento County or any surrounding county. Mitch talked again to Dave Kamanski, who said he didn't know where Phil would be, or why he would have kidnapped Claire.

"Why didn't I see something? Phil's a good friend. My partner. He wouldn't hurt Claire. Why would he?"

"Hell if I know, but he's unaccounted for and that's the only explanation."

"Phil adores Claire."

"How much?" Mitch demanded.

"That's not—"

"Dave, how well do you really know Philip Palmer?"

"He's been a cop for over fourteen years."

"Fourteen? He wasn't on the job when O'Brien was framed for murder?"

"What? What does that have to do with anything? Why aren't you looking for Claire?"

"When did he start with Sacramento PD?"

"I don't know—yeah, okay, it was during Tom's trial.

I was on leave, and when I returned he was on my squad. He wasn't even here during the murders. He lived in Los Angeles."

Mitch frowned. Maybe he was wrong and Palmer had nothing to do with the Taverton-O'Brien double murder. But why would he kidnap Claire *now*? Something had to have happened to make Palmer act *now,* and the only thing that even remotely fit in was that he knew about or was involved in O'Brien's frame job. He whispered to Grant, "Call Meg and have her follow up on Palmer being from Los Angeles."

To Dave, he said, "I need everything you know about Palmer. Family, history, where he went to school, where he grew up, police academy, college, anything. Fax it over." He gave Dave the fax number in Meg's office.

Grant pulled into FBI headquarters. Mitch walked directly to Meg's office. "Anything?"

"Palmer graduated from Los Angeles Police Academy, but never served in LAPD. Sac was his first assignment."

Odd, but not unheard of. "Fourteen years ago?"

"Yes."

Mitch frowned. He looked at his notes from his first conversation with Dave. "Palmer is nearly fifty. Isn't thirty-six a little old to join the academy?"

"I'd think."

"Dig deeper. There's something there."

"I have everyone on it, but we have a crisis with Collier right now. His attorney is here and I don't see how we can hold him. Matt went around with the U.S. Attorney on charges, and I think they're on the same page. Matt went in with Collier when his attorney arrived."

"Who's with Collier now besides Matt?"

"Richardson."

Bob Richardson was the special agent in charge. Mitch and Richardson had butted heads on more than one occasion, but Richardson had also gone to bat for him during Mitch's last round with the Office of Professional Responsibility. Besides, Mitch knew more about this case than anyone.

Meg handed him an envelope. "J. T. Caruso came through. This might come in handy."

Mitch glanced at the document and nodded. "Perfect."

He stalked into the interview room, Hans Vigo at his side. Richardson showed no reaction at their entrance.

Collier's attorney was saying, "Release my client or I'll file charges for false imprisonment, false arrest, failure to—"

"Shut up." Evidently, Richardson had had enough of Collier's attorney. They were playing hardball, and so was the FBI.

Claire's life was at stake. Collier knew something important, and Mitch was determined to get it out of him.

Hans Vigo said, "We have one offer for your client. He'd better take it, or we'll hold him."

"You can't hold him."

"Domestic terrorism," Richardson said.

"That's bullshit!" Collier screamed. "You fucking fascists. You think just because you have a badge you can wave around false charges and accuse me of terrorism? Where's the Department of Homeland Security? Bring it on, I'll have all your pensions in my bank account . . ."

"A sitting judge is dead. A developer. A congressman is missing. And the person who killed them is still out there. Do you think he's going to let you walk?" Mitch said. "Do you think you can disappear?"

Collier's Adam's apple was moving up and down, though he kept quiet. Oh, yeah, he was scared.

"You are protecting a killer, and we will find him. And you will be charged with accessory to attempted murder of a law enforcement officer."

Matt Elliott spoke. "We already have evidence that you worked in the same law firm as Thomas O'Brien's defense attorney. And"—he pulled papers out of a file folder—"we also know that you worked as an intern in the same law firm as Hamilton Drake, prior to your employment at Johnson & Mather. I've already cut one deal today, and I'm not too eager to cut another when I would rather see you rot in prison for what you did."

"I didn't do anything."

"Shut up," Collier's attorney said.

"It's nonsense. You don't know anything."

"We have a statement from Randolph Sizemore with the Western Innocence Project that you lied to him about your employment history when taking pro bono work."

"A slap on the wrist by the Bar."

Mitch slapped the statement Meg had handed him on the table in front of Collier. "Reny Willis, forensic pathologist, states that you instructed him on how to testify on the stand at O'Brien's trial." He flashed the other documents. "And helped him falsify the coroner's reports."

"He's lying," Collier said weakly.

Mitch was losing it. Collier didn't care that Claire's life was in danger. "A woman's life is at stake!" he exclaimed. "And if anything happens to her, you'll be just as guilty as Phil Palmer!"

Collier's face drained.

"You know him, don't you?" Mitch said. "You know who Palmer is. Tell us exactly how he plays into this and why he took Claire."

"I don't know," Collier said weakly, looking down at the table.

Richardson said, "The U.S. Attorney is ready to make a deal. We have D.A. Elliott here ready to sign away jurisdiction. With Reny Willis's statement, we can get subpoenas for anything we want—your house, your office. With Drake and Mancini dead, we have our best people working through their records. We already learned that Judge Drake arraigned Frank Lowe, and was likely the only one privy to Chase Taverton's plea arrangement with Lowe. They are all dead."

Matt said, "There is a manhunt on right now for Phil Palmer. If we find him before you get off your high horse, there is no deal. If we find him and Claire O'Brien is dead, we'll have you in for murder two."

"Bullshit," Collier's attorney said.

"Try me," Matt said.

Silence.

With every second that passed, Claire was at greater risk. Mitch forced himself to stay calm.

"You were doing a favor for a friend," Hans Vigo said, giving Collier an out. "Didn't think it was that big of a deal, a favor for a sitting judge, a judge who used to work for your old law firm. But after one thing, they asked another. And another."

Mitch picked up on the thread. "You got in so deep you didn't know how to get out. Oliver Maddox took up O'Brien's cause because he saw something in the files that didn't jibe. You panicked. But you didn't kill him, did you?"

"Don't answer," Collier's attorney said.

"But you know who did, you kept them informed of Maddox's investigation. You set the poor kid up. You listened to everything he learned, and when he got too close you sent him to his death."

"No," Collier whispered.

"Shut up," the attorney said.

Now Mitch wanted to smack the attorney more than Collier. "This is the only chance you're going to get to make a deal, and clear your conscience in the process." Mitch doubted Collier had a conscience, but he kept it to himself. Collier was weighing the pros and cons, Mitch saw it in his eyes.

Richardson said, "You have five minutes, then the deal's off the table. You'll be required to give up your license to practice law. You'll be required to answer truthfully all our questions, and assist us with information we uncover in the process of this investigation. In exchange, we will grant you immunity from prosecution. The U.S. Attorney is writing it up in my office as I speak. It's now or never. And I don't bluff."

"Leave me alone with my client," the attorney said.

The four men left the room. "He'll take it," Hans said.

"I hate letting him off," Matt said.

"Me too, but he may be the only one who can save Claire's life. And if he doesn't know where Palmer took Claire, she's going to die. I know it." Mitch was grim.

"If it's unconnected to this case, we just gave him immunity for nothing," Richardson said.

"Rest assured, we didn't," Hans said. "Collier knows

who killed Drake and Mancini, and he knows who framed O'Brien and why. There's a lot at stake here, but Claire O'Brien needs to stay our number one priority right now. And while I just came into this case today, I don't see how her kidnapping *isn't* connected. It's the timing. If Palmer wanted to kidnap Claire for an unrelated reason, he had many, better opportunities to do so over the years. But when she was in a houseful of friends and with an FBI bodyguard? His actions tell me that Palmer feels cornered about something—perhaps information that we have, or he thinks we have, about the Maddox murder or O'Brien frame."

Meg walked briskly down the hall. "Palmer entered the police academy in January of '94. But when the Los Angeles DMV faxed over his driver's license, I called them about a mistake. They double-checked. There's no mistake."

She held up an enlargement of a DMV photograph of Philip Palmer. A large black man smiled back at them. "Palmer?" Mitch asked. He hadn't met him before.

"The real Philip Palmer." She held up another photo. White guy. "This is the man who stole the dead Philip Palmer's identity and graduated from the L.A. Police Academy."

"Then who is that guy?"

"We're working on it. L.A. has his prints on file, but it's Saturday and they need to find someone to get into the archives. I'm also having the Sac PD run the prints they have for Palmer."

Meg's secretary, Bonnie, rushed up to them. "Here's the information you wanted from Stanford. Lexie just called it in."

"What's that?" Richardson asked.

"It's the list of everyone the police interviewed at Stanford about the disappearance of Jessica White, the girl who was on Maddox's flash drive." Meg scanned the list. "Drake, Riordan, and Mancini are *all* on the list. They were members of one of the fraternities that Jessica was seen at the night she went missing."

"This is perfect," Richardson said.

"Is Phil Palmer on it?" Mitch asked.

"No," she said. "Sorry. We ran all cars and property under his name, and there's nothing but his house on Robertson and the SUV found in the garage."

Mitch followed Richardson and Hans back into the interview room where Collier sweated.

"Time's up," Richardson said.

"We want it in writing before my client says anything," the attorney said.

"You'll have to be satisfied with it on tape," Richardson said, handing over a tape to the attorney. "The clock is ticking on a young woman's life, and I haven't the time to play any more games." He slammed the list of names in front of Collier.

"Do you know what this is?"

Collier frowned, read the list. Suddenly, his eyes widened. "I never knew."

"Knew what?"

"Phil Palmer. That's not his real name. I never knew he went to Stanford. I swear, all I knew was that Judge Drake had blackmailed someone into killing Taverton. I didn't know before they were dead, I swear to God, it was after the fact. After they were already dead, Hamilton asked me to sit on Reny Willis and coach him in how to falsify the coroner's report and testify in court. Hamilton had dirt on Willis—I don't know what it was, but it was serious enough that Willis was willing to help frame Tom O'Brien."

"Why did they want Taverton dead?"

Collier licked his lips. He was shaking. "Riordan, Hamilton, and Mancini—they killed Rose Van Alden and the judge forged a will so that she'd sell the land to Waterstone. She was old, she was stubborn."

"Where does Frank Lowe fit into it?"

"He saw Riordan leaving the old lady's house. He didn't know who he was at the time, he was a nobody, but Lowe later figured it out and kept his mouth shut. I guess he wanted to live. Then he was arrested and facing major time, and he talked to Taverton. Taverton brought in Judge Drake, not knowing he had a hand in Van Alden's death, and Hamilton called this guy from his fraternity. He told me later that they used this guy for murders. He was their own personal assassin. Hamilton thought that was funny."

"He's not laughing now," Mitch said. "His blood is spattered all over 4th Street."

Finger shaking, Collier tapped a name. "Bruce Langstrom. He changed his name to Philip Palmer, but they are one and the same." He stared at them, his face white. "I've only met him once, but he's the coldest bastard I've ever seen. He'll kill me. I'm not leaving this room until you have him in custody."

FORTY-TWO

Phil kept the large-screen television replaying her most private life while he bandaged her leg. Claire was numb inside. Her privacy, which had been so important to her especially since her father's conviction, had been violated in ways she'd never imagined.

This psychopath—someone she'd thought was a friend—had watched her for years. Getting undressed. Sleeping. Stretching. Doing crunches and push-ups and leg-lifts in her bra and panties. When Claire had thought she was alone.

Bile rose to her throat. Her life wasn't hers. He'd sullied it, every private moment. Her tears. Her laughter. Her friends. He'd watched her dress and undress. He'd seen her naked. He'd seen her try on new clothes, new bras, looking critically at her body in the mirror.

"How long?" Her voice was hollow.

"Long enough. I couldn't find a place for the camera in your McKinley Park house, not a well concealed place. And it was a lot harder getting in there undetected."

But Bill's house, and her first apartment.

The men she'd dated. Oh God, she'd slept with men in her bed. And Phil watched.

Ian walked into her room on-screen. Ian Clark, her first serious boyfriend.

"You saw everything?" she whispered.

"When you were nineteen you brought that boy home and gave him your virginity."

He slapped her so hard that her head whipped to the side.

He fast-forwarded the disk, then pressed play when it reached a spot he obviously anticipated. She was naked in bed going through the awkward motions of her first sexual encounter. They had both been seniors. Two days later, Ian had broken up with her for no reason. At least no good reason, nothing she understood at the time.

"I'm done," he said.

"What?"

"I just—it's not a good idea for us to see each other anymore."

"What do you mean? But—" He'd said he loved her. She thought she loved him too, at least that's how she felt when they were together. She hadn't told him, because she wasn't sure about anything in her life. She was still getting used to trusting someone, she'd thought she trusted him . . .

"I'm going away to college, and you're staying here. I don't want any ties."

"You lied to me."

He looked her dead in the eye. "Yeah, I did. I got what I wanted, and now it's over."

Ian had hurt her more than anyone . . . until Mitch. But what she'd felt for her first boyfriend was nothing compared to the complex emotions she had for Mitch.

Mitch had touched a part of her she hadn't seen or felt before. He'd brought out a better Claire, better all the way around because Mitch was the first person she had truly been herself with.

But he'd lied to her. Just like Ian, just like . . .

But her father hadn't lied. He'd told the truth and she hadn't believed him. Claire had seen what she wanted to see, the obvious, and blamed him.

She'd looked at the facts with Mitch, at the obvious, and accused him of using and manipulating her. And he had lied . . . but had he lied about what was most important? Had he lied about his feelings?

Did he love her like she loved him?

What was going to happen if he found her dead? After what she'd said to him. After he poured his heart out to her. She'd been angry with him, but mostly she'd been hurt. Hurt because she loved him so deeply.

More than anything, Claire wanted to live. She knew what Phil was doing. He was playing a psychological game to strip her of her spirit and will. She hardened her heart, ignored what was on the screen, pushed aside the theft of her privacy.

"Did you have anything to do with Ian breaking up with me?"

"He made his own choice. The right one."

"But you pushed him?"

"I've always protected you."

"You're sick."

He sighed. "I know."

That was the last answer she expected.

"You pushed Dave to tell me about Mitch."

"I didn't know he was a Fed. That was unfortunate. But Dave took care of it. I knew he would."

"Dave trusted you. I trusted you!"

"Then you only have yourself to blame for what's about to happen."

He finished taping her leg. It hurt like hell, but it wasn't bleeding anymore. She certainly wouldn't be able to run from him. He'd taken off her jeans, but he hadn't touched her anywhere but her leg.

Yet.

Her only hope was to find a weapon. Disarm him, perhaps, and shoot him. She'd have to shoot him. Could she?

She stared at the television, at her young naked body. Oh, yes, she could kill him . . .

Her teddy bear. The room she'd woken up in, a replica of her bedroom when her mother had still been alive.

The perfect frame. Another killer, someone without a connection to the victims. Someone like Phil Palmer. He hadn't moved to Sacramento until months after her mother was killed. How did he know what her room looked like? How had he gotten the picture of her and Amy? How had he found her teddy bear?

He'd been in her room before.

"You killed my mom."

"Yes, I did."

She reeled as if hit. She'd expected him to deny it, to yell at her, to slap her.

Her voice cracked, but she asked, "Why?"

All these years, she'd been friends with her mother's killer. She'd blamed her father, and ate dinner and went to ball games with the real killer. She'd been so wrong, both about her father and about Phil. Phil was Dave's partner. Phil had saved Dave's life, made a lifelong friend in Bill Kamanski. He'd practically been family.

It was all a lie. All an act. He was a brutal murderer who had slithered his way into her life.

She wanted to throw up. And she wanted to kill him. He'd stolen everything from her: her mother, her father, her privacy, her life. She had lost everything, grew up practically an orphan, angry and lost inside. Unable to love anyone, unable to trust . . .

Until Mitch.

"It was nothing personal. I was blackmailed into it." He sighed, as if it had been a minor irritation. "In college, I accidentally killed a girl. I didn't know anyone had seen me bury her body. But they're all dead now. I'm free. Or I will be free, as soon as I bury you."

He stared at her forlornly. "I protected you all these years. I was supposed to kill everyone in the house. When you walked in, I was already there, hiding in your room. Waiting for the perfect time. I heard the door and feared it was O'Brien. That would have ruined everything. But it was you. I'd already fallen in love with you—I'd spent hours in your bedroom that morning—though I would have had to kill you if you'd seen me. But you ran out. Good thing. That gave me enough time to kill them and leave. You calling your father was icing on the cake. I couldn't have planned it better myself. All I knew was that he was alone during his lunch hour while his wife was fucking another man. I did him a favor."

"You bastard! You're insane!" She pulled at her cuff; it tightened around her wrist. She tried to hit him with her free arm. He grabbed her wrist, holding it so tight it burned.

"It's time for you to shower. I don't touch any woman who's not clean."

She spat in his face.

He hit her and she tasted blood. Instead of swallowing it, she spat it in his face. He was going to kill her anyway, dammit, she wasn't going to let him rape her too. Glancing at the television she felt violated already.

He wiped off her bloody saliva with a tissue from his pocket.

"You were always feisty. So smart. But not intelligent enough to put all the pieces together, were you?"

He unlocked the handcuffs and pulled her into the bathroom. He turned on the shower.

"Take off your clothes," he told her.

"No."

He took a knife from his pocket and cut off her shirt, nicking her skin in the process. He cut off her bra, leaving her breasts exposed.

He stared at them. Tears welled in her eyes. She crossed her arms over her chest, trying to cover herself, but he brought up the knife and sliced her forearm. She dropped them to her side. He stared at her breasts. "So beautiful. Even more beautiful than on tape."

He reached out and touched one breast as if he were caressing a fragile glass figurine. She was shaking and closed her eyes. *Try for the knife, Claire. Try for the knife.*

Through half-opened eyes, she realized she wouldn't be able to disarm him. She couldn't stand on her wounded leg while kicking his arm, and his hand was at an angle that would be hard for her to grab, almost impossible to twist without using her bad leg for leverage.

She would wait for the right time. Claire didn't want

to die. She would live to tell the truth about Phil Palmer. She stood shaking in front of him, dressed only in her small bright pink panties.

"Don't move," he said, and cut off the panties.

Tears streamed down her face.

"Shower."

She stepped into the shower. Hot water stung the nicks on her chest and the gash on her arm. Her leg burned and she couldn't stop herself from crying out in pain. Maybe she could buy some time. She could withstand the pain if only she had more time!

He was watching her through the glass. Watching her shower. She turned her back on him, but didn't feel any safer or less violated.

"Use soap."

She obeyed, more to relax Phil and give herself time to think of an escape. How could she get out of here? Running was out of the question.

Kill or be killed.

You don't have a choice, Claire. First opportunity, you take it.

"You're done," he said after five minutes. His voice was thick. He was turned on by her nakedness. It made her ill.

When he handed her a towel, she noticed how dirty he was. His hands and fingernails were covered with dirt. Had he been gardening while she was drugged?

They'll never find us. At least not until they find your grave.

He'd been out digging her grave while she'd slept off the drugs. She wrapped the towel around her body. He only had a knife in his hand now. What happened to the gun? She didn't see it anywhere. She didn't remember where he'd put it. In a drawer? There, on the dresser.

"I know what you're thinking, Claire."

His breath was on her ear.

"Accept your fate."

He steered her at knifepoint to the bed. She let the towel drop to the floor "accidentally," counting on his sick obsession with her breasts to distract him.

She reached down to pick it up. "Don't," he whispered.

She turned to face him, defiant. He stared at her breasts. He reached out and touched her nipple. She resisted the need to slap his hand away.

"Sit," he said.

She sat on the edge of the bed. He leaned over her, his breath on her chest, and he reached for the cuffs that were attached to the bed.

"You hurt me," she said, pointing to the three nicks on her chest where his knife broke skin when he cut off her shirt.

"I'm sorry."

He actually sounded sincere.

"Please, Phil. Please don't kill me."

He gently touched her face. "I'm sorry I have to."

The handcuffs clicked around her wrist.

"I need to shower now. You really are beautiful."

He picked the gun up off the dresser, went into the bathroom, and shut the door.

The shower turned on again. Claire breathed a sigh of relief. She took the small fragment of soap she had clenched in her fist and rubbed it all around her imprisoned wrist. He'd been distracted by her breasts and hadn't ratcheted it too tight. She made her hand as long and narrow as possible, pulling her thumb in toward the middle. Between the loose cuff and the soap, she slipped out.

She didn't have a weapon, but she had time.

She slipped quietly out of his room, limping.

Get out of the house. Get out of the house now!

FORTY-THREE

It took the FBI twenty minutes to run a quick background check on Langstrom and find property he owned in rural eastern Sacramento County.

"Call the sheriff's department," Mitch said. "They may have a unit closer than we are."

Richardson said, "Belay that. Mitch, this guy is a cop. He's going to be listening for activity."

"They all have cell phones nowadays," Mitch said. "Can't we do this off the radio?"

"You head over there right now, I'll call the sheriff at home and get units sent over there without any chatter."

Hans interjected. "He's a cop and he's a sociopath. He'll be listening for chatter, as well as silence. When you talk to the sheriff, make sure he contacts only off-duty deputies, which will prevent *unusual* chatter."

"Point well taken," Richardson agreed.

Hans and Meg jumped in Mitch's car. Two more cars followed. Mitch flew down the road as fast as he dared while Meg typed the address into the GPS system. "I'll double-check the map," Hans said. GPS was, unfortunately, often wrong. If they were off by a street, it might delay them from reaching Claire in time.

Mitch merged onto the freeway. It was dark, and traffic was light on Saturday night. He turned on the hidden police lights built into the grill of the small sedan. Cars moved out of his way.

"Take Business 80 to 50 east, exit Power Inn Road, to Jackson Highway. Langstrom's property is off Dillard Road."

"I know where Dillard is," Mitch said, jaw tight. "It's faster to get off at Watt."

Hans was reading Langstrom's file in the backseat. "He dropped out of Stanford shortly after Jessica White went missing," he said. "Moved to L.A. His father is a renowned surgeon, Ander Langstrom. He died five years ago."

"Mother?" Meg asked.

"Died when Langstrom was eight."

"How did he steal an identity and go through the police academy?" Mitch asked. "Don't they do background checks anymore?"

"It's amazingly easy," Hans said. "My guess is Palmer died and Langstrom assumed his identity. Or he killed Palmer and destroyed the body sufficiently to prevent recognition, then went about living the guy's life. That's going to take a little more research. But Langstrom all but disappeared fifteen years ago. He has a residence in Los Angeles, files taxes—on a sizable inheritance—and is considered a recluse. Palmer has also paid taxes, on a much smaller income."

"None of this makes sense," Mitch said. "Why would Langstrom kill two people he doesn't know? Do you think Collier is credible, that Drake and his cohorts blackmailed Langstrom into murder?"

"As far-fetched as it sounds, it's the only thing that makes sense. Maybe it wasn't simple blackmail. It looks like Palmer has a sizable bank account. His income is higher than what I'd imagine a fifteen-year veteran of the police force would make. But I don't have his tax records. It'll take our finance people to make sense of it."

"An assassin," Meg said. "They brought him up here for a job."

"Why did he stay?" Mitch asked. "If he went back to L.A., he'd never have been connected to Taverton's murder. A hired gun. He could disappear."

"This is why." Hans handed Meg a photograph over the seat.

"Jessica White?"

"Doesn't she look familiar? I mean, I haven't seen Claire O'Brien in person, but I've seen her photograph and they certainly look a lot alike."

Mitch stole a glance at White's picture. The resemblance was there. Black hair and blue eyes and pale skin. "That might mean nothing." But Mitch didn't believe his own statement.

"Hold on. I found something."

Mitch glanced in the rearview mirror and saw Hans open his laptop and start pounding away on the keyboard. He asked, "What?"

"Let me pull up a photo if I can find it."

"Photo of who?"

"There's an odd thing in Langstrom's file. Sealed juvenile records."

"Not a criminal file," Hans added. "He was a witness. Damn, I can't access the file, but I have a name. State of California v. Bridget Lincoln."

"Did he testify for the state or the defense?" Meg asked.

"Don't know," Hans mumbled, typing frantically. "Bingo!"

He handed his laptop over to Meg.

"Shit, Hans, she looks just like Claire."

Mitch tried to look, but Meg said, "Keep your eyes on the road. You're going over ninety. There's Watt."

"I see it." He cut across lanes to exit.

"Trust me, she looks like Claire," Meg said.

"What happened to her?"

Hans said, "She went to prison for five years for statutory rape. She was the principal of a private K–8 school in Glendale. I'll bet a million bucks that Langstrom went to that school and was one of her victims."

"That's sick," Meg said.

"Men aren't the only pedophiles," Hans said. "Women pedophiles and rapists are rare, but they exist. It's usually a maternal situation instead of a violent attack. They provide a needed mother figure to the male victims—usually prepubescent without a mother in the home and often with a domineering or distant father—and in exchange for affection, they molest or manipulate the boys into engaging in sex with them. Bridget Lincoln wasn't a Mrs. Robinson seducing a college boy, she was a sexual predator.

"Langstrom fits the profile. Only child, mother died young, father successful and largely absent. Lincoln comes in, gives the young boy attention—it appears she preferred twelve- and thirteen-year-old boys—and when the one got too old, she traded for another. If Langstrom was already pre-wired a sociopath, the rejection could have set him off."

"But," Mitch asked, "as a boy, wouldn't he have a harder time coming forward?"

"Absolutely. Any victim of sexual abuse has a hard time telling authorities, but boys especially feel that they aren't men if they cry rape. And Langstrom doesn't seem to be the type to go to his father. I suspect that Ms. Lincoln preyed on the wrong boy—maybe one who had someone in the home who saw the signs and cared enough to do something about it. The police would have done an investigation, probably interviewed Langstrom. And he testified in court. He'd have felt humiliated and worthless and it would spur his anger, especially if he didn't receive decent counseling. And even if he had—" Hans shook his head.

"Don't sympathize with him," Mitch said.

"I'm not," Hans said. "But understanding his background gives us an advantage."

Meg said, "What you're saying, I think, is that Langstrom came to Sacramento to assassinate Taverton—either because of blackmail or money or both—and he saw Claire and fixated on her."

"Exactly. He returned later with a new identity as a cop. Got a job with Sacramento PD. Befriended Dave Kamanski, who was close to his age, and whose father had become the guardian of the minor Claire. He insinuated himself in all of their lives. And when everything started spiraling out of control, he took her."

"Why?" Mitch asked, slamming his fist on the dashboard. *Faster, faster.* The longer Langstrom had Claire . . .

"Because he couldn't leave her behind."

"What about the judge and Mancini?" Meg asked.

"Payback. I don't think Langstrom had anything to

do with drugging Claire at the Rabbit Hole. From what Mitch said, and the Lora Lane journals Grant found in Harper's car, Ms. Lane had drugged Claire because Harper told her to. When Langstrom found out about the attack on Claire, he snapped. He went after all of them, taking them out to avenge Claire and protect his identity."

"So he's not going to kill her?" Mitch asked.

"I don't know what he's going to do," Hans admitted. "But I don't see any good coming from this. Bridget Lincoln is dead. She was strangled two weeks after she was released from prison."

"You think Langstrom did it?"

"No one was arrested, but I don't have the police files. I don't know who they looked at or what evidence they had."

"Then what is he going to do with Claire?" Mitch said.

"I think he intends to kill her, then disappear. But first I think he has something specific in mind for her."

Hans didn't say it, but Mitch knew he was talking about sexual assault. Mitch forced himself not to speed more recklessly.

"Why now and not five years ago? Ten years ago?"

"Because he still felt like he had control over Claire and over his life. Even with his blackmailers dead, he probably assumes they have records about him and his crimes. He knows his duplicity will be exposed. And in his mind, he can't leave Claire. Unless she's dead."

Mitch had the accelerator floored. Dillard Road was one mile ahead. "Where off Dillard?" he asked through clenched teeth, not daring to take his eyes off the road.

"Two point six miles south turn left. Lemon Road. Go to the end, five miles. That's where he lives."

Fight, Claire.

Claire took the stairs as fast as she could, biting the inside of her cheek against the pain in her leg. She hated that she was naked, not just because of modesty, but because her skin was so pale. Even in the dark, she would be easy to spot. She wanted dark clothing for camouflage. And a gun.

She'd take what she could get. Freedom. She made it to the bottom of the stairs. The front door was ten feet away. Almost there.

The two deadbolts slid quietly into their slots. Good. She opened the front door.

An alarm pierced the night.

No!

She limped as fast as she could down the steps of the large farmhouse. A car was in the driveway. She couldn't count on there being keys in it, but it would provide a shield if Phil started shooting at her across the yard.

She reached the car as the alarm shut off, the silence ringing in her ears. She crouched behind the driver's side, where the wheel would block her feet from being seen by anyone looking under the car. It was dark, but a half moon illuminated the acreage. She glanced around, looking for anyplace to go, anyplace to hide. Blood dripped down her leg from the gunshot wound. She put pressure on it as she collected her thoughts.

"Claire!"

Phil stood silhouetted on the front porch. There was no easy place to hide. The house was thirty feet on the other side of the car. He would find her here.

She had to run, but she couldn't outrun him.

"Claire, I will find you. You're naked. You're injured. You aren't going to escape."

She looked around as best she could without exposing herself. She saw something in front of the car. Feet. She leaned down to see . . .

. . . a body. She'd thought she'd been awakened—or jolted out of her drug-induced loss of consciousness—by a gunshot. She was right. A man lay in front of the car. From the angle he had fallen, Claire suspected he was dead.

Was that man the owner of this car? He would have keys to the car. If she could get in, she could drive anywhere. Would he have left the keys in the car?

"Dammit, Claire, don't make this harder on yourself. You can't escape your fate."

He was closer. Claire didn't dare open the car door. The dome light would come on, exposing her position, and if the keys weren't in the ignition, she'd be toast.

She crawled around to the front of the car. She felt the man's pants for keys in his pockets. Nothing. But . . .

. . . he had a gun next to his hand. A 9mm. Was he a cop? Had he come here to rescue her, only to be shot by Phil?

No, the police would never send a lone cop to a scene like this. And if it was a routine patrol, or a neighbor calling, if he hadn't checked in they would have sent backup. Not a cop . . . but Claire couldn't dwell on who he was or why he was here. She reached for the gun. Instantly she felt more in control.

"Claire, time to stop the games."

He was standing behind the car.

You can't run from him. This is the only option.

Standing, Claire aimed the gun at Phil. She pressed the trigger.

Nothing.

Again and again.

Phil laughed. "I can't believe you didn't check to make sure there were bullets in the gun. I emptied the cartridge after I shot him. Couldn't be sure he was dead, didn't want him shooting me in the back."

Claire turned and ran. Limped. Her leg hurt, the pain blinding her, but she moved as fast as she could.

Phil was still laughing behind her. And gaining.

Please, please, please.

Claire didn't want to die. She stumbled, aiming for the bushes where she might be able to find some cover. She wanted time, dammit! Time with Mitch. Time with her dad. She wanted all the time back that Phil Palmer had stolen from her.

But how could she get away from a madman? She pushed through bushes and small trees, sharp branches and leaves cutting into her skin. She had one bad leg and a useless gun. She could hit him over the head with it. But to do that, she had to let him get close.

Her blood loss was making her dizzy. Where was he? She didn't hear him laughing anymore. She didn't hear anything except the echo of panic in her ears. She willed herself to calm down. If she wasn't calm, she couldn't think rationally, and couldn't find an escape route.

There was a shed twenty feet to her left. Could she make it? Would she find anything useful inside? Maybe cutting shears. Or a chain saw. She almost laughed at the thought, as if she'd found herself involuntarily in a B-horror flick. No, she'd be trapped over there. Stick to the bushes and trees, and keep moving.

"So predictable."

She jumped, tried to turn away from Phil. He'd gone around and come at her from the opposite direction.

He grabbed her by the arm and pulled her close. He'd pulled on jeans, but had on no shirt.

She swung her arm up and around, gun in hand. He clutched her wrist and slowed her momentum. Squeezed. The gun fell from her grasp.

His face was inches from hers; he'd pulled her up off the ground with angry strength. "I didn't want you to suffer, Claire. But you made me mad."

She screamed at the top of her lungs. Someone had to be around! Someone would hear her and call the police. He slapped her, once, twice, three times until she was on the ground. She felt around for the gun. It had fallen right here . . .

"You'll be better off dead," he told her.

"Fuck you!" she yelled. With her good leg, she kicked him. Made contact dead-on with his dick. He winced, bent over, and she stood, all her weight on the uninjured leg, gun in hand—this time holding the barrel.

He put his hands around her neck. She was startled, not expecting the intense and instant pain as her breath was stolen from her.

She used all her energy and coldcocked him with the gun. He released her, holding the back of his head, and she fell to the ground, greedily drawing in fresh air. She crawled away from him. He was on his knees, a cry of pain escaping his lungs.

Go, Claire! Go.

She continued moving away from him, unable to focus, but knowing if she was going to survive she couldn't be anywhere near him. Her head felt thick and her leg was slick with blood. She wanted to hold it, to stop the bleeding, but he'd come for her.

"Claire, you bitch!" he screamed, but he hadn't moved. She had. Or had she? Her mind was muddled, and she didn't know where he was.

She looked up and saw a backhoe in front of her. She almost laughed at the thought of using a slow machine as a getaway vehicle. She took a deep breath, put her hand on the metal, pulled herself up.

She turned. Where was Phil? She didn't see him. Her heart pounded. No, no, no. Where was he? She looked right, left—

"You found your grave."

He pushed her and suddenly she was falling . . .

. . . she hit mud, landing flat on her back. She was staring up at the starry sky, the half moon casting odd shadows in the hole she'd fallen into.

Hole?

You found your grave.

An engine roared to life. Dirt rained down on her . . .

She pulled herself to standing. Reached as high as she could. The hole was taller than she was. She tried to climb out, digging her toes into the dirt. But it was too hard. She couldn't get out.

More dirt came down on her head. A rock hit her, stunning her.

She screamed.

No one could hear her over the grave digger.

Mitch slammed on the brakes in Langstrom's driveway, behind a sedan. "I heard a scream."

"Wait for backup!" Meg said. "They're two minutes behind us."

Mitch ignored her and jumped from the car, gun drawn. He heard Meg swear under her breath, but she followed him out, Hans close behind her.

Silence.

They walked around the parked car. Mitch knelt and felt for a pulse on the body. He glanced at Meg and shook his head. Meg mouthed to him "Riordan."

Mitch pointed to the marks in the dirt and gravel of the drive. Meg didn't see what he saw, but she hadn't had as extensive training in tracking humans.

They kept low. There were voices, beyond the bushes. A hundred yards away. They were all vulnerable in the open, but Mitch couldn't wait for backup and a game plan. Saving Claire was the only thing on his mind.

"Fuck you!"

It was Claire's voice.

Mitch ran across the open space.

"Claire, you bitch!"

It was Langstrom, it had to be. Mitch continued toward where the voices came from. He couldn't see anyone yet, but they had to be near here.

A startled cry, then the sound of an engine.

He turned to the right and saw the backhoe on the far side of the property. A pile of dirt was being poured out . . . into a hole?

Where was Claire?

Mitch sprinted toward the backhoe. "FBI! Freeze!" He aimed his gun at Langstrom.

"If you shoot, she dies!" Langstrom shouted. A scoop full of dirt was held over the hole.

Claire was in there.

Mitch heard nothing over the motor. Was Claire still alive? Had he already killed her?

"Claire!" he shouted.

He thought he heard a faint cry from the hole, but it might have been his imagination and hope.

Mitch saw faint movement on the other side of the backhoe. Meg and Hans were circling around. Mitch needed to buy time. But he didn't know how injured Claire was. She could be dying in that hole. She could be suffocating . . .

"It's over, Langstrom," Mitch shouted. "Step down from the backhoe and surrender."

He laughed. "No, Special Fucking Agent. It's not over. It'll never be over until Bridget is dead."

Bridget? Who—the woman who was strangled. The one Hans suspected had molested the young Bruce Langstrom.

"She hurt you, didn't she?" Mitch said. He felt uncomfortable in this role. Hans had always been the one to talk to the psychopaths, working through their past and getting them to surrender or make a misstep. What if Mitch screwed this up? What if he said the wrong thing and Claire ended up dead because of him?

"You're not part of this. Go away."

"No," Mitch said. "I know about Bridget. She raped her male students and went to prison. You were one of her victims."

"Victim? Fuck you, Fed. I'm not a victim. I was never a victim! I loved her. I wanted her."

"Is that what you told the judge when you testified against her?"

"I never did that! I'd never hurt her. My father—he humiliated me. He did it, not me. He had shrinks come in and interpret what I said and change everything around."

"Shrinks. I can't stand them either. Come down, Bruce," Mitch said, trying to turn the conversation more personal. "Come down and we can talk about the damn shrinks." Even as he said it, Mitch knew Langstrom wasn't going to bite.

"You're transparent, Fed. You're going to back off, right now. Back off. Go back to your car. Drive away. Then I'll let Claire live."

She wasn't dead. At least, if Mitch could believe this killer, Claire wasn't yet dead. Mitch held on to the hope.

"You know I can't do that, Bruce. You're a cop. You wouldn't walk away either."

"Cop." He laughed. "I'm a hired gun, by both the government and the criminals who run it." He laughed, then it shut off abruptly. "Get away from me!" He released some of the dirt and Claire's scream from deep in the grave pierced the night, over the sound of the backhoe.

She was alive.

Mitch took a step backward. "Okay, Bruce. Okay. Look. I'm backing off."

Meg was in position.

"I'm backing off," Mitch repeated.

"It's better like this," Langstrom said.

In the rapidly fading light, Mitch saw movement in the backhoe. Was that a gun?

He hit the ground and rolled as a bullet whizzed past his head. Mitch had his gun out and aimed, but more gunfire rang through the air and Langstrom fell out of the backhoe.

The dirt in the scoop above Claire cascaded down.

"No!" Mitch jumped up and ran. "Claire!"

Damn motor, he couldn't hear her.

He ran to the edge of the hole. "Claire!"

He couldn't see her. Oh God, no, all that talking while she was dying . . . then he saw Claire's limp hand sticking out of the dirt.

He jumped down and began digging around her hand. Her arm. Her head.

"Claire!"

He pulled her head free of the dirt. She wasn't conscious. He felt for her pulse. Strong, but rapid. Blood coated her hands. Had she been shot? Where was the blood coming from? He checked for a head wound and found none.

"Hans! Meg! I need help."

The motor shut off.

"Mitch! Where are you? Mitch!"

"Down here! Call for an ambulance!"

Mitch dug away more dirt from Claire's body. She was naked. Her body was so cold. There were cuts, now filthy from the dirt, all over her arms and chest.

"I need help getting her out."

Meg jumped into the half-filled grave and rapidly scooped dirt away from Claire's body until Mitch could pull her free. He lifted her up and handed her to Hans, who was kneeling at the edge of the hole.

"Her leg's bleeding," Mitch said. It also appeared bandaged. What had that bastard done to her? Mitch wanted to kill Langstrom all over again. His eyes burned as Hans laid Claire down on the ground. Mitch pulled himself out of the hole, then helped Meg out. Both he and Hans removed their jackets and wrapped them around Claire.

Four more agents ran to the site. Meg gave the orders. "You two, secure the property. You, get the first-aid kit and blankets, stat. You, get the status of the ambulance."

Mitch smoothed Claire's hair away from her face. "Claire. Claire, come on, wake up. Please, Claire."

"She's lost a lot of blood," Hans said. He focused on removing the bandage. "The bleeding has mostly stopped, but we need to get the wound washed out and antibiotics administered ASAP."

"Claire, honey, please." Mitch swallowed thickly. He couldn't lose her. Dammit, he could *not* lose her like this. He would rather have her throw him out of her house in a rage than have her die in his arms. "Dammit, Claire. Yell at me. Hit me. Blame me. Just don't die on me. Don't do it." He pulled her into his arms, cradling her, taking comfort that her heart still beat, that her lungs still breathed.

He kissed her forehead, her cheek, her lips. "Claire," he whispered, "I need you. I need you back. Don't leave me. Don't leave me like this. I love you."

Sirens pierced the night. Thank God. "Claire, we're getting you help. You're going to be okay."

Mitch looked up. He'd forgotten that Hans and Meg were kneeling with him. He turned away from their inquisitive expressions. He didn't want to explain, but he said, "I love her. Go ahead, fire me."

Meg said, "I already figured that out." She took a deep breath. "I must have been a real bitch these last couple years if you think I'd fire you for falling in love."

Mitch stared at her. "What—"

"As far as I'm concerned, what you do on your own time is your business." She reached out, touched him. "You're a great agent, Mitch, flaws and all. I'm glad you're on my team."

Mitch nodded and stroked Claire's hair.

"She's going to be okay," Meg said. "She's a strong woman. I like her a lot."

FORTY-FOUR

Mitch stood to the side of the property with Meg and Hans. It was Sunday morning, dawn, and the evidence response team was getting to work on a grisly project. It reminded the three of their shared past. Only, this was somehow worse.

They had already identified seventeen possible grave sites. They excavated the most recent: The girl, sixteen or so, had been dead only a couple days. She had dark hair and fair skin.

Like Claire.

"It's come full circle, hasn't it?" Meg whispered. "Our first case together."

"Kosovo," Hans and Mitch said simultaneously. Thirteen years had passed since their horrifying weeks in Kosovo unearthing mass graves to identify human remains after the brutal civil war tore apart Yugoslavia. It still haunted all three of them.

"What do I say to her?" Mitch asked quietly. They had been upstairs and had put together what Bruce Langstrom had done. The young girl's room where evidence of a struggle told them Claire had been inside. The worn bear, her name on the door, the photo of a young

Claire and her friend on the wall—it didn't take a rocket scientist to surmise the room was a replica of Claire's childhood room.

The blood in the hallway where he'd shot her in the leg to prevent her from escaping. Her cut clothes in the bathroom, which matched up with the marks on her body when Mitch found her.

But it was the disk playing in a loop in the bedroom that had Mitch and even the seasoned, unflappable Hans Vigo speechless.

That bastard had been watching her for years. Filming her in the privacy of her own bedroom. Mitch wanted to kill him again—with his bare hands—for putting Claire through hell. For forcing her to watch her most intimate and private moments. Why? Some sick mind game? To demoralize her?

"Tell her you love her," Hans said.

"It's not going to be that easy."

"Nothing worth having is easy."

"How is she going to live knowing that he—"

"She will because she's a fighter," Hans said.

"And," Meg added, "she has you."

Mitch watched their evidence response team bring up another body and lay it on a bright yellow tarp. How do they stop monsters like Langstrom? So many victims. Innocent. Maybe he was supposed to be a cop. But the rules that favored killers like Langstrom would always be stacked against them. He didn't want to go back to a desk, more concerned with paperwork than criminals.

"I want the disk," he said.

"I can't—" Meg said.

"Just stop with the rules. I don't care if it's evidence.

He's dead! I have to protect Claire. If that gets out, it'll destroy her."

"I'll do it," Hans said.

"I can't ask you to—"

"You didn't. Trust me, Mitch. No one else will see it. Ever."

Hans turned and walked toward the house.

"Go back to the hospital," Meg said as they watched Hans enter Langstrom's house. "You'll want to be there when Claire wakes up."

"You need me here," Mitch said.

"Scram. Claire needs you more," Meg said.

"Thanks."

"By the way, a friend of mine called. He'd heard about you, might have a job you're interested in."

Mitch stared at her. "Am I fired?" Did he sound hopeful?

"No. I want you to stay. But—" Meg glanced down, then back at Mitch. "You've never been happy in the FBI. I saw it, but never addressed it, because I didn't want to lose you from my team. You're a great agent. But I want you to do something you really want to do, not what anyone else wants for you."

"I guess you know me better than I thought."

"You don't have to take it. And your job is safe, if you want to stay. Just give this guy a call and listen to what he has to say."

Mitch took the card Meg held out.

J. T. CARUSO

ROGAN-CARUSO PROTECTIVE SERVICES

"I'll listen," he said and walked to his car, leaving the dead, and the past, behind him.

* * *

Claire woke to soft voices. Her eyes opened half-way. She breathed as deeply as she could and smelled hospital.

She'd made it. Somehow, she got out of her grave and made it.

Memories of sound, voices, filtered in. Being buried with dirt. Screaming. Begging for her life. Then nothing but warmth. Being rocked. Someone holding her.

Don't die on me. Don't do it.

I need you.

I love you.

Mitch had been there. Claire had heard him, felt him.

"Mitch." Her throat was thick and raw.

"Honey."

It was her dad. She turned, saw Tom O'Brien sitting with Nelia Kincaid in her hospital room. He wore a bathrobe, but her dad was sitting up. Alive and well.

"Daddy?"

"You're okay." He took Claire's hand.

Nelia said, "I'll be right back." She left.

"Oh, Daddy, I don't know where to begin."

He fed her water through a straw.

"You don't have to say anything."

"He killed Mom."

"I know."

"He was in my room. He took my bear. He—"

"Shh. Don't."

Claire breathed deeply. "How'd they find out?"

"Mitch and the FBI put the information together, and they gave Don Collier a deal for Langstrom's name."

"Langstrom?"

"Phil Palmer's real name was Bruce Langstrom. He was an assassin, for lack of a better word. The FBI is going through countless records of Judge Drake, Richard Mancini, and Congressman Riordan. They're putting together a conspiracy going back nearly three decades. Political corruption, illegal land deals. Murder."

"Murder?"

"Seems they killed an old woman for her land. It's what started this, at least for us. Frank Lowe ratted out Riordan to Chase Taverton as part of a plea agreement. Judge Drake found out about it and had them killed. It was just chance that Lydia was having an affair with Taverton. If not Lydia, it would have been some other woman who died, another husband or ex-boyfriend framed."

Her dad held her hand.

"I'm so sorry," she said.

"This isn't your fault, or mine, or even your mother's. Blame those selfish bastards. Be satisfied that their crimes are being exposed now that they're dead."

"The time we lost—"

"Honey, believe me, I could hate for a long time if I think about what I lost. That's gone. I have you back, and that means more to me than anything in the world. I've regained my reputation. My innocence. My freedom. I can walk the streets again. And then there's Nelia."

His face softened and Claire squeezed his hand. "I'm glad you found someone who loves you."

He nodded. "And I'm glad you found someone who loves you."

"I—"

"Mitch told me everything last night after you were brought in."

"Everything?"

"More or less. Honey, he's a good man."

"I know." Her voice cracked. Mitch was more than just a good man. He was the love of her life.

The door opened and Mitch walked in. Nelia stood in the doorway. "Tom, you need to rest."

"Yes, ma'am." Tom leaned over and kissed Claire on the forehead. "Love you, Claire Beth."

"Love you too, Daddy."

Tom shuffled out arm in arm with Nelia.

Claire turned her head toward Mitch.

"You probably want to know what happened," he said.

She nodded. "Yeah. I missed a lot."

"Well, I guess I should start at the beginning." He sat down where her father had been sitting. "Apparently, thirty years ago, Bruce Langstrom—"

"Did you go in the house?" she whispered.

Mitch nodded.

Claire closed her eyes, unable to squeeze back burning tears. She wanted to disappear, to run away where no one knew who she was. Soon everybody would know, everyone would see all her secrets exposed, watch her have sex . . . oh, dear God, the Internet. It would be everywhere . . .

"Claire, don't do this to yourself."

"How can I face my dad? Everyone I work with, my friends, Dave and Bill—"

"It's gone. Destroyed. No one is going to see it. No one is going to talk about it."

"But it's evidence—"

"No it's not."

Claire looked at Mitch, saw that he spoke the truth. Her lips trembled. "I—Thank you."

"Don't do that. God, Claire, when I saw you in that grave, my life was over. I couldn't imagine not being given another chance to explain why I lied, to ask for your forgiveness, to tell you I love you. To ask for time to prove it."

She put her fingers to his lips. "I'm sorry, Mitch. I'm so sorry."

"Sorry? Sorry for what? I'm sorry I couldn't protect you. I'm sorry he hurt you. I would do anything to turn back time and stop it from happening." Mitch reached out for Claire, hesitated.

She took his hand and squeezed it.

"I was so mad and hurt when I found out the truth about you," she said.

"I know, and—"

"Let me finish, okay? I was hurt because I thought I had fallen in love with a lie, with someone who didn't exist. But it's you. Writer or damn FBI agent, it's still you. I love you, Mitch."

He let out a long breath, touched his head to hers. "I've been so worried. I need you, Claire. You showed me how lonely I was. How jaded. How miserable. When I'm with you, I see myself in a whole different light. I've been moving from job to job in the FBI—from Atlanta to Washington to Texas to Sacramento—never settling down, never happy, until I met you. I love you so much."

He kissed her lightly.

She sighed. "Aren't we a pair? I'd never have thought I could fall head over heels for someone like you, but now that I have, I couldn't imagine loving anyone else."

He smiled, touched her face.

"Can you do me a favor?"

"Anything."

"Can you check on my dogs and Neelix? They haven't eaten. They're probably—"

"I've already done it. I went by last night, and decided to stay. They missed you, I think."

She smiled. "They like you. They're good judges of character."

"I had a job offer."

"What kind of job?"

"Something that challenges me, that speaks to my sense of justice and fair play."

"Tell me."

"J. T. Caruso offered me a position at Rogan-Caruso."

"That's wonderful."

"You're okay with us working together?"

She nodded. "Absolutely. We'd make a good team."

"I agree. I won't lie to you again, Claire. Just promise me you'll trust me once more. I won't let you down."

"I trust you. No secrets, Mitch. You and me, no matter what, no secrets between us."

"I promise." He kissed her. "You won't regret loving me."

Can't get enough
of the edge-of-your-seat romantic suspense
from Allison Brennan?
Read on for an exclusive sneak peek at

SUDDEN DEATH

the first book in the new FBI trilogy

by

Allison Brennan

The murder had been ritualistic, brutal, and efficient.

There didn't appear to be any signs of a struggle, but here in the decrepit underside of Sacramento, that was difficult to determine. While the city did a fairly good job at keeping most of the streets clean, on the north side of downtown—away from the Capitol building and closer to the soup kitchen—the grime and unwanted bred. Here, the homeless weed through the garbage for something edible. Cardboard boxes had been pulled from the trash to shield them from an early heat wave.

Based on the lack of blood spatter, the victim had been prone when shot. But the victim had the same outward injuries as the other two known victims. His hamstrings had been cut clean through, incapacitating him.

"What are you thinking?" Sacramento PD Detective Dave Kamanski asked. He'd been the one to contact the local FBI office about the like-crime, and Meg was pleased to be able to work with someone she already knew and respected.

"His hamstrings weren't cut here. Not enough blood."

Kamanski frowned. "If the killer sliced his hamstrings first to prevent him from running, then shot him in the head, would there still be pooling?"

"I'm not a forensic expert," Meg said, "but my guess is that there would be some sort of spray or castoff." Without touching the victim, she inspected the deep gash in the back of his legs. She mimicked a slicing motion with her hand and then said, "I need the coroner's report, but it appears that the killer sliced right to left, cutting both legs with an even, fluid motion." She stood and said, "Turn around."

Kamanski did, looking over his shoulder at the tall blonde. She said, "I'm shorter than the killer and you're taller than the victim, but my guess is that the victim was walking somewhere, and the killer came and *slice,* cut the hamstrings. The vic went down on his knees—that should be obvious at the autopsy with early bruising or physical evidence of a collapse—and then even if the killer immediately sheathed the knife, there would be blood on the ground and castoff"—she looked to the left—"over there."

There was no noticeable blood on the ground or opposite brick wall. "But," she continued, "you'll want your crime scene unit to go over the area carefully."

"They're working it already," Kamanski said. "So you don't think he was killed here?"

He sounded skeptical, so Meg clarified. "No, he was definitely shot right here, as he lay prone—small caliber handgun is my guess, .22 caliber, behind the left ear. A .22 is very effective at close range."

Megan had seen far too many execution-style murders while she was part of the national Evidence Response Team that went to Kosovo ten years ago. Which led to the question of why disable the victim first if only to shoot him?

Megan already had the answer, if the evidence held true to the first two known victims: between the time the killer cut the victim's hamstrings to when he shot him, he'd received his sick pleasure from the torture. Debilitating the victim was simply to keep him from escaping.

"We need to find out where he was attacked and tortured."

"So this is connected with the cases on the hot sheet?"

"I can't say for sure, but the sliced hamstrings and the execution-style murder are two strong similarities. Neither detail was released to the media in either city of the first two killings, so I think it's probably the same guy. If the victim was tortured, that won't be obvious until the coroner strips the body."

The two previous victims had no visible marks until their clothing was removed and dozens of tiny pinpricks were obvious.

First Austin, Texas, then Las Vegas, Nevada. Now Sacramento. The only thing those three places had in common—on the surface—was that they were large cities. The victims were single, male, between the ages of thirty-five and forty-five, tortured and murdered in their homes. While most serial predators stayed within one race, the first victim was black and the second—and presumably the third—were white. The first vic owned his own business and, though divorced, was by all accounts a devoted father. The second vic had never married, but had a rap sheet for minor drug charges, and worked as a mechanic. There was some indication that he had a gambling problem, which delayed the local police from reporting the crime to the national database, mistakenly believing it was payback for an uncollected debt. The hot sheet possibly linking the two had only been sent out last week.

"The deputy coroner just pulled up," Kamanski said. "Let me clue him in and we'll be back."

"Great. The sooner we get the body moved, the better." Already, decomp had set in from the layers of clothing the dead man wore coupled with the already high late morning temperature.

Kamanski walked away, and Meg frowned at the body. Something else seemed—odd. Because the victim was homeless and had been living on the streets long enough to disappear into the backdrop of Sacramento, his age was indeterminate. His clothes hadn't been washed in weeks or longer, so his hands stood out.

"Tate," she called to the new special agent assigned to Squad Eight, the Violent Crimes/Major Offenders Unit of the Sacramento FBI. "Take pictures of his hands."

"I already photographed the body." But he squatted next to her and snapped a few shots with the digital camera, then with a film camera.

"They're clean," he said, surprised.

"Exactly. Another part of the ritual?" she wondered out loud. "Or had he fought back and scratched his attacker? Maybe scouring the hands was an attempt to get rid of evidence." She didn't have the hot sheet in front of her, but she didn't recall that the killer had cleansed his previous victims. If it was the same killer.

Under normal circumstances, Megan wouldn't be called out to a local homicide, but this murder matched two recent homicides in Texas and Nevada, prompting the Bureau to send out a nationwide alert about a possible serial murderer. Normally, such rather generic murders wouldn't have sparked the interest of the FBI, but the killer marked his victims in a very specific manner.

First, slicing the hamstrings to incapacitate the victim. Not fatal, but extremely debilitating and painful.

Next, restraint of some sort. Meg didn't touch the body because the coroner hadn't inspected it yet, but there were no obvious marks of restraint. Perhaps the wrists and ankles, which were concealed by his clothing.

Followed by prolonged torture. The hot sheet indicated that the first victim had been tortured for a minimum of two hours, the second victim four hours. But the torture itself was in dispute—there wasn't a lot of detail as to the method, only that needle marks were found on the victims but no known drugs were present. There was some obvious physical violence—the first victim had his fingers broken with a blunt object, the second victim's ribs had been cracked and broken from a beating. But no biological evidence had been found yet. The Quantico laboratory was assisting in processing trace evidence.

After the apparent torture, the victim was shot low in the back of the head, a classic and effective method of execution. There was no obvious postmortem ritual.

"It's as if he plays with them then suddenly shoots them dead."

"Excuse me?" Tate asked.

"Talking to myself," she muttered. "And it doesn't fit with this crime scene. He wasn't tortured here." She itched to look under his clothing to see if the needle marks matched up to the photographs she'd seen of one of the previous victims.

"Agent Elliott," Tate said.

She looked up, not realizing that she'd been staring at the body, trying to make sense of a senseless murder.

Senseless to you, Megan, not to the killer.

"Is the coroner ready?"

"I don't know. But look." He pointed to a chain under the victim.

Only three prongs on the chain, or necklace, were visible, but the pattern was immediately recognizable. Dog tags.

A veteran.

Meg had always prided herself on her even temper and logical approach to problems, but suddenly her vision blurred and she wanted blood—the blood of the killer, the blood of a society that didn't value those who fought for them. Men like her father . . .

She pushed him from her mind and focused on the homeless veteran. "Detective!" she called, wanting an ID as quickly as possible. Wanting to know how this soldier had ended up homeless and dead.

Detective Kamanski was at the edge of the crime scene talking to a small group of people. Uniformed officers were along the perimeter to keep the onlookers from getting too close. He glanced at Meg, then approached with a casually dressed young black man carrying a medical bag.

"Agent Elliott, this is Deputy Coroner Roland Banks."

Meg shook hands, then pointed to the chain. "I think those are dog tags. We might be able to get a quick ID on this victim."

"That'd be nice," Banks said. "We have a few dozen unidentified homeless filling the deep freeze right now."

While Banks did his job, Kamanski said, "I called in a detective who worked undercover down here for several months last year. He knows this area and the homeless better than anyone on the job."

"Good. We need an insider. If we do have a witness, it could be hard to get them to talk."

"Exactly. Abrahamson is on his way down."

Meg asked, "So how do you want to handle the investigation?"

"We'll need to have your boss and my boss talk, but I'm open. Joint task force?"

They both cracked a wry grin.

"Can you take care of the canvass and forensics? But if you need anything from our lab, let me know and I'll jump on it. And I'll start working the joint jurisdiction issues with Texas and Nevada, talk to both the locals and Feds and get copies of the files. It might help. Something connects these three men. It just doesn't seem random." To Banks she said, "I'd like to observe the autopsy."

"Probably first thing in the morning," the deputy coroner said. "They're already jammed up this afternoon."

"I'll be there. One thing I'm looking for are needle marks on the body. Very small, likely on the feet, neck, hands, and groin."

"The body is already in decomp, I don't know what we'll see underneath the clothes, but I'm not removing them here. The skin is already slipping."

"How long has he been dead?" Kamanski asked.

"In this heat? Decomp is telling me about twenty-four hours, but with this heat could be as few as six. I'll have to do some calculations, factor in his clothing, the position of the body—fortunately, he's not in direct sunlight. I'll take a wild stab—and I mean a not to put in your report guess—at six to ten hours. I know, he looks like twenty-four plus, but he's not."

Banks pulled out the dog tags. "Price, George L.," he read. "This looks like U.S. Army. No medical restrictions, blood type A negative. Christian. Have the social as well."

Both Meg and Kamanski wrote down the information. Tate snapped pictures. Banks put the chain down and Meg didn't hear anything. "Wait," she said.

"Excuse me?"

"There's only one tag."

Banks held up the chain. Carefully, Meg searched along the chain for another tag, as she said, "The two tags should be together. Either attached and separable, or the second tag on it's own small chain."

"There's only one tag," Banks said.

"Maybe he lost it," Kamanski offered.

"Not likely," she said, but she didn't discount the possibility. "Maybe the killer took it for a souvenir." Or another reason. Maybe he *did* lose it. Maybe he'd been injured or there was some other reason the second tag had been removed in the field when he was a soldier. It felt odd to Meg, but she didn't have any facts to base her instincts on so she kept her mouth shut.

An attractive brunette exited a nearby building across 12th Street and waved at Kamanski. "Dave, we found something you need to see," she said over the radio.

"That's Simone Charles, day shift supervisor for the CSU," Kamanski told Meg.

As Meg followed him over to where Simone waited, she used her BlackBerry to e-mail her boss about the victim's ID and the similarities to the two out-of-state murders. She added the single dog tag to the information and asked if the other two victims were also military.

Kamanski introduced them, and said, "So what did you find?"

"Follow me."

Instead of taking them inside the building, Simone walked past the door she had exited and down the alley a dozen feet. The alleyway was steep and narrow. To the right was a parking garage, to the left was the backside of a business. Ahead of them was the rectory attached to the Cathedral of the Blessed Sacrament, the oldest Catholic Church in the diocese.

She pointed toward the painted brick wall at the same time that Meg saw what had to be blood.

"Castoff," they said simultaneously. They were a good half-block from where the body was found.

Along the ground were bright yellow numbered cards and they told the story as Simone spoke. "We tested the wall, it came back positive for blood but we'll have to retest it in the lab. The victim was walking toward 11th Street, and the killer sliced his hamstrings, from right to left, and the blood spattered on the wall. But he had complete control of the knife, because there are no drops consistent with him holding the knife after the attack."

"Which means?" Kamanski asked.

"He sheathed it," Simone said. She demonstrated. "Slice—he can't avoid the spatter, probably because of the momentum and the suddenness of the attack—but he sliced, then stuck the knife right back in its case. Probably on his belt loop for ease of use."

She pointed to the numbered cards. "Those are from the victim. He fell here," she pointed to an area that had a pool of blood with two clean areas in between, where the victim had fallen to his knees. "Then was picked up and carried back that way." She started toward the building she'd exited, but then turned to the parking garage.

"I thought you left the building," Kamanski said.

"I did. Nothing there, but we're processing it anyway. It's the garage that I'm interested in."

"Wait," Meg said. "Did you say he was carried?"

Simone grinned. "Oh, yeah. Carried."

Meg looked at the ground, at the numbered markers, then saw what Simone saw. "No drag marks."

"Exactly," the criminalist said. "The guy couldn't have walked anywhere, so the killer would have to drag or carry him. The vic was pretty big, but I suppose a larger, strong male could have hoisted him over his shoulder." She frowned, looking down the alley.

"But then," Meg said, "the killer would have had his arms around the victim's legs." She demonstrated by pretending to haul something large onto her shoulder. "There wouldn't be this kind of blood trail. Maybe a few spots, but nothing this extensive."

"Yeah. Yeah I think you're right."

"That means there were two people?" Kamanski asked.

Meg nodded. "Carrying him probably under the arms. Lifting him up." She followed the blood spatters. "You can see some small, narrow drag marks in places—nothing deep, probably from his shoes." She made note to check the victim's shoes for scuffmarks.

Nowhere in the reports from the previous crime scenes had the investigators indicated there had been two potential suspects. Meg's heart beat rapidly with the new and valuable information.

The three of them followed the yellow markers into the parking garage. "I've already called for all security tapes, but there're many blind spots. The main entrance, exit, and all pedestrian entrances are covered, but not every inch of each parking floor. Still, we should be able to find the vehicle entering or exiting. The garage opens at 5 a.m., but it's unmanned—only those with card keys can get in."

"So the killer had a card key?"

Simone shrugged. "I don't know. He could have tricked the system, or walked in and stolen a pass from someone else's vehicle to get in. We'll figure that out when we get the tapes from security. Or he could have come in before the garage closed at 8 p.m."

Meg was cautiously optimistic. If they had tapes of the vehicle, they could have a view of the driver. Or passenger, if there were two.

In the center aisle of the garage, Simone stopped. Three parking spaces had been cleared and yellow crime scene tape was posted. "People aren't going to like me. I closed the garage as soon as we found the trail, but there were already some people parked inside. They're not going anywhere until I finish collecting evidence." She pointed to what first appeared like nothing.

Then Meg saw the blood. She glanced behind her and saw the trail of numbered yellow cards, and they stopped here. At the rear of the parking spot.

"My guess is van," Simone said. "But they couldn't have taken him anywhere, because the garage is closed at eight, chained, and opened at five. No in or out."

"So they parked here before eight at night and left the vehicle," Meg said. "Wouldn't security have towed it?"

Kamanski shook his head. "A lot of people will leave their cars overnight. Drinking at a bar, working late, whatever."

"We have the list—security does note the tag numbers, but not the location. There were twenty-one vehicles in the garage at eight-thirty last night when the parking supervisor made the rounds."

"How did they come back in unnoticed?"

"You can just walk in pretty easily from the street, just like we did. There's just that half-wall on the ground floor, plus walkways for pedestrians They brought him in, did whatever, and left him dead in the alley nearly a block away."

"Why didn't they just execute him in the garage?" Meg asked. "Why dump him in the alley? They had to cross 12th Street to do it."

"Downtown is dead most nights, especially on Sundays," Simone said. "I could run around here naked and no one would notice."

Kamanski raised an eyebrow but didn't say anything.

"I'd like a copy of the tapes," Meg said. "And your forensics report. With security cameras on the pedestrian entrance we should get a face, possibly a good shot and ID."

"That's what I'm thinking. No problem."

Meg frowned. "Is there any evidence that they took him out the same way?"

"Nooo," Simone said cautiously. "But after a little time, the injury would have clotted and there might not be blood evidence. We're still combing the crime scene—"

"What if," Meg interrupted, "they drove him out?" She walked briskly over to the where the garage exited into the alley. "They could have taken him in the van, drove cross 12th Street, put him out and shot him. A lot easier than carrying an incapacitated man half a block."

"Possible," Simone said. "Very possible."

As Meg walked back to the body with Detective Kamanski, she couldn't grasp the motive. Why go through such elaborate measures to kill a homeless veteran? Why the torture? Why kill him nearly a block from where he was kidnapped?

It seemed both foolish . . . and planned. Deliberate. Personal.

What did George Price have in common with Austin small business owner Duane Johnson and Las Vegas mechanic Dennis Perry?

Why were they tortured?

Why were they executed?

And if the MO held, Meg would probably not learn anything else about the killers until they were caught. They'd moved around the country with ease, and if they killed Price at dawn, they could be three hundred miles away by now.

Fortunately, they had a lot more information than at the two previous crime scenes. Security tapes, a larger crime scene, greater chance of witnesses. They just needed a little time and a lot of hard work, and Meg was confident they'd ID the killers. She was good at that—working each piece of the puzzle until an identity was confirmed, a suspect arrested, and a killer prosecuted.

Meg didn't know that in six hours, they'd have nothing. No tapes. No evidence. No body. And no jurisdiction.